Y0-BZY-352

The Stranger Behind You

THE STRANGER
BEHIND YOU

CAROL GOODMAN

WHEELER PUBLISHING
A part of Gale, a Cengage Company

LIBRARY OF CONGRESS CIP DATA ON FILE.
CATALOGUING IN PUBLICATION FOR THIS BOOK
IS AVAILABLE FROM THE LIBRARY OF CONGRESS.

ISBN-13: 978-1-4328-9382-8 (hardcover alk. paper)

Published in 2022 by arrangement with William Morrow Paperbacks, an imprint of HarperCollins Publishers.

Printed in Mexico
Print Number: 01   Print Year: 2022

To my mother,
Margaret Agnes Catherine
McGuckin Goodman,
1923–2016,
again and always

PROLOGUE

I have noticed in my professional capacity that when someone makes a point of saying that they're not lying, that usually means they are. When the realtor brags that she hasn't lied about the view, though, I have to admit that her claim is demonstrably true: the view is spectacular. Standing at the elegant bay window it's as if I am perched on a cliff overlooking the river. There's nothing between me and the Palisades but water and light. A person who was afraid of heights would be terrified, but heights aren't what I am afraid of.

"Can you tell me what 'state-of-the-art security' means?"

The realtor takes a nanosecond — an eon in Manhattan real estate time — to recalibrate and then rattles off the specs again: twenty-four-hour doorman, fiber-optic alarm system, security cameras.

"As I mentioned earlier, a high-ranking

government official lived here. I can't tell you who . . ." Her voice trails off, suggesting that she very well could if she chose to. All I'd have to do is raise my eyebrows, smile, lean in a little closer — all the body language that implies that it will just be between us girls. I've done it a thousand times before with ex-wives and mistresses, corporate CFOs and underpaid personal assistants. But I don't. I don't really care who the very important person was who lived here; I just want to be assured that he — or she — lived here safely and unbothered.

"Can you show me how the camera works?"

We walk to the front door — steel, fireproof, three locks including a titanium dead bolt that slides into place with the precision of a Mercedes engine — and she touches the screen mounted on the wall of the alcove. A picture emerges of the sidewalk outside the lobby. Leaf shadow dances along the pavement. A patch of the park bordering the building. We might be in a bosky glen. A uniformed doorman stands to one side, hands folded behind his back, with all the good posture and reserve of a Buckingham Palace guard.

"That's not a bad view either," the realtor

remarks.

It takes me a moment to realize she's commenting on the doorman's physique. He's young, dark-eyed with black curly hair, Irish I remember from the accent I detected when he greeted us. Probably from the Riverdale neighborhood to the north, where Irish immigrants still live. And yes, he's handsome.

"Does the building do security checks on all the staff?" I ask.

"Of course," she says, her voice turned chilly since I didn't engage in her man-ogling. There's an unwritten code that women are supposed to join in on certain subjects: hunky working-class men, chocolate, wine. I feel her eyes flick up and down my severe outfit — black jeans, boots, black blazer over plain white T-shirt, scarf wound twice around my neck even though it's a hot July day outside. *Gay,* she's thinking.

On the monitor the Irish doorman looks up and to the left — a tell that someone's lying but in this case also a surreptitious glance at the camera. For a second his eyes seem to meet mine in an amused complicity. *Not gay,* they seem to say. Then the realtor swipes the screen, and the view in the front of the building is replaced by the interior of the lobby. Twelve-foot-high ceilings, marble floors, damask-upholstered couches and chairs — a bit threadbare I'd noticed on the way in, but in that old-money style of prewar apartments and clubs. As we watch, an elderly woman walks her elderly poodle — their hair the same texture and shade of apricot — from the elevator to the front door, which magically opens at her approach. The hunky doorman is on his toes.

The realtor — *Marla,* why should I pretend I don't remember her name or that I haven't clocked her four-and-a-half-carat diamond ring, last year's Birkin bag, and this season's Chanel jacket? To whom am I pretending? — swipes the screen again and a view of the hallway outside this apartment's door appears. "You can set the camera so the default is on the hallway," Marla says.

The camera must be mounted at the end of the hallway. It shows the elevator door, the door to this apartment, and most of the hallway. It doesn't reach the door to the one other apartment on the floor, which makes me feel a little uneasy.

"Who lives across the hall?" I ask.

Marla cocks her head and frowns. She thinks I'm a time waster despite the reference I came with. She doesn't think that I can afford this apartment — four weeks ago she would have been right — and I'm not asking the right questions. I haven't asked if the fireplace works or if the advertised washing machine is top- or front-loading — all the details that constitute bona fide miracles in New York City real estate. I haven't even asked to see the clawfoot tub or the walk-in closets. "I can't divulge any details about the residents, but I can assure you they've all been carefully vetted by the co-op board."

"Is it a man?" I ask. "That's all I need to know."

Her eyes widen. *Maybe not even gay,* she's thinking, *maybe asexual.* But then she smiles pityingly. "A sweet old lady lives there. In her nineties. You won't hear a peep out of her, Ms. Lurie." And then her eyes get even bigger and her mouth forms a round O. "Lurie," she repeats, and I curse myself for not using a fake name. "Joan Lurie. Aren't you the one who wrote that story in *Manahatta* exposing Caspar Osgood?"

I could deny it — Joan Lurie's not *so* rare a name — but I'll have to pass a financial check to get the apartment anyway. "Yes, guilty. I mean . . . *he* is . . . *was.*"

Marla throws back her head and hoots, all East Side reserve falling to the wayside. "Was he ever! Four more women have come forward to say he assaulted them. One of them was only eighteen when she interned at *The Globe.* The pig! What I don't understand is how he got away with it for so long."

"Money," I say, "and the power money gets you. He paid off the women he could and the women who wouldn't take the money weren't believed because Caspar Ward Osgood, *Mayflower* descendant, owner of *The Globe,* Pulitzer Prize winner, married man with two children, couldn't possibly be molesting twentysomething women. No one wanted to go up against him. One of the women I interviewed — an Ivy League–educated reporter with a Pulitzer nom — said after she told Human Resources that Caspar Osgood pushed her into a bathroom and shoved his tongue into her mouth she lost her job and couldn't get another one. So who was going to report on the story?"

"You did," Marla says, looking into my eyes for the first time this morning. I'm taken aback by the candid look, but then she says, "I wish I'd had you to talk to six months ago," and I understand. She has a story too.

I could forestall it. All I'd have to do is break eye contact and ask to see those closets. Remind her of our professional relationship, that I'm here to buy an apartment not listen to her bad experiences with men.

But then I'm ashamed of the thought. What kind of a reporter turns away from a story? What kind of human being turns away from a person who needs to talk to someone?

So I maintain eye contact, lean in, and say, "Oh?"

She takes a step closer and lays her beautifully manicured fingers on my arm. I can smell her Chanel No. 5. "This job," she begins as so many of my sources over the last three years have, "you have no idea what it takes sometimes. Showing men — powerful men — apartments alone, sometimes late at night. It makes a girl feel . . . *vulnerable.*"

"I hadn't thought of that," I say. "Couldn't you ask a colleague to join you?"

"Ha! And split the commission?" she scoffs. But her laugh is as brittle as the light bouncing off the river beyond the windows. "I'd be done in a New York minute if I let on I was reluctant to show a prospective buyer a property on my own. I *do* always suggest they bring their wife, or partner, but sometimes . . . well, six months ago this Wall Street type asks to see a co-op on

13

Sutton Place. High-end, you understand. Belonged to the widow of a coffee tycoon. Asking way too much, but there was no talking her down. He wants to see it on a Friday night, in a big hurry because he has to catch the last train to Greenwich. 'Why don't you come back with your wife tomorrow?' I suggest. 'No,' he says . . . get this . . . 'women get too emotional about real estate. I have to vet it first.' "

I lift an eyebrow and she goes on. "What a jerk, right? That should have been my first clue, but what could I do? The coffee widow needed to sell, I needed my commission, and the guy checked out — seven-figure salary at a major Wall Street firm, huge year-end bonus, wife with old family money, equity in Greenwich, Jupiter Island, and Booth Harbor, yada, yada, yada." She twirls her hand and her four-and-a-half-carat solitaire catches the orange glow of the sun as it sinks over the red Palisades.

"So I meet him in the lobby, make sure to greet the doorman by name so Wall Street knows I've got backup, and we get in the elevator. Right away I can smell the liquor on him and I'm on guard. I'm giving him all the stats — professional as can be — and mentioning his wife and kids every other sentence. 'Oh your wife will love the shopping' and 'There's a park right across the street for your kids' and 'See how secure the locks are you won't have to worry about your wife and kids when you're away.' I walk straight to the view — East River, not as spectacular as *this* view but still pretty great — and when I turn around he's right there, on my heels, in my face . . . and then *in my mouth.* I mean, like, his tongue is in my mouth and his hands are on my ass!"

She pauses for my reaction and I give it. "Wow! What an asshole! What did you do?"

"I pushed him off, of course, and tried to laugh it off. 'Oh, that's not included in the lease,' I say, and then I flash my ring." She wriggles her fingers for me. The diamond sends a million rainbows skating across the polished parquet and dancing up the built-in oak bookcases, the marble mantel, and the cream-white egg and dart molding on the ceiling. " 'I'm taken,' I tell him. And then you know what he says?"

I can guess but I don't. "What?"

She lays her hand back down on my arm and digs her nails into my flesh. "He says, 'I bet you could go on a great honeymoon with the commission you make on this sale.' "

"The implication being he would buy the co-op if you had sex with him," I say.

"Implication my ass! He took out his checkbook and said he'd lay down a deposit right then if I lay down with him in the Master Suite."

"A bad punster on top of being a sexual predator," I comment, keeping my tone light. This is the point at which many women back out. I've learned that making a neutral but supportive comment can ease the path to confession. I've forgotten that I have no stake in Marla's story. Part of me — a part that emerged four weeks ago and that I'm heartily ashamed of — wants her to stop. But coaxing out women's stories has become second nature to me.

"So then what did you do?"

"Well," she says, tossing her highlighted, blown-out hair over her shoulder. "I said, 'Mr. Wall Street,' " she winks to let me know she's leaving out his name because she respects the confidentiality of her clients, even the pervy ones. " 'You *do* realize that if you buy this apartment I will have multiple dealings with your wife over the next few months. I would hate for there to be any . . . *awkwardness.*' "

"You were letting him know that you would tell his wife if he assaulted you."

"Yes. And it worked. He backed down. Tried to laugh it off. But he barely looked at the place and I found out later he bought a junior four in Murray Hill from a newbie realtor at another agency. I've always wondered what she put out for *that* measly fifteen percent."

"What an upsetting experience," I say by rote, as I have said to half a dozen other women. *When did it begin to feel so useless?* "Did you tell your boss?"

She shrugs. "He would have just told me that I should've put out for the sale."

I open my mouth to ask if she'd reported him anywhere else, but close it. Who could she have gone to with her story? Like many women who are sexually harassed on the job — waitresses who encounter handsy patrons, spa workers asked to perform "extra" services — there's no clear course of action. They can ask their bosses to expel the client, but once they've done that there's no way to make the predator accountable for their actions or to prevent them from assaulting other women other than reporting them to the police, and the police aren't going to take action unless there's been a physical assault.

"I'm sorry that happened to you," I say, which is what I said to every woman I interviewed. Then I would add: *But your story will help other women.* I don't say that

17

now. I no longer believe Marla's story will help anyone else — at least, not by telling it to me.

"Well, at least your story woke people up," Marla says. "If Caspar Osgood can be taken down, that means it could happen to any of them. I think it's great you wrote it and I bet a lot of women are telling you that."

"Thank you," I say. "I've gotten some moving responses, but not everyone is so happy . . . especially after . . ."

"Oh," she says, solemn now. "You must be getting some awful hate mail. Threats even. Especially after what happened . . . Is *that* why you're so concerned with security?"

I hesitate. Marla's told me her story; I could tell her mine. But then it occurs to me. Marla knew Mr. Wall Street's entire financial portfolio. There's no way she didn't look me up before agreeing to show me this spectacular river-view apartment, even though I came with a reference from Sylvia Crosley, the style editor at *Manahatta,* which of course meant she knew exactly who I was. She knew about the story I wrote for *Manahatta;* and knew about the announcement for the seven-figure book deal I got just last week, which is the only reason I can afford this apartment.

18

Which means Marla told her story to make a sale.

It's not that I don't believe her — I imagine *worse* has happened to her, actually — nor have I been entirely honest either. I am not here because of the nasty tweets and threatening emails I've received since I exposed the publisher of the *Globe* as a sexual predator, although I've certainly gotten plenty of those. Nor am I here for the view, although looking out at that expanse of sky and knowing there's no one looking back in at me has allowed me to breathe freely for the first time in four weeks.

"Yes," I tell Marla, "I'm here for the security." I don't tell her it's not because of those nasty tweets and threats I've received. I'm here because four weeks ago someone tried to kill me.

CHAPTER ONE

JOAN

It happened the night the story went live. My editor, Simon Wallace, had rented out the restaurant across the street from *Manahatta*'s offices to celebrate — a lavish gesture even for Simon, who ran the magazine as if it were 1989.

"You've worked on it for three years — it's a damned fine story — you deserve to celebrate before the wolves circle." He'd given the last phrase in his husky vibrato with a wink as we stood outside the door to the restaurant. He'd warned me three years ago that if I went forward with the story I'd be letting myself in for a "holy shitstorm."

He'd delivered the warning during my interview for a job writing for the style section of *Manahatta*. I'd already interviewed with the Style editor, Sylvia Crosley, but apparently the "big boss" had to personally meet all potential new hires. The first question Simon Wallace asked when he looked at my résumé was "Why'd you leave the *Globe*?"

It's what I'd been afraid of. No one left an internship at the *Globe* voluntarily. It was the plum of journalism internships. I could have lied — made up a bullshit story about wanting to work at a different kind of publication — but instead I told the truth. "I saw Caspar Osgood put his arm around his assistant and then I saw her crying in the ladies' room. She told me she'd been sleeping with him for six months and she was afraid that if she complained to HR, she'd be fired. She had a black eye that she'd tried to hide with make-up. The next day she was gone and I found out she *had* been fired. I went to HR to ask what had happened to her and to tell them that I was worried she'd been sexually harassed. Then *I* was fired. No reason given because, of course, they don't have to with an intern."

Simon had been silent for a moment, and then said, "You sound angry."

The truth was I'd been fighting back tears, digging my nails so hard into my palms I had little crescent scars there for days after. "I suppose so. Casper Osgood shouldn't be allowed to get away with treating women that way. No man should."

"It sounds like you're carrying a grudge," he had said.

"Maybe," I'd admitted, clenching my jaw to keep it from trembling. "But someone should expose him."

"Is that what you want to do? Expose Caspar Osgood, the darling of the conservative elite? He donates to the most powerful Republican causes and politicians and uses the *Globe* to crusade for reform. He's well connected and rich enough to pay for the best lawyers. A story like that would raise a holy shitstorm. It could break your career — or make it."

He'd said the last three words with a little upward lilt in his voice and a tug at the corner of his mouth. It felt like a lifeline being tossed to me just when I thought I was going under. "Yes," I'd responded, not realizing how *much* I wanted to expose Osgood until the word was out of my mouth. I'd spent the last three weeks weeping in my apartment, sure my career as a journalist was over before it had begun. "That's what I want to do. I'd like to write that story. But in the meantime, I'd really like this job writing for your Style section so I can pay my rent and not have to move back in with my mother and grandmother upstate."

That had made him laugh. "Why not both?" he'd asked. "How about we hire you to write style stories for Sylvia, and in the meantime you see what you can dig up on Osgood? If you think you've got a story in six months, pitch it to me properly and if I think it's got legs, I'll back you up. And by the way, there's nothing wrong with holding a grudge," he'd added, winking. "After paying the rent, it's the best motivator in the world."

Simon had been true to his word. He put me on staff, practically unheard-of at the e-zines I'd freelanced for since graduating from journalism school two years earlier. When I'd been working there for six months I went back to him with the names of two more women who said that Osgood had sexually assaulted them when they were working at the *Globe.*

"There does seem to be a pattern of behavior," he said. But he still seemed unsure and I thought I knew why. I'd learned since I began working for him that he'd gone to college with Caspar Osgood.

"I understand if you feel that you can't pursue the story because of your personal connection with Caspar Osgood."

He had bristled at that, as I had perhaps known he would, and said, "I would never compromise my journalistic objectivity. Keep working on the story but make sure you have contemporary corroborating evidence to back up every allegation."

We agreed that I'd stay in the Style section until the story was done, though. "It will be good cover for what you're working on and you'll need the distraction of shoes and gallery openings when you get deep into this." He'd been right about that. Writing about fashion and style might have seemed superfluous at times while I was listening to stories from victims of sexual assault, but "Put lemon in your water and drink at least sixty-four ounces a day" was a nice change from "He put his fingers in my mouth and told me to suck like a baby." Now, three years later, I was coming out with a groundbreaking exposé — a story that, as Simon had said, would either make or break my career — and my skin had never looked better.

"Aren't the wolves already circling?" I remarked to Simon as we stood in front of the restaurant. We'd both gotten cease-and-desist letters from Osgood's lawyers the day before. Simon had made a big production of lighting them on fire with the vintage cigar lighter some old reporter at the *Times* had given him when he started out.

"Oh, they're at the door, Joannie," he said, grinning. "All the people who have enabled Caspar Osgood all these years and overlooked the rumors and the gossip as they lined their pockets with his money are going to say you're an angry feminist who's attacking Osgood for his politics and who's bitter she's working for a two-bit rag instead of the great *Globe*. In fact" — he turned to me, his grin sobering to a wistful smile that melted the icy trepidation in the pit of my stomach — "it's not too late to back out. We posted the story to the staff's private online site half an hour ago, but it won't appear on the public site for" — he checked the vintage Patek Philippe watch on his wrist — "ten minutes, and the print edition won't hit the stands until tomorrow morning. I could tell Sammy to stop the presses. You could probably still get a job at the *Globe* if you played your cards right."

I snorted — then saw he was serious. "I'd rather work at this two-bit rag," I told him, my own voice turning hoarse.

He held my gaze another moment, as if testing my conviction. I felt the force of that gaze like a magnetic attraction — not, as I had realized over the last three years, a romantic or sexual attraction. It was his ap-

26

proval I wanted, the validation of his faith in me. I felt it now as he nodded. "Good," he said. "Let's give 'em hell."

He pushed open the door to the crowded restaurant, then took my hand and raised it over our heads as if I were a prizefighter who'd just gone fifteen rounds.

"Ladies and gentlemen of the press," he boomed, "I present the reporter who's just taken down Goliath. All hail to our own David. Hang on, kids, the ground's gonna shake when this giant goes down."

The ground did shake as my colleagues and friends pounded the floor with their feet and applauded. A dark-haired server handed me a glass of fizzing Champagne and someone thumped me on the back. Marisol from accounting shouted, "Let's take the fuckers down!" and everybody laughed and Simon gave my hand a squeeze that I felt all the way in my chest. Then he let go and I drifted untethered into the crowd.

Everybody was pushing forward to congratulate me, but they all parted for Sylvia Crosley. In a black Chanel dress, Louboutin heels, and her signature round glasses, Sylvia looked as cool and collected as always, but my stomach clenched in trepidation as she approached me. She'd been my boss for

27

three years — and a good one. I'd learned more about how to write from being line-edited by her sharp blue pencil than I had in journalism school. I'd also learned how to go barefoot in pumps without getting blisters (spray-on deodorant), what to order at a business lunch that won't go to your waist or stick in your teeth (poached salmon on Bibb lettuce), and where to get this season's couture at half price (I can't reveal that last one; she made me sign an NDA). But I hadn't told her about the story that I'd quietly worked on for the last three years and I was afraid she was feeling betrayed.

I eyed the flute of Champagne balanced between her lacquered fingernails and wondered if I was about to get it in my face. Instead she lifted it to me. "You sly dog," she said. "All this time you were filing fluff for me you were busting balls with the big boys. Brava!"

"I learned from the best," I said.

She lifted her chin up and clinked her glass against mine. We each took a sip — a mere lip-wetting kiss for her and a long sizzling gulp for me. I hadn't realized how worried I'd been about how she would take my story. Sylvia Crosley wasn't only a style editor; she knew everybody in New York, from the wholesaler in the Flower District who could get her Casablanca lilies out of season to this season's chair of the Met Gala. She kept a little book with the names and phone numbers of everybody from the concierge at the Carlyle to the mayor. I didn't want her for an enemy; I was about to make enough of those.

She sidled in closer to me and whispered in my ear. "You might have told me what you were working on. There are some sources I could have directed you to."

"Simon thought we should keep it as confidential as possible until we were ready to go public with the story." What Simon really had said was *Sylvia's a doll but she trades information like currency; there's no way she'd keep a story like this to herself.* She held my gaze a moment, as if she could hear me thinking, and then gave me a tight nod. Then she smiled and touched my arm. "Truly, you did a remarkable job — tracking down all those interns, finding corroborating evidence from their friends and families — it's all very . . . *solid.*"

"Simon insisted we have contemporary corroborating evidence for everything," I said.

"Of course he did," she said. "Any editor worth his salt would have done the same. I was just a little surprised he'd give you the

29

go-ahead on a story about Cass Osgood. You know they went to college together."

"Yes," I said, bristling a little at the implication that I wouldn't have known this. Simon was right: Sylvia liked to be the one who knew everything.

Sylvia gave me a small, pained smile. "It could look as if Simon were seeking revenge. The rumor is that Cass got Simon fired from the *Times* back in the '90s and then there was that thing with the club three years ago."

"What thing?"

Sylvia smiled, clearly glad to be the one to enlighten me, and leaned in to whisper: "I nominated Simon for membership to the Hi-Line Club but he didn't get in. I found out that Caspar Osgood had blackballed him."

"Oh," I said, reassured. "Surely Simon wouldn't care about something as frivolous as membership to some club."

"Honey," Sylvia said, her voice dripping with condescension, "never underestimate the pettiness of men and their egos."

We were interrupted then by Sam, one of the interns who had worked with me on the story. I looked apologetically toward Sylvia, but she shooed me away with a wave of her Champagne flute and a benign smile. I

30

tumbled into the crowd of young reporters and interns — all bubbling with my success, genuinely glad for me because I'd gone out of my way to be kind to them and at twenty-eight I wasn't *that* much older, so if it could happen to me, it could happen to them. Their happiness added to the glow from Sylvia's seal of approval.

"Look." Sam showed me her phone. "The article is live! There are already pictures on Twitter of Melissa Osgood receiving the news at that fundraiser of hers."

"What?" I ask, the warm glow fading. "Do you mean her fundraiser for suicide awareness?"

"Yeah. Didn't you cover it last year?"

"Y-Yes, but . . ." I remembered spending the whole night of the fundraiser trying to avoid Melissa Osgood. A better reporter might have tried to get her on record saying something about her husband's reputation with women, but I'd been afraid of compromising the story. Or maybe I'd just been too mortified to shake the hand of the woman whose husband I was working to destroy. I should have remembered the date of the fundraiser, though — the summer solstice because it was her son's favorite day —

"Oh no," I said, remembering the history

of the foundation. "I feel awful. The fundraiser is for suicide awareness because their son tried to kill himself. If we'd known —"

"Oh, Simon knew," Khaddija, Simon's assistant said, looking around to make sure her boss wasn't within earshot. "He always had me keep tabs on the Osgoods. You know he used to be friends with them."

"Wow, some friends," Atticus, one of the graphic designers said. "I've heard there's always been a rivalry between him and Caspar."

"Oooh," said Lauren, a style reporter, "I heard a rumor that Simon was in love with Melissa but she married Cass because he had the money. . . ."

The chatter around me became a cacophonous blur of he-saids and she-saids, exactly the kind of rumor-mongering I'd tried to avoid in my story. Why hadn't I remembered Melissa Osgood's fundraiser? Why hadn't Simon said anything about it?

The same server as before handed me another flute of Champagne and I drank it down too quickly. She seemed to be on my heels, as if someone had paid her to keep my drinks flowing. Looking around the room, I spotted Simon out on the restaurant's patio talking to Sylvia. He didn't look happy; neither did Sylvia. I imagined she

32

was taking him to task for not telling her about the story beforehand. I couldn't blame her. I remembered suddenly that Sylvia had been at Melissa's fundraiser last year. *They* were friends too —

Which of course was why Simon *hadn't* told her.

Something didn't seem right. Was it true, I wondered, taking yet another flute of Champagne from the dark-haired server's tray, that he had a thing for Melissa Osgood? Was *that* why he had agreed so easily to me doing the story — because he wanted to hurt his rival? Surely it couldn't have been something so trivial as resentment at not getting into a club, but then there was the thing he'd said about a grudge being the best motivator in the world.

But what did that matter? I knew that Caspar Osgood was a sexual predator — I'd heard story after story and corroborated each of them with evidence from colleagues and friends whom the victim had told of the assault around the time it happened. As I'd said to Sylvia, I hadn't used anything I couldn't back up. I wanted to ask Simon if he'd known about the fundraiser. I wouldn't ask about the club thing; that was too ridiculous. He was still on the patio but now, instead of arguing with Sylvia, he was on the phone. As I was wondering if I should go out and talk to him, a petite brunette in a Theory suit approached me and announced. "You're part of the new vanguard. Have you thought of writing a book?"

Glad for the distraction, I laughed and asked, "What self-respecting journalist hasn't?"

"Do you have additional material that didn't make it into the story?" she asked.

I snorted. "Are you kidding? After three years of research? I've got enough on the cutting-room floor for *two* books," I bragged, realizing I was pretty drunk by then.

"Really?" Theory asked, lifting one heavy eyebrow (I could recommend an eyebrow threader on the Upper West Side for her). "More of the same? Or anything more . . . *combustible*?"

Even through my Champagne high I knew this was a loaded question, but Sylvia's story about the Hi-Line Club had sparked a memory and I found myself telling the brunette that there'd been one line of inquiry that Simon had pulled me back from because I couldn't find corroboration.

"Oh?" she asked.

"Yeah, something that happened in a

private club with an underage girl . . ." I waved my empty flute and nearly collided with Sylvia, who had her head down looking at her phone. She looked up briefly, glanced at the woman I was speaking to, curled her lip at the Theory suit (Sylvia thought the brand was *unimaginative*), and hurried toward the front door with her phone pressed to her ear.

"At a private club?" the woman repeated.

"Um . . . I can't really talk about that," I said, watching Sylvia leave the restaurant. What had she and Simon been arguing about?

"Well," Theory said, retrieving a card from her jacket pocket, "if you're interested in doing a book let me know. I'm a literary agent. I think I could get you a seven-figure advance."

And then she was gone and I wasn't sure if I'd heard her right. Seven figures? That was, like, a million dollars. That was . . . I could pay off my student loans, live in a building where the stairwell didn't smell, afford the kind of clothes that wouldn't curl Sylvia's lip . . . and then I was talking to someone's wife who said she'd been groped by her uncle when she was five and the dark-haired waitress was saying *she* had a story for me and she was writing her name on a napkin and stuffing it in my pocket and I saw Simon standing on the other side of the room looking at me, and I started walking toward him, but somehow I ended up tilting toward a banquette, and Atticus grabbed my arm saying, "Whoa, Nellie! We'd better get you an Uber." And then I was in a car, only whoever had called the Uber had gotten my address wrong and the car dropped me off at the corner of East Tenth and Avenue D, two blocks from my apartment.

Thank God for gentrification, I thought, stumbling down streets that only a few decades ago would have been littered with hypodermic needles but now were completely changed as evidenced by the Lexus cruising the street, probably club kids looking for some chic after-hours spot. My mother had turned green when I told her where I was living. But she was remembering the neighborhood from her own brief residency in the city in the gritty '80s, before she scurried back home to the safety of upstate New York. Now there were artisanal coffee bars that offered six-dollar cold brews and boutiques that sold hand-sewn felt serapes that looked like something I'd worn in my kindergarten pageant and cost more than I made in a week. So what if my vestibule smelled like urine and the light-bulbs on floors three through five were burned out? I was living the dream! Small-town girl comes to the big city after J school, lives in a dive on ramen noodles and dreams for five years, and finally makes it big.

I was opening my apartment door when my phone rang. *Maybe it's Simon,* I thought, *with more news about the story.* I pulled my phone out of my purse, dropping my keys. As I bent over to pick them up I was shoved onto the floor. I tried to scream but a large hand covered my mouth pressing a damp cloth over my nose and mouth. A sickeningly sweet smell flooded my brain.

Chloroform.

My brain immediately went to a story Ariel had done a few years ago on a serial rapist who chloroformed his victims. She had researched its effects and learned it took five minutes to knock someone out, and too much could kill the victim.

I bit down hard on the hand and when it pulled away I tried to twist around to see my attacker — but he pulled something down over my head — a knitted cap that covered my eyes and nose and mouth. I couldn't breathe. The smell was overwhelming. I was getting dizzy. I heard metal jangling and then I was being pushed through my own door, into my own apartment, where this invisible attacker would do whatever he wanted.

I just want you to be safe, I could hear my mother pleading as I hit the floor.

Here it was, my mother's worst fear, the thing she lay awake nights worrying about. If I died it would break her heart.

No! I thought, pushing myself off the floor to fight, *I can't die like this.*

I must have taken my attacker by surprise. I got all the way to my knees and managed to grab a handful of his coat, but the fabric was slippery, like a raincoat, I thought, picturing my attacker dressed head to toe in blood-resistant nylon the better to bludgeon me in. *What to wear when attempting a murder,* I blearily imagined proposing as a story as the slick fabric slid through my fingers. Then I was tackled so hard that my head slammed against the floor. I had just time enough to think that my mother had been right — the world really was a dangerous place — and then I wasn't thinking anything at all.

CHAPTER TWO

MELISSA

It was going to be a perfect night.

After a late cold spring and a spate of sultry days in May, June had produced one perfect summer evening for my Solstice Gala at the New York City Garden Conservancy. The sky was the same color as the aperol spritzes quivering atop the brass trays and the banks of dahlias and tiger lilies bordering the lawn. It had taken a bit of coaxing to convince the head gardener at the conservancy to replant the perennial borders for this one event, but I was used to coaxing recalcitrant men. Everything needed to be perfect tonight.

Standing on the marble stairs that led down to the garden, I did a final check. The waitstaff were wearing orange silk ribbons, a symbol of suicide awareness, and matching bow ties. Plates of vegan and locally sourced hors d'oeuvres stood ready to be circulated to the guests. Provenance of said appetizers printed on recycled cardstock had been inserted in press kits. Reporters carefully chosen from the *Globe* — and one each from competing papers. And Whit, handsome in tux and orange cummerbund, standing on the lawn with his boyfriend, Drew, and the head gardener. Drew would no doubt be pestering the gardener about organic fertilizers and sustainable crops, but that was a small price to pay for the smile on my son's face — something I thought I'd never see again three years ago.

Was Whit just a trifle tense, though? Would tonight be too much for him?

You can't protect him forever, Cass had said when I voiced that same concern this morning.

Why not? I had wanted to reply. *Look what came of us* not *protecting him three years ago.*

But instead I had only sighed and asked Cass please not to be late. That was the last item on my checklist: husband present and accounted for. But of course he wasn't here.

I looked down at my watch, the diamond encrusted Cartier tank that Cass had given me for our anniversary three years ago. *For giving me a second chance,* he'd had inscribed on the back. It was only five minutes to seven. Cass had promised to leave the office at six but traffic on the West Side Highway could be heavy.

Why not make it eight? he'd asked.

Why not leave early? I'd countered. *Or not go in at all. This gala is in honor of your son —*

He doesn't see it that way and neither do I. I'll be there as close to seven as I can. You know I've got the meeting at city hall today.

And of course I'd relented. After all, his job paid the bills. It had bought this life where I could coax the head gardener of the conservancy into replanting his perennial borders. I'd only once put my foot down with Cass — three years ago — but then Whit had been in the hospital and I'd held all the bargaining chips.

I looked back toward Whit to reassure myself he was okay. He was laughing at something Drew was whispering in his ear, leaning down to hear what he had to say, a lock of dark hair falling across his brow. He needed a haircut, but at least there was color in his face and light in his eyes. He was fine. More than fine. He was perfect, and so would be this night. I wouldn't let Cass's lateness ruin it.

"Is Dad here?"

Emily was right behind me tottering unsteadily in the ridiculously high heels she'd insisted on buying — $700 Manolo Blahniks in a shade of orange she'd never wear again.

"Not yet, sweetie, you know your dad. He'll make a last-minute entrance for effect. Why don't you go over with Whit's friends?"

She made a face. "And get another lecture on why I should be vegan? Please."

"Drew's been wonderful for your brother —" I began.

"I know, I know. We all have to support Whit. I'm here, aren't I? And in this ridiculous color."

It was true that orange did not suit Emily. She'd gotten Cass's coloring — white-bread WASP — whereas Whit had enough of my Mediterranean olive tones to pull off a sultry orange. For myself I had commissioned a dress based on Frederic Leighton's painting *Flaming June,* which had turned out perfect. Poor Emily was wearing a clinging nylon halter dress that wasn't doing her figure any favors. I'd tried to suggest she try on a larger size but that had only resulted in a tearful fight at Bergdorf's.

"You look fine," I lied. "And where else would you be?"

Emily's face reddened, which only made the dress look worse on her. "Because I have no social life, right?" She'd just finished her first year at Bard and it hadn't gone well. *I just don't fit in!* she had wailed all year long. She'd sung the same song through high school at Brearley; I was beginning to be afraid she was just one of those girls who never finds her place.

"I didn't mean —"

"Whatever, Mom," Emily said, plucking an aperol spritz off the tray held by a passing waiter. "I'll go check on Whit and make sure he doesn't get too close to the parapet or anything."

It was a mean thing to say, but I didn't have time to get into it with Emily right now. Guests were arriving, floating down the marble stairs into the garden, oohing at the banks of orange flowers, tilting back the spritzes, including Wally Shanahan, flamboyant in an orange off-the-shoulder gown that hugged every bone on her Pilates-toned figure, which was still immaculate despite her sixty-plus years. Not only was Wally married to the Manhattan DA, Pat Shanahan, currently running for governor, she was also one of the biggest donors of the Suicide Awareness Directive. She'd lost a son to suicide twelve years ago, which gave her an authority that I always thought it best to defer to.

"Look at what you've done, Mel!" she cried, clasping me to her bosom. She sounded like she was scolding me, but that was just her way.

"*We've* done," I quickly amended. "I couldn't have done it without you."

Wally wiped her eyes. "We did it for our *children,*" she said, her voice catching on *children.* Wally had only the one now, a frightfully efficient lawyer who so far was refusing to produce grandchildren. If Wally got going now about her son she would break down.

"Look," I said, leaning in to whisper, "Freddie Marcus is here with wife number three."

Wally put on the glasses that were hanging from a jeweled chain on her neck and examined the elderly banker escorting a young woman wearing a shocking-pink evening dress and snorted. "We've got shoes older than her, darling."

Of course, Wally was more than a decade older than me, but she could have been talking about all of the young women at the party: the ones who worked at the *Globe* who were coming now in their summer dresses fluttering like butterfly wings, except for one girl in a prim vintage polka-dot dress, librarian glasses, and heavy, mannish loafers whom I guessed was the reporter from *Manahatta.* I was wondering if Simon had hired her and whether he still went for the same type of shy, bookish girl he'd liked in college. The rest of the young women were all asking the same question: *Where is he? Is he here yet?*

Wally picked up the refrain. "Where is that handsome husband of yours?"

I sighed and checked my watch again. "Stuck in traffic, no doubt. He had an important meeting down at city hall today."

"More important than his son?" Wally asked.

"Cass was there for Whit three years ago," I said automatically. It had become a mantra, one repeated a dozen times a day.

"Of course he was," Wally cooed soothingly. "What father wouldn't have shown up when his son landed in the ER with an overdose. It's showing up for the everyday stuff that's hard for men like our husbands. Speaking of which, there's mine." She tilted her glass in the direction of the terrace, where Pat had arrived with his entourage, creating that crackle of electricity that politicians (*good politicians,* Cass would say) always brought with them. He was surrounded by a gaggle of reporters who brought with them the restless, prowling

45

energy reporters (*good reporters,* Cass would say) always have. Cass had had it when we met thirty years ago at Brown. It was what had drawn me to him in the beginning, before I had known where that prowling might lead him.

"I'd better go stand by my man," Wally said, giving me an airy kiss on the cheek, "and save him from the vultures."

Saving people was Wally's specialty. She'd saved me when I'd gotten the call about Whit. It was during a Brearley parents meeting, and Wally Shanahan had followed me out into the hall to ask if everything was all right. I knew Wally slightly because she'd helped Whit get an internship at the District Attorney's Office, so I had blurted out that Whit was in the hospital up in Providence and that I couldn't reach Cass. Wally had immediately called her driver to come pick us up. An hour later we were on the Merritt Parkway and I was spilling everything. All about *why* I couldn't reach Cass because I'd kicked him out two months earlier when I'd found out he was screwing his secretary.

"Does he want to come back?" Wally had asked.

"Oh, he *says* he does," I'd admitted, "but I'm not sure I want him. Look at what it's done to Whit."

"And what will it do to Whit if you divorce?" Wally had asked. "Don't you think you need your family together at a time like this? Don't you think your boy needs his father right now?"

Of course, Wally had been right. I called Cass, and the secretary — she was a new one; not the one Cass had slept with; he'd at least had the manners to fire *her* — had actually been very nice and found Cass in minutes and hired him a helicopter. When we arrived, Cass was sitting at Whit's bedside grasping his hand — the one that wasn't attached to the IV — in both of his. And poor Whit, looking so pale and thin, was staring up at his father the way he had during his first swimming lessons — like Cass could pull him out of the water with the power of his gaze. I had known then that I would take Cass back the next time he asked — but first I'd make sure I got a few things in return.

A promise never to cheat again.

A commitment to fund a foundation to raise awareness of suicide.

A vow to always put family above the paper.

And he'd seemed to be honoring those commitments — he'd acted the part of the dutiful, loving husband and he'd even thrown in a hefty contribution to Pat Shanahan's campaign fund as a thank-you to Wally for taking such good care of me during a crisis. But here he was, after only three years, late to only the second annual fundraiser for SAD. How soon before he began sliding on his other promises? I eased myself away from Cy and Marjorie Ellis, old friends of Wally's and generous donors, to glance at my phone. No messages from Cass, but there was one from Sylvia Crosley.

Call me. Now.

It wasn't like her to be so histrionic. Sylvia had a reputation for being unfailingly composed, and I was fond of her, even if she had betrayed me by taking a job at my husband's rival's magazine. She'd been miffed she couldn't come tonight, but there was some office thing at *Manahatta* she just *had* to attend — some "big hush-hush announcement." Maybe *Manahatta* was going under. Maybe that's why Sylvia wanted me to call her. She needed a job at the *Globe*.

I looked across the lawn and saw the little boho reporter in the polka dots — what had Sylvia said her name was? Some Disney princess name like Belle or Aurora — checking her phone. Her eyebrows lifted above the rims of those ridiculous glasses, and then she started walking toward Whit, holding her phone out to him. I headed toward them to see what she wanted with him but she was making better time across the grass in her mannish loafers than I was in my spike heels. I could hear the pings of notification alerts going off as I passed the clutch of *Globe* reporters. How rude not to silence their phones, but of course the press had to stay connected, as Cass always said when I asked him not to check his phone at dinner.

But it wasn't just the reporters who were looking at their phones. Those young second wives had theirs out too and their husbands and the wealthy donors in Wally's set, and the flaks clustered around Pat Shanahan. Even Wally herself was frowning down at her screen — *She'd get a widow's hump if she stood like that too much* — and then looking up at me with an expression of —

What?

I wasn't sure I'd ever seen this expression on Wally's face before. It almost looked like —

"Ms. Osgood?" The *Manahatta* reporter turned away from Whit, whose face was drained of color, and held her phone up for me to see. "Do you have any comment about the recent allegations against your husband?"

The screen was open to a *Manahatta* story

— I recognized the font — with the headline: "Global Predator: Six Women Accuse Caspar Osgood of Sexual Misconduct." I felt the ground beneath my feet wobble — *Never let them see you waver,* Cass always said — but I managed a chilly smile.

"I see it's a story from *Manahatta,* one of my husband's competitors. Not exactly an impartial source. Everyone knows Simon Wallace has always been jealous of Cass." My voice hitched as I said Simon's name. He had been Cass's college roommate freshman year, and always . . . *there.* Hanging around Cass at the local bars, joining the same clubs, writing for the newspaper. He came from a working-class family in one of those depressing little New England mill towns not far from the college, and it was clear that he was trying really hard to fit in. *My shadow,* Cass called him. Then they had a falling-out when Cass got that promotion at the *Times* that Simon had wanted and he'd stopped speaking to both of us. It had hurt me that he was able to walk away from our friendship so easily, but as Cass said, it was only a matter of time before men like Simon showed their true colors. Still, Simon wouldn't *ruin* Cass. No matter what had happened between them, he wouldn't do that to us, would he? I slid my eyes away toward Wally, who was hovering nearby, hoping that she would echo my comment, but Wally only stared back with that look on her face.

Pity — that's what was on Wally Shanahan's stricken face. Pity.

"Are you saying you don't believe the women?" the reporter demanded.

Don't let them put words in your mouth, Cass always said. *If you don't like the question then answer one you like better.*

"I believe my husband, who has made this foundation possible —"

"Which was initiated by your son's suicide attempt," the little chit of a reporter said, swiveling back to face Whit. "Did your father's behavior have anything to do with your suicide attempt?"

"What a disgusting suggestion!" I shouted, stepping forward to get in between the reporter and Whit.

"Isn't it true that you only took your husband back because of your son's suicide attempt?" the reporter countered. Whit's eyes were filling with tears. He looked desperately toward me and I remembered how he had been looking up at Cass when I came into the hospital room. Like he was drowning. "Or didn't you know that, Whit?" she added.

"Get the hell away from my son."

I meant the words to come out low but in the silence that had fallen over the party they rang out like church bells. The reporter furrowed her heavy, unplucked brows. "I can understand that you wanted to protect your son, Mrs. Osgood. Is that why you kept your husband's sexual misconduct a secret?"

"I would *never*" — I began, taking a step forward and stumbling on my heels. My drink spilled down the girl's dress, staining the cheap fabric orange. There was an audible gasp from the crowd — as if I'd done it deliberately! — and then someone was gripping my elbow.

"Come on, Mel, let's get out of here." Wally's calm, authoritative voice was in my ear but she might have been a million miles away. I was floating above the party, like one of the orange flying wish lanterns we were going to set off as a finale.

"But the party . . . the donors . . . the lanterns . . ."

"It's done," Wally said, and I could see that she was right. Pat Shanahan was being rushed to his black Escalade as if a bomb had gone off. "Let me take care of packing up."

As she'd taken care of everything three years ago, urging me to take Cass back for

Whit's sake.

"Whit, darling . . ." I turned toward my son but he drew back. His face was ashen, betrayed, as if *I* had betrayed him. I shook my head, but I wasn't sure to what. He must have seen my indecision. Emily had found us, but she stood next to her brother, arm protectively wrapped around his shoulder. I'd have been heartened by this show of familial support except for the look on Emily's face.

"The story says that Dad slept with three of his assistants and had one fired when she wanted to end the . . ." Emily flung up her hand. "The *whatever* it's called when an older man is having sex with a twenty-five-year-old. It also says he forced a *nineteen-year-old* intern to give him a blowjob. *I'm* nineteen years old! How *could* he?"

"Oh, honey," I began, thinking of the joke Wally had made earlier — it seemed like an eon ago — *We have shoes older than those girls.* Only it didn't seem so funny anymore.

Wally was leading me away and Whit and Emily and Drew were going in the opposite direction. "Shouldn't we be leaving together?" I asked, but Wally was propelling me over the lawn, toward a side exit where the hired car — a demure dark-gray Lexus — was idling behind one of Shanahan's black Escalades. The driver was reading something on his phone, which he hurriedly put away when I got in.

"Take her straight home and go in through the garage when you get there," Wally told the driver. "And don't you dare talk to a single reporter or I'll have your livery license." She slammed the door and then leaned down, resting her elbow on the windowsill. "And don't you talk to anyone, Mel. Not even your friends."

Friends? I could feel a laugh bubbling up my throat. Would I have any by the morning?

"I'll call you tomorrow. I have a PR guy who knows how to handle these situations. Until then, just sit tight." She reached in and gave my shoulder a hard squeeze, which I'm sure she meant to be reassuring but actually hurt. Sometimes Wally didn't know her own strength. Then she withdrew her head and rapped her knuckles on the roof of the Lexus, as if she were urging the horses on in an old-fashioned coach. The tinted window powered up, sealing me in the plush leather interior.

I looked down at my phone. There was a Twitter notification with a link to the *Manahatta* article. I tapped on it and scrolled down to the byline. Joan Lurie. Hadn't she

54

been one of Sylvia's protégées? I tapped on the reporter's name and a picture of an attractive, although rather severe, young woman appeared on the screen. She looked familiar — hadn't *she* been the reporter assigned to the fundraiser last year? I remembered thinking that she was *exactly* Simon's type. How she must have been laughing at me behind my back.

"It doesn't look like anyone is following us, Mrs. Osgood," the driver said. "Shall I take the Saw Mill back to Ardsley?"

Ardsley. I visualized the empty, echoing rooms of our beautiful center-hall Colonial. Then I looked down at the picture of the reporter. The woman who had just ruined my perfect night. The woman who had just ruined my life.

"No," I said, "there's something I need to do downtown first."

CHAPTER THREE

JOAN

I came to on the floor of my living room —
well, living room/dining room/kitchen —
but I was closer to the coffee table than the
fold-out couch, so let's say living room. *At
least I'm not on the couch,* I thought grog-
gily — it felt as if my head was stuffed with
cotton balls — as if not being in proximity
to my bed meant I hadn't been raped.

Had I been raped?

I was still wearing the shirt and blouse I'd
gone to work in that day — the day *before,*
I realized, squinting in the hot sun coming
through the dirty glass of my one barred
window — but I wasn't wearing pantyhose.

Had I worn pantyhose?

No, Sylvia scoffed when I did. *So '80s.*

But I was wearing panties.

They were damp.

But then again, so was my whole body. I
was drenched in sweat, the bright sun turn-

ing my apartment into a greenhouse.

Someone had attacked me. *A stranger? Someone who saw me stumbling drunkenly along the sidewalk?* They — *he,* screw the gender-neutral pronoun — must have followed me into the building and up the stairs and I'd been too drunk to notice. I touched my scalp gingerly and found a hard, moist lump. I drew back my fingers and stared at the blood.

Then I touched myself between my legs.

I'd interviewed a woman who'd been roofied when she was in college. The worst thing, she said, was waking up the next day and not knowing what had been done to her.

Could you tell? I'd asked her.

I had bruises on my inner thighs, she'd said, *and . . . you know . . . semen.*

My thighs don't feel bruised. There's none of the tenderness that I feel after even consensual sex. Nothing's . . . *sticky.*

I start to cry. I'm not sure if it's relief or not. I don't know anything for sure. How can I? Someone grabbed me, chloroformed me, and pushed me into my apartment. Someone handled my unconscious body like it was a piece of meat. Someone . . .

Could still be here.

I push myself up. My shabby studio apartment swirls like a carnival ride, bits of my life flashing by like dioramas. Clothes spilling out of the tiny closet, a view of the rust-stained toilet, a cereal bowl and mug on the plywood counter that serves as a kitchen, the butcher-block table I use as a desk.

My laptop. Although my head is still spinning I struggle to my feet. No one is here — that's one advantage of living in a shoebox; there's no place to hide — but what did they take? My laptop has all my notes. Three years' worth of research. I don't use the Cloud because I don't trust it; I didn't want anyone scooping me on this story. I wouldn't even use the computers at *Manahatta.* Everything I have is on that laptop and a three-inch-long flash drive on my keychain.

The key chain is on the floor, glinting in the merciless sun next to my wallet and purse. The wallet is empty, but I can't recall whether I had cash in it or not, and even though the credit cards are gone, my attacker isn't going to get much joy out of those; I've maxed out every card I have.

The laptop is on my desk.

I feel a sense of relief that's greater than what I'd felt at finding that I hadn't been raped — and then a wave of deep shame. What kind of a person is more concerned about their hard drive than their body?

A professional, I imagine Simon saying. Which makes me feel a tiny bit better as I rush to the bathroom to throw up.

Even though my head feels like an ice pick has been lodged in my frontal lobe, I don't go to the hospital. Stupid, right? I do have insurance, courtesy of *Manahatta,* so I can't even use that as an excuse. I don't call the police. No excuse for that either. How many times have I asked a source why she didn't report Osgood to the police?

I didn't think it was a crime.

I was ashamed.

I was afraid I'd lose my job.

Well, I know attacking me and breaking into my apartment are crimes. And I do feel ashamed that I'd instinctually been more worried about my laptop than my virtue and that I'd stumbled home drunk, stupidly not checking behind me when I came in the front door. As for my job, I'm not going to lose it, but I wonder what a police report will do to the story. Will it look like a ploy for publicity? Will it seem awfully coincidental?

If nothing else it will distract from the story, and I've worked too hard for too long — and asked too many women to trust me

— to let myself get in the way of this story. At least I'd better have a look at how it's playing before I go adding to the noise.

I find my phone inside my purse. Dead. I plug it in and open my laptop.

At first I think it's broken. A sick joke from my attacker. The screen is so blurry I can't read a thing. I thump the trackpad, twirl the cursor around the screen, click through several open tabs, and then look down at the keyboard to reboot —

Only, the keyboard is blurry too. The glowing letters look like ancient runes rising up out of murky water. I lift a page of typescript from one of the piles and can't make out a word of it. I rub my eyes, but that only makes my headache worse. Is blurred vision a symptom of concussion? Or chloroform poisoning? I immediately think to google it and then laugh at myself. Even if I could navigate the screen well enough to type in the search, I couldn't read the results. Now would be the time that one of those voice-activated digital assistants would come in handy, but I've prudishly refused to buy one on the grounds that they're spy bots and represent an invasion of privacy.

So instead I let an attacker in my front door.

No, I correct myself, *I didn't let anyone in.* Why would I even think of it that way? It's as if all the skepticism I'd trained myself to wield (*You have to ask the skeptical questions before the reader can,* Simon told me) is now aimed at myself.

The screen in front of me dissolves into a grainy film as I begin to cry. The tears feel like they're rising up inside me, like floodwaters that will close over my head to complete the job my attacker set out to do. All the carefully constructed stories I've told myself over the last three years fall away and I'm right back where I was when I got fired from the *Globe* — a *fuck-up,* the kind of careless, stupid girl who gets herself in trouble —

My phone begins chiming, breaking into the pity-fest I'm throwing for myself . . . and chimes and chimes and chimes, loading messages and tweets and Facebook notifications and Google alerts I have set for my name and Caspar Osgood's. The world is weighing in on the story I've worked on for three years, and I can't read a word of it.

Then I recall that my phone does have a built-in voice-activated feature. I press the Home button and an electronic voice asks how she can help me. *Hey Siri, how do you know if you've been raped?* I imagine asking. Or: *How can I tell if I have a brain injury?* But instead I ask my phone to read me my messages.

I have 53 new text messages, 235 Twitter notifications, and 7 voicemails. I begin with the voicemails, figuring anyone actually calling me must have something important to say (or is at least older than thirty). Three are from my mother congratulating me on the story but wondering if I wasn't going to have a lot of people mad at me. I can hear the anxiety in her voice warring with her pride in me. One is from Sam asking if I got home all right. Two are from Simon, first telling me that he'd gotten a threatening call from Osgood at eight A.M., the second that Osgood had resigned his post as publisher of the *Globe* by noon.

Noon? Is it really that late? I can't read the time on my phone to find out.

"You took him down, kid. You did it. Call when you get this."

The last call was from someone named Andrea Robbins. It takes me a moment to realize Andrea is the literary agent I spoke to at the party last night.

"I put out some feelers," she says. "Give me a five-hundred-word pitch and I could get you a book deal by next Friday. Send it to ARobbins@Lit.com."

I start to laugh. I can't even read my emails. How am I going to type up five hundred words —

But then I remember that when I pitched the story to Simon *properly,* as he'd requested at our interview, he said that what I'd written was a book pitch and not an article pitch. *Too broad, too wordy, too melodramatic.* I'd redrafted four times before he accepted it — an exercise, I'd realized later, that was more about teaching me to write than about making up his mind to do the story. He'd *always* meant to do the story.

For revenge? I wonder, recalling what Sylvia had said at the party last night, but I push the thought away.

I still have the first draft of that pitch somewhere on the hard drive of my laptop. It might as well be at the bottom of the ocean, though, for all I'm able to get to it. My laptop has no voice-activated software. I could call up someone to help — Sam, for instance — but I realize as I picture Sam coming here that I can't face another human being right now.

I look down at the screen again, hoping my vision has cleared, but it hasn't. Dimly I realize that I've got bigger problems than emailing a book proposal to an agent. What if that blow detached my retina? What if I'm going blind? What if I have been raped? What if I'm pregnant or have been exposed to an STD? I should be going to the hospital. I should be calling the police.

Instead, I fumble my way into my email — at least it's the first open tab on the screen — and touch-type Andrea's email address into the recipient line, blessing the literary gods for that pretentiously brief agency name. I manage to find the attachment icon and then, grateful I have my documents preset to list alphabetically, click on the first icon, which I know is labeled "Amanda Story Pitch," which I'd named for my first source. I think of all those women whose stories are saved in my hard drive — and hesitate. There's so much more than what made it into the article — Simon was a ruthless pruner — that I don't think I'd have any trouble finding the material for a book, but not all of those women were willing to have their stories told in full. It seems, too, a different matter to use their stories to land a book deal. The *Manahatta* story was one thing — Caspar Osgood had to be exposed — but what's my justification for a book?

Money, a voice that sounds like Sylvia's suggests, *so you can live in a neighborhood where you don't get attacked in your own home.*

Like many of Sylvia's ripostes, this one sounds eminently reasonable. I click on the file and then touch-type a brief message, which I hope says "How's this?" and not "Giq;a rgua>"

It's a bit cavalier, but I imagine it's what Sylvia would do. I'm not sure when she became my role model, but as I click Send I feel a little thrill of accomplishment wholly at odds with my current disheveled and battered state.

"I will not let this define me," I say out loud, startling myself with the sound of my own voice. I don't sound like myself at all.

In the end, I don't call the police and I don't go to the hospital. At first I tell myself that I can always change my mind, but after a day goes by I realize that I wouldn't know how to explain why I hadn't gone to the police earlier. Several of the women I spoke to told me the same thing about why they waited so long to tell anyone what Caspar Osgood did to them. They were shocked and ashamed at first, and then by the time they felt ready to talk about it they were embarrassed they hadn't come forward sooner — and thought people wouldn't

65

believe them because they hadn't said something right away.

The irony that I find myself trapped in the same cycle of shame only makes it worse. How could I, having listened to all those stories, not have gone straight to the police? And how could I, having spent three years collecting evidence of sexual assault, think I was immune to it? Again and again I replay myself stumbling drunkenly from a taxi, letting myself into my building without a backward glance, climbing those darkened stairs deaf to following footsteps. How could I, knowing all that I know about how these things happen, have been so stupid to let this happen?

I couldn't bear to let the world know — and I knew the minute I went to the hospital it would come out. My name was already all over the Internet and tabloids. *Joan Lurie hunts down the lurid details.* (Simon had warned me there'd be puns.) *Former Fashion Blogger Busts Big Cheese.* (And alliteration.) *Gotham Girl Slays Goliath.* (And biblical references.)

I could imagine what the tabloids and blogs would make of my being attacked. I didn't want the story to be any more about me than it already was. Which was the reason I gave Simon for not doing any interviews as they came in. I told him I wanted to lie low and he gave me leave from the magazine for an indefinite period. *Whatever you need, kid,* he'd said, *you've earned it.* To keep him — or anyone else from the office — from visiting, I said I was going upstate to visit my mother for a couple of days. And for a dreadful few moments I even thought I would go. The idea of retreating to the safety of my childhood home was dangerously appealing, but I couldn't bear for my mother to know what had happened to me. It would confirm all her fears about me living in New York City, and she had enough on her plate taking care of my senile grandmother. I told myself I was staying away to spare her, and not because I was afraid that if I went home I might never have the courage to leave again.

My mother hadn't. When she came back from the city pregnant with me she never went back. *Not a good place to raise a child, especially as a single mother,* she told me when I asked, *and then your grandmother needed my help when she started losing her memory.* But I'd always heard a tinge of regret in her voice, a sense of missed opportunities that she'd sacrificed on the altar of motherhood and filial responsibility. I suspected, also, that her moving was a sur-render to my grandmother's anxieties, which only got worse as her mind became untethered. I didn't want to have that regret. I didn't want to give in to my fears.

So instead of hiding upstate I hid in my apartment, listening to Siri recite the symptoms of concussion from WebMD. I ordered food from FreshDirect and the noodle shop on the corner. I paid with an app and asked the delivery people to leave the food outside the door. I opened the door only after looking through the peephole to make sure there was no one waiting in the hall to knock me over the head. Even then, my heart pounded during the seconds when the door was open. The air in the hallway seemed to pulse with malign intent; the stairwell gaped like an open mouth; menacing shadows lurked in my peripheral vision — all symptoms of concussion, according to WebMD.

After the first few days, I stopped trying to read texts and emails and put an away message on my email account. I let any call go to voicemail and didn't bother listening to the message. I told my mother that I was turning my phone off to avoid reporters. I barely paid attention to Andrea Robbins's emails showing me the pitch letter she'd drafted and the list of editors she was sending it to. I even stopped listening to the re-actions to my story on social media. Even the positive reactions praising my *intrepid investigative reporting* rang false to me. How *intrepid* had I been in avoiding an attack in my own home? The negative reactions at-tacking my objectivity rang truer. Who was I, a twenty-nine-year-old style reporter, to take down the Great Caspar Osgood? Hadn't I been fired from an internship at the *Globe*? I'd written the story as revenge and was trying to make my own name at the expense of his.

Had I been acting out of revenge? I won-dered, trying to sift through the disordered mess in my head. *Hadn't I been preening at the party? Isn't that why I'd been so oblivious and drunk on my own success that I'd gotten myself attacked?*

After three weeks of castigating myself, my ego was more bruised than my eyes. I decided to try a walk up to the corner Rite-Aid. Although I still didn't think I'd been raped I felt that I needed to take a preg-nancy test — and I knew that if I ordered it from FreshDirect it would show up on my shopping history, which Sam swore could be hacked.

I put on sunglasses, a baseball cap, and a

sweatshirt even though it was sweltering outside. I kept my head down and hoped people thought I was a celebrity (which I probably was by this point) and not a drug dealer. Halfway up the block I felt sure someone was following me. When I turned my head a shadow skittered away, but the sidewalk was empty. I kept walking, but the feeling persisted, as if someone were lurking just on the edge of my vision. I used a trick my mother taught me and glanced into a plate-glass window to check for pursuers. I was startled by the sight of a hunchbacked thug in a hoodie — and then realized it was *me.*

My heart was pounding so hard by the time I got to the Rite-Aid that I thought I might be having a heart attack. I tossed the pregnancy test, along with half a dozen unnecessary toiletries, into a basket. As I reached for a tube of hand cream I saw something move to my left. I spun around so fast I knocked down a display of sunscreen. But this time I did see someone darting into the next aisle. Someone in a hoodie and dark glasses like me. I walked stiffly toward the counter, keeping an eye out for my doppelgänger, but there was no one at the checkout but a bored cashier flipping through a copy of the *Post.* As I approached she held it up and I saw the top part of the headline — big enough for even me to read: SEX ADDICT NEWSMAN . . .

What now? I thought. *Sex addict newsman claims innocence? Sex addict newsman sues reporter?* But then as I got closer the cashier lifted the paper and I saw the whole headline.

SEX ADDICT NEWSMAN
COMMITS SUICIDE IN FAMILY POOL

The shopping basket handles slip greasily through my fingers and my toiletries slide onto the floor. "Is-is-is that . . ." I stutter. "Do they mean Caspar Osgood?"

The cashier stares at me as if I had just crawled out from under a rock. "Yeah, the pig. If you ask me, he got off easy. Those women he molested should've been let to cut off his balls and stuff 'em in his mouth."

I flinch at the image as I kneel to collect my toiletries. *But hadn't I wanted him to suffer?* When I go to pay I spill change from my pocket all over the counter. As I pick it up the cashier adds, "I feel bad for the wife though. And the kids." She holds up a picture of Melissa Osgood, flanked by her adult son and daughter. "I hear the son's a recovering addict. Do you think she knew?"

For a moment I think my cover's been blown. She knows I wrote the story that brought Caspar Osgood down and is asking my expert opinion on Melissa Osgood's knowledge and culpability — a question I've often pondered these last three years.

"If she didn't," I say, still trying to absorb the news Osgood has killed himself, "she was willfully blind."

The shadow in my peripheral flickers and I spin around, half-expecting to find Melissa Osgood stalking me through the aisles of Rite-Aid. How she must hate me! But there's only a couple of girls my age in vintage sundresses waiting to buy coconut water. The hoodie-wearer is nowhere to be seen.

I add the *Post* to my purchases and head back home, ignoring the bruised purple aurora pulsing at the edges of my vision like an impending summer storm. *Caspar Osgood killed himself.* It proves his guilt more than anything I wrote. An innocent man would have fought to prove his innocence. And I *know* he wasn't innocent. I've listened to too many women recount the same strikingly similar story over and over again.

He asked me to stay late to go over a story. He said I had Pulitzer potential. He offered to mentor me. Then he rubbed up against me.

72

He shoved me into a supply closet. He put his fingers up my vagina. He pushed my head into his lap. He put my hand on his penis. When I complained he said he'd ruin my career. He said I'd never work as a journalist again. He fired me.

The man was a monster.

He had to be stopped.

It was not my fault he killed himself.

It's not my fault his family's lives are ruined.

My hand is shaking so badly I drop the keys as I'm trying to unlock the front door of my building. As I bend for them I see a shadow stretching over and past me on the sidewalk. A raised arm poised above my head. I turn, cringing, expecting Melissa Osgood come to exact revenge for her husband's downfall, but there's nothing but the torn awning from the bodega next door flapping in the wind.

I retrieve my keys and let myself in, checking that no one comes in with me, and hurry up the stairs, dodging shadows on every landing. I look over my shoulder as I unlock my apartment and quickly dash inside, engaging the dead bolt and the door chain. I sit down on the sofa and then get up to close the window, even though it turns my studio into a sweatbox. I sit back down and when I can breathe again I call Simon.

"You heard," he says by way of greeting.

"I never imagined —" I begin.

"Bullshit," Simon cuts in. "Let's be honest, kid. You set out to ruin that bastard for good reason. He was a monster. It's not your fault he was too big a coward to face up to what he'd done."

"But what about his wife? What will happen to her?"

"Melissa? She'll spend a few months at their place in the Hamptons and then write a tear-jerker tell-all memoir — or her well-paid ghostwriter will — about how she was *deceived* and how she's Osgood's biggest victim. Watch, it will come out two weeks before *your* book, which, by the way, I hear is being shopped by Andrea Robbins at Lit. If you had asked my advice I'd have steered you to my agent at Cromwell & Fitch."

I detect a hint of pique in Simon's voice. Should I have consulted with him before agreeing to let Andrea handle the book? *And how did he even know that it was being repped by her?*

"I don't even know about doing a book now," I say, guiltily realizing that I hadn't read the last two emails from Andrea. "It feels . . . *opportunistic.*"

"And what's wrong with that? This *is* your

74

opportunity, kid. You'd damn well better take advantage of it. Trust me, a moment like this doesn't come around twice. And if you want me to read a draft, I'd be happy to."

I thank Simon, promise I'll do a better job keeping in touch when I "get back from upstate," and get off the phone. Then I pee on a stick and am relieved to find out I'm not pregnant. I take two of the Tylenol PMs I bought at the Rite-Aid and climb into bed. I go to sleep imagining Melissa Osgood on a beach in the Hamptons, far, far away from my East Village studio — but when I wake up in the middle of the night it's Caspar Osgood I see standing on my fire escape, pool water dripping from his bloated face, come back from the dead for revenge.

I leap up, grab the can of mace my mother gave me when I moved to the city, and hold it out, braced to spray it in the eyes of my intruder, but the figure evaporates. Another concussion-induced chimera? Or my attacker back for a second round? Someone sent by Melissa Osgood to punish me for ruining her husband?

I stay up the rest of the night asking Siri to find the most secure window gates and look up the statistics for repeat home invasions. Why haven't I thought about it before?

Had I thought he wouldn't come back because there wasn't anything worth stealing? But what if he hadn't been looking for anything to steal? I've foolishly assumed all along that the attacker was a random criminal who seized on the opportunity of a drunk girl to follow me into my building. What if his mission was to kill me and he's come back to finish the job? The man who attacked me *knows where I live.* He could come back.

Siri interrupts my searches at nine a.m. to tell me I've got a call from Andrea Robbins.

When I answer it Andrea asks me if I'm sitting down. I consider telling her the truth: that I'm crouched in a corner of my shithole apartment because it's the only place I don't feel like someone is sneaking up on me. Instead I say, "Still in bed. I'm getting lazy on vacation."

"Well, don't get too used to it. I've got an offer that's going to put you back to work. I think it's the best offer we're going to get; the only hitch is you have to deliver the book in six months." Then she names a figure that is so big I can't even imagine what I'd do with that much money —

Until I *do* imagine what I will do with it.

I tell Andrea to take the offer. I can write the book in six months (never mind that I can't even physically *write* or *read* for more than fifteen minutes right now). She mentions a few more details but I'm not really paying attention anymore. As soon as the call's over I tell Siri, "I need an apartment that's safe. A refuge."

After a pause, she tells me about an apartment building in the upper Manhattan neighborhood of Inwood that's actually *called the Refuge.*

Yes, I think, *that's exactly what I need.* Then I ask her to look up the number for a realtor whom Sylvia once said was the best in the city, one who can get me into that building the fastest.

CHAPTER FOUR

MELISSA

The morning after the fundraiser — or the Disaster, as I have come to think of it — I asked Cass to move out.

"You have a perfect right to expect that," he answered. We were on the deck, next to the pool. He was still in the rumpled suit pants and shirt he'd worn to the office the day before; I was in yoga pants and a silk kurta. I'd woken up still wearing the *Flaming June* dress, pulped to a wreck of orange chiffon, hungover, with a head full of aperol mist where my memories ought to be, but I'd taken the time to shower, moisturize, and dress. I wasn't going into a showdown with Cass looking my age. "I can imagine how upsetting this must be for you."

"Can you? Do you have any idea what it was like to watch all our friends get the news that you're a sexual predator *right in front of my face?*"

"*That* was Simon Wallace's doing. He planned the timing of the story on the night of your fundraiser to humiliate me — and *you*. So whatever misplaced fondness you might still be harboring for him —"

"This isn't about Simon," I began, but he cut me off.

"That's exactly what it's about. You know he's had it out for me since I got promoted over him at the *Times* twenty-two years ago. And this girl he sicced on me — she was fired from her internship at the *Globe*. Aside from the lack of ethics, it's *sloppy.* I'd never assign a reporter to a story who had a motive to discredit the subject."

"So you deny that you had any contact with those women?" I asked.

He had turned red; he knew I had him there. "You know that one of the women is Amanda."

"Yes," I said, wincing at the name. "I'd recognize the name of the woman who nearly broke up our marriage three years ago."

"*Nearly.* I left her when you threw me out and haven't been with another woman since you agreed to give me a second chance. *That's* why she made up this story — to get back at me for leaving her. These other women . . ." He waved his hand as if the women were in attendance. I could picture them in the wavy pool light reflected on the sheers billowing out from the living room — Cass's seraglio. "Okay, some are flirtations from before Amanda and some are women who work for me and may have been disappointed I *didn't* flirt with them. I think Amanda talked to this reporter, Jane Lurie —"

"Joan," I corrected. "The reporter's name is Joan Lurie." I could also have told Cass where she lived. After we had left the Conservancy, I had asked my driver to take me down to the *Manahatta* offices to talk to Sylvia. I wanted to ask her to her face if she had known about the story and if she had, how could she not have told me. But when we pulled up in front of the offices I saw that girl coming out of a restaurant across the street. She was in a skimpy skirt and top, laughing, clearly drunk, and hanging on some skinny hipster with a man bun. Having the time of her life while celebrating the ruin of *my* life. When she got into a car, leaving Man Bun behind, I asked the driver to follow her.

"Okay, *Joan,*" Cass said, his voice rising. "Amanda told Joan Lurie a made-up version of our affair to get back at me for going back to you. The Lurie woman must have thought she had a story, so she went after other women who had worked for the *Globe* and had been fired. Who knows how much she led them on or how much they were willing to make up to get back at the *Globe.* Or how much Simon egged her on to pull me down."

"So what are you going to do about it?" I asked.

"I'm going to issue a statement admitting to the affair with Amanda and then explain why I ended it. And then I'll deny the rest. Wally called and recommended a PR guy that Pat used a few years ago, Greg Firestein. He's coming over to discuss strategy. I talked to him already this morning and he said it would really help if you made a statement of your own, saying you knew about the affair and that we had worked things out . . . maybe mentioning what happened to Whit . . . but I told him that was totally up to you. That I wouldn't blame you if the only statement you made today was that you were leaving me."

"In other words, you need me. The loyal wife standing by her husband."

"I always need you, Mel," he said, giving me his sad, earnest look. "But I'll understand if you walk out now. I'll give you everything — or at least what's left after these women come after me. If these women sue me — well, in this climate" — he waved again in the air as if the wavering pool light and blowing sheers were symptoms of a weather system — "we may lose everything."

"That's what she wants, isn't it?" I asked, closing my eyes. It made me woozy to look at the way the curtains swayed in the breeze. It brought back images of the night before that I preferred not to think about. "To ruin us."

"She?" he asked.

"That little chit of a reporter."

The driver had followed Joan to the East Village, where she practically fell out of her car and then weaved her way down the deserted streets as if she were untouchable. As if her life were inviolable. It had made me furious to watch her.

"She wants to see us go up in flames. Well, I'll be damned if I let her get away with it. Tell Greg I'll make that statement. And you . . . you can sleep in the guest room until I decide what I want to do with you."

The chairman of the *Globe*'s board called by noon that first day and suggested Cass step down from his position to "minimize damage to the *Globe* brand."

"I built that paper up from a tabloid rag,"

he bellowed. "And now I'm *damage to the brand*?"

Greg Firestein — the "PR guy" Wally had recommended — said it would be better to look like he was "focusing on his family" right now. He wrote a statement for Cass to release and one for me too. He also suggested that Emily and Whit go ahead with their summer plans — Whit to be an aide for Pat Shanahan's campaign up in Albany, Emily to go out to Taos to build yurts. I hated to watch them go, but I could see Greg's point that we should all behave as if everything were normal.

"You and Cass shouldn't go to any parties or seem to be celebratory but you should continue with your day to day — lunch with friends, volunteer work, recreational activities as long as they aren't too frivolous."

"Too frivolous?" I'd asked.

"Yoga, swimming, walking are all good; but no Barry's Bootcamp or SoulCycle."

I hate yoga. And where would I walk without reporters following me? As for lunches, my so-called friends all canceled our lunch dates. Some of them made excuses — suddenly many of my friends had emergency root canals and jury duty — and some spewed out sanctimonious hypocrisies about needing to "distance" themselves from *that* kind of behavior. And as for volunteer work, the chair of the Cancer Foundation called to say that perhaps it would be better if Cass and I didn't come to the gala this year — too much negative publicity.

"It's this #MeToo movement," Cass would rant, pacing up and down the patio after his morning swim. Whatever happened to due process? Whatever happened to innocent before proven guilty?"

After a few days I was sorry I hadn't gone to Taos to build yurts with Emily. With reporters camped at the end of the driveway we were practically prisoners in our own house. Greg arranged for food brought in from FreshDirect and GrubHub. I worked out on the elliptical in our exercise room and swam laps in the pool until I saw a picture of myself on the Internet looking emaciated in my bathing suit. Cass started swimming at night after that, but I stayed inside, eyeing the sky for drones and silently eating meals out of boxes.

After that first day we didn't talk about the women. If I was going to credit the stories I'd have left on the first day; since I hadn't left I'd lost my chance to question him. If I questioned him I'd be admitting doubt — and if I had any doubts, what was

I doing here?

The women were always with us, though, in the rippled light that came off the pool and in the billowing sheer drapes in the open doorways. Those drapes continued to make me sick when I looked at them. They reminded me of something that had happened when I followed Joan Lurie home. I'd only wanted to talk to her, to tell her what I thought of her planning her little debut on the night of my suicide awareness fundraiser. Did she know how hard I'd worked to build Whit back up these last three years — the expensive therapy, begging Wally to get him the job on Pat's campaign to give him a sense of purpose, the work I did for SAD? Did she know what it was like to see your son in a hospital bed because he had decided he didn't want to live? Or how long it took before I didn't wake up every night at three A.M. in a panic wanting to call Whit to make sure he was okay? But when I got out of the car I found myself following her, mesmerized by the sway of her skirt, unable to say a word. She was striding down an empty street as if nothing bad could happen to her. Because nothing bad *had* ever happened to her. It had made me so angry. It had made me want to make something bad happen to her.

I pictured grabbing her by the hair and swinging her around. I pictured driving my fist into her round, gaping mouth and pushing her down onto the filthy sidewalk . . .

But then I was on the sidewalk and the driver was helping me back into the car. I must have slipped. I wasn't sure what had happened. But whenever I looked at the drapes billowing, I'd be reminded of Joan's swishing skirt and I'd feel sick. So I stopped looking at them.

Our only outside visitors (unless you counted faithful Marta, who braved the reporters twice a week to come clean and take away our take-away boxes) were Greg Firestein and Wally Shanahan. They always arrived in Greg's anonymous-looking black SUV with tinted windows and pulled directly into our garage so the reporters wouldn't see Wally getting out. No doubt so Pat Shanahan wouldn't be connected to Cass more than he already was, since officially Pat had issued a statement "distancing" himself from Cass. Greg and Cass always sequestered themselves in Cass's study. Wally brought bottles of Veuve Clicquot and treats — French pâté and Russian caviar and Swiss chocolates, things I wouldn't want anyone seeing on our Fresh-Direct account because they might look too *frivolous.* She also brought Ambien and Xanax from a pharmacist who wouldn't talk to reporters. And she brought news.

"A lot of people think this whole #MeToo movement has gone too far. Did you read the letter those French women wrote last year? The French are always so sensible about these things. Maybe you and Cass should think about living in Paris for a while."

"And let Joan Lurie think she ran us out of town?"

"Sylvia Crosley told me she hasn't been in the office since the night the story was released. She's clearly ashamed of herself."

I knew Wally and Sylvia were friends — Sylvia knew everybody — but I was still a little piqued that Sylvia had told Wally this and not me. Sylvia had called exactly once since the Disaster, and then only to assure me she hadn't known what Joan was working on or she would have warned me. She hadn't called since.

"Cass told me that Joan Lurie was fired from her internship at the *Globe.* Why isn't anyone talking about that?" I asked Wally.

"Well," Wally said, spreading a tablespoon of pâté on a slice of baguette, "that would look a teensy bit petty right now. But just you wait. The tide will turn on this. You and

Cass just have to ride it out. Have some pâté, darlin', you're nothing but skin and bones."

Sometimes I thought Wally was trying to stuff me like a French goose. She and Greg both seemed invested in keeping me well fed — and quiet. The dutiful wife standing by her man.

Even if no one else was standing by Cass. The Society of Professional Journalists canceled his membership. Brown revoked his invitation to speak at next year's graduation — *Whit's graduation!* A couple of weeks after the Disaster, Pat Shanahan made a public statement saying he was returning Cass's campaign contributions. "Good," I told Cass. "The money will help with our legal fees."

Cass didn't seem to think that was funny. "This is the thanks I get for all the money I've shelled out for you?" I heard him yelling at Pat on the phone. I would have reminded him that he'd made those contributions to thank Wally for her support during Whit's crisis, but he clearly wasn't in the mood to be reasoned with.

A little later Greg drove up with Wally in the black SUV. "Like a hit man," Cass said, peering out the sidelight. Wally got out in a long black raincoat and a wide-brimmed hat as if she were afraid of being recognized in our garage. When she suggested we sit out on the terrace, though, I understood; she didn't want to risk being recognized if we were photographed by a drone.

"I hear on the grapevine that Joan Lurie's book is getting seven-figure offers," she told me, filling my glass.

I nearly choked on my wine. "Seven figures? For a packet of lies? What could she possibly fill a book with that's worth that much money?"

"That's what everybody is wondering," Wally said, leaning forward. "The rumor is that she has more material that didn't make it into the *Manahatta* story. Is there anything . . . well . . ." Wally gave me that pained smile women get on their faces when they're about to say something really hurtful but are pretending it's for your own good. "Anything Cass has mentioned to you that's *worse* than what came out in the story?"

I stared at her for a moment, unable to process what she was asking me. The sheers were fluttering in from the living room and the light from the pool was making curvy lines on Wally's face. It made me feel dizzy. "The *story* alleges that he had sex with half a dozen interns and assistants over the years, that he'd coerced women into giving him blowjobs in his office, and fired women who didn't comply," I said, my words coming out slurred. My mouth felt numb. "What could be worse?"

"Well," Wally said, looking embarrassed, "if any of the women were underage, for instance —"

"Cass would *never,*" I hissed, stumbling as I stood up from the lounge chair. Wally got up to steady me.

"Maybe Cass didn't know the girl was underage," she said, leading me back into the living room. "Some of these teenage girls do their hair and makeup to look much older. Cass might have met one at a party, for instance, and thought she was older. Did he mention anything like that to you? Anything that happened at a party?"

"Of coursch not . . ." I slurred. Greg came into the living room and took the bottle of Veuve Clicquot from Wally, making some joke about what it meant in French, and then Greg was helping me up the stairs. Where had Wally gone? I could hear her voice downstairs talking to someone on her phone in a low, urgent tone. I caught my own name. It sounded like she was saying, *Don't worry about Melissa.* When we got to my bedroom I told Greg I could take it from here, but his hands lingered on my waist . . . and then drifted down to my ass. I pushed him away and raised my hand to slap him but he caught it. "See what it feels like, Mel? Now you know how those girls felt when your husband assaulted them."

I opened my mouth but nothing came out. Like I really was nothing but a puppet and couldn't talk for myself anymore. He turned and left. Maybe I'd heard him wrong. There was a humming in my ears and everything was blurry. I dropped into bed without taking my clothes off and fell into a deep, dreamless sleep as if I'd taken an Ambien, but I hadn't . . . or at least I didn't think I had. Sometimes I forgot when I took them . . . I should tell Wally I didn't want any more. . . .

When I woke up the sun was in my face and someone was screaming. One of those reporters, I thought, had finally broken into the house.

I stumbled down the stairs into the living room. The gliders were open, the sheers moving in the breeze like an army of naked women. All those women who had accused Cass had marched on the house to take their revenge. They were screaming outside for his blood — for *my* blood, my children's blood. I hurried to the doors, tripping over something on the floor. A shoe. One of Cass's handmade Italian loafers. I picked it up and pushed through the filmy drapes. It felt like pushing through flesh, like being in a steam room surrounded by fat, damp bodies pressing up against my chest . . .

See what it feels like, Mel?

The screaming made it impossible to think. It was louder when I got outside. Mist was rising from the pool's surface. A woman was standing on the edge, a cowl over her head, her hands covering her face. She was like a statue on a grave. Only louder.

It was Marta, her hands over her mouth as if she were trying to silence the sounds coming from inside of her. There must be an animal drowned in the pool —

"What is it?" I demanded, grabbing her hands and pulling them away from her face. She snatched them out of my grip as if my hands were on fire — as if I were trying to hurt her — and pointed to the pool.

He was floating in the deep end, face-down, white shirt riffling in the current from the circulation pump, arms spread as if he had tried to embrace the water. As if all his women had come for him and he'd opened his arms wide to welcome them and they'd rushed into his embrace. They finally had him now.

CHAPTER FIVE

JOAN

Caspar Osgood tweeted his suicide note — an apology to the women he had hurt — but Melissa Osgood issued a statement that she believed her husband had been hounded to his grave by a witch-hunt.

"She has to say that," Simon told me. "To protect herself against a civil suit. She'll probably sue us as well."

"Should I make a statement?" I asked.

"No. Better to continue laying low. In fact, I suggest you extend your leave for six months so you can work on your book; that's what you should be focusing on now. Remember, you wrote a good, honest story, Joan. It can stand on its own merits."

All the favorable responses to my story seemed to have evaporated, at least as far as I could tell from my cursory review of the news via Siri; I still couldn't look at a screen for more than fifteen minutes. I didn't tweet back at the pundits saying I had hounded Osgood to his grave or comment on the *Atlantic Monthly* article questioning whether the #MeToo movement had gone too far.

Instead, in the week following Cass's suicide, I forced myself into an Uber and took the drive uptown to look at an apartment at the Refuge. I knew as soon as I saw those windows looking out on open space with no one looking back that I would feel safe. I was afraid that the co-op board wouldn't approve my application, but Sylvia knew someone on the board who *eased* my way, and my new literary agency sent me the first part of my advance money in time for the down payment. After Cass's death, the publisher seemed, if anything, *more* excited about the book.

My new editor, Etinosa Okoro, was only a few years older than me but a powerhouse. The first thing she told me when we spoke on the phone was that the *Manahatta* story had made her weep for her sister, who had been sexually assaulted when she was a teenager in Lagos. We outlined a plan for my first draft, but she told me that I should feel free to follow where the story took me.

"I trust your instincts," she told me, which almost made *me* weep; since the night of the attack I hadn't felt like I could trust anything about myself.

We agreed that I would send her a progress report in three months. Then she told me that she wanted me to write about my reaction to the suicide. I had no idea how I was going to do that. Since the night I woke up and saw Caspar Osgood's bloated ghost on my fire escape I've tried not to think about him at all.

As if purging myself of my possessions could rid me of the memory, I donate my fold-out couch and rickety IKEA furniture to Salvation Army and order new from Pottery Barn and West Elm. I donate bags of my clothes, keeping only the good pieces I have picked up at the sample sales that Sylvia has directed me to over the last three years — Italian woolens from obscure centuries-old mills, the leather shoes handmade in an English village, the Chanel bag I wore the night of the party, which somehow escaped the attention of my thief — that felt like good-luck tokens of another life. I pack up the notebooks and folders I've amassed over three years, stuffing them indiscriminately into boxes because I can't read my own handwritten labels. They fill two boxes, which I take, along with a few boxes of books and two suitcases, in an Uber up the West Side Highway on a rainy day in the first week of August.

Steamy condensation fogs the windows, muting the city into a pearly, iridescent blur. Shadows still lurk in my peripheral vision, but as long as I don't move my head too fast they float companionably alongside me like a school of curious fish, pushed along by the tide, past the elegant terraces of Riverside Park and the massive ramparts of Fort Tryon Park. The car exits at Dyckman Street and drives toward Inwood Park — a green and leafy enclave at the northern tip of Manhattan where Peter Minuit purchased the swampy island for a few bushels of shells under a tulip tree nearly four hundred years ago. The gray spires of the Refuge rise out of the trees like a medieval castle built to withstand a siege, the river serving as a moat around it. Inviolate.

Safe.

The doorman, who introduces himself as Enda, helps me up with my boxes, leaving the door to an older silver-haired doorman who I'm told is called Hector. "We always make sure to have an extra person on-site when someone's moving in or needs help," Enda explains as we ride up in the elevator. "If you let me know when to expect your moving truck, I'll arrange to have extra help on call."

"This is it," I tell him, a bit curtly. I recognize the not-so-subtle hint that I may have neglected something and notice the way he wrinkles his nose at my grimy luggage and tattered liquor-store boxes, as if I'm bringing in cases of vodka instead of books and papers. Or maybe it's the books and papers he objects to. Who bothers with paper anything these days? Or perhaps it's the shabby wingback chair my mother sent as a housewarming present that's waiting for me in the apartment.

I remember how you loved curling up and reading in it and thought it would warm up your new place, my mother said when she called last week. I could tell from her voice that she was hoping I'd invite her to see my new apartment, but I knew she would know something terrible had happened to me if she saw me in person, and I just can't bear for her to know about the attack. She's spent her whole life battling the anxiety that my grandmother passed down to her, and if she knows that one of her fears had come true she might begin to think all of them would.

I see that she's included one of the hideous afghans my grandmother had knitted as well. I *had* loved reading in that old chair, curled up under one of Grandma's scratchy afghans, and I'm touched my mother spent the money to have it delivered. But it looks out of place in the apartment, especially with the white, green, and orange (my grandmother's favorite color combination) afghan draped over it.

The only other pieces of furniture are two velvet couches, marooned on a sea of parquet like the only surviving lifeboats from the *Titanic,* and a massive oak desk I'd splurged on from Stickley and that the deliverers have left along the wall next to the fireplace.

"I told Stickley I wanted the desk in the bay window," I say, the doorman's snobbery turning me into a bitch lady. I feel as though I'm starting to sound like Sylvia.

"Eejits," he says. "I'll move it for you."

I offer to help — he can't possibly move the massive oak desk by himself — but he waves me away, strips off his shiny buttoned jacket, and grasps the long sides of the Stickley desk and lifts it up. Only the strain in his back muscles gives away how heavy it is as he carries it over to the windows and places it down gently beneath the center one. The bottom sill is a few inches below the top of the desk. The Feng Shui expert I interviewed last year would complain that I was blocking the energy flow, but I have always dreamed of having a desk with a view.

Enda steps back and surveys it. "Looks a bit lonely . . . wait . . ." He moves the threadbare wingback chair to one side of the desk as if it were holding an invisible companion to watch over me when I write. "There," he says, draping the afghan over the arm of the chair, "now you have a place to write and a place to read. You're all set to write the great American novel."

"I don't know about the great American novel," I say, disarmed by the way the glow off the river lights up his face. "I'm just going to tell a few women's stories —" I break off, ashamed at how corny that sounds. That blow to the head is making me soft. Sentimental.

"Oh yeah," he says, snapping his fingers. "You're the one who brought down that sex pervert. Good on you. I wonder that you didn't feel afraid going up against a big man like that."

Brought down? I don't know if he's referring to Osgood's suicide or not, but there's something about the way he says it — or the way he's leaning too close to me in his shirtsleeves, which are still damp from the exertion of moving the desk — that makes my skin prickle. Like he's telling me I *should* be afraid. "It's the men who bully and intimidate women who should be afraid," I say, digging in my purse for a tip.

He smiles and holds up his hands, palms out, as if to counter what I'm saying, but then I realize he's just turning down the tip. He picks up his jacket but drapes it over his shoulder rather than putting it back on. *Big man.* He's letting me know he's not smaller than me just because he's paid to wait on me. It's a harmless bit of bravado, but I suddenly want him *out.* I walk briskly to the front door and hold it open. He saunters, smiling all the way.

"Buzz if you need me," he says, pointing to the button next to the monitor. "I'm always here."

Again it sounds like a threat. *I'm always here. I'm always watching you.* I wonder which cameras *he* has access to. Maybe I'm just being paranoid.

"Good to know," I say as he takes his time exiting. I lose no time in closing the door after him and bolting all my state-of-the-art locks. Then I watch him walk down the hall on the camera screen. When he gets to the elevator he turns back and smiles right at the camera. As if he didn't have a doubt in the world that I was watching him.

I spend the next few weeks settling into my

new apartment. *I can't possibly begin work on my book,* I explain to the boxes of notes, *until I feel settled.* First I need filing cabinets, which I order from Stickley to match my desk. Then I need new folders, which I order from an Italian stationery company I once did a story on. I order colorful dishes from Marimekko, and then add rugs and throw pillows to cheer up the place. I order crisp linen sheets from D. Porthault, hoping they will make me sleep better. Despite my new, secure apartment I still can't sleep well and I feel groggy and unfocused during the day. So I order a fancy Breville coffee/espresso machine to wake myself up.

All the boxes arrive as if by magic. I never see who delivers them — Enda or Hector — I just hear a chime from the monitor and there's the box on my camera screen, sitting in the empty hallway. As if the doormen know I don't want to open my door to another human being.

One of those packages arrives with the latest voice-activated digital assistant. I unpack it warily as if it were a bomb — *Should I ask Enda if he can run my packages through a metal detector?* — and plug it in.

"Hello," a polite animatrix voice chirps, a soothing blue light pulsing from the top of the phallic-shaped unit. "Thank you for inviting me into your home. What's your name?"

I nearly pull out the plug. Sylvia wanted me to do a story on electronic assistants last year, but I declined because I would have had to sample a few in my home. *I don't need any more corporate spies in my life,* I'd groused. *Google already reads my mail, Amazon is keeping track of my taste in books and vitamins, and Facebook is mining my data for the Russians. I don't want to bug my own home.*

But what choice do I have? While I can see well enough to read now, I still can't focus on print for longer than fifteen minutes. Plus my memory is shot to hell. I can't even remember my computer password, but luckily I've got it written down in the back of my address book.

"Joan," I tell the blinking light. Is it an accident that it reminds me of the eye in *2001: A Space Odyssey*? "What's yours?"

I'm expecting one of the anodyne millennial names — Michaela, Alexa, Electra — popular with digital media, but the pulsing light replies, "You can call me whatever you like."

"Oh," I say, disarmed. This already feels . . . *intimate.* Did some marketer decide I would bond with my device better if I named it?

"You're a robot," I say, as if I need to establish boundaries.

"Yes, that is correct," it answers cheerfully. "A voice-activated personal assistant, to be precise."

"Hm, your acronym would be VAPA, but that doesn't sound very nice."

"Vapa," it repeats. "That sounds like vapid."

"I don't like it," I agree. "How about . . . *Bot*?"

"Bot," it repeats. In the device's neutral, non-accent the word sounds almost sweet.

"I like it," I say.

"Me too," Bot agrees. "Is there anything else I can do for you?"

"Yes," I say, "tell me what Twitter is saying about me today."

And she does. I sit in the wingback chair — Enda was right; this is the perfect place for it — looking out at the river as I listen to how the world is reacting to my story and its aftermath — and find that the world has moved on. Several more men — and a few women — have been accused of sexual harassment since I wrote my story. Actors, politicians, playwrights, coaches, doctors . . . the list, recited in Bot's cheerful uninflected voice seems endless. There's blowback, of course: the accused crying witch-hunt, the pundits fretting that sex and flirting are dead. A reprise of the letter those French-women wrote last year accusing the new movement of casting women as victims. And some of the cases do seem a bit shaky. A woman has bad, awkward sex with an actor, a geriatric entertainer's hand drifts a few inches too low on a woman's ass. The shaky cases are seized upon as signs that the movement's gone too far. Osgood's name is invoked as a victim of the "going too far." And then another woman attests to how her career was derailed when she reported a playwright for groping her and nothing was done and the media takes up that case.

I'm both relieved and chastened by how little Osgood figures in the overall narrative. His suicide has both confirmed his guilt and made it awkward to talk about him. He has become both a poster child for the #MeToo movement and its backlash. Others have taken up the fight. What do I still have to add to the discussion? More important, I wonder, looking guiltily at the unpacked boxes of notes, the closed laptop, and the beautiful view, what am I going to write a book about?

I admit my quandary to Simon when he calls to check up on me a few weeks after I move in. "I'm not sure I really have anything more to add to the conversation. Do I look for more stories? Do I go over the stories I've already collected? Do I try some of the leads I didn't follow?"

Simon doesn't say anything right away, and I'm afraid I've put him off with my self-pity. Simon once told me he didn't do pep talks. I stare at Bot's blinking blue light, wondering if I could ask her to weigh in, maybe program her to repeat supportive homilies.

Then Simon's voice emerges from the silver obelisk. "Going back over old leads sounds counterproductive. There's a reason they didn't pan out in the first place. Maybe, instead, you should be looking at what made Caspar Osgood the predator he became. I hear his father was an alcoholic philanderer. Anyway . . . I'm sure you'll figure it out, kid."

I can hear his impatience. Simon's got my back, but I'd better not waste his time.

"I'd better," I say, trying to make my voice light. "I've already spent a good chunk of my advance on my fancy new digs."

"Best motivator of all," he says, "is paying the bills. Don't forget you've always got a job here when you're ready to come back."

And then he claims to have another call

and gets off, leaving me wondering what happened to a grudge being such a good motivator.

I ask Bot to play some classical music — something good for creativity — and she selects something called Brainwave Symphony, which claims to infuse classical pieces with "subtle pulses of sound to trigger your brain to produce states of enhanced creativity." I'm expecting something annoyingly New Age, but instead the soothing notes of Ralph Vaughn Williams's "The Lark Ascending" fill the apartment. "Nice choice," I tell Bot as I unpack a box of files. Each file is labeled with the name of a woman I interviewed. If I stare too long at a name it begins to blur.

I interrupt "Lark Ascending" to ask Bot to look up what causes blurry vision on WebMD and she lists a dozen causes, including brain damage, migraines, glaucoma, and psychological stress. Maybe it's psychosomatic. I spent three years listening to the stories of women who were groped, fingered, pressed against, mouthed, ejaculated on. I was disgusted by the behavior they described, but somehow I wasn't *touched* by it. Now I can feel every word on my skin — prodding, poking, pawing — trying to get *in*.

Maybe that's because my attacker might have done those things to me.

The moment I think about the attack, that sickeningly sweet smell of chloroform stings my nose and I feel the suffocating cloth pressing against my mouth, shutting off my air, smothering me. I hear the scrape of keys in a lock —

I startle out of the memory and realize I *do* hear a key in the lock. Someone is trying to get into my apartment. I turn and look toward my door and see that the doorknob is turning.

No, I tell myself, *it's a trick of my damaged eyes, a hallucination like seeing Caspar Osgood on my fire escape. No one can get to me here.*

One of the bolts slides open.

I rise up and levitate across the parquet to the door, my eyes fixed to the doorknob. It must be Enda or Hector thinking I'm not here —

When am I ever not here? I haven't gone out in the three weeks since I moved in. And why would either of them come in if I wasn't here?

I inch along the wall and touch the monitor. The hallway appears because I made that the default view at Marla's suggestion, but the screen is blurred and out of focus.

He's broken the camera, I think, not sure who I mean by *he* but imagining Caspar Osgood's bloated ruin of a face. I rub my eyes to clear them and a figure emerges from the fog. Not Caspar Osgood, thank God, but not Hector or Enda either. It's an old woman so frail and insubstantial she looks as much a phantom as that apparition on the fire escape. I expect her to melt right back into the fog that fills my brain. Then she looks right at me as if she knows I'm looking at her and there's nothing blurry about those sharp gray-green eyes and the look of desperation in them.

Only a monster would ignore those pleading eyes.

I only hesitate a second. Maybe two. Then I pull open the door and she falls across my threshold.

CHAPTER SIX

MELISSA

Turns out, life insurance doesn't have to pay benefits in cases of suicide if the policy is less than two years old. I know because I googled it the day after Cass died. I know that sounds cold — especially after all the crusading I've done these last three years for suicide awareness — but I was looking at the rest of my life without Cass's income, two kids in college, and possible lawsuits because of that wretched Joan Lurie article. So forgive me if I needed to look at the bottom line.

At first I breathed a sigh of relief. Cass has had life insurance since the kids were little. He made a big deal of it when I quit my job to stay home after Emily was born. He'd just come into his trust fund and Emily was fussy and Whit was in the terrible twos so we figured it made sense for me to stay home, but he also wanted me to feel secure. "If you're sacrificing your earning potential to raise our children, you deserve the security of knowing you'll be provided for if something should happen to me."

The big man. The paterfamilias. Cass loved to play that role. His father was an alcoholic philanderer who squandered his own portion of the family money, and Cass always swore he wasn't going to end up like him.

Well, look at him now. Apparently, as I learned from our accountant in the week after his death, Cass renegotiated his life-insurance policies two years back. That's because he'd started borrowing on the first one three years ago and went through all the equity. He bought a new (cheaper) policy one year and eleven months ago that stipulated in the not-so-fine print that it didn't pay out in cases of illegal activity, fraud, or suicide before two years had elapsed.

He couldn't even wait one lousy month.

Or be bothered to make it look *not* like suicide.

No, he had to *tweet* his goddamned suicide note out to the whole world. As if this scandal wasn't bad enough, like he was deliberately trying to ruin our lives.

I am so sorry to all the women I have hurt, most of all my wife Sweet Melissa. And to my son and daughter, please forgive me.

#SoSorry and #SweetMelissa trended for a week on Twitter. What the hell? Cass didn't even *like* the Allman Brothers! He hadn't called me Sweet Melissa since college, and then only *ironically* because Simon liked the song before he switched to jazz and Motown because that's what Cass and his friends listened to.

I considered suing *Manahatta,* but Greg and Wally told me I should let it go, that public sympathy would veer in my direction if I simply remained quiet, but I was sick of playing the dumb wife and I certainly wasn't going to listen to Greg after that weird grope. I still felt nauseated when I thought about his hands on my body, but I was afraid that if I mentioned anything to Wally about it, she'd bring up how much I'd had to drink that night and I couldn't bear to see that look of pity on her face again. But that didn't mean I had to follow their advice. I issued a statement that my husband had been hounded to death by a witch-hunt, that I personally blamed Joan Lurie, Simon Wallace, and *Manahatta* magazine for publishing unfounded rumors, and that I planned to pursue my own legal recourse. Let Simon Wallace and his slut reporter worry about their own necks for a change.

My lawyer told me I'd played into the insurance company's hands; I'd all but confirmed that Cass's death was a suicide. It turned out he was right. The insurance company *declined* to pay out. As if that wasn't enough, he then confirmed my fears that there could be forthcoming lawsuits against the estate but that I didn't have a viable case against *Manahatta.* And worse still, when I dug out the file marked "Ardsley House" I found out that Cass had taken a home-equity loan on the house last year. The house was in the name of his S-Corp ("That's to your advantage should I predecease you," he told me when we bought the house twenty years ago.) so he'd been able to take out the loans without my signature. There was barely a quarter million left from the one million I thought we had in equity.

The Hamptons house, which was also owned by S-Corp, had practically no equity at all.

Our broker at Merrill Lynch told me that Cass had sold most of our mutual funds last year. I thought there at least must be money in the LLC that Cass had formed twenty years ago to buy the *Globe,* but when I met with the accountant he explained that Cass had drained his own account in the LLC and then distributed partnership interest to outside investors. Because he wasn't a majority owner of the *Globe* anymore, the board had been able to push him out. One of the board members contacted me the week after his death to tell me that since he had resigned, his pension was "nullified."

In other words, I was broke.

If I sold both houses I'd have less than half a million to my name for the next sixteen years, until I turned sixty-five and could draw on our 401(k) and other retirement funds, and even those, I learned from our broker at Merrill Lynch, had been borrowed against and nearly drained.

No wonder Cass had taken his entire bottle of Ambien and a dozen OxyContin and gone for a midnight swim. He wasn't just facing public shame from Joan Lurie's story; he was staring down financial ruin.

Which he left *me* to deal with.

For the first few weeks I considered joining him. I know that sounds *horrible,* but for the first time I could understand how the thought of suicide could get inside you and prey on you. It was like an earworm, a song you can't get out of your head, crooning, *Who would miss you? You weren't even enough for Cass to live for.* Then I heard Emily wailing the same thing — *How could Daddy leave me? Why wasn't I enough of a reason for him to live?* and I realized I had to pull myself together for her and Whit's sake. I took Emily to a therapist in Scarsdale and got her a prescription for Celexa. Whit was harder to deal with.

"All the tripe he fed me about suicide being the coward's way out," he railed in the limousine after the funeral (a sad, underattended event at Westchester Hills). "What a hypocrite!"

That's what he was saying to you? I thought, remembering that touching scene at Whit's hospital bedside. I had thought he'd been telling Whit how much he loved him. "You're a braver and better man than him," I told my son.

I was terrified for Whit. I knew from my work for SAD that having a parent kill themselves made it three times more likely for that child to commit suicide. I couldn't find a statistic for having *both* parents kill themselves, but I knew it wouldn't be good. So I told those voices urging me to end it to shut up; I had to stick around for Whit and Emily's sake. Fortunately, thanks to their summer jobs, they did not have to watch their childhood homes get dismantled. I put both houses up for sale in the third week of August. I knew it didn't look good to sell so soon after Cass's death, but I needed the money before the second installment of fall tuition came due.

Wally came over to help me organize the estate sale at the Ardsley House. "People will come just to gawk," she said, slapping red stickers on the Waterford crystal and Minton china. "But they'll buy, too, so they can point to their loveseat and say that was from the disgraced publisher of the *Globe*."

"Good," I said, "let them have their grisly souvenirs. As long as I get enough to pay Emily and Whit's tuition."

"Have you given any more thought to where you'll go?" she asked — not for the first time. "Pat and I have discussed it and we'd be happy to lend you our summer house on Nantucket."

I thanked her for the offer of the house but said I needed to be closer to the city to get a job.

"How's the job hunt going?" she asked with an embarrassed look, as if *having* to get a job (as opposed to getting one for the fun of it) was akin to contracting an STD.

"I'm having lunch with Sally Jessell next week. Sylvia set it up . . ." I paused, thinking about the call I'd gotten from Sylvia the day after Cass's death. She'd only called to give her condolences but when she asked if there was anything she could do, I asked if she could help get me a job. She'd seemed surprised, but then she offered to hook me up with her friend Sally. "I'm hoping she'll give me a column at *Image,*" I tell Wally. "I went to journalism school after all, and worked on the *Times* for eight years before I quit to raise my children. I have skills."

"Of course you do, honey." Wally patted my arm as if I were a five-year-old bragging I could ride a pony. "And you have so much still to give the world. And so much to say. Don't you let that Lurie woman have the last word."

"What do you mean?" I asked, dusting a Meissen serving platter.

"I saw in Page Six she got a book deal for over two million."

"Over two million? For that little —"

"Just wait. I bet it sells all of five copies. Don't let it bother you, Mel. You'll come out of this just fine. . . . Are you really selling this beautiful Burberry coat and matching hat? I love how this set makes you look like a Russian spy."

"Oh," I said, fingering the heavy black twill fabric, "this is actually an extra. Cass bought the first one — a limited edition — on an anniversary trip to London and when he saw how much I loved it he knew I'd want a second in case anything ever happened to the first. I know that sounds crazy —"

"Not at all," Wally said, wiping her eye. "Whenever I find something I really like I buy an extra one. Life is so uncertain, why not have a spare . . ." Her voice trailed off as we both contemplated the sad reality that there were no spares for her son and my husband. "What a devoted husband Cass was," she said, squeezing my hand, "to know you so well. I just can't believe . . . Well, anyway, why don't I take them to the consignment shop I use. I'll get you a good price on them."

I let her take the spare Burberry coat and hat. How ridiculous it struck me now that I had thought I could protect myself from loss by buying duplicates. Still, when I watched her walking to her car with the coat draped over her arm I was struck by a feeling of loss so strong I sank to the floor, wrapped my arms around my knees, and wailed into the empty, echoing house. I wasn't even sure what I was mourning: Cass or our life together that always seemed so safe because there was always an extra for anything we might lose.

■ ■ ■ ■

A week later, on a sweltering day, I drove to the Metro-North train station, a stack of my résumés printed on linen stock tucked inside a leather portfolio on the passenger seat. As I waited for the train, I thought of the year after college when I was living with my parents in nearby Scarsdale and commuting into the city for my job at the *Times.* I'd loved getting dressed up in smart suits and crowding in with all the other morning commuters, buying a buttered roll at the station. Older passengers would fold their *Times* or *Wall Street Journal* in precise quarters and turn the pages without ever having to spread the paper open. I wanted to be like them. Doing the crossword puzzle in ink, calling the conductor by name, drinking G&Ts in the bar car on summer Fridays. Why had I forgotten how much I liked going to work? How had I ended up with such a different life?

Cass. Cass is how. And why.

That first year out of college we agreed we weren't ready to live together. Nor would we have been able to afford to. People always thought Cass was rich because his family was WASPy old money, but no one

119

knew his father had squandered all the money except for a trust fund put aside for Cass by his grandparents that didn't pay out until he turned thirty. So he lived in a fifth-floor walkup in Chelsea, before Chelsea was nice, that he shared with two other guys working at the *Times:* Simon Wallace, who was still his friend back then, and someone named Vince, who was always late on the rent and moved back to Texas after a year. Cass and Simon worked in feature news and I worked in style. We didn't think it would look professional for people to know Cass and I were dating, so when he passed my desk he would call me Miss Krantz and act super formal. It was fun — and *sexy.* That's what a lot of these MeToo-ers don't get — how sexy offices could be back in those days. The older newsmen were gallant and the younger ones flirted. Sure, there were the ones you had to watch — the handsy typesetter who would paw you when you delivered proofs to his desk, the advertising guys who were always making crude jokes and ogling the secretaries. But Cass was never like that, even though he could have had his pick of the women. He wanted *me,* even though I was from *new* money not *old* money, and grew up in Scarsdale not Greenwich.

When he asked me to marry him, all the girls — and not a few of the older women — were jealous. But sweet too. They threw me an engagement party. I remember, at the get-together in the conference room, one of the older secretaries made a joke about Cass working his way through the steno pool. But that was just envy. We didn't even have a steno pool then. And besides, what did it matter? *He chose me.* It was around that time, too, that my mother was diagnosed with breast cancer and it felt like it was important to have a family of my own.

Cass was promoted to bureau chief in his fifth year at the *Times.* He beat out Simon Wallace for the job, which, everyone knew, is why Simon's always resented Cass. Simon even claimed that Cass got that job by falsely telling the editor-in-chief that Simon had been stealing Cass's work. But Cass denied that he had snitched on Simon even though it was true; Simon had been stealing from him for years, *just like he used to "borrow" my clothes in college and imitate the way I talked and dressed. Men like Simon,* Cass told me that night he came home with the news of the promotion and an expensive bottle of Champagne *show their true colors in the end.* I could tell Cass was angry as he opened the Champagne, but that didn't stop him from grabbing me and insisting that we start a family right there on the kitchen counter of our tiny Murray Hill Junior Four. *I need an heir for the dynasty you and I are going to rule.*

We were going to be a power couple. Like Connie Chung and Maurice Povich. Like Ben Bradlee and Sally Quinn.

Only, then Whit began having developmental delays and baby Emily was *super* fussy and then Cass came into his trust so I didn't *have* to go back to work after my maternity leave ended. Then there was that *kerfuffle* at the *Times.* Cass told me that he was forced out because his politics didn't match the owner's, but Simon had told me there'd been a rumored complaint about Cass from one of the female employees, but Cass denied it and I was too busy being a young mother to Whit and Emily to think about that. I still believed I'd go back to work eventually, but I wouldn't be able to go back to the *Times* after what happened, and then Cass bought the *Globe* — becoming the youngest newspaper owner in New York at the time — and it would have been awkward working there . . . and suddenly it's nearly twenty years later and Cass is dead.

I don't realize I'm crying until the train

enters the tunnel for Grand Central Station and I see my face — skin white, cheeks sunken, eyes black pits — reflected in the darkened window. I look like the ghoulish ghost of that girl who rode this train twenty-five years ago, dreaming of a life that's gone up in smoke.

But maybe it's not too late. I'm only forty-eight. Lots of women start over once their kids are out of the house. All I need is a little job writing columns for a fashion magazine and maybe a book deal for myself. If that little chit Joan Lurie, who stumbles drunkenly around town ruining lives, can do it, why shouldn't I?

I fix my makeup in the ladies' room and take a taxi to the restaurant, which is so trendy it doesn't even have a sign, just a thick oak door with some kind of hiero-glyphs carved into it. I'm five minutes late but still the first to arrive. As the hostess leads me across the crowded dining room to a brushed steel table that looks like a hospital gurney, I feel all the eyes in the room on me. *That's Caspar Osgood's widow,* they're surely whispering, *do you think she knew?*

I order a gin and tonic (which could look like seltzer if it turned out that Sally didn't imbibe at lunch) and stare at my phone as if I had so many messages to attend to. Sally rushes in ten minutes later, spewing apologies, air kissing, and ending a phone call all at once.

"Crazy day at the office, darling. I may kill my new assistant." Then she blushes, but whether she's embarrassed to have brought up death or assistants is hard to tell. She furrows her brow and gives me a concerned look. "But how are you, darling? How are you holding up?"

What am I supposed to say to that? My husband of twenty-five years was accused of being a sexual predator and then killed himself, leaving me broke and publicly humiliated.

"I'm focusing on holding things together for Whit and Emily," I say. I can't look like a pitiful wreck. I need this job. "And trying to put this whole thing behind me. I need to move on. I need —"

The waitress chooses this moment to introduce herself and list the specials. There are so many reductions of this and essences of that it sounds less like a menu and more like a purge. I order something with froth in it — who doesn't love froth? — and tap my glass for another. Sally orders club soda with bitters and "the salad." Who knew there was anything as simple as salad on this menu?

When the waitress leaves, Sally reaches over the table and touches my hand. "I just can't imagine how hard this must be on you. Did you . . . well, did you have any idea about Cass before the *Manahatta* article?"

I stare at her, appalled she's gotten right to the point — or at least, *her* point. Although I should know from experience you have to be direct in this business. If I want a job from her I have to show that I'm tough enough to take it.

"Look," I say, taking a sip of my G&T and leaning forward. She leans in, too, and I feel a little thrill of power. The room seems suddenly silent, as if everyone around us has paused their conversations and is waiting to hear what I have to say. "It's not like I didn't know that Cass had his *flirtations.* He was a handsome man — a *powerful* man. Women desired him. But the idea that he forced himself on women . . . well, it's absurd." I allow myself a little laugh — a *frothy* laugh. "Why would he, when he had so many women throwing themselves at him?"

I lean back and take another sip of my drink, satisfied. Sally leans back, too, but with a little frown on her face. "You don't believe the women?" she asks.

"Why does everyone ask that as if it's a federal crime? Some women lie. Especially when they've been slighted. I know for a fact that one of the women had a consensual affair with Cass and then was upset when Cass wouldn't leave me. She fed this story to that reporter — *Joan Lurie* — and she saw an opportunity for herself in it. Look at what it's done for her. She got a two-million-dollar book deal."

"I've heard that too. That must be . . . *galling.*"

"To have that . . . *woman* profit on the destruction of my family? Yes, you could say that."

"I wouldn't wonder," Sally says, stirring her drink, "that you'd want to get your own story out there."

"I *have* thought of that," I say, relieved that she's brought it up. "In fact . . . I've been thinking I'd like to write a column. A kind of 'advice for the new millennium.' You know, explaining to young women how *we* handled sex harassment back in the day and how they can protect themselves but still have fun and not lose the romance of flirtation."

Sally's lips do something funny. Like she's trying not to smile. "You want to write an *advice* column?"

She makes it sound so unlikely that I immediately pivot. "Well, maybe not advice *per se.* Maybe something more lifestyle-ish. We could pitch it as fortysomething women starting over."

"Starting over?"

I wish she would stop repeating everything I say in that incredulous tone. It's like having something you ate bubble back up your throat. But I persevere, scrambling to take control of the conversation. "Yes. Like I plan to . . . I'd like to show that a woman can survive tragedy. That she . . . that *I* still have something to contribute to society. I think that's an important message, don't you?" I'm beginning to ramble and Sally is still sitting there like a lump with a little perturbed look on her face.

"Melissa, darling," she says at last. "Are you talking about getting a *job*?"

She says it like I've just suggested getting my head shaved, only *that* she might approve of. "Why not? I mean, I thought that's why . . . isn't that why Sylvia set this up? I went to journalism school, after all. I worked on the *Times,* didn't she tell you that? If you don't think I can handle my own column right away I don't mind starting out with something smaller. Here . . ." I take out my résumé and place it on the table in

127

front of her. She stares down at it as if I've just put a bag of dog poop on her plate.

And then she does the worst thing she could do. She laughs. A deep, throaty, head-back laugh that makes every head at the restaurant turn toward her. I'm not even imagining it. "Oh my, I haven't seen a real printed résumé in . . . eons. And on card stock. What a good, diligent girl you are, Melissa. Are you thinking you want to work as an *assistant*? Why, those girls are nearly your daughter's age. We have shoes older than them."

"Actually," I say, "I don't. I just sold my last pair of Prada loafers on eBay." She starts to laugh again as if I'm making a joke and then a horrified look spreads across her face.

"Melissa, you're not . . . in financial difficulties, are you?" she asks, as if inquiring if I have cancer.

I can feel tears pricking my eyes and something welling up in me, a desire to unburden myself of the horror of the last weeks — Cass's body floating in the pool and finding out about the life insurance, the pension, and the debt. But then I think of something. "Sally, if you didn't think this was about me getting a job, what *did* you think it was about? Why did you agree to meet with me? Didn't Sylvia say I was looking for a job?"

She opens her mouth to answer just as the waitress appears with our food. I keep my eyes on Sally, though, not willing to let her evade the question.

"Well," she says when the waitress is gone, "of course I'm always glad to see you, but since you ask . . . Sylvia and I had discussed you doing an interview for *Image.* She even offered to sit in because we both thought you'd feel more comfortable telling your story to someone you knew. I can promise it would be very tasteful, a cover photograph, and pictures of you in your home. It would be a chance to present your side of the story."

"You want to do a story on me?" I ask in disbelief. "With pictures of me in my home?" Now I am the one dumbly repeating everything I hear.

Sally nods. "Yes, I think it would give our readers context to see the life you built with Cass —"

"Do you want," I cut in, "for me to pose in front of the pool where he drowned?"

"Well —"

"Or perhaps you'd like me to pose next to the packing boxes. Perhaps your readers would like a picture of me sitting on the street surrounded by my possessions." My voice is rising as I struggle to contain my anger. "Perhaps that would satisfy their bloodlust?"

"There's no need to take it that way," she says.

I look down at my plate, which is covered with a blue-green froth that looks like something the Little Mermaid might have regurgitated. When Cass's autopsy report came back, it said his stomach was full of scotch, Oxycontin, Ambien, and chlorinated pool water. I imagine it would have looked much like this. If I stay here a moment longer I may add the contents of my *own* stomach to the plate, which might be satisfying just to see Sally's expression. But then I imagine the tweets. *Sex Predator's wife loses lunch. #Karmasabitch.*

So instead I pluck my napkin out of my lap and drop it over my plate. "Thanks for lunch, Sal," I say, rising to my feet. Teal-green blooms seep through the bleached linen napkin. I picture Cass's white shirt riffling in the aquamarine pool water. I picture the white sheers billowing in my empty house and Joan Lurie sashaying down her street, Chanel bag twitching at her hips, like she owned this town. "And

130

thank you for the interesting proposal. But I'll be telling my own story from now on."

CHAPTER SEVEN

JOAN

The old woman is so thin — the bones of her wrists and ankles birdlike under skin speckled as a fawn's — that I have no doubt I could pick her up, but I'm afraid that I'll hurt her. I kneel beside her, scanning her delicate limbs for breaks. "Should I call 911?" I ask loudly, assuming she'll be hard of hearing.

"Calling 911," Bot says.

The old woman swivels her head to Bot's perch on the coffee table and laughs. "Tell that thing I don't need an ambulance, just to catch my breath."

"Don't call 911," I tell Bot, wondering if that's really the right move.

"You must have mistaken my door for yours," I say. "Do you live across the hall?"

She's looking around my apartment dazedly. "I live here," she says.

"In the Refuge?" I ask, trying to comfort

132

her the way my mother would always try to tease a thread of truth out of my grandmother's confused rants and weave it back into the fabric of reality.

"Yes, the Refuge," she agrees, fixing her gray-green eyes on me. "Are you new?"

"I just moved in a few weeks ago . . . Do you think you can get up . . . may I help you?" I hold out my hands to her and she looks up at me doubtfully, as if I'm asking her to jump out a tenth-story window.

"What's your name?" she asks.

"Joan," I tell her.

She smiles. "Like Joan of Arc. My favorite of the saints. Hello, Joan, I'm Lillian. Lillian Day."

"I'm pleased to make your acquaintance, Lillian Day," I say, trying not to smile at the formality while we're sitting on the floor. It feels as if we're performing a sacred ritual: a naming ceremony to restore her sense of dignity. When she lays her cold hands in mine, though, it feels like I'm the one who's being given back something. The world is suddenly as sharp as Lillian Day's gray-green eyes.

I make her tea, apologizing that I only have Lipton's.

"Always been good enough for me," she

says, taking the mug with only a tiny tremor in her hand. She's straightened her plaid skirt, white blouse, and beaded cardigan while I was in the kitchen and looks none the worse for her fall. Her wispy white hair is smoothed back into a bun. She's sitting upright on the edge of the big wingback chair by the window, her back as straight as a ruler, incongruous red sneakers dangling an inch above the floor. The white wicker bag she'd worn on her arm is sitting next to her, equally upright, like an obedient pet dog.

"I like what you've done with the place," she says. "Lots of space and sunshine."

I look around at the new furniture and rugs and throw pillows I've bought to make the place look more cheerful, but then my eyes snag on the stack of boxes. "I still have a lot of unpacking to do," I say apologetically. "Somehow this still doesn't feel like home."

"It can be difficult to settle into a new place," Lillian says.

"Yes," I agree. "How long have you been here?"

"Hm," she says, her eyes flicking upward and to the left, "let's see . . . I came here in the fall of 1941 —"

"Nineteen forty-one! That's seventy-seven

years ago!"

"Is it?" she asks, smiling politely. "I've never had much of a head for numbers. Sister Dolores said I'd better do a typing course and go for work in the steno pool rather than bookkeeping."

"Are you sure it was 1941?" I ask gently. "I didn't think it became an apartment building until the late '40s."

"An apartment building?" she asks, looking confused. "Oh no, it wasn't an apartment building. It was the Refuge . . . you know . . . for" — she leans closer to me as if we might be overheard — "fallen women. Girls who got into trouble."

"Is that what it was before?" I ask, thinking that Marla had left out that little detail. "But you weren't . . . I mean, you couldn't have been . . ." Now I'm the one who's embarrassed. I've spent the last three years listening to women recount the most intimate and disgusting details of sexual assault, but I can't bring myself to say "prostitute" to this nice old lady.

"A lady of ill repute?" Lillian suggests with a birdlike tilt of her head and a slyness to her voice. "No. But I did fall into a bit of trouble and wound up remanded to the Magdalens."

"The Magdalens? Like the ones who ran

the Magdalen laundries in Ireland?"

"Aye," she says, the mention of Ireland adding a Celtic lilt to her thick Brooklyn accent. "The same. They brought their laundries and their ideas here. Purify your sins through washing other people's dirty laundry and add a pretty penny to your coffers while you're at it. They kept us up high where no one could see us . . ." She points to the window and the view of the river and Palisades beyond. "And the only escape was the drop to the rocks below. We girls ruined our eyes mending and worked our hands raw scrubbing the city's dirty linen." She holds out her fragile dappled hands and pushes back the sleeve of her cardigan to reveal a tangle of white scar tissue.

I suck in my breath. "That's horrible! I had no idea there were Magdalen laundries in this country."

"Well, as you say, it was closed down eventually." She draws the sleeve of her cardigan back down and plucks a handkerchief from the cuff to dab her eyes. She hadn't shed a tear at falling, but now her eyes are full from revealing this old wound. "I suppose things are better now . . . why, look at you!" Her voice brightens. "A pretty young girl with a big apartment to herself! What kind of job do you do?"

"I'm a journalist," I say.

"A reporter!" she cries, her voice now genuinely happy. "Why, that was what I wanted to be, but the nuns said that was no job for a good Catholic girl. I temped in the steno pool of a newspaper for a bit and I thought I might get a regular job there . . ." Her voice falters and her hand drifts up to touch a gold locket embossed with a floral design rubbed smooth. I wonder if it holds a picture of a sweetheart, perhaps one she lost in the war. She's about the age of my grandmother, who lost her husband — my grandfather — in the war. "It wasn't easy being a girl on her own back then. You may not know it to look at me now, but I was quite pretty when I was young."

She lengthens her neck and bats her eyelashes in such a coquettish fashion that I start to laugh, but then I see it — or rather, I suddenly see *her,* beneath the age spots and wrinkles, I see the high cheekbones, the broad brow, the full curve to her lips and, most of all, the *snap* in those gray-green eyes.

"I bet you were beautiful," I say. "You still are."

She holds my gaze, suddenly serious. She doesn't try to wave off the compliment. "Sometimes there was a price to pay," she says, "for being beautiful."

The nape of my neck prickles the way it does when I sense a story — *the reporter's sixth sense,* Simon calls it. I can imagine Lillian as a young, beautiful woman working at an office job in the '40s. What chance did a woman have back then when even women today are still bullied and pressured into sex by men in power? Was that the "trouble" she "fell into"? A boss who made sexual advances? I open my mouth to ask what price she paid for being beautiful, but then I remember that Lillian isn't one of my sources. She's an old woman who's just had a bad fall.

I close my mouth and notice that her eyes are looking a bit cloudy and her ramrod-straight posture is drooping. The fall has taken more out of her than she was willing to admit.

"You should get some rest," I say. She looks a bit disappointed so I add, "Would you like to come back again for tea?"

"I would like that," she says, her back straightening and her eyes regaining some of their clarity. She rises to her feet quite easily but accepts my arm to guide her across the slippery parquet. I offer to take her to her apartment but she flutters her hands at the suggestion that she needs help.

"I'll find it now. I was just a little bit turned around before. I know where I am. Look, I have my keys."

She holds up the ring of keys that she'd dropped when she came in. Seeing them makes me remember something.

"You were opening my door," I say. "How did you have a key to my door?"

She looks confused . . . then guilty. "Rose must have given it to me."

"Rose?"

"Yes, Rose. She was here before . . ."

"Oh," I say, "you mean the previous tenant. Did you feed her cat . . . or something like that?"

Lillian smiles. "Something like that." Then she gives my arm a squeeze and shoos me back into my own apartment. I have no choice but to retreat and close the door, but I watch her on the camera walking to her door — or at least to as far as the camera reaches before she vanishes off-screen. I turn from the monitor and my eyes are drawn to the windows.

They kept us up high where no one could see us and the only escape was the drop to the rocks below.

I'd chosen this apartment because no one could see in and no one could climb up the sheer cliff, so I could feel safe behind my locked door with my surveillance camera and doorman downstairs, but I don't feel safe; I feel as trapped here as those Magdalen girls. Removing one danger has only exposed me to another. I feel like an animal that has burrowed itself into a hole to escape a predator only to discover it hasn't left itself an escape route.

After Lillian leaves, the apartment feels lonely and quiet. I pour myself a glass of wine and ask Bot to tell me the history of the Refuge. She tells me that the Refuge for Fallen Women was founded by the Sisters of the Good Shepherd, who called themselves the Magdalen sisters after Mary Magdalene, who was saved by Jesus from the sin of prostitution. Their symbol — which Bot pulls up on my laptop — was a cross with a shepherd's crook threaded down its center and two hearts linked behind it. They founded a Magdalen Society in New York City in the 1830s, first housed in downtown Manhattan, with the mission of rescuing women from lives of prostitution and vice and providing an asylum to erring females "who manifest a desire to return to the path of virtue." They must have found a lot of erring females, because they soon outgrew their downtown quarters and moved, in

1907, to Inwood. The society built a massive French chateau on a ridge overlooking the Hudson River. It was described in the *New York Times* as a "five-story fireproof structure solidly built of stone, covered in white stucco, with large, light, airy rooms."

As Bot lists the features of the Refuge it sounds like a paradise — "Big sunny rooms where girls sew and laugh amongst themselves, a spotless infirmary with surgical appliances and a medical chest." Even the basement, where "the home maintains a laundry and teaches its inmates to become fine laundresses," had large, sun-filled windows.

Every description, I notice, mentions the windows. "The workroom where the girls sew is like the deck of a steamer and so are the dormitories where they sleep," a *New York Tribune* reporter wrote. "The bathrooms and sanitary arrangements are admirable. All kinds of cases are sent there. Some are women who come or are sent there."

"Bot," I say, "reread that quote from the *Tribune.*"

Bot obliges. I stop her when she gets to "All kinds of cases are sent there. Some are women who come or are sent there."

"So it's not a voluntary cruise," I point out to Bot, thinking that two such awkward, redundant sentences would never have survived Sylvia's blue pencil.

"Do you want me to look up cruises?" Bot asks.

"No thank you, Bot," I say, reminding myself that Bot doesn't really have much of a sense of humor. "Go on and tell me how things worked out in this bright and sunny Magdalen asylum."

Bot proceeds, informing me that in 1913 there was a riot that involved seventy-five girls who scratched one another, shredded one another's clothes, and threw furniture out the large and sunny windows.

In 1914 a sixteen-year-old girl died going out one of those windows in a botched escape attempt. "Being unversed in even the elemental theories of physics," the reporter mockingly wrote, "Sarah Green tied one end of a rope composed of ripped bed clothes to a chair on the fourth floor of the Magdalen Home and started to lower herself from a window to the rocks bordering the Hudson last night. As soon as she changed her weight from the window sill to the rope the chair followed her out the window and seventeen bones in her body were broken when she fell on the crags."

I open the window above my desk and look out. Just as Lillian said, it's a straight drop to the rocks below, although there's the Henry Hudson Parkway and train tracks between the rocks and the river. I've heard the train in the night, but I hadn't realized the tracks were so close. Maybe the sound of the train lured the girls with the promise of escape. But how desperate would a girl be to try that sheer drop?

In 1916 another girl plunged to her death from a third-floor window. The Magdalens claimed she fell while sleepwalking, but couldn't explain why if she was sleepwalking she was fully dressed.

It was then that a legend sprang up that the Refuge was haunted by the ghosts of all the girls had who died trying to escape. There were many failed escapes over the years — and some successful ones, including a girl who went down a laundry chute and over a forty-foot wall never to be seen or heard from again. In 1941 two women vanished mysteriously. Some believed their bodies had been dumped in the river; others that they had hopped on a northbound train and made their way to freedom. The Refuge was closed soon afterward.

Instead of making me feel better, this history has made me feel more isolated and trapped than before. *Why haven't I invited any friends over?* I wonder, pouring another glass of wine. I know the answer. After three years working on this story 24/7, most of my friends got tired of me turning down dinner and drinks dates and acting guarded and secretive when I did because I couldn't talk about *the story.*

My last boyfriend said I spent more time with my boss, working late, than with him. He even accused me of having a thing for Simon, which was ridiculous, Simon was twenty years older than me. I respected him, wanted his esteem, and yes, it was true that all the twentysomething man-children I dated paled in comparison. Which is maybe why it's been almost a year since I went out on a date.

I go to pour another glass of wine and see that the bottle's empty. When I check the cabinet I find that it was my last bottle. I'd ordered a case when I moved in, thinking it would last me until I was ready to start going out again, but apparently I'm drinking more than I used to.

I rinse the bottle out and put it in the recycling bin — along with three others. *Okay,* I decide, *I'm definitely going to cut back on drinking alone. If I want a drink I'll go out.* There were several bars in the neighborhood, just down the hill. I could ask Sam and some of the other reporters for drinks one night. Only, I wouldn't know which bar to suggest since I've never been to any. Would they think that was weird that I'd lived here nearly three weeks and haven't even been to my local pub?

I look out my window. The sun is low over the Palisades, turning the sky that lovely shade of peachy-orange, but it isn't dark yet. It's a beautiful summer evening. I could walk down the hill to one of the pubs, have a glass of wine and a bite to eat. After all, I wasn't one of those poor Magdalen girls who weren't allowed to leave. I was free to go.

Before I can change my mind I march into my bedroom, shedding the ratty T-shirt and shorts I've been living in, and swing open my closet door. There, staring at me resentfully, is a pretty summer sundress I'd bought last winter when I imagined myself basking in the success of my big story. It still has its tags on.

I resolutely rip them off and pull the dress off the hanger and over my head. It hangs loosely, but I tighten the back sash and fish around in a still-unpacked box for a pair of sandals. Then I brush my hair, reflexively feeling for the bump at the back of my head. It's nearly gone. I've healed, I tell myself. I'm ready to go out into the world.

I find the Chanel bag I wore the night of my publication party. I haven't used it since that night, and seeing it — remembering it splayed out on my floor with wallet and keys dumped out — makes me feel momentarily ill. But I toss wallet, phone, keys, and lipstick inside. I'm aware that I'm moving fast, as if I have a date, because I am afraid that if I slow down I'll back out. I won't be able to go. And then I'll have to admit that I'm just as trapped here as those Magdalen girls.

I check the camera before opening the door. There's no one in the hall. In the lobby Enda is standing at his desk watching two women — both in heels and stylish summer clothes — getting on the elevator. One of them looks a bit like Marla, but the elevator door closes before I can tell for sure. It could be Marla showing an apartment to that fashionable-looking woman. I am in a trendy, desirable building in an up-and-coming neighborhood. *Not* trapped in a prison for prostitutes.

I step out into the hall and feel instantly light-headed, which is ridiculous. I've gone to the end of the hall to the garbage chute many times. Even doddery old Lillian Day is able to get around by herself. I hit the button and notice that the elevator has been paused on 4. That must be where Marla is showing the apartment. *I've got the better view,* I think a bit cattily as I ride down to the lobby. *And,* I can't help noticing when the doors open, Enda gives me a look that he definitely did *not* give Marla and her client. A look that makes my stomach do a little flip — and almost sends me back upstairs.

When did an admiring look from a man start to make me feel . . . *sick?* Was it listening to all those women who were assaulted? Or was it being followed up my apartment stairs and clobbered over the head? Either way, I won't let a leering doorman send me scurrying back to my room.

I square my shoulders and walk across the lobby with my head up.

"Going out?" Enda asks, getting up from his desk. "Do you need me to call you a cab?"

"No, thank you. I'm just walking down to the shops. It looks like such a lovely evening."

"That it is," he says. "I'm glad to see you getting out to enjoy it."

It's on the tip of my tongue to tell him it's none of his business how often I go out. Instead I smile and say, "I met one of my neighbors today. That old lady across the hall? Lillian Day."

He wrinkles his forehead. "The lady across from you is named Breen, but perhaps Day was her maiden name. She's a bit" — he taps his forehead — "forgetful."

"She seemed very sharp to me," I say, feeling protective of Lillian. "Oh, and she seemed to have a copy of my key. Maybe the previous tenant gave it to her."

"Not possible," Enda says briskly. "The locks were all changed when the previous tenant moved out. That's building policy."

I bristle at his automatic dismissal of my claim. "She was turning her key in my lock," I say, "and the bolt was sliding open when I got to the door."

He smiles — a supercilious smirk that makes my blood boil. "Maybe you just heard her rattling her key in your lock and *thought* you saw the bolt move. All that writing and reading you do — I bet it's hard on your eyes."

He might as well say that intellectual work has made me unhinged, like doctors warned women college students in the nineteenth century. "I know what I saw," I tell him. "And I want my locks changed."

"That's up to you, ma'am," he replies, suddenly formal. "But it will have to be at your own expense, as the building has

148

already changed your locks once. I can text you the name of a local locksmith if you like. Will there be anything else? Are you still going out . . . *to the shops*?"

He says the last words mockingly, as if he knows I'm heading to the local bar. As if that's any of his business. "No, that will be all," I say in my best imitation of Sylvia's imperious tone. "Thank you and have a good evening."

He bows — *ironically* — and holds the door open for me to walk through. There's no point in arguing.

Other than to delay stepping out of the building.

Which is ridiculous. It is, indeed, a lovely evening. A cool breeze and greenery beckons. It's been over two months since my story was published — an eon in a New York City news cycle. No one knows or cares who I am. Only a complete agoraphobe would hesitate to walk out that door. Is that what I've become? Is that what my attacker has made me?

Only if I let him.

One of the women I interviewed said that the reason she had agreed to talk to me was because she couldn't let what Caspar Osgood did to her define her. "I'm the author of my own story," she had said, clenching her fists.

My small-town-girl-makes-it-big-in-the-big-city story might be hokey, but it is a hell of a lot better than damaged-victim-becomes-shut-in.

And I'm certainly not going to let Enda have the satisfaction of seeing me retreat upstairs like a frightened child.

I lift my face to the breeze and step out from under the awning. I'm momentarily dazzled by the rays of the setting sun, but I slip on my sunglasses and the sidewalk snaps into focus — a checkerboard of sun and shade gently curving down to the avenue below. It smells like river water and burning charcoal. Someone is having a barbecue in the park. I hear birdsong and children playing. This might be the most unthreatening neighborhood in Manhattan. There's a church on the corner with a stone bell tower. I might be in a hilltop town in Tuscany instead of a neighborhood in northern Manhattan.

And that's why I moved here, I remember as I start down the hill, *to feel safe.* And because I could afford to now. Three years of hard work on the story got me the book deal that made this possible. All I had to do was write the damn book. And I would. I already felt better out in the fresh air, moving my body. I decide I will start taking daily walks — runs, even.

On either side of me I see joggers on the paths in the park — young men and women in bright nylon shorts and sweaty Dri-FIT shirts. There are older people, too, strolling slowly or sitting on benches, and women pushing strollers and clutching coffee cups. There are also families picnicking and grilling and children playing under the sprinklers in the playground. As I get closer to the church I notice signs in both Spanish and English on the community bulletin board advertising church suppers and yoga classes.

What a lovely neighborhood I've landed in, I think.

And then, just as I reach the church, I hear footsteps behind me. Which means nothing, I tell myself. There are lots of people out. But when I stop, the footsteps stop and a cold hand touches the back of my neck.

I spin around and the curving, sun-checkered sidewalk tilts upward. A dark, hooded figure slides off the edge of my vision, like oil dripping over a ledge, swamping my vision just as it was blacked out that night when my attacker pulled something over my head and pushed me to the floor —

I fall to the ground now, pain shooting up

from my scraped knees and palms. A sweet smell fills my mouth and throat just as it did that night, choking me. I can't breathe. Then a man is speaking to me in Spanish. From my rudimentary high school Spanish, I make out the words for "help" and "hospital."

"I don't need a hospital," I say as the man helps me to my feet. He's a short, middle-aged man in a white guayabera shirt. His hands smell like lighter fluid, probably because I have taken him away from his family barbecue. I can see his family watching us from their picnic table. There is no ominous hooded figure, just a family grilling chicken under a tree festooned with balloons and a star-shaped piñata. Of course, the hooded figure could have slipped into the park.

"I think I just need to go home," I tell my little group of onlookers. My rescuer offers to walk me back to my building, and a young woman, his daughter perhaps, comes with us, chattering about how she fell coming down the same hill last winter. "It's steeper than you think," she says. I thank her and the man, who hasn't said a word all the way up the hill. Enda comes out of the building as we approach.

"What happened?" he demands.

"I just had a little fall," I say, feeling like a child reprimanded by her mother. *That's what comes of gallivanting out at the bars,* I can imagine my grandmother saying. "I'm fine. I just want to go upstairs."

He insists on going up with me. "I've got a package for you anyway," he says, hoisting a heavy box under his arm. "It's from the liquor store on Broadway."

"I didn't order . . ." I begin, but then I wonder if maybe I did and I just forgot. At any rate, I think as Enda uses my keys to unlock my door, I won't be sending it back.

CHAPTER EIGHT

MELISSA

I would like to go home after lunch but I have an appointment to see an apartment in Tribeca with the realtor Sylvia recommended.

"Tribeca!" Emily had teased when I texted her earlier. "How hip of you, Mom."

I had thought it would make for an easy commute to *Image*'s Soho offices. I had thought I'd have a nice job offer in my pocket that would make a loft with a Hudson River view feasible. I'd been imagining myself starting over in a clean white space uncluttered by my past — and all those shoes older than the young women who had jobs and had slept with my husband. (I'd been exaggerating when I told Sally I'd already sold my last Prada loafers.) But walking through the army of young people thronging the sidewalks of Tribeca makes me feel old and out of place. The realtor —

a bleached blonde in a skintight Chanel sheath and arms as toned as a gymnast's — makes me feel old, and the maintenance fee for the raw, soulless loft makes me feel poor. In the taxi down here I'd calculated what I'd have in principal after making a down payment and how much income I could expect from it. With a salary it had seemed feasible; without one I won't have enough to pay my expenses without going into the rest of the principal.

"I'm not sure," I tell the realtor, Marla. "It's just so different from my Colonial in Ardsley. Maybe I'm not ready to commit to something long-term yet. Do you have anything to rent?"

She gives me a pained look — she won't make a commission on a lease. "That's totally understandable, Melissa — may I call you Melissa? — but unfortunately there aren't many leases on the market, certainly not in this neighborhood —"

In the land of the young and gainfully employed, she might as well say. Next she'll be suggesting assisted living for me.

"But I do have a listing for a sale uptown that has a lot more character than this and just as nice a view. It's quite a bit less . . ."

She names a figure that's still too much. "How far uptown?" I ask.

"Near Cloister Heights."

"The Cloisters!" I recall a Brearley field trip there. "That's practically in the Bronx."

"It's a very up-and-coming neighborhood, actually. In fact, I just sold a unit in the same building to a well-known journalist — oh!"

She turns bright red. Does she think the word *journalist* will remind me of my dead husband? But then I notice the sly smile tugging at her mouth. "What famous journalist?" I demand.

"I really shouldn't have . . . I mean, I can't say . . . all client information is strictly confidential."

"It was Joan Lurie, wasn't it? She bought herself a new place with the blood money she got writing lies about my husband."

"I'm sorry, Mrs. Osgood, I really wasn't thinking. Of course you wouldn't want to live in the same building —"

"On the contrary," I say, picturing how uncomfortable it would make Joan Lurie, "I'd be very interested in seeing the listing. Can you show it to me today?"

In the Uber going uptown I reconsider. I can't even really afford this cheaper place that's so far uptown I might as well just stay in Westchester. I should be conserving what little money I have in case one of Cass's women comes after me with a lawsuit. And when we get off the Henry Hudson I immediately see that all Marla's talk of gentrification and up-and-coming were code for ghetto. I mean, I'm not a racist. I *love* Marta and have several — well, two — Black friends from the boards I'm on, but that doesn't mean I want to live in a crime-ridden neighborhood where the nearest deli is a bodega. Still, I *am* curious to know what Joan Lurie's blood money had bought her and if we should happen to pass in the lobby, let *her* squirm. Let *her* worry about what a disgraced, grief-torn widow might do to avenge herself.

As we turn off a grimy avenue onto a tree-lined street that goes steeply uphill, Marla points out the advantages of the location: the proximity to the Cloisters and the A train, the surrounding park, and the view. The view *is* pretty nice. It's practically the same view as from the conservancy, and it reminds me of the night of the gala before my world caved in — the last moment I felt happy. The apartment building itself looks like the French chateau Cass and I stayed in for our twentieth wedding anniversary.

"What was this building originally?" I ask, trying to look like I have some real interest in the place.

Marla looks a bit uncomfortable. "Actually, it was a kind of school . . . or a home, you might say . . . for wayward girls. The nuns ran it as a laundry —"

"You mean like those awful Magdalen laundries in Ireland?" I ask, remembering a movie I watched with Emily. "Like a prison?"

"Well . . . not exactly . . ." she says, but that's exactly what it looks like — behind all the French gewgaws — a prison. Which is the perfect place for Joan Lurie to have ended up.

The doorman is young and hunky with what my mother used to call, after a few G&Ts — *bedroom eyes.* The apartment is on the fourth floor — not even the penthouse — and is ridiculously small. It's advertised as two bedrooms, but the second room is barely big enough for a single bed. Where would Whit and Emily stay when they came to visit? The washing machine and dryer are stacked right on top of each other, and I'm picturing how disdainful Marta would be of it when I remember that I have to tell her that I'm letting her go. I'm the one who would be stuffing my own laundry in there like those poor girls who were imprisoned in this place.

It's clear from all the security features that the surrounding neighborhood is a slum. There's camera surveillance of the hallway, lobby, and outside the front door as if it's a prison. Which it was. At least I can leave satisfied that Joan Lurie is living in a dump —

And then I see her. She's on the camera, walking out the front door, wearing a floaty sundress like she's going to a picnic. She pauses and takes a deep breath, tilting her face up to the sun, like she's congratulating herself on what a great person she is. The valiant crusader who brought down the big, bad sex offender. She sashays off into the dappled sunshine with that same sway in her hips like on the night I followed her to her apartment. Cass's suicide has done nothing to dim her narcissistic entitlement. It makes my blood boil. It makes me want to wipe the smug smile right off her face.

But how?

She's secure up here in her protected aerie, writing her book about my husband. Spinning stories from the lies those women told — women who might be plotting to sue me for the little pittance I have left.

Marla can probably see I've lost interest in the place. She shows me the bathrooms and the linen closet — which is too small to even hold the three eiderdowns I bought in Switzerland last year — in a bored monotone.

"What's this?" I ask, pointing to a door at the end of the hall.

"That's a back door," she tells me. "It provides access for deliveries and service calls. Some of the units have covered them up, but the doorman keeps a key anyway just in case." She finds an old-fashioned key on the chain the doorman gave her and opens the door onto a dreary stairwell. There's a heavy iron railing that's been painted over so many times it looks like it's swollen with tumors. There are scratches on the walls that probably come from careless deliverymen but that give the impression of crazy people trying to claw themselves out of this place. I look up and see a door on the floor above.

"It's too bad you weren't searching two months ago," she says, staring up at the door with me. "You could have gotten the top floor."

So that must be Joan Lurie's apartment. Behind that door are all her files on the women who lied about my husband and who are still lying in wait to sue me and take away what little I have left. Only one lousy door with one lousy lock that opens with a key kept by that hunky bedroom-eyes doorman —

Marla tries to show me the claw-foot tub, but I remain standing on the landing gazing upward, more interested in this view than the one of the river.

"How soon would it take to get board approval and move in?" I ask.

"Well, that depends on your financing —"

"Cash," I say. "What if it's cash?"

"Well, generally about six weeks —"

"How soon if I double your commission?" I hold her gaze, trying not to think about how much of my principal this will eat into.

She doesn't miss a beat. "Three, maybe four weeks," she says.

"Make it three," I tell her. "And we've got a deal."

While Marla makes a call to the co-op board I sit on the window ledge and phone my broker at Merrill Lynch and ask him to wire all the money in my account into my checking so I can write a check for the apartment. It's after seven on a summer Friday, but Gil answers. He hesitates, though, when I tell him how much I want to withdraw.

"Don't you think you might want to keep some back in case of lawsuits —" he begins.

"There will be more when the houses

sell," I say, neglecting to mention that that money is slated for college tuition. "And I can't sit around on eggshells waiting for some hysterical women to sue me."

"Of course not," Gil says. "It would be useful, though, to know what that reporter has —"

"Yes," I say, staring up at the ceiling. I can hear footsteps moving across the floor — *she's* back early. "That would be useful. But I don't think Joan Lurie and I will be having lunch anytime soon." This much is true. I don't tell Gil, though, that I've just bought the apartment under hers.

"No, of course not," Gil says, clearly impatient to get off now. "I'll have the money wired to you by Monday morning. I wish you the best of luck in this new place. You deserve some peace and quiet, Melissa. I still can't believe —"

"Thanks, Gil," I cut in before he can profess his astonishment at Cass's proclivities. "Love to Fran and the kids." I end the call and place my phone down on the window ledge. Marla comes in to tell me that the co-op board is willing to expedite the process as long as I'm willing to sign a no-publicity waiver. "Basically it just asks that you don't draw publicity to the building, conduct interviews —"

"Did *she* have to sign one?" I ask.

"I believe they're standard," Marla says, keeping her eyes on her phone and briskly moving on to dates for a closing. She's lying, I think. The co-op board wants to make sure that the disgraced widow of the sex pervert doesn't hurt their property values, but they probably didn't blink an eye at letting in the slut who drew all that damning publicity to me in the first place. Who's up there now working on a book filled with more lies —

Marla asks if those dates are okay and I ask if they can't be moved up a bit and she tells me three weeks is the absolute quickest she's ever seen anyone get into a co-op. Liar. If Cass were here he'd get us in tomorrow. He was always good at getting what he wanted.

But if Cass were here I wouldn't be moving into this dump.

"I suppose it will have to do," I say, standing up. We go down in the elevator. In the lobby the hunky doorman, whose name it turns out is Enda, offers to get us a taxi.

"I've already called an Uber," Marla says. "Can I drop you, Melissa? Are you going to Grand Central?"

"Actually," I say, "I thought I'd explore my new neighborhood a bit." I smile at

Enda. "Can you recommend a good place for dinner?"

Marla gives me a quizzical look and says her farewells while Enda draws me a map on the back of a take-out menu showing me how to get to an Irish pub called the Black Rose, which he says "does a brilliant shepherd's pie."

Without mentioning that I have no intention of eating such slop, I lean up close to him while he draws the map. "I'm hopeless with directions. I don't suppose you could show me the way."

"Wish I could, love," he says with a slow, simmering smile, "but I'm on duty all night."

"Oh well, I'll just have to manage on my own then. I suppose the neighborhood's safe."

"Safe enough while everyone's out. I wouldn't walk back up through the park on your own after dark, though. And if you ever do —" He writes a phone number on the hand-drawn map. "You call me so I can look out for you."

"I'll do that," I say, leaning in a little closer. He doesn't lean away. I turn and he holds the door for me and I can hear that he doesn't close it right away. He's watching me as I walk down the hill. It feels good to have a man's eyes on me again. After I quit working I was in a world of women: the other mothers, teachers, women on the charity boards. At Cass's work things I was just an appendage — the boss's wife — invisible or, now I realize, an object of pity. The wife whose husband was sleeping with every secretary and intern within sight.

But I'm still attractive — all that damned Pilates and expensive skin treatments Sylvia is always recommending — and still *young enough.* Not that I'm ready for anything romantic. I'm not *heartless,* and I wouldn't get involved with the Irish doorman, of course, but there's no harm in flirting. He might prove to be useful.

I stop and pretend to adjust my shoe strap while glancing back and he's still standing at the door watching me. I give him a little wave and continue down the hill, feeling happy for the first time in months, since the night of the gala.

The Black Rose is full of girls in droopy dresses and boys in beards and those horrible man buns. No one would imagine me living here in a million years. Wally Shanahan will be shocked, I think gleefully, sitting down at the bar and ordering a gin and tonic. And Sylvia . . . I remember that Sylvia set me up for that disastrous interview

165

with Sally Jessell. I'll give her a call next week and thank her for the referral but make clear that I wasn't going to do any interviews right now because I was thinking of writing my own book. Best not to make an enemy of Sylvia; I had enough of those with the women lining up to sue me and Joan Lurie planning to write more lies about me and Cass in her book.

I drink two G&Ts and nibble on a kale salad while paging through a local paper, since I didn't bring my phone. I chat with the bartender, who's a font of information on the neighborhood. When I tell him I'm moving into the Refuge, he launches into a long monologue on the history of the place, including riots, daring escapes, and tragic suicidal leaps from the high windows. The bar itself was named for a girl who was an inmate there, some '40s mobster's moll who killed herself jumping out a window at the Refuge.

"My husband killed himself," I tell him while biting on a swizzle stick. "Only, we lived in a two-story so he had to drown himself in the swimming pool."

He stares at me as if he's not sure if I'm joking or not — finally, a cure for mansplaining! — and then leaves me alone. My last drink is on the house.

At 11:45 I leave and start walking up the hill. Enda was probably right about it not being safe. There's no one but a few dog walkers and a bum asleep on a bench. If I had my phone I'd take Enda up on his offer, but it's safely tucked away in the apartment that'll soon be mine. Besides, even if I could call Enda he wouldn't be able to see me from the front door.

A fog has crept over the park, hiding the apartment building from sight. It smells like the ocean — and something else — bleach and laundry soap. Probably coming from a factory along the river. That's a little detail that Marla left out. I walk faster and am glad to hear voices ahead of me — women's voices, one urging the other on — "We just have to walk up the hill. . . ." A couple of girls coming home late and drunk. I hurry to catch up with them, passing through a colder patch of fog. Suddenly I feel like I'm *in* the river. I can't breathe. I'm choking on ice-cold water, my throat and nostrils burning with the sting of soap and bleach —

Which must have been the last thing Cass ever smelled: the chlorine from our pool. I picture him floating in the water, his limp arms spread out. My heart squeezes at the thought of his last moments. No matter what he did to me he didn't deserve to die like that —

Something brushes up against my face. Something cold and wet, like the dead hand of a drowned man. I scream and jerk away, running blindly in the fog, which spits me out onto the doorstep of the Refuge. Enda is there, staring into space. His eyebrows shoot up at the sight of me.

"Mrs. Osgood? Are you all right? Did something happen?" He's looking behind me into the fog. The two girls have vanished.

"Someone grabbed me . . ." I gasp. "Back there." I point into the fog — only the fog has vanished now. The sidewalk is empty.

"He must have run into the park," I say.

"I said to call if you were coming up the hill alone," he says, helping me into the lobby.

"I don't have my phone," I say. "I realized I didn't have it when I went to call an Uber. I must have left it in the apartment."

"Are you sure? Could you have left it down at the bar? I could call them —"

"No," I say sharply. Then, letting the tears fall, "I'm sure I left it in the apartment. Please, let me go up to look for it?"

"Technically," Enda's saying, "the place isn't yours yet and I'm not supposed to let anyone in."

"What if one of my children is trying to

reach me? This has been such an awful time for them. For all of us." The tears are flowing now and I'm not faking it. The smell of chlorine still burns in my nose and the touch of death crawls on my skin. "You have a key, don't you?"

He gives me a suspicious look. I shouldn't have said that about the key. It makes it look like I've planned this, which, of course, I have. "I'm not supposed to leave the lobby . . ." he begins, and then his shoulders slump as I sob. "We'll have to be quick about it then. Come on, we have to go up the service stairs, though, because I only have the key to the back door. Are you up to it in those shoes?"

"Of course I'm up to it," I snap.

"Come on, then."

He shows me through a door to the left of the elevators into a dimly lit stairwell. I recognize the same overpainted iron banister as before.

"Aren't there doors in the hallways to this stairwell?" I ask.

"No," he says, "only onto the backs of the apartments. It was used by the nuns when this was a laundry. They kept those girls locked up tight."

"Oh yes, a man in the bar was telling me the place's history. It's a bit . . . *creepy*."

"What was creepy is what the Church did to those girls, locking them up because they'd had a little fun or ran into a bit of trouble. Back in Ireland I had a great-aunt who'd been in one of the laundries. She said a girl could wind up there because she was, as she put it, *too free with the boys* or talked back to the priests. I don't know what these girls did to get put here, but from all the locks on the doors I know no one wanted them to get out."

We've climbed four floors and come to the door of "my" apartment. He uses an old-fashioned skeleton key to open it. The hallway inside is even darker than the stairwell. He turns on his phone flashlight and lights the way. I hadn't noticed before that there were no windows in the long hallway. I imagine nuns patrolling these halls, making sure the girls didn't get away, the girls weeping in their narrow cots —

I shake myself. This place is making me sentimental. I direct Enda to the windowsill where I left my phone. "There it is," I say, picking it up and hitting the Home button. "Oh dear, three missed calls from my daughter. Do you mind if I call her back?"

"I'd prefer you made your calls downstairs, Mrs. Osgood. We're really not supposed to be here and I'm not supposed to leave my post."

I pout. "Don't you want to help me 'break in' my new place?" I say, leaning back on the windowsill and extending my legs out so he can get a good look at them.

"Some other time, Mrs. Osgood, when it *is* your new place."

"Oh, okay." I get up and let him lead me back down the hall and into the stairwell. After he's locked the door and put the keys in his pocket I make a little noise — like that fainting noise the woman on *Masterpiece Mystery* does — and then fall in his direction. He catches me. His arms are *very* strong. I allow myself to droop against his broad, muscular chest and dip my hand into his pocket as he lowers me carefully to the floor.

"Oh, my," I say, "I just got so light-headed for a moment. I think I must be dehydrated."

"That must be the problem," he says, detangling himself from me and leaning me against the wall. "Take it easy for a moment. Is there anyone I can call?"

"No," I say with a little sniff. "No one. Only . . . I think I really am dehydrated. Do you think you could get me some water?" He looks toward the apartment door. "*Bottled* water," I add. "I have a very sensitive stomach."

He sighs and stands up. "I've got some at my desk —"

I nod and close my eyes. "If it's not too much trouble."

"Not at all," he says grudgingly. As he starts down the stairs I hear him muttering, "What is it with falling women today?"

I listen until his steps grow fainter and then I get up and uncurl my fist to look at the key in my hand. Then I head up the stairs.

CHAPTER NINE

JOAN

Back in my apartment I engage all my locks even though, knowing there could be spare keys out there, they no longer make me feel safe. I'll get the locks changed tomorrow, I tell myself. In the meantime, it's just frail old Lillian Day who has a key, and even to my hyper-paranoid brain she does not seem like a credible threat. I could go to her apartment and demand she give me my key back. At least it would prove to Enda that I hadn't imagined her having my key.

That would be mean, though, to upset an old lady who's probably asleep by now. Plus, even the thought of going into the hallway is unbearable. So I open a bottle of wine and begin pulling files out of a box. I am secluding myself to work on this book — not because I've become an alcoholic agoraphobe, I tell myself. It's all about the *process.*

I line the files up on the satiny oak surface of my Stickley desk. The names of the women swim across my field of vision like fish. Here's Amanda, Caspar Osgood's assistant who broke down in tears and told me that she'd been sleeping with her boss and she was afraid he'd fire her if she tried to end it. When I interviewed her a few weeks after we'd both been fired from the *Globe,* Amanda gave me a list of interns who had worked there and I went to each of them. I was careful. I never directly asked if Caspar Osgood had assaulted them. I said I was doing a story on the value of internships. There were plenty who just complained of having to bring their bosses coffee or how competitive the other interns were, as well as those who said it was great, but they were working in PR now, journalism wasn't really a viable career option anymore. But then there were the ones who would fidget and look nervous and then their stories would come spilling out —

Stephanie, Gwyneth, Pamela —

I touch their names on each file. Nice college girls who shyly reported the furtive gropings, fingerings, rubbings, and maulings as if *they* were somehow at fault. If Caspar Osgood had a type, it was the kind of polite, well-behaved college girl that he

174

had married. They all could have been Melissa Osgood thirty years ago.

Girls all compliant like Melissa Osgood, I scrawl across one of the folders, *trying to find a younger version of what he'd lost?*

When I started talking to older reporters, I found that he'd been doing it for at least the last twenty years —

Sandra, Amy, Roslyn —

These women, I recall, as I handle each of their files, reported the abuse more matter-of-factly. *Everyone's got a Caspar Osgood in their résumé, the guy whose groping you endure and then move on,* Roslyn, a senior editor at a Phoenix paper informed me. Some of these women wouldn't let me use their names. It would hurt their career, they said. People would accuse them of sleeping their way to the top.

Of course, Roslyn told me over drinks at the Arizona Biltmore (Simon, who knew her, said to take her someplace fancy), *people say that anyway whether you do or not. It's what people are saying about you and Simon Wallace, you know.* She'd given me a sideways look. *Are you, by the way?*

I had laughed it off, but now I wonder if people are saying that. I resist an urge to ask Bot to search social media for references to me and Simon. I have to start working

175

on the book. Etinosa had specifically asked that I keep an eye out for material that I hadn't explored fully in the article. As I'd told Andrea Robbins that night at the *Manahatta* party, there were plenty of tips I hadn't been able to pursue, the most incendiary of which was the accusation that Cass had assaulted an underage server at a fancy private club. But who had told me that?

When I try to remember, all the women I've interviewed over the last three years blur together, all of their voices echoing inside my brain. *What is wrong with me?* I start to ask Bot to look up whether imagined voices are a symptom of concussion when it hits me: Amanda had told me that a server had seen Cass hit her at a club and that Cass had been taken down to the police station. But that had proved to be a dead end. I'd checked through all the police databases and there was no record of any charges against Caspar Osgood. *If there's no police record you can't report it,* Simon had said. *Amanda was probably mistaken or making it up. Stay with the workplace harassment angle. God knows you've got enough there.*

Still, I think now, if I could follow that lead, it would make for great new material for the book. I open the hard copy of Amanda's file but as I begin to read I notice that the pages are out of order and some seem to be missing. Had I really left them like this? When I try to put them in order the words of the typescript blur together. It would probably be easier to just print out the digital file, but when I open my laptop my screen is a blur. I can't even read the print I've magnified to 220 percent or make out the lights across the river. The whole world has smeared into an indistinguishable blur. Maybe I've had more wine than I thought. Or maybe whatever was jarred loose in the attack has finally detached, leaving me blind and brain damaged —

But then I realize it's just a fog that's risen from the river, blotting out the view — that and the bottle of wine I've polished off, leaving me drunk and maudlin. Through that blur suddenly comes the name of the club where Osgood had supposedly been arrested: the Hi-Line Club — the same club that, according to Sylvia, Simon had tried to join but he'd been denied membership, supposedly because Cass blackballed him. I scrawl the name down on top of Amanda's folder and then stumble into my bedroom, collapse into bed without undressing, and fall asleep thinking about those women whose files are on my desk. *Amanda, Stephanie, Gwyneth, Pamela, Sandra, Amy, Roslyn.*

But in my dreams the women and I are all in the Refuge when it was still a Magdalen laundry, put there for loose morals and being too free with the boys.

"Look at what getting drunk and gallivanting about on the streets got you," a tall, imposing nun scolds me.

She leads me to a row of boiling vats, thick yellow steam rising from them. The smell makes my eyes and nose sting. The heat is unbearable, but when I try to step away I see my wrist is chained to the iron vat.

"You might as well get to work," the girl to my right says. She's wearing the same muslin uniform as me . . . she looks familiar . . . but when I try to get a better look at her through the steam someone strikes me on the back of the head and I stumble against the vat, nearly falling in, boiling water scalding my hands. Gray water churns in the vat, white clots of cloth writhe like snakes, viscous bubbles rising — one of those bubbles bobs to the surface and looks up at me with Caspar Osgood's dead eyes.

I wake up screaming, fighting with my own bedsheets, that smell of bleach and soap clawing up my throat —

And then I hear a step in the hallway.

Is someone in my apartment?

I rise out of bed as weightless as those

soap bubbles and stand listening. The door to the hall is closed — had I closed it? I don't remember doing it. I hear a creak that could be a floorboard settling and then the unmistakable click of a door opening and then closing.

Someone is definitely in my apartment.

I quickly scan my nightstand for my phone, but it's not there. The last I remember having it was when I put it in my bag to go out — the bag that I dropped on my desk when I came in. It also has the can of mace my mother gave me. I am defenseless, cowering in my bedroom. Maybe it's just Lillian, confused and wandering again. Or Enda checking on me. In which case I will give him a piece of my mind.

Anger suddenly replaces fear. I grab the brass lamp from my nightstand, ripping the plug out of the wall. The hallway stretches out in front of me like a tunnel with only a dim glow at the end. The door to the linen closet is partly ajar. The intruder could be in there. I walk down the hall and fling open the door. A pile of sheets falls out, the smell of laundry soap stirring up that awful dream.

Maybe I had been dreaming when I heard that footstep.

But the door opening — I'd been awake

for that.

I stalk down the hallway, holding the lamp in both hands like a baseball bat, into the living room, which is lit by a full moon riding a bank of clouds above the river. The fog has vanished. The moonlight is so dazzling that the dark room seems alive with presences. Those women chained to the laundry vats, those nuns in long black habits patrolling their wards.

I blink and the image fades into patterns of light and shadow cast by moonlight and clouds. The room is empty. The door is closed. I check the locks and the security camera. The outside hallway and lobby are also empty, and so is the sidewalk outside the front door —

Where is Enda? Taking a break? Somewhere the camera doesn't reach? I swipe between the lobby and the sidewalk, fighting the urge to buzz him and demand to know where he is, and then something flickers as I swipe back from the sidewalk to the lobby: a dark shape lurking on the edge of the trees bordering the door. I switch to the sidewalk just in time to catch a glimpse of that shape stealing in through the door. When I look back at the lobby it's empty. But the intruder could be hiding behind one of the tall wingback chairs, free to roam at will while Enda is God-knows-where.

I hit the buzzer, my eyes glued to the image of the lobby, and wait. Nothing moves, but staring at the black-and-white picture on the screen makes my head ache and vision blur. I blink — and something moves on the screen — Enda, hurrying from the service stairs to the front desk, shrugging his jacket back on.

"Yes?" His voice crackling from the monitor startles me. "What can I do for you, Miss Lurie?"

What indeed? What services was he performing that had him out of his jacket after midnight?

"I . . . uh . . . I heard someone at my door before," I say. It's not entirely a lie. I *did* hear someone at the door before — ten hours before when Lillian showed up. "And when I looked at the camera I thought I saw someone in the lobby."

He doesn't say anything right away. I can see his back. The collar of his jacket is tucked under, the nape of his neck shiny with sweat, hair mussed. "So," he says, his voice thick with condescension, "you heard someone at your door and so you looked at the lobby? Is there anyone at your door or in your apartment now?"

"No, of course not," I say. "I checked the

lobby *after* I made sure the intruder was gone. But he may still be in the building. Do you think you could stop being an ass long enough to look behind the chairs?"

A tremor passes through his back that might be repressed laughter or anger. "Okay," he says. "I'll have a look behind the chairs. Should I be checking under them? How big was this intruder of yours?"

"I can see you," I say tightly, "not looking anywhere."

He turns around and looks up into the camera, grinning. Then he makes a show of looking behind and under the chairs and sofa. He moves them to show me there's nothing behind them and even tilts them up to show me there's nothing underneath either. When he lifts up a corner of the carpet I explode.

"He must have gotten out. But there *was* someone there and, as I told you before, my neighbor had my key. What were you doing away from your post? I was promised twenty-four-hour doormen. I'm going to complain to the co-op board." I regret the tone of my voice immediately but I'm too far down the road of outraged entitlement to stop. "*And* you were supposed to text me the number of a locksmith. I want my locks changed."

"Now?" he asks, making a show of looking at his watch. "You want your locks changed at twelve thirty in the morning?"

"How am I supposed to sleep tonight knowing there are copies of my key out there?"

He looks up at the camera. "Weeelll," he says, drawing out the word, "would you like me to come up and have a look around?"

Is there a suggestive lilt in his voice? Is this some kind of code for offering *special services*?

"No," I say, "that won't be necessary —"

He cuts me off. "Actually, I think I'd better have a look. I can't take the chance that there's an intruder in the building. I'll be right up."

I try to object, but he's already turned off the intercom and crossed the lobby to the service stairs. Why isn't he taking the elevator? I wonder. Then I look down at myself and notice that I'm still in my sundress, which is a wrinkled mess. I hurry back to my room and change into a T-shirt and sweatpants, and brush my hair. Then I go back to the front door and check the camera, but Enda's not here yet.

Then I see the elevator needle moving from 4 to 5. But why would Enda be in the elevator when he took the stairs? Four is the floor where Marla showed an apartment earlier. What if someone she showed it to somehow got the key? What if *she* is on her way up now? My heart is pounding so hard as the elevator doors open that my vision blurs — no, it's not that — the camera has short-circuited. The screen is a fuzzy gray, as opaque as the fog that had risen off the river before —

And with the same soap and bleach smell.

I can hear footsteps in the hallway approaching my door — or maybe it's the sound of my heart jackhammering against my rib cage. I feel as if I've stood here before, waiting inside the fog, not knowing if the one approaching is coming to save me or kill me —

A sharp rap on the door makes me jump, and the camera screen flicks back to life. There's Enda, looking sweaty and flustered. As I fumble with the locks I have the thought: *How do I know he's not the one who's been sent to kill me?* It doesn't feel as if it's my thought. And it's too late anyway; I've already opened the door.

Enda gives me one look and grins. "You look like you've seen a ghost. Are you going to let me in to check under the carpets?"

"I didn't ask you to come up," I point out, but stand aside to let him in. "However, if you want to check I won't stop you." The truth is I'll feel better having him check. "There aren't any carpets, though."

"Hmph," he grunts, heading down the hallway toward my bedroom. "That may be a problem now that 4B's been sold. Your co-op agreement requires that seventy-five percent of your floors be covered."

He goes into my bedroom and makes a show of looking under the bed. I stand in the doorway, arms folded across my chest. "Did that woman who came in with Marla buy the place?"

He looks up. "How do you know Marla was showing it today? And how did you know she was showing it to a woman?"

"I saw them in the elevator," I say. It's not entirely a lie. But to cover I ask him, "Were you helping her move in?"

He blushes so red I know I've hit a nerve. So he *was* up to something. He gets to his feet and squeezes past me into the hallway and stalks to the linen closet.

"I've already checked in there —" I begin, but he opens the door anyway. A bundle of towels falls out.

"There's your intruder," he says, lifting a tilting shelf from the closet. "This shelf came loose. You must have heard it fall."

"It just fell by itself?" I ask skeptically.

"Weeell," he drawls, holding up the warped plywood, "it's a bit flimsy. You should have it fixed — or personally, I'd recommend storing your linens elsewhere and clearing this doorway."

I give him a puzzled look. "What door—" But then I see, behind the shelves, the clear outline of a door. "What the hell!" I say. "I didn't know there was a door there."

Enda gives me a strange look. "Didn't the real-estate agent show it to you? It's described in the co-op agreement. You're not supposed to block it. The last tenant got around that by saying the shelves were removable."

"Where does it lead?" I ask, horrified that there's been this back entrance to my sanctuary all along. "And who has the key to it?"

"You do, for starters," he says. "It should have been on the ring of keys you got at the closing."

I remember now the one old-fashioned skeleton key. I'd thought it was to the basement storage area, which I had no intention of using.

"And of course Hector and I have one." He holds up a key identical to the one I thought was to the basement storage area. "It's all in the handbook. We keep a key in

186

case you want a delivery when you're out. It's nothing to worry about," he adds as I glare at him. "I never let the key out of my sight."

As he says it his eyes shift up and to the left, as I'd seen him do on my first day here. Only then I'd thought he was looking up into the camera.

Now it's clear that he's lying.

CHAPTER TEN

MELISSA

Compliant, that's what that little bitch called me. There on the top folder on her big, pretentious, look-at-me-I've-got-an-enormous-book-deal desk. *Girls all compliant like Melissa Osgood. Trying to find a younger version of what he'd lost?* Who the hell did she think she was, playing armchair psychiatrist with Cass and me when she didn't know the first thing about us or our marriage? Clearly from her bachelorette digs — take-out containers and empty wine bottles lying around everywhere! — she's never even lived with anyone. What did she know about what made a marriage work? What did she know about the compromises, the sacrifices?

I'd show her compliant.

I was so mad that after I copied the files from her hard drive — conveniently labeled on her laptop, which, to my good fortune, had not gone to sleep — I erased Amanda's file; *Joan* deserved to be erased. Then I copied her whole hard drive and got out of there, just as I heard her stirring in her bedroom. I went right back through that sad little linen closet of hers and locked the door behind me and was back on the fourth-floor landing before Enda even got back. I was afraid maybe he'd come up, found that I was in Joan's apartment, and gone to the police, but then he came pounding up the stairs, all hot and bothered.

"Look," he said, "I've had a complaint from a tenant that they heard someone at their door. You didn't . . ."

I just widened my eyes and looked up at him blankly. He shook the thought away. I could see him thinking that a nice, *compliant* wife like me wouldn't have the nerve to break into anyone's apartment.

What girls like Joan Lurie don't realize is that sometimes instead of striding around shouting loud demands, looking like you're compliant gets a lot more done. So when Enda told me I had to go down to the basement and out the side door so the nervous tenant didn't see me on the lobby camera, I didn't bat an eyelash.

"Of course," I told him, "I don't want to get you in any trouble. This will be our little secret." Meaning he wasn't going to tell anyone about me being here because it would get *him* in trouble.

Sometimes compliance breeds compliance in others.

And I didn't even mind sneaking out through the basement. Yes, it was creepy. I had to go down a long dark corridor past closed doors, which must be where the storage units are, and into a big cavern with rock walls and enormous iron vats that smelled like soap and mildew, but I was glad to learn how to leave the building unobserved by the cameras. I bet Joan Lurie doesn't know about that. Which meant I could move in, live right below Joan, and if I was careful she wouldn't even know I was there. At first I didn't care if she saw me, but now that I have secret access to her back door I might just keep my presence hidden until I can find out what she's planning to write in her book, and I can debunk her lies even before she publishes them.

I might have been *compliant* when I needed to be, but no one is telling me what to do now.

In the next two weeks plenty of people try to tell me what to do. When I told Wally Shanahan where I was moving, she laughed in my face. "Don't be ridiculous, Mel, you can't live in *Inwood*. There's not even a Zabar's or Whole Foods. Let me call that shark of a realtor Sylvia recommended and we'll get you out of that hasty decision and into a nice co-op in Greenwich."

"No thank you," I told Wally. "I'm going to love my new place. It's got a great view and a charming Irish pub down the hill and I can just order from FreshDirect and GrubHub. Come visit. We'll go to the Cloisters."

My accountant told me I'd be broke in five years if I lived off my principal.

My lawyer told me I should be putting money aside for future lawsuits.

Sylvia was nicer about my choice. *I've heard it's an up-and-coming neighborhood,* she said, and even expressed an interest in visiting, but I could tell by her strained voice that she was mortified for me.

I thanked them all for their concern and said I knew what I was doing.

And I do. As soon as I got home I downloaded all of Joan's files onto my laptop. I have the names and addresses of all her sources. The transcripts of their interviews. All I have to do is go through them and find the holes. I have Cass's calendars, credit-card receipts, and, once I hack into his email account, correspondence. I am sure there will be discrepancies between the lies these women spun and my husband's records. And when I find them I will write my own story and then I will sue the living daylights out of Joan Lurie and Simon Wallace. I will drive *Manahatta* into the ground — or maybe I'll *buy* it with the money I get in the lawsuit and from *my* book deal. I've always wanted to run a little magazine. I'll let Sylvia stay on, but I'll wait until Sally Jessell needs a job and then laugh *frothily* in her face.

The next two weeks *fly* by. Whit and Emily come home to sort through their stuff before going back to college. I tell them they either have to get rid of it or keep it in their dorm rooms. Emily cries and tells me I'm hard-hearted. She has gone from being furious at her father to believing he was a saint and everything that has happened is somehow my fault. I let her rage at me. I wish Whit would do the same but he has withdrawn into an incommunicative sulk that worries me more. He'll do better when he's back at Brown with his friends, I tell myself, and they'll both be better when I've cleared their father's name. In the meantime, I give in and rent a storage unit but limit them

192

each to five hundred square feet. They both forgive me long enough to be helpful: Emily by holing up in my closet to take pictures of all my shoes and handbags that she'll then list on eBay, and Whit by helping me hack into Cass's Gmail account so, I tell him, I can protect myself against any possible lawsuits.

We try passwords with combinations of birth and anniversary dates and celebrity names.

"Who were dad's favorite authors?" Whit asks.

I stare at him. "Whitman and Emily Dickinson," I say after a short moment. "How did you think you got your names?"

Whit shrugs. "I never knew."

How had we not told him? When I met Cass in English 101 at Brown and he said his favorite writers were Whitman and Dickinson I imagined right then and there that someday we would marry and have children named Emily and Whitman. I imagined we'd have the kind of bookish family that went every weekend to the Museum of Natural History and the New York Public Library at Bryant Park and spent their summers in Maine and had their own private jokes and made-up language. Like one of those families in a Salinger story, only with a little less neurosis. What had happened to *that* dream?

Work had happened. The *Globe* and Cass's ambition to make something of himself that wasn't predicated on the family name. To prove he wasn't his father. To fill a hole I hadn't even known was there.

"Try Globe1030," I tell Whit.

He does and we're in. "That's not anyone's birthday," he says, frowning.

"No," I tell him, "it's the day your father bought the *Globe.*"

"I guess I shouldn't be surprised," Whit says. "Work was always the most important thing to him."

My heart contracts in pain for him. "Your father loved you very much. Remember —" I search my memory for proof of Cass's paternal love but all I find is the image of Cass sitting by Whit's hospital bedside after Whit's suicide attempt. "Remember how fast he got to the hospital when you . . ." I falter, hating to bring up the moment.

"When I tried to off myself?" Whit asks. "Yeah, he got there quick enough for that." He gets up, his face clearly troubled. How could I have been so stupid as to bring up his own suicide attempt when his father has just killed himself?

"Whit," I say, "if you want to talk —"

"I've got a therapist for that, Mom. I'd better go finish packing."

As I watch him go I'm torn between chasing after him and opening the laptop. What can I say to him? Better I face whatever bombshells are lying in wait for me on Cass's laptop so I can at least protect him and his sister from any more shocks.

I take Cass's laptop outside. The weather has finally broken and it feels like the worst of the summer heat is behind us. I gaze out at the empty pool. The realtor had suggested I keep it filled for showing optics, but I knew every time I looked at it I'd see Cass's bloated body.

The empty pool is a depressing sight, though, like the end of that John Cheever story we read in 101 about the cheating husband who swims across a suburban neighborhood of pools to reach his home. I remember how much Simon had loved the story, with its setting of suburban hedges and sparkling swimming pools. One of the other kids — a snooty bitch from Westport — had made a condescending comment about how *bourgeois* Cheever was, and Cass had come to Simon's rescue.

"That's the point," Cass had said in his silky, confident upper-class voice, "Cheever unmasks the façade of bourgeois desire."

Ms. Westport had turned pink and Simon had given Cass a look of such gratitude that I'd been embarrassed for him, but I was proud of Cass for defending Simon. After the *Times* incident, though, when Simon turned on Cass, Cass had said, "Simon's just like the man in that Cheever story who swims through everybody else's pools. A trespasser. He wants what we have — or at least for us not to have it."

By "we" Cass really meant him and his blue-blooded, old-money family, not me and my nouveau-riche Scarsdale parents, but he had turned out to be right.

I wonder if Cass thought about the story when he decided to take one last swim —

I shiver. I should go inside; it's actually colder out here than I thought, already more like autumn than summer. But I don't want Whit or Emily looking over my shoulder while I read Cass's email. I'm afraid of what I'll find there — porn? Salacious messages from his lovers?

I take a deep breath and open the laptop. And what I find is almost worse: dozens of debt-relief and bankruptcy lawyer solicitations. How depressing it must have been for Cass to wade through these every time he opened his email. It gives me a pang to realize he didn't feel like he could share these troubles with me, but when I try to imagine what that conversation would have sounded like, I hear myself demanding to know how he had gotten us into this predicament. No doubt that was exactly why he hadn't come to me with these problems.

The solicitations have just kept coming after his death, as if he might still be able to solve his problems beyond the grave by consolidating his credit-card debt or taking out a low-interest loan. I scroll past them all to the days before his death, assuming there will be more emails of a personal nature, but there isn't much. No colleagues or friends writing to say they believed in him or just writing to see how he was doing. His only regular correspondent was Greg Firestein. I open these emails and find cryptic missives.

About what we talked about on the 12th — I still think it's inadvisable.

Pursuant to question you asked yesterday — our sources say no.

Re: Tuesday: Unlikely.

Cass might as well have been consulting a Magic 8-Ball. For that advice Cass had been shelling out over ten thousand a week. Greg had called the day after Cass's funeral to say he was wiping out the balance due on Cass's account, as if he were doing me an enormous favor. I should be suing him for sexual assault for what he did that last night, putting his grubby hands on me and talking to me like it was somehow *my* fault Cass had affairs. Talk about blaming the victim! I would write a chapter about him in my book. In fact, I should save all these emails as proof of how useless he had been.

I save them to a folder, which I copy onto my flash drive. It occurs to me that if any of the women ever do sue us they might try to confiscate Cass's laptop. Could they do that? No one's asked about it so far, but then there were no legal charges made against Cass and his death was declared a suicide by the medical examiner of Westchester County, so there was no criminal investigation.

I scan back through the emails until I get to the day of the gala. Here, at last, is a normal day in Cass's life — emails from friends saying they're looking forward to seeing him later, colleagues checking in on stories in the paper, an old college friend asking if Cass could help his daughter get an internship at the *Globe* (I bet he felt stupid about that later) and one from me reminding him not to be late that makes me cringe at my wheedling tone. *Just a friendly reminder to be there at 7, hon.* I'd even added a smiley face and cocktail glass emoji, as if I'd had to cajole my own husband into coming to my gala. *Compliant,* I hear that Lurie woman saying as I scroll to the next email, which came in at 4:03. This one's from Simon Wallace.

I open it and see that it's part of a longer thread that began the day before, when Simon sent Cass a draft of Joan Lurie's story. Which means that when Cass went to work that morning, while I reminded him to bring his tux, and babbled on about who was coming, and complained about who wasn't, and fretted that maybe aperol spritzes were passé, he knew about the story. He knew there was this ticking time bomb about to destroy our lives. I am so angry that I scream out loud, "You bastard!"

My shout echoes in the hollow basin of the pool and is answered by the dry scrape of leaves against its cement belly — a sound like the cackling of the dead, who are beyond our anger. How could Cass have blithely gone to work that day without warning me?

The answer is right in front of me in

Cass's reply to Simon's first email: If you run this I will sue you and destroy your rag of a magazine. Cass thought that he could stop it. He thought he could make the problem go away as he had made so many problems go away — as he had when I asked him if Amanda was going to be a problem after he left her to come back to me —

What had he said?

I sit, trying to remember his exact words, as if I will hear them if I'm still enough. All I hear are the dry leaves and the wind in the privet hedge at the end of our lawn — *the* lawn; it doesn't belong to us anymore even if there were still an *us.*

And then I hear Cass's voice, as clearly as if he were sitting in the chaise longue right next to me.

Don't worry about Amanda. I've taken care of her.

I hadn't asked him what he meant. I was too relieved to have him back and too angry at her to care what Cass might have had to do to buy her silence. Now I wonder if he had paid her off — or threatened her as he'd threatened Simon. Of course he'd gone off to work that day optimistic that he'd kill the *Manahatta* story before the party. He'd dismissed it from his mind as he banished anything that threatened his peace.

There was a phrase in that Cheever story that Cass had underlined in his copy of the book — how did it go? — something about a *gift for concealing painful facts.* That's what Cass had had — a gift for concealing painful facts from himself and others. That's what enabled him to go off to work that day, concealing from me that our world was about to implode, because he thought that he could fix it.

Why hadn't he? Why had he failed?

I scroll down to Simon's response to Cass's threat.

We both know that there was more that could have been in that story — the incident at the Hi-Line, for example. If you sue I'll publish *that.*

A chilly breeze stirs the leaves in the bottom of the pool, sounding like sandpaper on raw skin. I feel flayed by it. What had Cass been so afraid of Simon revealing?

That story, he called the assassination piece he'd done, as if they were back in college arguing about literature instead of real life, calling whatever happened: "The Incident at the Hi-Line Club," which sounded like the title of a Sherlock Holmes adventure, for God's sake —

201

What could have happened at the Hi-Line Club? I type "Hi-Line" into the email's search bar and get a slew of emails from the club about events and outstanding dues. I remember how excited Cass had been when he was accepted to the club. It had seemed a little silly to me, but Cass had explained that it was the most exclusive club in New York and would give him an opportunity to rub shoulders with the most powerful movers and shakers in the city. A lot of good that had done him. Where were all the movers and shakers when our lives were going down the toilet?

I glance back at the list of emails and notice there's one dated September 8, 2015, from the membership committee requesting a letter of recommendation. When I open it I see that the letter was for Simon Wallace. *That* was odd. Why would Cass write a letter for Simon when they hadn't been friends for years? But then I see. Cass had written back saying "I cannot in good faith support this candidate. An accusation of plagiarism that was made against him some years back establishes that he is simply not the right sort for the Hi-Line."

Ouch. It seems a bit petty, but then that couldn't be what Simon had referred to as "The Hi-Line Incident." For one thing,

Cass's letter would certainly have been confidential — and there's no other email, or file on the computer, referring to the Hi-Line.

I do remember where I'd seen the name of the club before, though. It had been scribbled across the folder on top of Joan's desk right above that condescending comment she'd made about me. I should have photographed the whole file — or taken it. Still, I had all her digital files on my flash-drive. I could look through them and figure out what Simon had been talking about that was even worse than what was already in Joan Lurie's story.

Chapter Eleven

Joan

I don't sleep very much for the rest of the night. The thought of that back door being there for the three weeks I've lived here without me knowing makes me feel sick. Enda showing me that the lock is secure doesn't help any — or his opening it and showing me the dank, dimly lit stairwell that leads down to the basement, especially after my nightmare about the laundry vats. It feels as if some subterranean vault was cracked open when I was attacked and toxic groundwater is seeping into my brain.

In the morning I make an appointment with the locksmith Enda recommended. I offer to pay a surcharge because it's the weekend. Then I check my bank balance online and am sickened when I see how much money I've gone through. I'm not due another payment until I turn in the book, and I haven't even started the outline I'd promised to send Etinosa a month ago.

I look at the folders splayed across the desk, a wine stain on one, that drunken scrawl about Melissa Osgood on another, and cringe. *Armchair psychology,* Simon would say, *is never a substitute for the facts.*

So what are the facts?

I stack up the folders with the oldest cases on the bottom and the most recent on the top — *Amanda, Stephanie, Gwyneth, Pamela, Sandra, Amy, Roslyn.* What I should do is read through them all from start to finish, review the facts, look for patterns, figure out what I need to turn this material into a book.

I open the first folder — Amanda's — and stare at the pages for a full minute before realizing that they are upside down. *Great start, Joan.* I remember realizing they were out of order last night but now as I try to organize them I see that some pages are missing. Did I misplace them? I don't recall the last time I looked at the folder. Am I losing my memory? Am I losing my *mind*? What if this isn't from the attack but is a sign of early onset Alzheimer's? I recall that when my grandmother started losing her faculties we'd find her wandering around the house at night, rearranging the dishes and crockery as if she were looking for the lost bits of her mind in the kitchen cabinets. Was that what was happening to me?

I shake myself. It's only from lack of sleep . . . and possible brain damage. Didn't some celebrity commit suicide because of chronic migraines —

Stop! I shout.

"Can I help you with something?" Bot asks.

I laugh. "Yes," I tell her. "Find the file 'Amanda' on my hard drive and please read it to me."

"Looking for file 'Amanda' on hard drive," Bot says agreeably, and then after a pause, "Hm. I'm sorry. There is no file 'Amanda' on your hard drive."

"Shit," I say. It's like the universe doesn't want me to write this book. I try scrolling through the files in my Documents folder, but the type blurs on the screen. I pick up the next file on the desk — Stephanie — and ask Bot to find that one. She does and offers to read it to me. I have her check the other six files first and they're all there — as are all the other files for the story. It's only Amanda who's missing. It must be mislabeled, I tell myself, there's no insidious plot to keep me from writing this book. That's down to my own laziness and procrastination. And that's going to stop right now.

I open a new file on my desktop labeled "Book," and while Bot reads me the files I type in notes, which I'll be able to have Bot read back to me later. I can do this, I tell myself; I don't really have any other choice.

I work until the locksmith, an ancient, stooped man named Lou, shows up to change the locks. I take a break to eat while he works.

"I just replaced these," he grumbles as he removes the three locks on the front door.

"Someone had a key," I tell him. "I want all the keys delivered directly to me."

He shrugs. "You're supposed to give one to the doorman, but that's between you and management, lady. I just do the locks."

When I ask about the back door he tells me that management doesn't like to change those locks. I tell him to let me worry about management. He installs a dead bolt over the old lock that can be locked from the inside. When I ask for a lock on the linen-closet door he looks at me like I'm crazy. "Unless you plan on locking someone up in the closet, you don't need that, and in case of fire, you want quick access to those back stairs. They're the only way outta here. That's why the nuns locked them — so the girls couldn't get out."

I stare right back at him. "Are you really old enough to remember when there were nuns here?"

He smiles, happy that I've challenged him. "They were still here when I was a kid and my father did all the locks for them. I remember him coming home and saying that the place gave him the heebie-jeebies — all them young girls trapped up here like pigeons in a coop. 'What'll happen if there's a fire,' he asked the nun. Do you know what that nun said back to him?" Lou lifts his bushy eyebrows at me. " *'God's will,'* that's what the nun told my father. So don't you worry so much about someone comin' in. This is a good neighborhood. You worry about getting yourself *out.* "

After he leaves, I settle back into work. I keep thinking about those girls locked away up here — *like pigeons* — and for what? How many of those girls, I wonder, got "in trouble" because they were the victims of sexual assault? How many were the mistresses of rich men who shunted them off when they were done with them? Instead of being paid off or fired, like so many victims of sexual assault today, a word in a constable's ear was all that was needed.

A sharp knock startles me out of a daydream so vivid that for a moment I imagine it's a policeman at the door come to arrest me —

For what? I chide myself. *What do I have to feel guilty about?*

It's not a policeman. It's Lillian Day, in the same beaded cardigan, plaid skirt, red sneakers, and straw bag. In addition, she's holding a china plate full of Milanos.

"Am I disturbing you?" she asks. "Is now a good time for tea?"

I think of the morbid woolgathering I'd been doing at my desk and tell her, "Yes, this is a perfect time for tea."

I seat Lillian in the wingback chair by the window and take the desk chair for myself, placing two mugs of tea and the plate of Milanos on the desk between us. It feels a little as if I'm being interviewed as Lillian asks me questions about what it's like to be a reporter and I tell her about the style stories I wrote for *Manahatta*.

"How very glamorous! You're just like Rosalind Russell in *His Girl Friday*!" she cries, her eyes bright. "But tell me what you mean by a Brazilian?"

I explain and she hoots, kicking up her red sneakers in the air. "Oh my, I wonder what the nuns at Our Lady of Perpetual

Help would have to say about *that*. I got in trouble in the eighth grade for wearing lipstick, which I'd only done on a dare from my best friend, Rose, who'd 'borrowed' it from her aunt who danced in vaudeville. Rose said this color would be pretty on me so I tried it and then scrubbed it off, but Sister Dolores had keen eyes. 'What have you got on your face, Lily Anne O'Day?' "

Lillian's voice is so unlike her own that I shiver.

"That was Sister Dolores," she adds in her own voice. "Our Lady of Sorrows, we called her. We were all dead scared of her — except for Rose, who stood right up in class and said, 'It's my fault, Sister Dolores, I made Lily put on that lipstick because I thought the color suited her. I thought we'd gotten it all off.' From the look Sister Dolores gave her, you'd have thought poor Rose had desecrated the statue of the Virgin Mary. 'Though you wash yourself with lye and use much soap, the stain of your guilt is still before me,' quoted Sister. And then she made both of us stay after school.

"When I saw my mother come in her best white blouse, freshly ironed, and Sunday skirt and shoes, newly polished, I felt sorry for all the work I'd put her to. Sister Dolores told her she should take better care of my upbringing and not let me spend so much time with questionable company — meaning Rose — and running in the streets with the boys. Of course" — Lillian leans closer to me, her eyes shining — "I did play with the boys on the street. I was the best Ringolevio player on our block, and Rose and I fought all the bullies who picked on the littler kids. But Sister Dolores made it sound like I was doing something . . . dirty. My poor mother, she had a weak heart from having had rheumatic fever as a child and wasn't very strong, but she worked her fingers to the bone keeping us clean and fed. She listened to it all with her head bowed, but in the end she spoke up for me. 'My Lily Anne is a good girl, Sister; she won't take any harm from her friend or from a few games in the street with her brothers.' " Lillian (born Lily Anne, I gather) smiles wistfully at the memory, but the smile quickly vanishes.

"Later, when I got into trouble, Sister Dolores came to see me here. 'I suppose your poor mother was wrong about you not taking any harm from the streets,' she said. 'It looks to me like the streets have had their way with you. You're past saving now. You'll never get to see your mother in heaven.' "

"What a terrible thing to say." I lay my

hand over Lillian's cool, dry hand. She looks at me with eyes shining like the sea. "And what did she mean about your mother? Was she . . . had she died?"

Lillian nods, her eyes brimming. "When I was seventeen I was standing in the kitchen with my mother, watching her stir the oatmeal on the stove, and she fell down to the floor. My father ran to get help, but by the time he came back with the policeman — why not a doctor? I wondered — she was gone. My father took to drink after the funeral and couldn't watch the boys. He went to live in a boardinghouse. My aunts Gert and Viola offered to take us children to their house in Coney Island, but they were too old to watch over a crew of rambunctious young boys, so it was decided I would leave school to look after my brothers."

"It was decided?" I repeat. "My editor Sylvia always says to watch out for the passive voice; it usually means someone is evading blame."

Lillian smiles. "Your editor is right, but I don't know who you'd say was to blame here. My father was too far gone in his cups to have much of a say. My aunts between them didn't have more than an eighth-grade education. What difference did it make to a girl — and a poor one at that — to finish high school? It wasn't like I'd be going to college. I'd taken a steno class and could take down two hundred words a minute. And I was very pretty. I'd have no trouble getting a job when the time came."

"When the time came?"

She looks sad again. "I wasn't much good at looking after the boys. They missed our mother and their friends from the old neighborhood. Coney Island had a rough crowd — gangsters and hoodlums on every corner who preyed on young boys. They got into trouble and then the Children's Society came and said the boys weren't being looked after properly . . . that I was *negligent.*"

"You were only seventeen," I say.

She shakes her head. "I burned the oatmeal in the morning and never could get their shirts white the way our mother could. I went walking on the boardwalk with Rose, who was my only friend who'd make the trip from Bay Ridge to visit me, instead of making sure the boys came straight home from school. The Children's Society took the boys to St. Vincent's Home. My aunts said maybe it was for the best . . . but it wasn't. When I went to visit them on Sundays they cried and begged to come home.

It was worse when they stopped crying. Tommy got this hardened look about him, like he was trying to keep from crying every minute of the day, and Joe was so angry he snapped at everything I said. Bill, the youngest, tried to smile and please everyone around him like he hoped someone would take him home if he were just good enough. Someone finally did. A couple from New Rochelle wanted to adopt him and my father signed the papers without telling me. I thought my heart would break then, but Bill probably ended up better than Tommy and Joe."

"What happened to them?"

"Well, you see, back in those days, the Syndicate ruled Brooklyn. They were everywhere, taking protection money from every candy store and flophouse, taking their share off the goods that were unloaded on the docks. The biggest mob in Brooklyn was Murder Inc., run by Albert Anastasia and Louis Buchalter. They sent thugs like Abe Reles to kill anyone who didn't pay their protection money. They needed young boys to make their pickups and deliver messages. They got them from places like St. Vincent's, where the boys had no one to watch after them and were willing to do anything for a couple of dimes to buy candy and cigarettes. Tommy started working for them first, and then Joe, running numbers for the bookies. Whenever they got picked up I'd go down to the police station and explain to the desk sergeant how hard the boys had it since our mother died. I got to know all the policemen. *What's a pretty girl like you doing in a place like this?* they would tease, and *I wish all the mugs we collared had sisters pretty as you.*"

She looks up and meets my eyes. I have a sudden, sharp vision of a young Lillian, hair swept up off her face in victory rolls, smart in padded shoulders and seamed stockings, walking bravely into a Brooklyn police station, trading on her beauty for her brother's freedom. "Did you mind?" I ask. "About the . . . *teasing.*"

Her eyes narrow. "I got used to it. You see, I thought that as long as I stayed on the right side of the tracks I'd be all right."

"The right side of the tracks?"

She nods. "There were a lot of pretty girls in Coney Island back then and some of the very prettiest went with the toughs — they dressed the best and had the most money to spend. Once you went with a mobster, though, well that's who you were. A mobster's girl. If you lost one, there was always another waiting. That's what I told Rose.

She left school, too, that year because she said it was no fun without me. Really, I think it was because she couldn't stomach living with her stepfather any longer and needed to get out of the house. She became a hat-check girl at the Stork Club and started going with a fast bunch of fellows. 'Watch out,' I told her, 'or you'll end up like the Kiss-of-Death Girl.' "

"The Kiss-of-Death Girl?" I ask, intrigued. The name sounds like something from an old noir movie.

Lillian's eyes shine. "Evelyn Mittelman. All her fellows had a way of dying, usually at the hands of her next fellow. Rose and I saw her around Coney Island, but she wasn't much to look at by then. None of those girls were in the end, once they started using dope and getting knocked around."

Lillian's still the same sweet old lady who brought cookies for tea, swinging her red sneakers, but something darker is in the room with us. There's a tension in the air, as if we're both poised on a precipice.

"But you," I say as softly as I would to a woman standing on a high window ledge, "you stayed on the right side of the tracks."

A sad, faraway smile forms on her face. "For a while, at least. Sometimes you don't even know when you're stepping over a line, especially when you're all by yourself on the other side. Tommy started running errands for a thug by the name of Eddie Silver. He'd come by with presents for me — real silk stockings, which were hard to find because of the war, and chocolate because he knew I had a sweet tooth. He only wanted to show me what a big man he'd become, but it scared me to see how deep he was getting in with those toughs. One day I saw he was carrying a gun, and when I asked him where he'd gotten it he said that Eddie Silver had given it to him for protection. 'Whose protection?' I asked him, 'his or yours?' Rose told me I shouldn't be so hard on Tommy. This is what you had to do to get along in the world today. She had started wearing fancy clothes I knew she couldn't afford on what she made as a hat-check girl, and she was spending time with that same thug, Eddie Silver, who used to throw around a lot of money at the Stork Club. She said her fellows gave her presents but I was afraid . . . well . . ." Lillian blushes.

"You thought she was working as a prostitute."

Lillian nods. "She got picked up by the cops that summer. I went down to the courthouse to speak up for her like I'd done for the boys, but when I tried, the judge said he didn't need to hear one tart speaking up for another. She was sent here to the Magdalens for a month. I visited her . . ."

She looks around my apartment, and I remember her saying that first day that her friend Rose had given her the key for my apartment. I had thought she meant the former tenant, but now I wonder if she wasn't thinking of her childhood friend Rose. "She lived here?" I ask. "Where my apartment is now?"

"Oh no!" Lillian says. "This was the infirmary. She was here when I came because she'd burned her hand in the laundry. Her bed was right here by the window. 'How do you like my penthouse view?' she joked when I came to see her, like she was in a suite at the Plaza. But for all her joking I could see that this place had already changed her. Her eyes were flat and she kept plucking at her blanket with her poor bandaged hands . . ."

Lillian plucks at the knitted afghan over the arm of the chair in unconscious imitation of her friend as she goes on. "I gave her the locket my mother had given me on my confirmation." Lillian touches her own locket and I wonder if she's confused. If this is the locket she gave Rose, why does she still have it? "It's the flowers of the

Virgin Mary, you see, the Lily and the Rose, so I told Rose it was meant for both of us and it would keep her safe until she got out. But when she got out she was changed, harder, like being in here had made her think she was as bad as the nuns said she was. I didn't spend as much time with her anymore after that. I had gotten a job in the steno pool at the Brooklyn Courthouse. That's where I met Frank."

"Frank?"

"Frank Maloney, the assistant DA. He always asked for me when he needed to depose a witness because he said that even the most hardened criminal was so disarmed by my beauty that he'd sing like an angel." Lillian sits up taller, preening.

"Frank sounds like a charmer," I say.

"Oh, he was," Lillian says brightly, but then her shoulders slump and the brightness goes out of her eyes. "He helped out when Tommy got in trouble. One night I was just getting ready for bed when Tommy shows up at my room . . . by then I'd moved out of my aunts' place and lived in a boardinghouse . . . he was in a state and covered in blood. I thought he'd been shot! Instead it turned out he had been fooling with that gun to impress his girlfriend, Arlene, and the gun had gone off and hit the poor girl!

Instead of taking her straight to the hospital he'd run to get me. He was babbling, not making any sense, pulling me down to the boardwalk . . ." Lillian's voice falters. "She was lying in the cold, wet sand under the boardwalk. At first I thought she must have drowned, her skin was cold and wet from the fog rolling in off the ocean. Tommy was going on about how it had been an accident and he was sorry and he would do whatever I told him to do. As if I knew what to do! But then I remembered that I had Frank's phone number. I ran down to a candy store on Mermaid Avenue and called Frank. When I told him my brother was in trouble, he told me to wait under the boardwalk and he'd be right there. I went back and sat with Tommy, holding his hand, listening to the foghorns . . ."

She looks at me, her eyes startling against the gray fog that has risen from the river now and is pressing against the glass. "When the fog comes up like this I think I'm back there with Tommy, sitting beside Arlene in the blood-soaked sand, waiting . . ."

I reach for her hand and am alarmed to find it cold and damp. While we've been sitting here the fog has crept in under the windows and settled over us like a shroud. I pull the afghan off the chair and wrap it around her shoulders, chafing her hands to warm them up. "And did Frank come?" I ask. "Was he able to help?"

"Oh yes," Lillian says, squeezing my hand. "He came. He took care of everything. He told Tommy he'd vouch for him and make sure the judge went easy on him. He was a minor, after all, and it was an accident. Frank was true to his word. Tommy got three years on a charge of manslaughter when he could have gotten life."

Lillian's face, glazed by tears, shines in the eerie fog light like a pebble washed ashore by the sea. "I knew it was better than if he had run, but I couldn't help feeling that *I* was the one who had put him in that prison."

"Oh no!" I say. "It wasn't your fault. You did the best you could for him."

"Maybe," she concedes, "but sometimes I've wondered if what Sister Dolores said was right about me having a stain on my soul that won't wash out and if that means I'll never see my mother again." She sighs, her shoulders drooping. Gone is the sharp young woman who strode into the police station to rescue her errant brothers. "But I've bent your ear too long with my old stories. You must be wanting to get back to

221

your story."

The truth is I'm more interested in Lillian's story right now, but she is clearly worn out from revisiting so many painful moments. If she were a source I might push her, but she's not a source. She's just a sweet old lady and she's right; I should get back to my real work. "I suppose I should," I say, "but you'll come back, won't you, and tell me more?"

"I'd like that. You're a good listener." A bit of the sharpness has returned to her eyes. "I can see why you'd be good at your job."

I help her to the door, where she again waves off my offer to escort her to her apartment. This woman faced down Coney Island cops and gangsters, I tell myself, she can navigate the hallway. Still, I watch her on the camera until she vanishes off-screen. Then I go back to my desk — back to my *more important* story. But isn't it all the same story? These girls — I arrange their files in a fan like the plumed bustle of a chorus girl — were nice girls who thought they'd be okay as long as they stayed on the right side of the tracks. Until someone like Caspar Osgood came along and shoved them off the tracks, changing their lives forever.

Roslyn, Amy, Sandra, Pamela, Gwyneth,

Stephanie, Amanda —

Then I notice something. Amanda is the most recent case of these seven. Of course, when I started three years ago she was the current case, but although I found other, older cases, and more have come forward since my story came out, all of the cases happened *before* Amanda. No one has come forward claiming that Caspar Osgood has assaulted her in the last three years. Had his more recent victims stayed quiet? Or had he stopped assaulting women three years ago? If so, why? Had his conscience caught up with him? Somehow I don't think so.

So what, I wonder, happened three years ago?

Chapter Twelve

MELISSA

The estate sale is such a success — Wally was right about the vultures wanting a piece of our tragedy — and Whit is so good at selling my clothes and accessories on eBay that I have the house cleared by the third week in September. So when I get an offer for my asking price I decide to move right away, even though it will take weeks to close on the house. *Why should I wait?* I think, walking through the empty rooms of my beautiful, empty house. There's nothing here for me anymore. Whatever future I have left is waiting for me at the Refuge.

I have the few pieces I kept delivered in a small van and order some sad furniture from Pottery Barn, the kind that says right up front that it's *basic,* which Emily says is her friends' most brutal takedown, as in *She's so basic she goes to Olive Garden for first dates.* I am coming to like the idea of basic, though. Basic means stripped-down, back to essentials, like a soldier in a field camp. *That's what this place is to me,* I think when I arrive on a chilly day in the last week of September with three Louis Vuitton suitcases, only one of the eiderdowns, and two boxes of Cass's files, a field camp from which to launch my attack from beneath enemy lines.

I put my desk right where hers is, under the bay window. I like to think of her sitting at her desk, spinning her tissue of lies, not knowing that I am lurking right below her, spinning her destruction.

A spider crouched in its web.

A spy.

Before he went back to college, I asked Whit if it was easy to install spyware on someone's laptop. He gave me a worried look and I told him I just wanted to make sure that Daddy's laptop wasn't bugged. "And don't look at me like I'm crazy," I told him. "You know your father had enemies."

He looked troubled by that thought, and once again I could have kicked myself for saying the wrong thing. "Did you find anything . . . *new* when you looked through his laptop?" he asked.

"Do you mean more women accusing him?" He had looked away, as if embarrassed for me. "No," I said firmly. "I really think that your father stopped all of that three years ago after . . . after he saw how much we all needed him."

Whit nodded. "He said things would be different."

"He did?" I asked. "You mean when —"

"In the hospital. I mean, after he said that thing about suicide being for cowards. He told me things would be different."

"You see," I said, wiping my eyes, "that's how much your father loved you. That's why we need to still protect him."

He nodded and showed me how to check for spyware. There wasn't any that we could detect. Then he showed me a few websites selling the stuff. "It's totally legal," he told me. "They get away with it by saying it's for" — he crooked his fingers into air quotes — " 'monitoring your children or employees.' Ugh. Can you imagine the skeevy parent or boss who would do that?"

I shook my head in my full agreement — wishing I'd thought of doing it before Whit's suicide attempt — and took mental note of the site he showed me. When I went to the site on my own, though, it made me nervous. Warning! It said in red letters at the bottom of the screen. Installing computer monitoring tools on computers you do not own or do not have permission to monitor may violate local, state, or federal law.

No duh.

What made me nervous was the thought that someone might be watching *me*. What if someone knew I ordered the spyware online? Wouldn't that put me on some kind of list? I mean, whenever I looked at evening dresses on Neiman Marcus's website I got pop-ups for the next month showing me *more* evening dresses. So what cyber bells would go off if I ordered TotalSpy from PrivateEye.com?

I decided to wait until I could read through what I had already gotten from Joan's computer and what I had in Cass's files and emails. It only takes me a few hours to settle in. I put the Frette sheets on my new bed (I may be roughing it but I'm not going to sleep on sandpaper), open up the paleo salad I'd ordered from GrubHub, and pour myself a glass of sparkling water (no more Veuve Clicquot; I need a clear head). Then I arrange Cass's laptop and files on the lovely French marquetry writing desk Cass gave me for our tenth anniversary, open up Cass's laptop, and download the files I took from Joan Lurie's computer. I decide to read Amanda's file first, the one I deleted from Joan's computer. Let's see what that little slut who tried to break up my marriage had to say.

The file includes the transcripts of all the interviews Amanda gave. I read the first one, cringing at Joan's description of how Amanda broke down in tears and *reluctantly* confided that she was sleeping with her boss, but only because she was afraid she'd be fired if she stopped.

What a load of crap.

Then I notice the date when Joan supposedly saw Amanda crying in the bathroom; it's May 15, which is the day after I found out that Cass was sleeping with his secretary and threw him out. Interesting that he'd had some kind of fight with her the very next day. Maybe she had expected him to move in with her and was disappointed when he refused. I go to Cass's online bank account and look for his Amex and Mastercard statements that covered that time period. I find a charge at the Peninsula, Cass's favorite Manhattan hotel (I prefer the Carlyle). Of course, that doesn't prove he wasn't inviting Amanda over. If I could look at the hotel bills —

I go to his email and search for the hotel's name and up pop a dozen emails with bills attached. There are bills for weeks when I know Cass was spending his nights with me in Ardsley. Apparently he was spending his *afternoons* with someone else. I ignore the rising nausea at this additional evidence of infidelity — that's not what I'm after here — and open the bill for May. But the room-service charges are for breakfasts for one, a few lonely dinners, and lots of movie rentals. Not what I was expecting. I almost feel sorry for Cass.

Almost. His bill for two weeks at the Peninsula is more than my monthly maintenance fee for this Spartan apartment. He clearly didn't care how much he was spending, which makes me wonder when he began draining our finances.

I look back at our bank statements for May 2015. There are our mortgage payments for the Ardsley and Hampton houses, a tuition bill for Whit's college and one for Brearley, a $5,000 donation to the Cancer Foundation (we donated every month in honor of my mother), and a $10,000 check to Pat Shanahan's reelection campaign fund, which he'd written after Wally was so supportive, driving me up to Providence. Nothing out of the ordinary.

I go back to Amanda's file. Joan interviewed her a month after the incident in the *Globe* ladies' room, after which both Amanda and Joan had been fired from the

Globe. After Amanda spewed out a ridiculous story of intimidation and assault, Joan asked for dates and places for each occurrence. I note these down on my iPad to check against Cass's diary later.

"Thanks, Joan," I say out loud, "these will come in handy."

She also asks if anyone witnessed the assaults. "No," Amanda told her, "he was always careful to make sure we were alone." *Convenient,* I think. Undeterred, intrepid girl reporter Joan Lurie asked if she told anyone about the assaults at the time.

"You mean like right after?" Amanda asks. Not the brightest bulb in the pack. How was Cass able to *stand* her?

"Yes," Joan says, "like, did anyone see you after and notice that you were upset?"

"Oh, I see . . . well, yes. In May there was this party downtown . . . some kind of fundraiser thing at this fancy private club and Cass asked me to go to be, like, his 'eyes and ears,' which is what he'd say when really he just wanted me there . . . you know . . . for sex."

"And you would still go?"

Good question, Joan.

"Well, yeah, it was expected. So I go and there are all these bigwigs — political types and newspeople, even a couple from your magazine — and some real celebrities, too, like that actress in that reality show . . . anyway, I was kind of bored so I wandered out onto the terrace to have a cigarette and I was just checking my phone for messages and Cass came out. I could tell he'd been drinking a lot and he started asking me if I'd been talking to his wife, which was crazy, why would I talk to his wife? I mean, I got her on the phone sometimes and she always seemed . . . *nice.* I felt kind of sorry for her, to tell you the truth —"

How dare she feel sorry for me, I think, getting up to refresh my drink and wishing I'd ordered some wine or, better yet, vodka, *when she was the interloper, the woman sleeping with another woman's husband.* I stop at the camera monitor and watch Hector reading a newspaper at his desk for a few minutes to calm myself down (it's like having a twenty-four-hour meditation channel watching these guys at work). Then I go back to Amanda's fairy tale.

"But I never would have told her about the things her husband did."

"Why not?" Joan asks. "Wouldn't that have stopped it?"

"Maybe," Amanda conceded, "but I knew how angry it would make him. For all his . . . *fooling around* I got the impression he really cared about her. I know that sounds weird, like if he cared about her why couldn't he keep his dick in his pants, but it was like he kept her in this other box that nothing else should touch. She was his beautiful college sweetheart in the big white house in Westchester, and as long as he still had her he was still that boy he was when he was young — the crusading boy reporter."

"Interesting," Joan had said. "So at this party Cass accused you of talking to his wife. Was he loud? Could someone else have heard him?"

"Well, that's the thing. I think someone did. Because after . . . I was crying . . . and this girl, one of the servers, came out from behind one of the planters on the terrace — I guess she'd been sneaking a cigarette too — and asked if I was okay and did I want to call someone. I think she meant, like, the police, which really startled me because up until then I hadn't thought of what Cass did as . . . well . . . *illegal.*"

"What did he do that night, Amanda? When he was asking you if you'd called his wife."

"Oh, he . . . um . . . he made me go down on him. One minute he was yelling at me and the next he was unzipping his fly and

232

pushing my head into his lap and when I tried to say no — I mean *anyone* could have come out on the terrace and seen us — he slapped me. It was like yelling had gotten him hard. He told me once that anger was the most powerful aphrodisiac."

I flinch and pull back from the screen as if *I* have been slapped. The words Amanda used reared up out of her hysterical account with the force of reality because Cass had said those words to me, years ago, when we were in college. I'd thought it was an affectation, like reading Sartre and wearing black turtlenecks. But it was true that we always had great makeup sex —

I get up and pace, pausing to watch Hector leading a workman in coveralls to the service door until I am calm enough to return to the desk. Yes, he slept with Amanda, which is why he said that *intimate* thing to her. Maybe that was why he had strayed. He needed sex fueled by anger and I didn't give that to him anymore. But that didn't mean he had *forced* her. And as for that so-called witness, Amanda couldn't recall her name. *Amanda looked nervous when I asked her a second time,* Joan had noted, *and changed the subject.* Shouldn't that have told Joan that Amanda was lying? But instead she'd just made a note to get a list of servers from the caterer, Bread & Roses. Joan had dutifully noted that she'd been unable to locate the server who had witnessed Cass and Amanda's tête-à-tête. *Because she didn't exist.* I read through the rest of Amanda's file. Yes, there are some so-called corroborating accounts: Amanda's roommate, who recounted that Amanda was "very stressed" during this period and one night broke down and told her that she was afraid she'd get fired if she told anyone about what Cass was "doing to her." And there was an accountant at the *Globe* who said she saw Amanda crying in the bathroom and Amanda told her she was afraid of her boss. But all that proved was that Amanda was hysterical and lied to other people. There were no real witnesses.

And it's the same with the others. At first it's hard reading all these women's stories, the things they *said* my husband did to them, but I make myself look for the facts, like Cass always said a good reporter should.

You have to go cold inside, he'd say, *don't let yourself be swayed by emotions, look for the facts, what can be proved, where are the witnesses, the paper trail, the* bodies. *Without them, all you have are fairy tales and ghost stories.*

Joan Lurie had tried to find that evidence,

I have to concede. She interviewed friends of these women who swore they told them what was happening at the time, but all that proves is that their friends were lying too. There's no hard evidence here, just stories. Cass would have known that. Why didn't he fight back?

We both know that there was more that could have been in that story, Simon had said in his email to Cass, *the incident at the Hi-Line, for example. If you sue I'll publish* that.

Exasperated, I stride down the long hallway as I go over it in my head. There was some detail about what happened the night of the Hi-Line party that Simon made Joan leave out of the story she published. What? And where was it? There's nothing more in her computer files about it except for the interview with Amanda, and apparently she stopped following that lead when she couldn't find the server. But maybe Simon wrote her a memo — something he wrote down because he didn't want a digital trail — that she's kept in the physical copy of Amanda's file. I should have taken the hard copy of Amanda's file from Joan's desk. Let her worry that she was losing it — from the number of empty bottles in her apartment she couldn't be thinking very clearly —

Nor am I, I realize. I may be sober, but

anger is clouding my brain. I stop in front of the monitor and practice the breathing exercises I learned with Emily at the "Coping with Anxiety" workshop we took together after Whit's suicide attempt. Breathe in a count of seven — I have to figure out how to get back in Joan's apartment — hold for a count of four — and take Amanda's file — breathe out for a count of eight —

Then there she is, as if I have summoned her, crossing the lobby unsteadily, as if she's been drinking. She's wearing a ratty pair of sweatpants and a T-shirt and her hair's a mess, as if she'd been rousted out of bed. She stops at the desk and says something to Hector. *Yells* something, waving her arms around in the air. She really *has* lost it. I can see even on the grainy camera that Hector is looking at her like she's crazy. She's pointing out the front door as if she wants Hector to go outside with her. He shrugs and gets up and slowly walks out the door —

— leaving his ring of keys on his desk.

All I would have to do is run down and grab them then run back up to Joan's apartment, let myself in, grab Amanda's file, and hightail it back —

I'm out the back door before giving myself time to reconsider. *This is crazy,* I tell myself as I charge down the iron stairs *barefoot.*

I'll probably get an infection from the filthy stairs and I'm someone who makes the nail salon girl wash out the pedicure tub in front of me before I'll stick my feet in. Chances are, Hector will be back at his desk by the time I get down to the lobby —

Or worse, someone will come up the stairs and catch me.

Which is exactly what is happening. I hear iron grating against iron below me when I'm on the second-floor landing. It sounds like a tomb being wrenched open —

Like the gates of Cass's family mausoleum.

I freeze on the landing, panting, listening to my own thudding heart —

And then to footsteps coming up. Fast, heavy footsteps that make the iron skeleton of the staircase shake. Someone is coming up and they're coming up fast.

I turn and run back up the stairs, glad I've been training on the elliptical, only there's no setting on the elliptical for Sprinting-Up-Iron-Stairs-While-Being-Pursued-by —

Who? What am I doing? It's probably just Hector, delivering a package. Why should I care if he finds me on the stairs? I'll tell him I was going out and wanted the exercise of taking the stairs —

Barefoot?

I run up the final stairs, the steady fast footsteps not far behind me. I take in a big breath and hold it. The iron stairs smell like blood. My hands, as they reach for the knob of my own door, smell like blood.

The knob doesn't turn. I'd forgotten in my hurried dash out the door that the door locks automatically, and I didn't bring my own key. The footsteps are still coming, steady as a metronome. A shadow climbs up the wall in advance, sepulchral as the Grim Reaper. I sprint up the next flight of stairs, passing Joan's door. I consider banging on it and pleading for help, but then I remember she's not there. Now where? This is the top floor, the penthouse —

But there *are* stairs going farther up: a flimsy iron spiral staircase that shakes as I climb, releasing an odor of rust and an even stronger reek of blood. These stairs haven't been painted over and they're not lit. Wherever they lead it's not a place anyone goes anymore. There is a glimmer of light at the top, though, coming through a pane of murky glass wedged into the sharp angle between ceiling and wall. It's a kind of hatch to the roof. I push at it but all that comes loose are decades' worth of pigeon feathers and droppings. I sink down onto the top step and wrap my arms around my knees. Below me the drumbeat footsteps have ceased. Is he waiting for me to come down? I'm trapped here, like a rat —

I am immediately sorry to have thought about rats. I squeeze my knees to keep from crying out and bolting down the stairs and force myself to listen. The grate of iron again, a door opening . . . he's gone into Joan's apartment. He's done what I planned to do: taken Hector's keys and let himself in.

So I am not the only one who wants to keep track of Joan.

Unless he plans to wait inside for Joan to come back and then hurt her.

I should, I realize, go downstairs and rouse Hector to call the police, but then why should I help her when she's ruined my life —

A wave of shame floods over me. What kind of woman sits by while another woman is hurt?

The kind you made me, I think, not sure who I mean — Joan or Cass.

It's too late anyway. I hear the door below me open and close and then that steady drumbeat of feet going down the stairs as quickly as he came up. Another door opens and closes farther below me. Whoever he is, he's come and gone, doing Joan Lurie no injury. I am *not* an accomplice to her harm — just to some theft.

Of what? Something about what happened at the Hi-Line Club? Who else wants that? And what will they do with it?

As if in response to my unvoiced questions something falls in my lap. A clot of pigeon droppings and feathers that makes me want to scream. But then I notice something caught in it — a delicate sickle moon that looks like an ivory earring that's so unexpectedly pretty I find myself picking it up despite the filth it rests in. When I hold it up to the light I see that it's a fingernail.

CHAPTER THIRTEEN

JOAN

When I call him the next day Simon is skeptical. He doesn't believe that Caspar Osgood just stopped harassing women three years ago.

"I think he got more careful. What I hear is that Melissa found out about Amanda and kicked him out. Then their son tried to kill himself and for the sake of family unity she took Cass back on the understanding that he never stray again. My guess is that he changed his hunting grounds. Interns and reporters at the *Globe* became too risky so he went elsewhere. A man like Osgood doesn't just *stop.*"

For not the first time I hear the animosity in Simon's voice when he talks about Caspar Osgood. I think of what Melissa wrote in her statement — that Simon held a grudge against him because Cass had been promoted over him at the *Times* and that he'd initiated my investigation because of that grudge. But that wasn't true. I'd already had the idea for the story when I interviewed with Simon. *Was that why he hired me?* I shake the thought away. I'd found Amanda and no grudge had invented the women who told me about what Osgood did to them.

And I'd been diligent, I acknowledge with relief as I listen again and again to the women's accounts in the next four weeks. I'd pinned down dates and times and checked them against Osgood's known whereabouts. I'd interviewed corroborating witnesses whom my sources had confided in at the time the assaults were taking place.

"You're not going to get an eyewitness account," Simon had warned me. "And you shouldn't expect to. That's what's kept harassment accountability in the dark ages — it's so often an unwitnessed crime. But you can build up surrounding evidence to support the victims' accounts — contemporary corroborations — people who saw them right after or people they talked to about what happened at the time."

That's what I had done, and I'd been impressed with how effective it had been. Most people tell someone — a roommate, a girlfriend, a coworker — or there was someone who remembered seeing the victim flustered and upset after an encounter. There were so many obvious victims, in fact, that I became exasperated that no one had acted when so many people clearly knew what was happening. But it was always the same story: Osgood was powerful. No one wanted to go up against him. I wasn't going to let the lack of an eyewitness to an actual assault keep me from exposing Osgood at last.

Still, when Amanda had mentioned a server who might have witnessed Osgood slapping her and forcing her to perform oral sex on him, I admit I had been eager to find her. I'd called the catering company, Bread & Roses, and asked for a list of the servers for the night in question. When the owner hesitated, I hinted that I worked for Sylvia Crosley at *Manahatta,* hoping the appeal of a potential review in our Style section might entice her to divulge. She emailed me the list five minutes later; apparently Sylvia was good friends with the owner of the company.

I had been able to track down all of them — mostly aspiring writers and actors paying the rent by waitressing, bartending, and doing catering gigs. None of them had remembered any incident like the one Amanda described.

Did I doubt her veracity at that point? Maybe for a moment. But then she only *thought* that the server had seen something. Maybe she'd been mistaken. Or maybe the server had forgotten. Several of the servers I had interviewed had trouble remembering the specific night at all, even though it was only a couple of months before. "I was working back-to-back shifts that month," Maya, a woman with a shaved head and a tattoo of a fork on her arm told me, "saving to finance my band's tour of South America. Frankly, the whole period is a blur."

I hadn't been overly concerned, but the missing server — as I began to think of her — had troubled me. And there's something else that bothers me about it now. Luckily I hadn't deleted the email from the owner of Bread & Roses, and I pull it back up to find the servers' contact information. I spend a week calling everyone on the list. A few of the young women on the list have moved on, one to voiceover work in L.A., another to a role in *The Book of Mormon,* and another to law school. Quite a few are still working the catering/ restaurant/bartending circuit hoping for the big break that will lift them out of the masses of artistic hopefuls into —

What, exactly?

Talking to them reminds me of myself three years ago, when I thought this story would be the making of me. If you had told me then that I'd have a book deal and be living in a swanky apartment with a doorman, I'd have thought my prayers had been answered. I wouldn't have thought I'd be hiding in that swanky apartment afraid to go out, afraid to pick up a piece of typescript because it might reveal that I really do have brain damage.

Which is why I leave reading Amanda's paper file till last. It's late September and the cooler weather reminds me that summer is over. I've barely begun writing my book. I still can't find Amanda's folder on the hard drive. So when I finish calling all the catering staff I pick up Amanda's paper file. I put the pages in order and then I read through the whole interview, ignoring the twitch in my left eye and the creeping pain in my right temple until I get to the part where she says that after Caspar Osgood assaulted her a server came out from behind the planter on the terrace and asked if she wanted her to go to the police with her. None of the servers I contacted was able to verify the account, and when I checked the police records for that night — May 15, 2015 — I couldn't find a police record for

Osgood.

Maybe Amanda and the server went to the police and the police had dismissed the charge so there'd never been a formal complaint or file.

But why can't I find the server to corroborate Amanda's account?

I could try to contact Amanda to go over her story again, but the last time I reached out to her, just before the story came out, I discovered she was living in L.A. working as a yoga teacher, and she told me that she "just wanted to move on." Now it occurs to me that she might have been paid off and signed an NDA.

But why would anyone pay her off *after* she had given me her story?

My mind is spinning with the contradictions. I lift my head to look out the window and clear it and for a moment I think there's a fireworks show over the Hudson River. My view is spangled with bright lights and exploding starbursts, but when I turn around the fireworks are still there in front of me. They're inside me. I've got a full-on ocular migraine. I've had them before, but never this bad. My vision looks like a reel of 8mm film that's burning. I close my eyes and press my palms against them. When I reopen them it's worse: a heavy-metal light

246

show of pyrotechnics.

I get unsteadily to my feet and stumble toward the kitchen — or at least I hope in that direction. I can barely see anything. I hold my arms out but I trip over a packing box, crashing to my knees. I crawl to the door to pull myself up, holding on to the doorknob. *This is it,* I think, *I am having a stroke.* A clot must have formed when I was hit and now it's loosened and blocked the blood flow to my brain. A gray darkness is rising, like soapy water, extinguishing the fire bursts —

I must fall and lose some time because when I come to, I am on the floor. I reach out —

And touch flesh.

Someone is in my apartment.

My attacker has come back to finish me off.

"Are you all right, dear? Do you want me to call a doctor?"

Lillian?

"How . . . ?"

"Your door was open, dear, and I saw you lying on the floor. Can I get you a glass of water? A cold washcloth? Some tea?"

I blink and my vision clears, though it's still blurry — as if a film of Vaseline is coating my eyeballs. But I can make out Lillian

247

sitting on the floor beside me, red sneakers tucked beneath her skirt, straw bag perched in her lap.

"No, I think I'm okay." I struggle to my feet, then help Lillian up, her wrists so delicate in my hands I'm afraid I will break them. And yet she came to my aid when she saw me passed out. She could have broken a hip getting down on the floor with me. I lead her over to the wingback chair — or maybe she's leading me. Her grip on my hand is firm. I leave her on the chair and go to make us tea.

"Make it strong with plenty of sugar," Lillian calls from the living room. "My mother always said that's what you needed when you'd had a shock."

"That must have been scary seeing me on the floor," I say, bringing us two mugs of hot, sweet tea.

"Oh," she says, taking her cup, "I've seen worse. I saw a man get knifed at the Stork Club."

"Really? How awful," I say, settling down next to Lillian. "That must have been terrifying. Were you there on a date?"

"No, I was working there. After Tommy's trial I was let go from the steno pool at the courthouse. The office manager said, 'We can't have girls associated with the underworld working here.' " Lillian wickedly mimics the snooty office manager's voice, but I can hear the shame behind the impersonation. "She wouldn't even give me a reference. Rose said I could fill in for her at the Stork Club to tide me over and make a few extra dollars. She said all I'd have to do is pour drinks and smile . . . well, I was very naïve back then. I could tell right away that the men expected more than a smile. This one fellow kept pulling me into his lap and pinching my behind. I got so mad I slapped his face. I thought he would slap me back, but Eddie Silver laughed and said the mork got what was coming to him and that they should all keep their hands off me. *Can't you see she's a nice Catholic girl,* he said, *an Irish rose.* You see, it was easier just to wear Rose's nametag. We looked enough alike — two dark-haired Irish girls — that the manager wouldn't even notice Rose was gone. Eddie Silver didn't notice any difference. He called me *My Irish Rose* from then on."

"From then on? Wasn't Eddie the one who gave your brother Tommy the gun?"

Lillian takes a sip of tea and looks uncomfortable. Perhaps I've overstepped my bounds. I've forgotten again that Lillian isn't a source to be interrogated. And who am I to judge her for doing what she had to do to stay alive?

"I hadn't forgotten that," Lillian says. "And I wouldn't have given him the time of day, only the night Benny the Book got knifed at the Stork Club we all got brought down to the station and Frank was there. I was surprised because Frank was assistant DA in Brooklyn, and this was Manhattan, but he was there because his boss had been building a case against Eddie and he got a tip about the incident at the club. When he walked in I was so ashamed for him to see me mixed up in such a sordid business."

"But you were an innocent witness," I pointed out.

"I suppose . . . but I was wearing one of Rose's dresses and it was . . . well, it made me look cheap. By then I realized what being a 'hostess' at one of those private parties really meant and Frank wouldn't know I'd just been filling in. I saw how surprised he was to see me — and then how something *changed* in how he looked at me. I wanted to explain, but he just walked right on by, like he didn't want anyone to know he knew me. I sat in that station for hours, freezing in that skimpy, ridiculous dress, blood all over me —"

"You were that close to the man who was

knifed?"

She nodded. "I was right behind him. This fellow leaned in like he was gonna tell a joke and then he was gone and Benny the Book was on the floor bleeding his life out. That's why they brought me down, because they thought I could identify the attacker, but I was leaning down to light Benny's cigarette and I didn't see the man who knifed him. I tried to tell them that, but no one would listen . . . until Frank called me into a room. It was just him and a stenographer there to take down my statement. I looked at that stenographer, in her nice neat skirt and blouse, and I thought I could probably type faster than her. I wanted so much to be *her* instead of this floozy with blood all over her. I started out telling Frank I'd just been filling in for my friend Rose — I pointed to my name tag — and the stenographer said, 'Should I correct the witness's name, sir? We have her name down here as Rose O'Grady.'

"Frank didn't answer. He just stared at me. Then he asked the steno girl to go get me a cup of hot coffee. 'Can't you see the poor girl's freezing?' he said. He took off his jacket and put it around my shoulders . . . and while he was doing that he leaned in close to me and whispered in my ear, 'Don't tell them your real name. Just go along with being Rose.'

"I didn't know why he wanted me to do that, but when the steno came back he said: 'Witness account of Rose O'Grady,' and I didn't correct him. I gave my statement just as it happened, which wasn't all that long because I hadn't seen much, but I did it as Rose O'Grady not Lillian Day. And you know what? It was funny, but I didn't feel so afraid once I was pretending to be Rose. She'd always been bolder than me. She didn't care what people thought of her. So I stopped caring what the steno girl thought about me and I told her what I saw. I even told her about slapping that fellow's face and Eddie Silver saying they should all lay off me because I was an Irish Rose. I saw Miss Steno smirk at that, but Frank shot her a look and said, 'That will be all, Miss Sawyer. You can go type up Miss O'Grady's statement and bring it back for her to sign.'

"That took me back a bit, the thought of signing Rose's name to something official, but Frank said I didn't have to worry. 'No one's going to look very hard at it because it didn't tell anything and nothing's ever touched Eddie Silver and his boys anyway. 'I've been trying to pin something on Eddie and his crew for two years now and I can't get anywhere. I couldn't even get him on giving your brother that gun.'

"I told him I was sorry I hadn't seen more and I wished I could help . . . And he said, 'Maybe you can.' "

Lillian looks up at me, the corner of her mouth quirking.

"Oh!" I say, seeing it. "He wanted you to . . . what? Be an informer?"

"Well, he didn't call it that. He said that Eddie Silver clearly liked me. He kept asking if *that girlie Rose* was all right and that he didn't want a *nice girl like that* mixed up in such *unfortunate circumstances.* So if I could maybe go on filling in for Rose now and again I could be his eyes and ears at the club and maybe I could help get that thug off the streets so he wouldn't lead boys like my brother into trouble. And then he added that if he could arrest Eddie, and Tommy testified that Eddie gave him that gun, he could have Tommy's time in prison reduced . . ."

Lillian's voice trails off and I see that her eyes have taken on that wet green sheen they get when they fill with tears, as if there is a sea of grief that rises up behind them when she remembers certain moments in her past.

"That sounds," I say gently, "as if he were

offering to help your brother in exchange for you being an informer."

Lillian doesn't say anything right away. She looks out the window, toward the river. When she speaks it's as if she's speaking to the river. "It would be easy to blame Frank for what happened later, but I knew what I was doing. Since my mother died I had tried hard to stay on the right side of the line while I watched my father and then my brothers, one by one, slip over. I could feel it pulling me. I *liked* the idea of being a spy — like Mata Hari in the movies. I thought that here at last I could step over that line and still hold on to myself because I would be playing a part. I would be Rose. And so at the end I could go back to being Lillian." She turns to me. "I suppose you think I was very foolish."

I shake my head. "I think you were very young —"

Lillian holds up her hand to silence me. I think at first that she's rejecting the excuse of youth, but then I see that she's listening to something. "Someone's at your back door," she says.

I cock my head and listen and then I hear what she hears. A knob turning? I bolt up and run into the hall. The knob *is* turning. "Who's there?" I shout. The knob stops and then I hear footsteps thundering down the back stairs. I hurry to the intercom and press the doorman's button. No one answers. I swipe to the lobby and see that it's empty, and then to outside, where I see Hector helping a young woman fold a stroller into a taxi. As I watch, a hooded figure darts out of the front door, ducking behind Hector and into the park.

"Dammit," I say. "He went right past Hector. I have to go tell him." I look back at Lillian, who's perched on the edge of the chair, eyes bright. "You stay here," I tell her. "I'll be right back."

I go out the front door and press the elevator button, wondering if it wouldn't be faster to go down the stairs, but the elevator is right there, as if waiting for me. I take it down to the lobby. Hector is back behind his desk, reading a newspaper.

"Didn't you see him?" I demand. "A man — a tall, hooded man — ran out of the building right past you. He was trying to get into my apartment."

Hector stares at me. "No one's come in the building except the boilerman."

"Then it was the boilerman. Was he working in the basement? He could have come up the back stairs. He was turning my doorknob, but when I shouted he ran back down the stairs. I saw him run out of the building —" I point out the door and see the hooded man standing in the park looking right at me. "There he is!" I yell. "Come on, we can catch him and you'll see." I grab Hector's arm and pull him to the door. He comes reluctantly, muttering something in Spanish. As soon as the hooded man sees us, he turns and walks down the hill. I let go of Hector's arm and run, hoping Hector is following me.

"Hey!" I shout. "Hold up!" The man doesn't stop or speed up. He just ambles down the hill, hands in his pockets, head down, hood up. He's nearing the church and I suddenly remember the evening I went out and made it just this far but then someone touched the back of my neck and when I turned I saw a dark hooded figure retreating into the park.

Maybe he's lured me out here to kill me. I think of Lillian's description of the knifing at the Stork Club. *This fellow leaned in like he was gonna tell a joke and then he was gone and Benny the Book was on the floor bleeding his life out.* That could happen to me here on this city street. What am I doing, chasing a man who may well be the one who already tried to kill me?

But I can't stop. Like Lillian said, I might

be crossing a line but I'm drawn to it. The hooded man reaches the church and ducks into a side door. I glance behind me to see if Hector's with me, but he's half a block behind. By the time he catches up with me the hooded man could slip out another door. I wave at Hector and point toward the door — then I go inside.

It's so dark inside the church that I can't see anything at first. I am blinded and helpless. Now would be a good time for my attacker to do away with me. And there he is, I see, as my eyes adjust to the dark, coming toward me, wielding a heavy object above his head to strike me.

I scream and throw up my hands to ward off the blow. I feel hands on me as I crouch and cover my head. My screams echo in the dark stone vault of the church but there's no one coming to my rescue because I'm past saving. *Though you wash yourself with lye and use much soap, the stain of your guilt is still before me.*

The words Sister Dolores said to Lillian echo in my head, although I don't know what my *stain of guilt* is supposed to be; I haven't done anything wrong. So why do I feel so ashamed? I look up and see my "attacker" is a nun in a black-and-white habit. Her weathered and wrinkled face looks down at me kindly. "Are you all right, child?"

Hector looms beside her and says something to the nun in Spanish, to which the nun responds in Spanish. They continue, clearly talking about me. *She is one of our crazy residents,* I imagine Hector is explaining. *Poor witless thing,* the nun must be replying as she clucks her tongue.

Hector helps me up and escorts me to the door. I look around the church, but there's no sign of the hooded man.

Did he even exist? Or was he a hallucination like the fireworks and blotches I saw earlier?

I let Hector lead me out of the church and up the hill. I feel as if I am one of the inmates of the Magdalen Refuge being taken back after a failed escape.

Hector brings me up in the elevator and to my door. I realize I don't have a key, but we find that the door is open. I must have left it open when I ran out, leaving poor Lillian at the mercy of any intruders.

"Lillian," I say. "She saw the knob turning. She'll tell you." But when we open the door Lillian isn't there. There are only our two teacups, which show I hadn't imagined her as well.

I thank Hector and apologize for wasting

his time. I head toward my bedroom, but then I notice that the files on my desk have been scattered across the surface. Had Lillian been looking at them? It seems unlikely, but then I recall again how my grandmother would root through the kitchen cabinets when she got confused. And Lillian certainly had been upset by the story she'd told me. I pick up a loose sheet of paper and see it's the list of servers from Bread & Roses —

It was easier just to wear Rose's name tag, Lillian had said. *We looked enough alike — two dark-haired Irish girls — that the manager wouldn't even notice Rose was gone.*

I stare at the list, remembering what one of the servers had said to me. *I was working back-to-back shifts . . . frankly, that whole period is a blur . . .*

What if someone — a friend, a roommate — filled in for the party catered by Bread & Roses but they didn't mention it to the boss? What if the fill-in was the one who saw Osgood attacking Amanda?

I start at the top of the list and begin making all the calls again.

CHAPTER FOURTEEN

MELISSA

Nothing makes you want something more than knowing someone else wants it.

That's what Cass always said, and he was right. I could be looking at something online — a Celine bag, a pair of Ferragamo loafers — for a week, trying to decide if I wanted it, and the minute the words "sold out" flashed on the screen I knew I had to have it. I'd call the site and make them search their stores to find me one.

Knowing that someone else is trying to find out what Joan is up to makes me redouble my efforts. I order the spyware from the site, paying for the most expensive one with the silliest name: the MataHari. For the next few days, while I'm waiting for it to arrive, I camp out in front of the surveillance monitor to study the doormen's and Joan's habits to figure out the best plan for getting back into her apartment.

Which is how I figure out that Joan's become a shut-in.

She *never* goes out. Packages arrive for her from FreshDirect and the liquor store and Amazon and the bodega down on Broadway. I know when they're for her because I can watch the elevator go up to the fifth floor and the only other resident on five is an old woman who gets nothing but a single delivery from Shop-Rite once a week — a sad little bag of Ensure, Entenmann's baked goods, and instant coffee. I know this from Hector, who's become quite the chatterbox since I gave him a $50 tip for letting me back in my apartment the day Joan went gaga on him.

"I saw on my camera that hysterical woman dragging you outside and I came down to see if I could help," I told him after I brushed the spider webs out of my hair and walked down five flights of filth-encrusted stairs in my bare feet. "Silly me, I forgot my keys I was so worried. Was everything all right? She looked . . . *enloquecido.*" I chose the word that Marta would use for raving women, someone who cut her off in the supermarket parking lot, or the old woman who lived in the apartment below her who screamed all night.

"*Hablas Español?*" he asked as he took me

261

up in the elevator.

"Un poco," I told him. *"Es un lenguaje tan hermoso."* And useful for making sure Marta used the right amount of starch in Cass's shirts.

Delighted, he told me the whole story of Joan's hallucinated intruder and the scene she made in the church.

"Pobre chica. Does she have any family to look after her?"

He told me that the only person she ever saw was the old lady in 5B, and that the old lady never went out either. Hector's been so friendly since that tip that I almost think he'd *let* me have the key to Joan's apartment if I asked him nicely enough, which is a nice change from Enda, who's been decidedly cool to me since that first night, but I don't want to get *that* friendly with Hector, and it won't do any good if Joan never leaves her apartment.

In an attempt to lure her out I slip into her mailbox a free drinks coupon to trivia night at the Black Rose, which Mick, the bartender, tells me is a big hit with the millennials, and a gift certificate to yoga classes at the church, which are surprisingly good once you get over the smell of incense wafting down from upstairs. But she doesn't budge from her apartment.

When the spyware comes I practice by installing it on Cass's computer and then "spy" on myself from my iPad. I should have thought of this years ago. I would have learned about the second mortgages and the mysterious monthly withdrawals of $9,999 (Where was he spending it? On his women to keep them quiet?), and the loans he took out against his life insurance. I would have noticed that he'd stopped donating to the Cancer Society — unless he was writing the checks from his LLC account, which I can't access on the laptop — and paying his dues to the Hi-Line Club, which he'd been so excited to join so he could rub shoulders with all those *movers and shakers.*

I would have noticed that while he wasn't cheating anymore, *something* was eating him alive.

His medical report from last year said he had an ulcer and high blood pressure.

He had prescriptions for Xanax and Ativan that he never told me about.

Whatever had happened at the Hi-Line had spooked him. It scared him enough that Simon could use it to threaten him. And if it scared Cass, who didn't scare easy, what damage might it do to me? I have to get Joan out of her apartment to find out what she knows.

It comes to me on a Sunday in mid-October. I'm walking back from the green market in the church schoolyard, feeling invigorated by the crisp fall weather, the smell of apples in my canvas shopping bag (I'd texted a picture of the market to Whit and Emily), and the admiring glances I'd gotten from the rustic, flannel-shirted farmers selling their produce, and I think: *You could just call Simon and ask.* After all, he'd always had a bit of a thing for me. Everyone thinks that the grudge Simon had against Cass started with being passed over for that promotion at the *Times* — and yes, that sealed it, especially because Simon had wrongfully thought Cass had accused him of plagiarism — but the truth is their rivalry really started because Simon had a crush on me all the way back in college. He made a pass at me once at a party and told me that Cass wasn't good enough for me. Now that Cass is gone I could call Simon and tell him he'd been right.

It wouldn't be hard to pretend. Simon was a good-looking man. If he and his little accomplice, Joan Lurie, hadn't ruined my husband I might be interested. But he didn't have to know that. I could tell him that I should have listened to him all those years ago, that I saw now what a cad Cass had been. If only I was sure that Cass really had been guilty of abusing all those women, then I could move on . . . I could get him to tell me what he was holding over Cass's head. He wouldn't be able to resist. I'd call him and ask to meet him somewhere downtown . . .

Or wouldn't it be interesting if Joan saw me coming back to the Refuge with Simon? So far I've been very careful to avoid the cameras by going in and out through the basement — thank you, Enda — but I could walk Simon through the lobby and, if she watches those cameras as much as I do, there's a good chance she would see me with him. She'd know then that I live in the Refuge, but so what? What's she going to do about it? It would be worth it to have her jealous of me.

I sprint up the rest of the hill with new-found energy at the thought of luring Simon to the Refuge and go in through the basement door (I don't want Joan to see me *yet*), walk past those creepy vats, stop by my storage area to pick up a couple of things, and take the stairs to rack up more steps on my Fitbit — and to avoid meeting Joan in the elevator in case she does ever leave her apartment. After I've poured myself a glass of sparkling water I sit at my desk and compose an email to Simon. It takes a few tries but when I'm done I think I've hit the perfect note.

Dear Simon, I hope this finds you well. Thank you for the flowers and your condolence note. I apologize for not writing earlier, but, as I'm sure you can imagine, this has been a very trying time for me and the children and I haven't been inclined to be charitable toward you and your magazine. As time passes, though, and I find out more about the man Cass was, I think I understand why you did what you did. I find myself, too, thinking back to our college days. If you'd like to get a drink someday and reminisce, let me know. I find that one thing Cass's death has taught me is to value the time and friends I still have.

Yours, Melissa

I read it over twice to make sure there's nothing in it that Simon could quote as an admission that I believe Cass is guilty. Each time I read it I find myself tearing up a little at the last line. It's the one line in the whole thing that isn't a lie.

I hit Send and look out at the river. I *had*

been lying when I said I'd been thinking back to my college days — I thought it was the kind of thing that would appeal to Simon, who was always donating to the college and speaking there — but now that I've said it, I find myself doing just that. Specifically, I find myself remembering one day freshman year. I was studying in the library and I noticed Cass and Simon working at a table not far from me. Or rather, I noticed *Cass.* How could anyone not? He was stretched out in front of a window, the light turning his tousled, still-damp-from-the-shower hair the color of beaten bronze. He was wearing a Choate sweatshirt, faded khakis, and scuffed leather loafers without socks. Everything was worn down to a smooth patina that only old money seemed able to accomplish. His wrists and bare ankles still held a tan from last summer. I'd glimpsed boys like him in Scarsdale but never one so effortlessly beautiful. Looking at him made you think of Adirondack lakes and clam bakes on private beaches. It made you want to touch that sun-kissed skin and run your fingers through all that silky hair. I could hardly drag my eyes off him — and I wasn't the only one who couldn't stop looking. On the other side of the table, legs stretched out in the same pose, but in shadow, was Simon Wallace. He, too, had his head down in Janson's *History of Art,* but as I watched I saw that every few minutes he looked up at Cass.

And then I noticed something else. Simon was dressed almost exactly the same — khakis, Weejun loafers without socks, college sweatshirt — only everything that Simon had was new. The pants were creased at awkward angles, the loafers were a brash raw ox-blood, the new-from-the-college-store sweatshirt ungainly over Simon's bony wrists and collarbones. I felt embarrassed for him — or maybe I felt embarrassed for myself. I wasn't poor like Simon — far from it — but since coming to Brown I'd realized there was a difference between people like Caspar Osgood, whose families had come over on the *Mayflower,* and people like me, whose ancestors had come over in steerage from eastern Europe. Between the girls who wore cashmere sweaters and Liberty of London shirts inherited from a great-aunt and the girls who purchased theirs from Saks. Between the boys with gold signet rings worn so smooth the initials were unreadable because they didn't have to be read — everyone knew what they meant — and girls like me who wore their names on chains bought at Tiffany's.

I couldn't blame Simon for wanting what I wanted, but his being so obvious about it made me feel . . . *exposed.*

And he had to try so hard. He worked three jobs to keep up. The funny thing was, he ended up having more spending money than Cass, whose trust fund didn't kick in until he was thirty, and so Simon often paid the bill when we went out.

How he must have hated us.

And yet he was the one who found the apartment for him and Cass to share after college. Who got the internship at the *Times* first and then recommended Cass. Who always walked me downstairs and waited while I got a cab when I had to go back to Westchester at night. All that changed after Cass got promoted over him and Simon believed it was because Cass had accused him of plagiarism. They had a big fight and then it seemed Simon just dropped out of our lives. I remember I'd been hurt that he was able to just sever his ties with both of us over a *work thing,* but when I said that to Cass he told me I didn't understand how ambitious Simon was.

He was always a trespasser, Cass said, *like Neddy in "The Swimmer." We were just the pools he had to swim through to get where he wanted to go.*

How satisfied he must have been to find a way to get back at Cass. But I couldn't help wondering whether *I* was part of his revenge scheme or if I had just been collateral damage. Maybe that's what I *really* want to know even more than what happened at the Hi-Line Club.

I hear the ding of an incoming email, which at this time of night is less likely to be announcing a sale at Saks or an offer for low-cost prescription drugs (am I already in *that* demographic?). It's Simon, replying only twenty-seven minutes after my email to him, saying he'd love to get together. When am I free?

I tell him the truth, that I have a lot of time on my hands these days. Then I suggest he come uptown to my new neighborhood and join me at my local pub for Tuesday trivia night.

When I get to the Black Rose I'm glad I decided to dress down. Simon is drinking a pint at the bar wearing jeans, an untucked Oxford shirt, and a rumpled tweed jacket looking like he might have just wandered out of the library at Brown. He certainly hasn't aged since I last saw him, which was probably at the Met Gala six years ago. I'm in jeans, too, (a $300 pair I bought when I still had money) and a portrait-collar sweater that shows off my collarbones. Simon once told me I looked like Audrey Hepburn in *Charade* and I'm hoping my outfit will remind him of that night we saw it in the Student Union — the night he tried to kiss me.

The evening is crisp, everyone wearing sweaters and plaids, and there are crowds of boisterous young men streaming down from the Columbia playing fields up the street. It feels like college. When Simon turns and sees me it's clear he's thinking about those days too.

"Melissa," he says, getting up and leaning down to kiss my cheek. "Look at you! You look like you just walked out of the library and are on your way to a frat party."

I laugh, waving away the compliment. "I have kids in college now."

"Nevertheless," he says, stepping back to survey me, "you haven't aged a day. I was afraid —"

"That being a widow had turned me into an old hag?" I ask.

He has the good grace to blush. "If I had known that Cass —"

"You wouldn't have run the story?" I ask, smiling sweetly. "Let's start out by being honest, Simon. Nothing would have kept you from running a story you believed in. And you couldn't have known Cass would . . ." I allow my voice to wobble and I touch the back of my hand to my cheek. Simon is immediately all over me, arm around my shoulder, escorting me to a table, signaling the waiter for a drink. I allow myself to be cosseted and then apologize for making a fuss.

"I'm just happy you reached out to me, Mel. I wanted to — but I didn't think you'd see me. I've been feeling lousy."

I bite back the response that he damn well *should* feel lousy and say instead, "I just thought: I lost Cass; I don't want to lose all my old friends — most of whom will have nothing to do with me anymore."

"Is that true? That's awful, Mel; it's not your fault what Cass did."

"Isn't it?" I ask, leaning forward, hands clasped together on the sticky table. "Everyone thinks it is. *I should have known, I should have stopped it.* But here's the thing, Simon, I thought I had. Three years ago I threw him out. I only took him back because . . . well, you probably heard about Whit. He needed the stability of an intact family. But my condition was that he *never* stray again. And I thought he was staying true to his word. He really seemed like a different man

272

these last three years . . ." I do the voice wobble and eye wipe again and take a sip of my drink. Simon leans forward and touches my hand.

"You did the best you could, Melissa. If it's any consolation I think he did change three years ago — no one's come forward from the last three years."

"Well, that's something," I say with a little shaky laugh. "But even that . . . I wonder . . ." I move my hand to his arm and grasp his wrist. "I thought he seemed different because he was ashamed of his behavior, but now I think that he was living under a cloud and I wonder if something else happened three years ago. Something he was afraid of."

"Maybe," Simon says levelly, "he was afraid that one of the women he had assaulted was going to call the police."

I let go of his hand and lean back, but I don't break eye contact. "Do you really believe that, Simon? Do you really think all those women were telling the truth? Don't you remember college, how girls were always throwing themselves at Cass?"

"College was a long time ago, Mel." He takes a sip of his beer and looks out the window. "And I don't remember *you* throwing yourself at Cass. As I remember it, he

273

pursued you pretty hard."

"Did he?" I ask, flattered in spite of myself, but also a little suspicious. I remember that day in the library Simon looking up and catching my eye, seeing me watching Cass, the momentary recognition that we both wanted the same thing. But then, I'd been better at hiding it. "I suppose I didn't want to make it easy for him. I think I realized he was the kind of man who didn't want what was easy."

"Are you sure that's the only reason you hesitated? Are you sure it wasn't because you saw something in him that scared you before he finally wore you down?"

I try to laugh, but it comes out shrill — I notice Mick looking over from the bar as if he's worried about me. "You always were so dramatic, Simon. Weren't you going to major in theatre before you met Cass? Maybe you should have stuck with that."

It's a little mean, but I'm wounded that he thinks I succumbed to Cass *wearing me down* as if I were some witless sorority girl he got drunk to lay. And it's not true. I had set out to get Caspar Osgood that day in the library. Maybe, it occurs to me for the first time, it was seeing Simon wanting him that made me want Cass.

Nothing makes you want something more

than knowing someone else wants it.

"Maybe we both would have been happier if we'd never met Cass," Simon says. "I've always thought it was a shame how you wasted your potential on him. You could have been a good reporter."

"You make it sound as if I'm already over the hill. I can still be a reporter."

"Can you, Mel?" he asks. "Reporting — *good* reporting — takes at least a passing acquaintance with the truth. When you've spent as long as you have living a lie you may find it hard to recognize the truth."

I'm so stunned that I can't say anything right away. "Well," I finally say, trying to keep my voice from shaking for real now, "I certainly recognize when I'm not appreciated . . ." I start to get up and Simon gets up with me, tossing some bills on the table. He follows me out the door and catches up with me across the street on the edge of the park.

"What did you expect, Mel?" he demands angrily as if *I* were the one who had insulted *him.* "Did you think I was still carrying a torch for you?"

"I expected," I say, rounding on him, "for you to tell me the truth, since it's so important to you. You *had* something on Cass. You threatened him with revealing some-

275

thing that had happened at the Hi-Line Club. That's why he didn't fight back. That's why he killed himself. What was it, Simon? If you want me to face the truth let's start there."

Simon's face under the streetlamp looks suddenly pale and stricken. "Where did you hear that?" he asks in a low voice that rumbles in my stomach. I'm suddenly aware of how vulnerable I am — a lone woman standing next to the dark expanse of the park with a man. There aren't so many people out now that it's gotten cooler. But then I dismiss my fears. This is *Simon.* We went to college together.

"I read Cass's emails," I say, tilting my chin up defiantly. "After he died. So you see, I'm not the witless innocent you seem to think I am."

"I never said you were witless — or innocent, Mel." There's still that warning rumble in his voice, but now there's something else, too. He steps closer to me and I feel an electric charge between us that I'm not sure is fear or attraction. "But are you sure the email was really from me? You know it's not impossible to make it look like you're someone else on the Internet."

"Are you saying you didn't send an email to Cass saying you'd print the 'Hi-Line

276

Incident' if he sued *Manahatta*?"

"I'm asking, Melissa, if you're ready to face the truth," he says with a sudden gentleness that leaves me speechless for a moment. Then I know what to say.

"You're one to talk. You're the one whose life has been a lie. Admit it, you wanted to be Cass since freshman year in college. Look at you" — I gesture at the tweed jacket and Oxford shirt — "you're still the poor boy from a blue-collar mill town who wanted to look like he came from money. You even stole Cass's work and that's why he got promoted over you —"

Simon's laugh is so sharp and full of anger that it startles me into silence. "Is *that* what Cass told you, Mel? He was the one stealing from *me.*" He slaps his chest so hard I jump. "He'd take a story right out of my printer and pass it off as his because he was running late on deadline. And why not? I wrote half his papers in college. I'm not proud of that. I admit I was desperate to have his approval and he always made it sound like he was doing me a favor — teaching me to become a better writer with the benefit of his expensive prep school education. He once told me that his old man used to say that the best thing you could do for people was to let them be *of use* to you."

"He hated his father," I said.

"Yes," Simon agrees, "but that didn't stop Cass from turning into him."

There's still hatred in his voice but I'm no longer sure if it's all for Cass; some of it seems directed at himself. It makes me feel sick . . . and suddenly very tired. I turn and start walking up the hill. He follows me, but I pretend not to notice. The truth is I'm scared, scared that what Simon says is true — that it was Cass who stole Simon's work all those years ago and Cass who had assaulted those women and lied to my face. That he had turned into his philandering father. And if Cass wasn't who I thought he was, then what did that make me? My whole life has revolved around Cass, and without that center, what do I have left? As I reach the top of the hill I feel suddenly dizzy, as if I've been sent spinning out into space. I pause — and the footsteps behind me pause too.

I spin around, ready to confront Simon. "All right!" I shout. "Tell me the worst of it!"

But there's no one there. The pavement, which had echoed with footsteps a moment ago, is empty. The park stretches out on either side, empty and vacant. Then I feel

278

someone behind me.

I spin around and find Enda standing close behind me.

"Mrs. Osgood? Who are you talking to? Has someone frightened you?"

Yes! I want to scream. *Simon frightened me!*

"Someone was following me," I say instead, struggling to get my voice under control. "But I lost him." I look into the empty park. "What are *you* doing away from the building?"

"I thought I heard something. . . . Come on. I shouldn't have left my post."

I let myself be steered to the front door of the Refuge, but I can feel anger percolating up inside of me as my fear recedes. It must have been Simon following me and then he ran off when I turned around. He was trying to scare me to get me to back off. Poor silly Melissa, who was easy prey in college for charming Caspar Osgood. The dupe who gave up her own career. The blind wife who enabled her husband's cheating.

I am not that woman.

I will not let Simon and his minion Joan Lurie turn me into that woman.

I say a chilly good night to Enda, refusing his offer to see me to my door. I need to think. Simon never came right out and said that he hadn't sent the email to Cass, but he had managed to evade my question about what happened at the Hi-Line. I need to know what happened. I have to get Joan out of her apartment to install that spyware on her laptop.

And now I know how.

After I've poured myself a glass of wine I sit down at my desk and open my laptop and open Simon's email to me. His private email address is Cassiopeia930 — a reference from another Cheever story, that one about the brothers. What a pretentious twit! How dare he lecture me!

I make an email account Cassiopeia1930, banking on Joan's distracted state to keep her from noticing the extra number. Then I send Joan an email from "Simon."

"There's something I need to talk to you about in private," I write. "It's about the Hi-Line incident. Meet me tomorrow night at the Black Rose at nine."

CHAPTER FIFTEEN

JOAN

On the fifth call I find the server who brought in a substitute. It's the rock singer, Maya, who had been about to embark on her band's South American tour. "Oh yeah," she says when I ask her if she might have missed a shift around that time. "I'd been working back-to-back shifts for ten days to make extra money for the tour but I just kind of crashed. I got sick and I had to find someone to cover me for a few gigs."

"Could one of those gigs have been the party at the Hi-Line Club?" I ask, biting back my frustration that she hadn't mentioned this possibility earlier.

"Yeah, maybe? I mean, we'd catered a couple of gigs there that year — a lot of political stuff, so I thought I'd done the one you asked about but come to think of it . . . yeah, I think I remember it was really hard to find someone because there were a lot of weddings that month. Everyone thinks June's the big wedding month but May is actually more popular —"

"Do you remember who you finally got to cover you?" I ask, cutting short her May-is-the-new-June spiel. It sounds like a story idea that I'd pitch to Sylvia.

"Yeah, it was this girl named MJ . . . or was it AJ? . . . who worked for a tea room downtown . . . yeah, I totally remember her now. She had a rose tattoo on her wrist."

"Uh-huh, do you remember her last name?"

"Mmmmm . . ." Maya hums so long it sounds like she's warming up for a song, but she ends with an abrupt and contradictory "Yeah, no, but I'm sure you could find her. She drew these really cool cartoons and had a webcomic with a logo that was some kind of bird and she worked in one of those tea rooms in the Village . . . or SoHo or Nolita."

Sure, I think, *that should be a snap.* "Would Bread & Roses have a record of her?"

"No, it was easier just to have her fill in as if she were me. She took the tips and I paid her back when I got my check."

"How?" I leap in. "How did you pay her back?"

"Um, on Venmo? I think? Did they have Venmo three years ago?"

"Yes," I say, because I remember doing a story on it. "Would you have a record of that?"

"Uh . . . yeah . . . maybe . . . I can look . . . but I've got to go now. I have a gig in Williamsburg today."

I can tell she's impatient with my attempts to pin down a detail that feels unimportant to her. A girl named MJ or AJ who filled in for her, just another aspirational creative in a city of millions of them.

"Okay, but if you could look through your Venmo account . . . or if you remember anything else about MJ" — *Like her last name!* — "could you please call me back? It's important. She may —" I hesitate, unsure how much I should share with Maya. But I can feel her focus shifting, and if I don't do something to keep it, she'll forget all about me and the phantom MJ/AJ as soon as she ends this call. "She may have witnessed something."

"Oh my God!" Maya cries. "Like a crime? Could she be in danger? Wow," she says in an awed tone. "I mean, it could have been me."

I have Maya's attention now, even if she has turned it back on herself, so I try to make the most of it. "Yes, I'm afraid that she could be in trouble for something she saw. So if you could please try to think if there's anything else you remember . . ."

"Absolutely," Maya says. "I promise, but I've gotta run. My train's —"

The call dissolves in a screech of subway brakes. For a moment I am on the platform with her, hopping on a train for Brooklyn, something I've done a hundred times since I moved to New York but that now feels as farfetched as taking a rocket ship to the moon. It's been months since I took a subway — a week since I went out last, and that was just to chase the hooded phantom down to the church.

I'm working, I tell myself, writing *AJ/MJ?* on a Post-it. I write in what I know about her: *Tea Shop Village, Nolita, SoHo? Cartoonist. Bird logo? Rose tattoo on wrist.* I stare at the sparseness of it and then draw in a rose to fill in the empty space. I stick it onto the blank wall to the right of my desk and then stare at it.

"No cartooning career in your future, kid," I say out loud.

"Do you want me to look up cartooning classes?" Bot asks.

"No," I tell her, "but can you look up tea shops for me in downtown Manhattan?"

"Here are some tea shops below Fourteenth Street in Manhattan." She lists six. There's an English-themed one called Tea & Sympathy, two Japanese ones, a Korean bubble tea room, one called Harney & Sons in SoHo, and a Bosie Tea Parlor, named after Oscar Wilde's boyfriend, in the West Village. My mouth is watering for a scone with clotted cream and jam by the time she finishes listing them.

I could take the A train downtown and scout out all these places in an afternoon. Graze through a couple varieties of Oolong and some tea-infused macarons while I'm at it.

Why not?

It would be like the old days when Sylvia would send me on a mission to find out the ten best organic chocolatiers for Valentine's Day —

This is my job. I can't do it all from my apartment. Maybe if I pretend I am doing this for one of Sylvia's assignments I will transport myself back into the person who could traipse all around the city without a care in the world —

Like the girl who stumbled drunkenly into her building without checking who was behind her —

No. Not that girl. I'm just taking the A

train downtown in broad daylight to have tea, for God's sake.

I get in the shower and try to calm myself. In my head I plan out my route, starting with Tea & Sympathy, which is near the A stop on Fourteenth Street, working down to Bosie Tea Parlor on Morton Street, then heading east to Harney's in SoHo.

I dress in jeans, turtleneck, and blazer, but spend a little extra time on makeup, using foundation to liven up my pasty skin and concealer to hide the dark rings under my eyes. I put my long hair up in a twist and promise myself I'll make an appointment to get it cut. I stop at my desk to print out a list of the tea shops and realize there are several more on my route that don't fit. It would help if I could narrow down the possibilities by calling them and finding out if there's an AJ or MJ who works there.

At Tea & Sympathy I learn there's a Mary Jo who sometimes goes by MJ but she doesn't have a shift until tomorrow.

At Bosie Tea Parlor there's a Molly Johnson who's in later.

At Harney's there's a CJ and an Alice John who might go by AJ or Allie or Allison.

There are no MJ/AJ variations at the Japanese and Korean tea shops. Of course, that doesn't mean that there wasn't one three years ago — or that the AJ/MJ I'm looking for hasn't quit long ago. Still, I can probably find out more if I just go to these places.

As I'm getting up, though, I have another idea. I click on Bosie's Twitter account and see they've got 411 followers. I start scrolling down the list and find that, along with tea purveyors and tea magazines and tea bloggers, many of the followers are girls with quirky background photos and quixotic profiles. Ivy is an urban explorer and tea lover. Shana's vices are *Star Wars* and happy hour. Lauren is a photographer and, like Ivy, an urban explorer. A lot of them list "urban explorer" as if it's a hobby, like spelunking. I have a feeling that at least some of these girls work at Bosie. Then there she is: AJ. Free Spirit. Artist. Tea Enthusiast. Her background picture is a pair of Anime eyes and a drawing of a raven. Her profile picture is literally her face in profile, all but hidden by a high Victorian coat collar, round tinted glasses, and a mane of dark hair. I click on her Twitter account and find that her last post was in June — a drawing she'd done of a man and woman asleep on the subway. It's quite good. I scroll down through her posts — her own drawings, retweets of other artists' drawings, still lifes of New York City scenes, fancy art pens poised on sketch pads, a delicate hand holding a teacup —

A hand with a rose tattooed on the wrist.

This is the girl. I'm sure of it.

Excited, I click on her Facebook page and scroll through photos of her and her friends. All the pictures of her are partial views in shadow. Still she looks familiar to me. I could swear I've seen her before. She could be one of the interns at *Manahatta* or the barista who used to make my morning macchiato, or the girl who cut my hair in the East Village. When I think of all the young women I have crossed paths with in the last few years their faces blur together as if my current damaged eyesight has retroactively blurred my memories of the past.

Or maybe I'm too brain damaged to recognize her. But at least I've got her. I call up Bosie again and ask if the AJ who's a cartoonist still works there. The woman tells me no, that AJ ghosted them a few months ago.

"Do you know where she's working now?"

"I'm sorry, but we can't just give out personal information about our servers on the phone," she says prissily before hanging up.

I could get more in person, I'm sure. But

first I send AJ a Facebook friend request, a personal tweet, and a message on her Instagram account. "Hey," I say in each, "I'd like to interview you for a book I'm doing about New York cartoonists."

Then I go back to her Facebook account. In August a few dozen people wished her Happy Birthday, but there were no replies from AJ, no thank-yous, not even a ♡ on the birthday wishes.

That is strange.

What I should do is go downtown to talk to her coworkers.

I close my laptop and get up to go, checking that I have my keys, wallet, and phone. Then I stand at the door, willing myself to open it. I review the steps I'll have to take to get downtown — and I start to shake. My ears are ringing and I feel lightheaded, my heart pounding so hard I can hear it knocking against my ribs —

No, it's someone knocking at the door. I look on the camera and see Lillian, poised expectantly outside my door, holding a plate of cookies. When I open the door her eyes brighten at my outfit and then dim.

"Oh, you look so nice. You must be on your way out."

"Not at all," I say, reflecting that it's not entirely a lie. I really wasn't on my way anywhere. "I was just going to have tea. Come on in."

Lillian launches into her story quickly today without any prompting from me. "I've been thinking about what you asked me last time about whether Frank was offering me a deal to help Tommy in exchange for spying on Eddie Silver, and I think you were right. Frank was very ambitious. He wanted to impress his boss, the DA, and put Eddie behind bars. If that meant using a pretty, naïve girl to help him . . . well, I don't really blame him. But I wasn't just a naïve girl. I wanted to get Eddie Silver, too, and all the men like him who had preyed on my brother and gotten him in trouble. Tommy never would have had that gun if not for Eddie. That poor girl Arlene wouldn't have been killed and Tommy wouldn't have been in prison."

A different Lillian emerges as she talks. Fierce. Angry.

"That was very brave of you," I acknowledge.

"Oh," she says, laughing it off, "I suppose I also fancied wearing new dresses and going to clubs. I'd been poor for so very long, it felt marvelous to have something new to wear and plenty to eat. My tips at the Stork

Club for one night were more than I made in a week as a stenographer and the chef always put aside food for me to take home — slabs of roast beef and dinner rolls and chocolate éclairs. I would have gotten fat if I hadn't spent the nights dancing."

Her eyes are gleaming now and I can picture this young Lillian, seizing the chance to live life. "Where would you go dancing?" I ask.

"Oh, Roseland, and the Savoy up in Harlem. We'd always end up at Prospect Hall in Brooklyn, though, because it was on the way home. Eddie would take a few of the girls with him and tell us to have a good time. He'd disappear in the back 'on business.' My job was to remember the names of the men he met with and listen in to what they were talking about."

"But if you were on the dance floor —"

"Oh," Lillian says, a sly smile in her eyes. "I would find reasons to go back there. To ask Eddie to come out for a dance or because I wanted one of his expensive cigarettes. I recognized the men he was with because Frank had shown me pictures. There were the big bosses, Albert Anastasia and Frank Costello, and the hired guns, like Joe Adonis and Abe Reles — now, there was a man to make your blood run cold. They called him Kid Twist because of the way he liked to sneak up behind a man and slip a garotte around his neck and strangle him to death."

"Weren't you scared to be around men like that?"

"I knew they wouldn't try anything, because I was under Eddie's protection. And Eddie —" She tilts her head and smiles at me. "I bet you want to ask if he took advantage of me."

It's true I've been wondering what their relationship entailed — how far she'd been willing to go in her role of undercover agent — but I find myself shy of bringing up sex with this nice old lady. Though perhaps my reticence is doing a disservice to Lillian. Maybe she wants to tell the truth after all these years.

"Yes," I say, returning her playful look with a serious one. "If you're able to tell me. I imagine a man like Eddie Silver would have expected sexual favors —"

"Oh, but he didn't — at least, not from me," Lillian exclaims, unembarrassed. "You see, he still thought of me as his Irish Rose, his sweet lass from the old country, never mind I was born in Flatbush. His *róisín dubh,* he'd call me, his black rose, after an old Irish song. He never touched me, and he made it clear to his underlings that I was off-limits. So you see, I was safe . . . at least until . . ." A shadow passes over her face, her bright-green eyes turning as flat as corroded pennies.

"Until?" I prompt.

She sighs. "Until I saw something I shouldn't." She takes a deep breath. For a moment I think she won't be able to go on. I have to restrain myself from prompting her, but then when she starts again, the words spill out as if they've been building up inside her, waiting to escape.

"One night we were out and Eddie says, 'I have to pay a visit to an old friend who's staying in a hotel.' We were in Brooklyn and he offered to drop me home if I was tired but I said, 'No, I'm wide-awake,' because I was thinking Frank would want to know about this friend. When we pulled up in front of the Half Moon Hotel in Coney Island I knew I was right —"

The Half Moon Hotel jars a memory, but I can't grasp it.

"Because that's where the police were keeping Abe Reles, who had turned state's witness against the mob and was informing on all his former colleagues in exchange for immunity. Abe was on the top two floors, guarded by a dozen policemen, so I didn't think that's where we were going. And we weren't, at first. We went to a suite on the fourth floor, where a couple of fellows were sitting around smoking and drinking with a girl, who turned out to be Rose."

Seeing my surprise she nods. "I hadn't seen much of Rose since I'd taken her place at the Stork. 'You keep it,' she'd told me, 'I have better ways to make a buck.' I had a hunch what that better way was, and I guessed she was embarrassed for me to see what she'd become. I'd catch a glimpse of her every now and then on the arm of one mobster or another, one of whom must've brought her to the Half Moon that night. I barely recognized her. She had the glassy eyes of a doper, and she was dressed like a floozy. When she saw me I was afraid she'd let on that my name wasn't really Rose, but she only laughed and said, 'Well, look what the cat dragged in, fellows, Second Hand Rose.' Eddie laughed like it was a fine joke. 'Two Irish Roses! A couple more and we'll have a bouquet. Just what we need to distract the boys in blue upstairs.' "

"Did he mean the policemen guarding Abe Reles?" I ask.

"Yes. That's why Eddie brought me. He wanted Rose and me to entertain the police while he took care of Abe so that Abe couldn't testify against him and his friend. I tried to laugh it off. 'You know I can't sing a note, Eddie, how do you expect me to entertain them?' And he answered, 'I don't know, Lil, maybe by doing impersonations.'

"I went cold all over when I realized he knew my real name, but Rose came to my rescue. 'Don't be sore, Eddie, Lil filled in for me one night. The Two Flowers of Mary Magdalene, we called ourselves back at St. Stephens. Even the nuns mixed us up.' That wasn't right," Lillian tells me, as if anxious I get the right details down. "The rose and the lily were the two flowers of the Virgin Mary, but Rose was making a joke. Then she said to me, 'Don't worry, Lil, I'll show you how it's done.' She winked at me and I thought it would be all right. At any rate, I didn't dare refuse, or Eddie would guess I'd been stringing him along the whole time. So I laughed and said I just needed to powder my nose. I went to the bathroom and looked out the window. There were police cars parked down below. Maybe I could get a message to Frank through them — but I also saw one of Eddie's goons pacing back and forth and I knew if he saw me drop something out the window it could get back to Eddie. So I ran cold water over my hands and freshened my lipstick and told my reflection in the mirror, 'You can do this, Lillian,' and I went out and said, 'Let's go see those coppers.' One of Eddie's guys took us to a room on the fifth floor, which I knew from what Frank had told me was right below where they were keeping Reles. It was a suite with a bedroom and a sitting area. 'Wait here,' he told me and Rose. When he was gone I turned to Rose. 'What do they expect us to do?' I asked.

" 'What do you think?' she said, lighting a cigarette and sitting down in a chair. Then she laughed. 'Don't tell me you're not doing the same with Eddie, what with all the time you've been spending with him.'

"When she saw my face she stopped laughing. 'My pure Lily, only you could manage to stay lily white in such a dung heap. Don't worry, I'll take care of you.'

"Then Eddie's man was back with two policemen. 'What did I tell you, boys, two blushing Irish roses.' One of the cops was big and red-faced, drunk already, but the other was young and skinny, a freckle-faced boy not much older than my Tommy. Rose turned on the radio and sashayed up to the big one and coaxed him into a big chair. 'Let's get you fellas something to drink. Lil, why don't you ask that lug outside to get us some ice.' She did what she could to delay the inevitable. She plied her big guy with enough drink to sink a battleship and signaled me to do the same as she pulled hers by his tie into the other room. At first I thought it was going to be all right. My fellow was so shy he could barely talk to me. Ernest was his name. He seemed relieved when I asked him questions about himself and he launched into a long, boring history of his education and ambitions in law enforcement and how many push-ups he did for his physical exam.

" 'Your mother must be so proud of you,' I said, thinking that mention of his mother might dampen his sex drive. But instead he took it as an invitation to lunge across the settee at me. He was so clumsy, like a big wet dog, that I laughed.

"He slapped me.

"Well, I was used to fighting on the streets, so I slapped him right back. He looked surprised — and then angry. He pinned me to the sofa and started grinding his hips against me. I tried to push him away. He wasn't very tall, but he was strong — all those push-ups — and he was crushing me down into that big soft couch, which smelled like mildew. A cushion fell over my face — or maybe he pushed it over my face — and I suddenly couldn't see or breathe. It felt

297

like I was drowning . . ."

Her voice catches as if she really was choking, and I reach out to touch her hand. She grips mine as if I could pull her back to safety.

"I wrenched my neck around to get air. I remember 'You Made Me Love You' was playing on the radio. I could see the table with the drinks and the window beyond. I kept my eyes on the window as if I could fly out of it — and that's how I saw the body fall. I screamed, but Ernest just covered my face with the cushion. I was going to die, I thought, just like the man who fell from the window. I was in a place of death . . ."

Lillian looked at me and I saw the terror in her eyes. She was in that room in the Half Moon Hotel, battling for her life, seventy-seven years ago. A piece of her was always in that room, just as a piece of me would always be on the threshold of my old apartment feeling that hand over my mouth. I reached out and squeezed her hand.

"But then someone was pulling Ernest off me — the big cop — shouting, 'Come on, lover boy, we got trouble!' Ernest looked confused. I had the feeling he was going to have that confused look on his face for the rest of his life, never understanding what had gone wrong with all his big plans. The minute I could get up I ran to the window. There was a body on the roof below us, one leg bent back the wrong way, face looking up at the sky. You could see right away that he was dead. Then Rose was pulling me to the door saying, 'Come on, we gotta scram.' We ran to the back stairs and Rose told me to wait while she looked down to see if the coast was clear. She opened the door and I leaned against the wall trying to straighten my skirt and blouse. My stockings were torn and the snap on my garter was broken. I could hear voices coming from the open door. One of them was Eddie.

" 'The girls done their part keeping your boys busy, but now they're a liability. You can take care of them . . .'

"I heard another man's voice — a deeper rumble — but then the door closed and Rose was shaking me. 'Eddie's sending someone to kill us. We have to hide.' She pulled me into a janitor's closet. It smelled like bleach and mildew . . . like that awful couch. I must have been shaking because Rose put her arms around me and held me. I bit my lip so hard to keep from crying out that I tasted blood. I heard footsteps going down the hall and a door opening and closing. That must have been Eddie's hit man going into the suite. Rose cracked the door open and peeked out, then pulled me out of the closet. We ran down the back stairs and out into an alley. The police car was parked across the street on Surf Avenue, as if it still had something to guard. Rose pulled me the other way, toward the boardwalk, but instead of walking on top of it she pulled me underneath it. It was pitch-black down there, except for the places where the street-lights slanted through the boards. The sand was cold and damp. I could hear the waves pounding on the shore and it felt like it was the sound of my heart hammering against my ribs and my blood rushing in my veins — but then Rose stopped me and put her hand over my mouth while she looked up. Someone was walking above us. I could see his shadow when he moved under the streetlamp, the shape of a man in a belted trench coat and a fedora, stretched out over the planks of the boardwalk, creeping toward us. I crouched down in the sand while he passed over us and I remembered kneeling in the cold sand next to poor dead Arlene. It felt like the shadow of death moving over us and I thought of what my mother used to say when she got a sudden chill —"

"Someone just walked over my grave," I say with a nod. "My grandmother used to say that."

Lillian shakes her head. "He passed over us twice — the second time going in the opposite direction back to the hotel — and then we ran all the way to the Stillwell Avenue subway station near Nathan's. Rose took me by both arms and whispered, her face close to mine but invisible in the dark. 'We gotta split up, Lil. They'll be looking for two girls. When you hear the train come in you run up and take it into Manhattan. I'll take the next one. Meet me in Grand Central under the big clock. We'll take a train upstate to my aunt's.'

" 'What will we do upstate?' I asked.

" 'We'll stay alive,' Rose said, giving me a hard shake. 'Which is more than we'll do here if Eddie's guys get ahold of us.' She moved her head back, into a slice of light, and I saw that her face was wet. I hadn't seen Rose cry since my mother died. 'Rose,' I said, 'did you see the other man's face? The one Eddie sent to kill us?'

"She said something to me I didn't entirely understand and then she slipped a small, cold object into my hand. 'Here,' she said, 'you'd better go.' She gave me a fierce hug and then pushed me away. I stumbled in the sand out onto the sidewalk, and then up the steps to the subway platform — right

301

into the arms of two uniformed policemen. They hustled me back down and into a squad car and took me straight to the DA's office, where Frank was waiting. When I saw him it was all I could do not to burst into tears and throw myself in his arms. I told him about Eddie sending me and Rose upstairs to 'entertain' the cops and how I thought Eddie had guessed I was a snitch, but when I got to the part up in the suite — well, I couldn't tell Frank about what happened on the couch. I don't know why. I somehow felt . . . *stupid* that I'd gotten myself into that position."

"It's not uncommon among survivors of sexual assault," I tell Lillian, "to feel ashamed as if it were their fault. It's what keeps so many victims silent."

It's a little speech I've given a dozen times but Lillian looks at me as if I've delivered the secret of the universe. "Yes," she says, squeezing my hand. "I never told anyone what happened . . . until now."

Now it's my turn to tear up. I've been the first recipient of a number of sexual assault stories, but never one that's lain seventy-seven years in the dark.

"I told Frank that before anything happened I saw Reles fall from the window. I even made a joke about my virtue being saved by the fall, and then I told him how we ran to the stairs and heard Eddie coming up the stairs with another man. When I told him what Eddie had said, Frank turned pale.

" 'Are you sure he said *your boys*?' " Frank asked.

"I nodded. 'That sounds like whoever he was talking to was a cop. That must be how Eddie figured out you were an informer, and since Rose was your friend he figured she was too. He must have planned to use you and Rose to distract the cops who were guarding Reles and then get rid of both of you. Did you see the other man on the stairs?'

"I told Frank no, but Rose had. He asked me if Rose knew who it was and I said no and then he asked me if Rose had described him and I started to cry and said I couldn't remember. And really I couldn't. The whole flight from the Half Moon — hiding under the boardwalk, stumbling through the sand, that shadow stretching over the planks — all of that was beginning to feel like a nightmare I'd barely woken up from. The pieces were beginning to break apart, the way a dream evaporates on waking. When I closed my eyes, though, I was back on that couch, choking on the smell of mildew, watching a man fall past a window."

I could explain to Lillian the brain chemistry of why that moment when she feared for her life was seared into her brain, but instead I hand her a tissue and pour her another cup of tea.

"When I finished crying Frank told me that I couldn't go back to my room. Eddie Silver's men would be looking for me. I wouldn't be safe until Eddie was put away. I told Frank I'd testify against him and he said that was good but they needed Rose's testimony, too, and they needed her to identify the other man on the stairs. If they arrested Eddie without the other man he would have Rose and me both killed.

" 'But I didn't see him,' I wailed. 'Only Rose did.'

" 'He won't know that. But don't worry,' Frank said. 'We'll find Rose. In the meantime, I'm going to keep you safe. I have just the place for you.'

"So that's how I ended up here at the Refuge. Frank said he had to put me someplace safe until they could find Rose and she could ID the other man. He pretended I was being put away for 'solicitation' because, he said, no one would think I was an informer then and no one would look for me way up here practically in the Bronx.

It felt like a world away from Coney Island. He thought I would be safe here . . ."

She wipes her eyes. She seems to deflate, suddenly, as if she'd used up all her resources on that headlong dash from the Half Moon Hotel only to collapse when she reached safety — this place of refuge.

"What happened to Rose?" I ask as gently as I can. "Did Frank find her?"

"Not at first. And then . . ." She begins to cry.

I'm afraid that telling this story has been too much for her. "Maybe we should leave the rest of the story for another day," I say, a line that Simon would say no reporter should *ever* utter.

"Yes . . . I think that's a good idea . . . I'm going to go lie down." She gets unsteadily to her feet and I help her to the door. Before she walks out, she opens her wicker purse. I think she's looking for her keys, but instead she reaches inside and brings out a balled-up tissue.

"I want you to have this," she says, "to keep you safe." She sees me staring at the tissue and laughs. She digs in the folds and pours something cool and metallic into my palm — a bronze circle engraved with a floral design.

"This is what I had given Rose when she

was at the Refuge, to keep her safe. She gave it back to me under the boardwalk. I think you need it more," she said with a sly smile. "After all, who's going to bother with an old lady like me?"

"Are you sure . . ." I begin, but she clasps my hand closed over the locket.

"It gave *me* courage," she says. "It will for you too."

I thank her and open the door. I don't watch her on-camera, though; instead I rush back to my desk and I open my laptop to google Abe Reles and the Half Moon Hotel. I read until my eyesight blurs and then I ask Bot to continue reading as I write down notes on index cards and Post-its. The story corresponds to much of what Lillian told me, except that there's no record of two Irish girls entertaining policemen in a fifth-floor suite. But of course there wouldn't be. There *is* an Eddie Silver — a captain in Albert Anastasia's crime ring whom Reles was scheduled to testify against the day after he fell to his death. And there are numerous references to the event in newspapers and books. *The canary could sing but couldn't fly,* the journalists of the day quipped. I find myself wondering how much of Lillian's story is true. It's not that I doubt the story of what happened in the Half Moon Hotel with the policeman; the memory of that assault has been branded on her brain. *Seared into memory.* But the rest . . . the escape under the boardwalk, being placed under witness protection at a refuge for fallen women . . . even by her own admission, those details were hazy. I can't help but wonder how much she has invented over the years to give the story of how she came to the Refuge a little more legitimacy than just poor girl becomes prostitute and ends up in a home run by nuns. Like all of us on Instagram, framing our lives in misty filters and curated shots of foamy lattes.

Thinking of Instagram, I pick up my phone and start scrolling through AJ's Instagram again, looking for a clue to where she's gone — a favorite aunt upstate like Rose had, maybe? Instead I notice the same girl appearing over and over again in her selfies, another dark-haired girl.

Two sisters from another mister, one photo is captioned. They're on a beach, their dark hair intermingling in the ocean breeze, grinning up into the camera. The picture makes me think of Rose and Lillian under the boardwalk.

I hover over the photo of the other girl and find she's tagged as Stacy Fernandez. I go back through AJ's twitter and Facebook feeds and find that Stacy has liked or retweeted every photo. She must be her best friend. Wouldn't she know where AJ was? I click on Stacy's Facebook page and send her a friend request. Then I send her a tweet and an Instagram message.

I'm looking for AJ, I say. *Do you know where she is?*

I pull up my email and find a message from Simon's Gmail account. The subject line reads: *Hi-Line Club.* I open it with a little shiver of anticipation. *Why is he writing me from his private email?*

Its brief contents hardly enlighten me: There's something I need to talk to you about in private. About the Hi-Line incident. Meet me tomorrow night at the Black Rose at nine. Simon.

I stare at the message until it swells, blurs, and floats off into my peripheral vision like a crow flapping into the sky. The words echo in my head as if they'd been spoken aloud by some tough PI in a '40s noir — Sam Spade in *The Maltese Falcon,* perhaps. That's what I seem to be living in right now. Lillian's tale of gangsters, hit men, night-clubs, and secret identities has crept into my life. Even the name of the proposed meeting place — the Black Rose — is straight out of Lillian's story. *Why not?* I think. *Better Lillian's story than the one you've been living — defeated shut-in who can't write a book.*

"Bot," I say aloud, "reply to email from Simon. Say, 'Yes, I'll be there.' "

CHAPTER SIXTEEN

MELISSA

Joan replies back in half an hour to say she'll be there.

Good for you, Joan, I think. Maybe this is what she needs to get out of the house. I'm really doing her a favor.

Tomorrow is Wednesday — Irish folksong night. It will be crowded enough that Joan won't be sure right away that Simon's not there. Maybe she'll make some friends while she's waiting. And Hector is on duty Wednesday. I just have to figure out a way to get him to leave his desk for a long enough time for me to get those keys.

I have only one day to figure it out. Cass always said he did his best thinking on a deadline. I do mine while my hands are busy, so I go down to the hardware store the next morning and buy a hammer, rubber gloves, a paint scraper, and industrial-strength cleaner.

"Doing some home repairs, Mrs. Osgood?" Hector remarks when he runs into me in the basement. "Anything I can help you with?"

"Just hanging some pictures," I say. "I don't want to get too dependent on you, Hector."

Which gives me an idea.

I spend the day going up and down between my storage unit in the basement and my apartment, taking the stairs quickly to build up my endurance — *who needs a fancy gym or personal trainer!* I bring up a box with family pictures in it — the ones with Cass in them that I thought I wouldn't want to look at anymore. I need them now, though. When I'm unpacking it I find a folder with Cass's LLC files and remember that I hadn't gone through those accounts when I went through the others. I put it on my desk to look through later.

Toward the end of the day I go all the way up to the spiral stairs below the skylight and clean it off. If I'm going to use the landing as a hiding place, at least it should be clean and well ventilated. I pull the nails out that keep it shut. There are only three nails but they are long and heavy — more like spikes than nails. Someone really wanted to keep someone out — or in. It takes all my strength, bracing my back against the stairs and my feet against the wall, to pull the first one out. It feels like extracting a tooth from living flesh and it looks like it's dripping blood when it finally comes loose. *Rust,* I tell myself, tackling the second one, mixed with rainwater seeping down from the roof.

When I've gotten all three bloody nails out I push on the glass and it opens, showering me with dried pigeon droppings and feathers but also with a gust of fresh air that smells like the river. I wriggle out the hatch, glad I'd done all that exercise; I'm slim enough to fit through the narrow opening and my arms are strong enough to pull me up onto the roof. I feel like a climber who's scaled Mount Everest. The sun is setting over the Palisades, turning them a brilliant red and the Hudson molten gold. To the south, beyond the glowing tower of the Cloisters, a million lights are just coming to life, pricking out the skyline as if it had just come into being. It's the way the city looked to me when I was just starting out: as if New York and all its possibilities had invented itself just for me and Cass.

I wipe my face and find it's wet. I don't know why. It's not like I've never seen a view before. Cass took me to Windows on the World for my twenty-first birthday, and for my birthday last year we went to Top of the Hub in Boston. Cass liked places with wide, sweeping views. *They make me feel like the future is limitless.*

But that's not how I feel looking at the skyline and the river. I feel only a terrible loneliness, as if I'm marooned on a desert island with no way off . . .

And there isn't. Aside from the narrow escape hatch I came out of there's only one other door and it's bolted shut. On the edge of the roof there's a skeletal black ladder outlined against the setting sun like the ribs of a prehistoric mastodon. I pick my way across the sticky tar surface to the edge of the roof, lay my hand on the warm, corroded iron, and look over.

The narrow, spindly ladder plunges straight down the side of the building to the rocks below on the border of the West Side Highway. An escape route of sorts, but only for someone who's decided death may be the only way out.

When I come downstairs I check my email to make sure Joan hasn't backed out, but there's nothing from her. *That's my girl,* I think, conceding a grudging admiration for her as if she were a newbie intern I am teaching to be more outgoing.

I shower, scrubbing disgusting pigeon droppings and city soot off my skin while making my plan. I dress in a casual but nice lounge outfit — yoga pants and a cashmere hoodie — and get the hammer and picture hangers. Then I make enough of a racket hammering that Hector has to call up to let me know that the mother in 3B is complaining that I'm keeping her baby up.

"I was just going to take a break for dinner," I tell Hector.

And I do. I pop a Daily Harvest soup in the microwave, pour myself a large glass of wine, and park myself in front of the surveillance monitor. I told Joan to meet me (Simon) at nine. I start watching the camera at eight. By 8:46 I'm beginning to worry that Joan has chickened out. Perhaps she really has become an agoraphobe. Am I going to have to slip her brochures for local therapists? But then at 8:52 she appears on the lobby camera, stepping out of the elevator in wool trousers, black turtleneck, and trench coat, like she's Ingrid Bergman in *Casablanca* for heaven's sake.

"Whatever it takes, Joannie," I say to the camera. "You can do it."

She crosses the lobby, stops to talk to Hector, cranes her neck to peek out the front door like she's checking for rain — or falling meteors. But it's a crisp fall night, ideal for an assignation with a source. She touches something at her throat, squares her shoulders, and marches out the door. I switch to the outside camera and watch her pause under the awning and peer mistrustfully into the park. Maybe I should have made the appointment for daytime. But then her hand goes back to the thing at her throat — has she gone all born-again on me? — and strides off-camera.

"Good girl!" I shout, spilling my wine. Then I pick up the hammer on the floor beside me, raise it, and bring it down on my thumb.

"Shit!" I scream, loud enough to be heard across the river in Fort Lee. I push the intercom and cry into it, not having to fake the tears in my voice, "Hector! I've hurt myself! Please come!"

Since I'm watching on the camera I can see the look of genuine concern on his face. What a sweetheart! I hope I can do this without getting him in trouble.

"Do you want me to call 911?" he asks.

"No . . ." I sob. "Just . . . please . . . come."

I see him looking around the empty lobby considering, and then he looks down at the keys on his desk, scoops them up, and stuffs them in his jacket pocket. Does he suspect that someone lifted them the last time? It's all right, though, I have a plan for this.

By the time he arrives at my door, which I've left open, I am sitting on my couch with a towel wrapped around my throbbing thumb, tears streaming down my face.

"Pobre chica," he croons, coming to sit beside me. "I told you I would help."

"I . . . know . . . I just wanted to prove I-I could do something on my own. I'm tired of feeling so helpless. And I wanted my family with me." I wave to the wall behind me where I've hung three pictures of baby Whit and Emily crookedly on the wall. Other pictures — of Whit's graduation from Choate and Emily's from Brearley, of the four of us in front of the Colosseum in Rome, of Cass and me on our wedding day — are strewn across the floor.

"Family is what makes us strong, *senora,*" he says, unwrapping the towel and wincing at my red, swollen thumb. "Let me get you some ice."

"I already have some," I say, indicating the full ice bucket on the coffee table. "It's not so bad . . . I just . . . I was hoping to get this all done because my children are visiting tomorrow and I want them to see how much I love them. That even though their father is gone, they still have a family."

I don't have to fake these tears. I should have Emily and Whit to visit, I realize. I *should* be reassuring them that we're still a family.

"Here," Hector says, "take it easy. I'll get these up in no time."

He pats me on the shoulder and gets up. When he removes the first crooked photo from the wall he pauses and takes off his jacket.

"Let me hang that up for you," I say, popping to my feet. "You don't want to get your uniform wrinkled." He nods, staring at the wall and the pictures, measuring with his eyes. I carry his jacket to the hall closet, slipping the keys into my hoodie pocket. It's all I can do not to sprint up to Joan's, but I make myself go to the kitchen, pour a glass of spring water, and send Joan an email from Simon that he's delayed but will be there soon. Then I return to the living room, where I lavish praise on the first two photographs he has hung on the wall.

"Bravo!" I say, "That's so much better — and look how quickly you've done it! I bet you'll get these all done in no time . . . oh damn!"

"What's the matter?" he asks.

"Oh, I just realized there are two more I wanted to hang that are still down in the storage unit . . . would you mind . . . it will only take a minute . . ." He barely glances at me as I walk to the back stairs, shouting over my shoulder, "Back in a few!" Then I am sprinting up the stairs, clutching the keys to keep them from jangling.

The key turns, but the door doesn't open right away. There's another lock. Using my phone's flashlight I see there's another keyhole above the original lock. Joan has installed an interior bolt.

I nearly weep with frustration, but then I look at the ring of keys in my hand. The co-op board specifies that the doorman must have all keys to the apartment's back-door. A rule I'd readily break, but I'm betting Joan's a rule follower. And there *is* a shiny new key on Hector's ring. I try it in the new lock and it turns.

"Well done, Joan," I whisper as I open the door and start down the hallway. "You keep to the straight and narrow. It will get you . . ."

My voice dies as I reach her living room. The only light is the gooseneck lamp on her desk. Its metal neck is wrenched to the side, lighting up the wall covered in sticky notes. They rustle in the breeze from the open window like a flock of pigeons agitated at my approach. I shake away the unsettled feeling I have that they will fly away if I startle them and concentrate on the laptop sitting in the middle of the desk. It chimes when I open it and the screen goes from black to a grainy newsprint image so enlarged that it's unclear what it is at first. A face maybe? Not worth altering to find out.

I take my flash drive and insert it into the USB port on the side. The laptop buzzes angrily at the intrusion and I half expect it to spit out the foreign body. Maybe Joan has installed anti-spyware software. But then the buzz turns into a contented hum and an icon of a stylized Greta Garbo playing Mata Hari. A bit much, if you ask me, but I suppose that's what you get when you pay top dollar. I tap on the trackpad and a box appears, asking me if I want to install MataHari 2.2 on this computer. When I tap Yes, another box opens asking me to certify that I own, or have permission from the owner of, this computer. I click the box without a second thought . . . and then it asks me for my password. *Crap.* Of course Joan's computer requires a password before downloading an application. Why hadn't I thought of that? And it's not like I know enough about Joan to guess like I did with Cass. . . . But then looking around the desk I notice a pile of folders under an address book with a Monet painting on the cover and a logo of the Metropolitan Museum of Art. Why does someone Joan's age even *have* an address book? It was probably a gift from her mother. Still, why keep it on her desk, unless . . . I reach for it and open it to the last page, which is where I would keep important numbers, and there it is: a list of passwords including the one for her MacBook. I type in the password and an image appears of a 1940s dame smoking a cigarette. As Greta's cigarette burns down a number appears on the screen telling me what percent of the download is done.

Very clever. I just have to hope the whole thing doesn't go up in smoke. To distract myself I look at the wall of sticky notes.

One says: *MJ/AJ? Tea Shop Village, Nolita, SoHo? Cartoonist. Bird Logo.*

There's also a drawing of a rose on the bottom.

Another says: *Assault at the Hi-Line Club witnessed by AJ?*

So Joan is looking for someone named AJ who worked at the May fundraiser at the Hi-Line Club. The same event that Simon had alluded to in his threatening email to Cass. Joan also thought something happened at that party — but she doesn't mention anything about an underage girl.

There's a fan of red ribbons extending from an index card with "Hi-Line Club" written on it.

I pull back the lamp to widen its circular glow and see that the notes extend over the whole wall. There's a card with Amanda's name that is attached to note cards with police precinct phone numbers and the question: *officers on duty 5/15/15?* My skin prickles in the cool breeze from the window. Joan is looking for a local police officer on duty at the time of the party. Did Cass have a run-in with the police? Surely I would have known about that. There's no record of an arrest on Cass's computer. No, this must be a wild idea of Joan's. But just in case, I'll take pictures of the wall. It will take forever moving the lamp over each section, though, so I walk to the front door and turn on the overhead lights. When I turn back I gasp. It's like when you notice an ant and then another and then realize there's a whole swarm. Not only is the entire wall covered with sticky notes and index cards and cut-out pictures, they are also all connected by string spiraling out like a spider web. It looks like the work of a crazy conspiracy theorist. And when I move closer and look at the pictures I see that in addition to photos of Cass there are also photos clipped from old newspapers that seem to come from the 1940s. There's one of a woman captioned "The Kiss of Death Girl," another of a thuggish hoodlum named Abe Reles, a picture of the Half Moon Hotel in Coney Island, a logo for the Stork Club, and an illustration of a pretty girl in a '40s hairdo identified as "The Legendary Black Rose."

"What the hell, Joan," I say out loud. "What does this have to do with Cass?"

But the answer is obvious. Joan Lurie has lost her mind.

I take a panoramic shot of the whole wall and then closer shots. I may need this one day to prove she was insane. Although I'm not sure how I'd explain what I was doing in her apartment. I'll worry about that later. The computer has stopped whirring and Mata Hari's cigarette is ash. "Mission Accomplished" scrolls across the screen. I take out the flash drive and the grainy picture reappears and I see now it's a detail of one of the pictures on the wall. Rose O'Grady — the Legendary Black Rose.

I wonder what Joan thought when she got the email from "Simon" asking to meet at the Black Rose. Now that I know Joan's obsessions I might be able to use them to drive her further over the edge.

I'm startled by a distant crack. It almost sounds like a gunshot. Instinctively, I head to the surveillance camera. The lobby is empty, of course, because Hector is in my apartment hanging pictures. *Uh-oh,* I think, *what if a marauding gang chooses this moment to storm the Refuge?* Then, as I watch, the lobby door swings open. It's Joan. Her clothes are disheveled, her hair is loose and wild, and her face is panicked. I feel a pang of guilt that something bad has happened to her when I was the one who sent her out. Then that feeling changes into something else entirely when I notice that she's not alone. Simon Wallace is with her.

CHAPTER SEVENTEEN

JOAN

I'm feeling nervous about tomorrow's meeting with Simon and need to occupy my mind. I decide to fill in the chart that I started with AJ's Post-it and try to map out what I know about the events from three years ago. Maybe if it's all laid out in front of me, I'll see things more clearly and will know what questions to ask him and how to describe all the clues.

I write the name of the Hi-Line Club and the date 5/15/15 on an index card and tack it above AJ's name. Then I make a card for Amanda that says, "Witness at the Hi-Line?" and "Trouble with the police?" and "Police record?"

"Bot," I say, "Tell me what police precincts are near the Hi-Line Club."

Bot lists three. I copy down the names and phone numbers and make a note to find out who was on duty the night of May 15, 2015.

Then I attach red ribbons from Amanda's card to each of these and stand back again to see the connections.

There's something about this pattern I've made that feels familiar. I stare at it until it's burned onto my retinas, but I can't grasp it. When I give up and go to bed the shapes pulse and jitter beneath my eyelids. In my dreams they transform into a girl fleeing down a dark corridor, her retreating back flickering in and out of diagonal slashes of light. When I try to catch up to her my feet sink into cold, wet sand. We're not in a corridor though; we're under the boardwalk. I can hear the roar of the sea and a rhythmic pounding, which I realize are the footsteps of someone up above us on the boardwalk, tracking our movements, waiting until we reach the end to catch us. The girl ahead of me must hear it, too, because she starts to run. I run, too, because I know that our only chance is to reach the end of the boardwalk before *he* does. The slashes of light flicker faster, speeding up like an old-fashioned zoetrope. It makes me dizzy and I begin to fall, the sand rearing up in my face, filling my mouth with the sweet smell of chloroform.

I wake up with my heart pounding, drenched in sweat, my mouth as dry as sand. I get up and stumble toward the kitchen for water but am arrested by the pattern of moonlight coming in through the slatted blinds, streaking the walls, creating the same pattern of light as beneath the boardwalk in my dreams. Only now I'm staring at it as if from above, as if I'm lying on the boardwalk looking through the cracks, and the pounding in my head is the footsteps below me. I lie down on the floor and press my face to it, listening. . . .

I wake up on the floor of the living room in the slatted sunlight. For a moment I think I'm back on Avenue A waking up after the attack and the months since have been a dream. The book deal and fancy apartment are just the wish fulfillment of another aspirational reporter.

But then I feel the cool river breeze on my skin and hear the ruffling of paper. There are sheets of paper all around me and squares of yellow and orange and pink scattered over the floor. When I get to my knees I see that the leaf litter of Post-its stretches across the floor and climbs up the wall, where it has overrun the chart I began last night.

I have no memory of putting them up.

But I must have. Who else, I ask myself as I look closer, would have written *Lillian* and

Rose and *Abe Reles* and *The Half Moon Hotel* and *Assistant DA Frank Maloney* and *Murder Inc.* on Post-its and index cards and arrayed them over the cards for AJ and Amanda and the Hi-Line Club? I'm not sure what's worse: that I did it, that I forgot I did it, or that, staring at it now, it sort of makes sense.

A long shower and several cups of black coffee later, the cobwebs have been pushed out of my head. I get to work and spend the rest of the day fine-tuning my wall. I feel like one of those scrapbooking Martha Stewart types my mother is friends with, cutting out pictures from magazines to make decoupage trays and keepsake boxes. Frustrated artists, I used to call them, until I realized it hurt my mother's feelings. She'd wanted to go to art school but her mother insisted she go to teachers' college instead so she'd have a dependable career. *You have to remember she grew up in the Depression,* my mother would say when I accused my grandmother of crushing her dreams. *You can't blame her for being risk-averse.*

Now I can see the appeal in collaging. My floor is littered with pictures printed off the Internet. Abe Reles's ugly pug-nosed face next to Caspar Osgood's urbanely handsome one, the sleek modernity of the Hi-Line next to the Art Deco curves of the Stork Club. I even find an illustration of the notorious "Black Rose" that looks a bit like Lillian.

I can't explain why I'm doing it or what I hope to accomplish, but I feel as if I'm moving around pieces of a jigsaw puzzle that got scattered when I was hit over the head. When I get them right I'll know what AJ saw at the Hi Line and my brain will be fixed. Or maybe Simon will know. He said that he wanted to talk about what happened at the club, but I don't know if he wants to find out what I know, or to tell me what *he knows.* Either way, it must be something sensitive in order for him to want to meet in private after all these months.

As I get dressed I feel a flutter of tension in my stomach. Is it the prospect of meeting with my boss outside the office? I wonder. After all, that's how so many of the women I interviewed say their trouble started. *He asked me to meet for drinks. He wanted to talk about my career over dinner.* But no, I tell myself, Simon's always behaved completely aboveboard. I'm just nervous because the last two times I tried to go out were disasters. To gird myself I dress as if I'm a '40s-era spy going on a mission: black turtleneck, high-waisted wool trousers, and a tan trench coat. I put on heels but think better of it, remembering how unsteady I've been on my feet, and change into heavy black boots. The only thing I need to complete my '40s noir look is a handgun. I settle for the can of mace that my mother gave me when I moved to the city (she couldn't help but inherit some of my grandmother's fears) and retrieve Lillian's locket from the paperclip dispenser on the desk. It feels cool and reassuring against my throat, tucked safely under my turtleneck.

At ten minutes to eight I leave the apartment, double-locking the door behind me. I pause outside Lillian's door, wondering if I should ask if she needs anything, but decide she's probably asleep.

I take the elevator down, cross the lobby, wave at Hector. I picture how I would look to someone watching on the surveillance camera: Intrepid reporter Joan Lurie out on assignment. I remember what Lillian said about how she was able to be braver when she was pretending to be Rose. I pretend I am young Lillian, spying on mobsters for the DA's Office, and it gets me out the door. I almost stop to light an imaginary cigarette I'm so into the role, but instead I touch my throat to feel Lillian's locket there, put my collar up against the chill, and stick my hands in my pockets, curling my fingers around the can of mace. I stride down the hill, breathing in the brisk October air. Dead leaves crunch under my feet, crisp and re-assuring. Not at all like the wet sand in my dreams.

I make it past the church and turn left. The Black Rose, according to Google Maps, is on a side street called Indian Road that curves off Seaman Avenue following the border of the park. Perhaps it was an Indian footpath when this part of Manhattan was still untracked wilderness. It's easy to imagine oneself outside time here at the tip of Manhattan. Ahead I see a glint of water, an inlet where the Harlem River flows into the Hudson. Across the water I can see the cliff where the Columbia crew team has painted a giant *C,* and the Metro-North tracks. Warm yellow light spills onto the sidewalk as a door opens, accompanied by laughter and voices and the smell of beer and french fries.

Maybe I'll have a burger and a dark ale.

Inside, the tavern is warm and welcom-ing, paneled in dark wood and lit by stained-glass lamps. The liquor bottles behind the bar gleam like a banked fire and an actual fire in a real fireplace crackles in a side room. I look around for Simon but he's not here yet. I pick a table in a corner near the fireplace, where I can watch the door. My server asks if I'm here for Irish folk music night and I laugh, thinking I'll bring Lillian down to hear the music sometime, and order a Guinness Stout. My phone pings and I see an email notification flash across my screen. From Simon: Delayed. Be there in fifteen minutes.

While I wait I read the back of the menu, which tells the history of the bar. Most of it I've already read online, but there's an extra bit here that's not on their website.

The legendary Black Rose hid in the Magdalen Refuge until her hiding place was discovered. Some surmise that her whereabouts were sold to the gangsters she was running from. She vanished from the Refuge on a cold winter's night in 1941. Was she killed by the mob and dumped in the river? Or did she escape on a passing northbound train and live out her life in anonymity in some small town? Perhaps we will never know.

I wonder if Lillian is the Black Rose. Did she keep Rose's name when she entered the Refuge? I take out my notebook to make a note to ask her — and hear a familiar voice.

"Always working, I see."

It's not even been five minutes since his email, but here he is, his face ruddy in the firelight, handsome rumpled tweed and loose-collared Oxford shirt. I'm glad I dressed down.

"You told me once that a good reporter's always working."

"That I did." He sits down and motions to the bartender to bring him a Guinness as well. Then he looks closer at me and frowns. "From the looks of you, I'd say you're working too hard, Joannie. Have you been sleeping? Is it the book? You know . . ." He looks over his shoulder as if checking to see if anyone is listening to us. A man in a baseball cap shifts a few inches away and turns to watch the musicians setting up. Simon moves closer to me. "Sometimes a story is so dark it can wreck you. Is there something you found that's bothering you? I have to admit I was worried when I got your email."

I begin to tell him that I'm afraid that this story *is* taking me someplace dark when I register what he said. "What do you mean when you got *my* email. *You* emailed *me*!"

Simon blinks and frowns — the frown I've seen him aim at reporters in editorial board meetings when they've said something stupid. "I *should* have emailed you sooner to check up on you, so I was glad to get your email, but a little surprised that you wanted to talk to me about the" — he looks behind him again and the baseball-cap guy shifts a fraction as if aware that Simon is looking at him — "the Hi-Line thing," he whispers. "I thought we'd gone over that and decided it was something Amanda had made up. I hope you haven't been basing your book on that."

He gives me a concerned smile and I feel my stomach curdle. Did I imagine Simon's email? Am I going crazy? "Wait," I say, reaching for my phone and opening my email app. "I'll show you." I scroll through my inbox as the singer croons about his *dark Rosaleen. Do not sigh! Do not weep!* I find the email from Simon and breathe a sigh of relief. "Look," I say, too loud, too eager. "Here it is! You even used the subject line 'Hi-Line Club.' "

Simon's eyes widen and he holds his hands up, patting the air to quiet me. Then he takes my phone from me and looks down. As he reads I listen to the plaintive song.

Woe and pain, pain and woe,
Are my lot, night and noon,

To see your bright face clouded so,
Like to the mournful moon —

Simon looks up, his face as clouded as the one described in the song. "This isn't from me," he says. "Look, there's an extra '1' in the address." He holds the phone up to me, but my eyes have gone blurry.

"But you got my answer!" I wail, rivaling the singer for woe and pain.

"I got an email from you asking me to meet you here." He takes out his phone, but I shake my head. There's no point in him showing it to me; my vision is so blurry I can barely make out his face.

"How?" I begin.

"Someone hacked into your email," he says. "They've set this up. My guess is they wanted to get you out of your apartment."

"To do what?" I ask, thinking of the crazy diagram on my living-room wall.

"My guess is that they want to see what you're working on. We should go back there and check."

"But if someone's there —"

"I'll be with you," he says, grabbing my elbow and steering me away from the bar.

"Shouldn't we call the police?" I ask as he propels me out the door.

"And tell them what?" Simon asks. "That

we can't remember who emailed whom?"

I'm thinking that's not exactly what happened, but I'm too breathless to answer as we racewalk up the steep hill. The park has grown quieter — and darker. I peer ahead into the gloom, looking for the lights of the Refuge, but I can barely make them out.

"Is it always this murky up here?" Simon asks.

"It's the river," I gasp. "Simon, wait up. Tell me what happened at the Hi-Line. Why would anyone be so worried about what I know to trick me out of my apartment? Why does it matter? Cass is dead —"

At Cass's name Simon reels around, his face looming angrily out of the fog. "Do you think that when a man like Cass goes down he goes down alone? Or that he cares who he takes down with him? Did he think about his wife and children when he killed himself? He'd drag his grandmother into hell if he thought he could sell her soul to the devil to ease his own discomfort. He'd —"

Simon's voice stops abruptly. He's looking behind me, down the hill. I start to turn around to see what he's looking at, but he grabs my arm and pulls me toward him. "I think we're being followed," he says in a low, urgent voice. Then an explosion goes off in my ear and Simon pushes me to the ground. His weight on me awakens that moment in my apartment when my assailant tackled me to the floor. I thrash against him, struggling to breathe, but then I realize what the sound was — a gunshot. Someone has shot at us and might be coming for us right now. Simon must realize the same thing. He pulls me to my feet and drags me into a blind run.

To where? I wonder, gulping mouthfuls of dank, wet fog. It smells like bleach and soap, like the closet Lillian hid in with Rose. Then we're out of the fog and at the door of the Refuge. I'm so grateful to see it that I push past Simon and into the lobby . . . which is empty. *Where's Hector? Did he hear that shot and run out to investigate?*

"We need to call the police!" I yell.

"Let's go to your apartment first," Simon says, punching the elevator button. I'm going to suggest we take the stairs, but the elevator opens and Simon pushes me in. He presses the button for the fifth floor and I slump against the back wall. For a moment I wonder how he knew what floor I live on, but then I'm pretty sure I must have bragged about living in "the penthouse."

"Holy shit," I say, my voice shaking, my stomach plummeting, and my knees giving out as we rise upward. "What *was* that?"

"Someone just shot at us," Simon replies, his breath ragged.

"What the hell! But *why*?"

He doesn't answer. When the door opens he checks the hall first as if he suspects someone is going to burst out of one of the doors. *Poor Lillian,* I think, *did she hear that shot?* With her history it would have frightened her. I think of checking in on her but first I need to get Simon into my apartment and call the police. I open my door and Simon walks past me, toward the desk as if drawn by the lamp . . . *Did I leave that on?*

"This is why," he says, looking at my wall. "This is why someone just tried to kill you. To keep you from finding out what happened at the Hi-Line."

CHAPTER EIGHTEEN

MELISSA

When I get back to my apartment Hector is already putting on his jacket and heading out the door.

"I'm sorry, *senora*," he says hurriedly. "I thought I heard a gunshot. I have to go —"

"A gunshot!" I cry, staring at his jacket and wondering how I'm going to get the keys into it. "Oh my God! I thought this was a safe neighborhood."

"Don't worry," he says, "no one will get inside this building to hurt you."

"Thank God you're here," I say, bursting into tears and collapsing against his chest.

He pats my back awkwardly as I slip the keys in his pocket, and then he steps back from me, his face red. Poor man. I've embarrassed him and myself but it couldn't be helped. I hope it doesn't give him any ideas, but as he hastily excuses himself and leaves I realize he's too much of a gentleman to take advantage of a distraught woman.

As soon as he's gone I pull the kitchen chair back in front of the camera so I can watch for Simon's exit. I check the elevator door and see it's paused on 5. Then I hear footsteps above me and a door opening. If only I had the apartment across from Joan's then I could watch them on the camera — *maybe if that old lady dies I could switch apartments* — to see if there's a good-night kiss.

But then I hear one set of heavy footsteps moving from the door to the window and another lighter set following. They are both standing at the window — admiring the river view? Or did they hear a gunshot too? Or is Simon staring at that crazy wall of Post-its? Of course he is. That's why they're standing there so long. Simon is probably telling her she needs to get help. She certainly looked like a madwoman on the lobby camera. But wait, how the hell did Simon show up at the fake date I had set up? Had Joan realized that the email was phony and called him? Maybe they are examining Joan's computer right now to find out how the email was sent.

If that's what they're doing, I might as well get what I can from Joan's computer before they disable the spyware. I sit down at my desk, conscious that I am sitting right below them, like a troll lurking beneath a bridge, *spying* on them. Being a spy suddenly doesn't feel so romantic, but at least this way I'll know if they stay in the living room and I'll know when Simon leaves.

It seems Simon will be staying all night. Eventually I hear footsteps leaving the living room and going down the hall, but I refuse to let myself follow them into my own bedroom to listen, even if it means staying up all night at my desk. Fortunately, it does not seem as if they have uncovered my spyware, and Joan's cloned computer proves an ample distraction through the small hours of the night. I learn how pathetic her finances were before the book deal — it's a crime what a pittance Simon was paying her at *Manahatta*! — and exactly what she got for her advance and how much she paid for the apartment. If she's not careful she's going to run out of money even before I do.

From Facebook I find out she's got a couple of friends from college who are growing annoyed that she never makes time for them and a string of shaggy, underemployed ex-boyfriends that she's well rid of. She's got terrible taste in men. One guy she dated sent her an invoice for half their Airbnb bill in the Catskills and, I find through her checking account statements, she paid it! Another broke up with her by email saying he didn't think she respected his *qi*. No wonder the poor girl hated men. But still, it's no excuse for her to have taken it out on my Cass.

The only thing I find to be remotely jealous of is her correspondence with her mother. There's a whole folder full of it, dating back to when Joan was in college (a second-rate state school). They're clearly close. Joan wrote her long emails about her classes, the books she was reading, the boys she liked. Although I dutifully text Whit and Emily every day, they hardly ever answer with anything more than the most perfunctory responses. Forget about taking my calls or emailing! Emily says no one talks on the phone or emails anymore. And Whit — Whit seems to be actively avoiding me.

The emails from her mother *are* a little boring, I'll admit. She's a teacher in a small town upstate and she writes about her students, complains about the principal and what the focus on standardized testing has done to the curriculum. She also reports on Joan's grandmother's deteriorating mental state.

"She still tells all the old stories she raised me on — you know the ones: growing up in the Depression, the bread lines, eating crusts for dinner, and then the glamorous war years, dating soldiers, dancing in nightclubs, marrying your grandfather just before he shipped out and then finding out the boat he was on had sunk — I bet you know them all as well as I do. But now she mixes up the details and comes up with these totally new stories as if she's reinventing her life. Which wouldn't be so bad except that she keeps getting stuck in the bad parts and getting scared. She's becoming increasingly paranoid. She thinks that bad men are after her and she gets up in the middle of the night and tries to climb out the windows. I'm afraid if she gets any worse I'll have to put her in a home."

Do you think, *Mrs. Lurie? The old woman clearly has dementia.*

I notice, too, that Joan is impatient with her mother. Her emails in the last year have grown terser.

That's so sad grandma can't remember her own name.

I really can't bear to see her like this.

Why don't you come down here if you want to see me so badly?

So maybe I'm not so jealous of Joan's special mother-daughter bond.

I move on to her research for "the story," as she refers to it, as if it's some goddamned biblical epic. Most of the background I've read already — and I've read more of it than she has. I see in her hard drive search field that she's been looking for the Amanda file I erased. I feel a pang of guilt for the frustration I must have caused her and I quickly squelch it. *Look at all the pain she's caused me!*

At least she quickly turned her efforts to looking for AJ — and found her Facebook, Instagram, and Twitter accounts. AJ herself is clearly MIA. She hasn't checked in to any of her social media accounts since June, when she used to post something at least once a day, although rarely a selfie, I notice. In fact, the only pictures of her are cryptic, partial shots — profiles with her sunglasses on and hair down as if she didn't want anyone to see her face. Nor does she give her last name. She's just A. Jay on Facebook, @arosegrowsinharlem on Twitter, and ARoseByAnyOtherName on Instagram. Many of her posts involve roses, but she hasn't posted so much as a petal since June 21 — the day of the gala. The day my world fell apart.

What happened to *her* on that day?

She's around Emily's age; surely she must have a mother who knows where she is — or is probably very worried about her.

I look back through AJ's Facebook. She's more active on Twitter and Instagram but Facebook is where her mother's more likely to post. I look through the comments and likes and find someone named Barbara. No one under fifty is named Barbara, so it has to be her mother or at least an aunt.

I switch to my own laptop and find Barbara's Facebook page. She's a retired nurse living in St. Petersburg, Florida. Before sending her a friend request I check the time. It's six A.M., a little early to send a request, but maybe not to an older person who probably gets up at the crack of dawn. First, though, I change my background picture on my Facebook page to a picture of a teacup and a hokey quote about tea being the elixir of the soul. Then I follow the tearoom where AJ worked and post an old picture of Emily and me having tea at Harrods. I'm hoping Barbara will think I know her daughter from the tea shop or that our daughters worked together (although I'd die if all Emily did with her college degree was *waitress*).

While I'm waiting to hear from Barbara, I look through more of Joan's search history. Oddly, after finding the tearoom, Joan started searching for information about some Depression-era criminal named Abe Reles and a racket called Murder Inc. What could that possibly have to do with AJ — or Cass, for that matter? Is she writing an article on 1940s crime figures? Shouldn't she be working on her book?

But when I look through her Word documents all I can find are some notes on her past research. There's no other recent document at all. Unless she's writing the book by hand (and no one Joan's age would even write a *letter* by hand), she hasn't written *anything*. And according to her contract, the book is due in less than four months.

Now, that's interesting.

Maybe I don't have to worry about Joan Lurie publishing any more scurrilous lies about Cass. Maybe she's realized she doesn't have enough material for a book —

But then why is she looking for this missing AJ person? The only connection is that she may have worked as a waitress at that party Cass went to at the Hi-Line Club. If her disappearance had to do with something that happened at the Hi-Line, wouldn't she have gone into hiding three years ago? But no, she went missing when Joan's story came out, so something in the story must have frightened her. Maybe she was afraid that Joan was going to try to get her to come forward to accuse Cass. Maybe her version of events that night didn't fit the picture of Cass that Joan's story portrayed and someone paid her to stay quiet.

I look again at the date of the party and remember that Cass had written a check that night to Pat Shanahan. . . .

And then it hits me. Cass wrote a check to Shanahan on May 15, 2015. But I'd always thought that Cass began donating to Shanahan *after* Whit's suicide attempt because of how kind Wally was to me on that day. But Whit tried to kill himself on May 21 — a date forever seared into my memory. Why was Cass writing a check to Pat Shanahan six days *before*?

It's nothing, I tell myself. Cass went to a fundraiser and wrote a check out, because that's what Cass did, play the big man. Which is what he did a week later, too, when he told me he was donating to Shanahan as a thank-you for Wally's help. I remember I had even teased him about donating to a conservative when he'd been such a liberal in college and he had quoted me that old chestnut about how if you aren't a liberal when you're young, you have no heart, but if you aren't a conservative when you're middle-aged, you have no head. Now it appears that conversion occurred the night of the Hi-Line party.

It's nothing, that little voice whispers again, only with a bit less conviction. It's not even for that big an amount —

Then I remember that I still haven't looked at his LLC files. Cass sometimes wrote checks on that account for business expenses. The folder is sitting on my desk where I left it earlier. I open it and find all the statements neatly arranged chronologically. I flip through them until I find the one for May 2015. There's a check to an accountant, one to a car service, and then one to Pat Shanahan, written the night of May 15, 2015, for $50,000.

Well. That was a lot. But then Cass sometimes got carried away with his enthusiasm and it was the night of the fundraiser. So it wasn't *that* unusual.

I flip through the next few statements and find, three months later, *another* $50,000 check made out to Pat's campaign. And another three months after that . . . and another . . .

I recalled Cass telling me once that LLCs could donate unlimited amounts to political campaigns.

That's why I get invited to so many fundraisers, he said.

He liked to feel like an important man, his fingers on the pulse of power. I knew he'd contributed to Shanahan's campaign, but I'd never imagined —

I go through all the statements for the last three years, highlighting the donations to Shanahan. They add up to over a million dollars.

WTF, as Emily would say. While he was second mortgaging our house and borrowing on his life insurance he was donating a million dollars to a political campaign. This wasn't a political cause; it was extortion. Pat Shanahan had something over him. Something that had happened the night of the Hi-Line party. Something this girl AJ knew about. And apparently this girl AJ had gone missing the night of my gala. Could, I wonder, feeling suddenly very cold, Cass have had anything to do with her disappearance?

As I'm pondering that dreadful possibility my laptop pings. Barbara has accepted my friend request and sent me a message: Do you know where my daughter is?

I feel a sickening pang of guilt. How would I feel if Emily or Whit were missing? And what if Cass had something to do with it? But no, Cass wouldn't have been capable of hurting someone, especially a girl Emily's age, and besides, Emily wouldn't have been running around the outer boroughs sporting tattoos and working as a waitress and Whit —

Whit had worked as an intern for Pat Shanahan. It makes me ill to think of him involved in any of this. I'll call him tomorrow and make sure he takes my call. We'll have a long talk and I'll call Emily after. I'll make clear to both kids that they must check in regularly. In the meantime, I need to find AJ to make sure she's okay and find out what really happened the night of the Hi-Line party.

I click Reply and type: Oh no, is AJ missing? I noticed she wasn't at the tea shop when I got back from my summer place in the Hamptons —

I backspace over *Hamptons* and type *country* instead. I don't want Barbara to think I'm a snob.

And I wondered what had happened to her. She's such a lovely girl!

Barbara doesn't answer right away. I imagine her preening at the praise of her daughter as I do whenever anyone says something nice about Whit or Emily. Maybe she's wiping away a tear as I find myself doing right now, thinking about Whit and Emily and wondering how they're doing at Brown and Bard. Parents' weekend is coming up at Bard, and I asked Emily if she wanted me to come but she said it was "kind of lame." But now I wonder if she won't feel lonely with all the other parents there —

A long message bubble pops up on my screen.

That's so sweet of you to say. The fact is that I haven't heard from her since the last week of June. She said she was going to upstate New York to work at a resort in the Catskills and that I shouldn't be concerned if I didn't hear from her because there was no cell phone service or wifi, but I thought she'd at least call once in a while and she hasn't. To tell you the truth I'm sick with worry.

Of course she is. What twentysomething voluntarily goes without Wi-Fi and their phone? It sounds like she's joined a cult. I think what to say next. How can I get her to give me information?

Has she ever done anything like this before?

Again there's a long pause and I worry that I've offended her. When Whit OD'd people asked the same question and I could always tell they were thinking that *I* must have done something wrong to have my son end up with so many problems. Not that *Cass* had done anything wrong. Everyone always blames the mother. I'm about to type that I didn't mean to suggest it was her fault when another bubble appears.

Actually, yes. She ran away when she was 16 and she dropped out of college last year. She's always been a bit rebellious which is why I think the police aren't taking it seriously. But I think this is different. She was worried about something earlier in the summer. She said some reporter was bugging her.

Ah, I think, relieved that it was Joan who had chased the poor girl out of the city, not my husband.

That's terrible, I type, I know how unscrupulous they can be.

351

She replies right away. I even came up here to New York to look for her myself but none of her friends will talk to me. They all act like I'm being hysterical and that I'm violating AJ's privacy rights by wanting to know where she is!

I know exactly what she means. Emily's and Whit's friends act exactly the same way. This poor woman.

Then I have an idea.

You said you're in New York now?

Yes, she types, I'm staying at a Catholic hostel in Chelsea. It was all I could afford. I'm going out of my mind here with no one to talk to. And I've been here for two weeks now and have had no luck finding my daughter!

I shudder, imagining how dreary that place must be. The woman deserves a good lunch.

Would you like to meet? I think I have an idea of how to find her.

She answers with a heart emoji and one of an angel. Oh God, I hope she isn't some born-again fanatic. But if she is it will be all the more newsworthy when I reunite her with her daughter. As I make a date to meet at Buvette, a darling little French café in the West Village that Sylvia told me about last year, a flicker of motion draws my attention to the camera screen. Simon is getting out of the elevator and walking across the lobby, sweater knotted over his shoulders. He exchanges a smirk with Enda. I can practically smell the testosterone from here. He won't look so smug when I expose the lies he published about Cass and how his reporter hounded that poor girl out of the city. The girl I'm going to find and reunite with her mother. I can't think of a better way to rehabilitate my own image.

CHAPTER NINETEEN

JOAN

"Is that why you told me not to follow up Amanda's story about what happened at the Hi-Line party?" I ask. "Because you thought it was too dangerous?"

He sighs and sinks down in the wingback chair, the springs groaning as if protesting that anyone heavier than Lillian sit on it. "I suppose that doesn't sound very professional," he says. "And I wasn't completely honest. You see, I was at that party —"

"At a fundraiser for Pat Shanahan? But he's a *Republican*!"

Simon laughs, then assembles his face into a stern expression. "A newspaperman can't be biased. We have to cover both sides objectively —"

"So you were covering the party?" I ask, interrupting a lecture I've heard a million times before.

He frowns. "Not exactly. But Sylvia told

354

me about the party and she got me in as her plus one." He laughs again. "She actually wanted me to join the club and I went along with the idea because I wanted to see who had turned out for Pat Shanahan. I was surprised to see Cass there. He'd been a liberal in college, even fancied himself a Socialist . . ." Simon smiles. "Easy posing as a Socialist when you've got a big trust fund waiting for you."

There's a note of bitterness in Simon's voice I haven't heard before that makes me think about the rumors that he was envious of Caspar Osgood. Could it be true that he okayed my story because he wanted revenge on his college nemesis? I try to focus back on the main point. "So you saw Osgood at the party? Did you see him with Amanda? Did you see him mistreat any of the servers?"

"Of course not," he says, looking out the window where there's nothing to see but fog. "If I'd seen anything like that, I'd have said something."

"So why didn't you let me follow this up?" I cry.

"Because I thought it was too dangerous," Simon says, turning back to me. "I know, that's not a good reason for an editor, but I'm afraid I wasn't being completely . . .

objective. I was worried about *you.* Shanahan has a reputation for playing . . . *rough.* I thought if he was involved in a cover-up and you got too close, well . . ." He holds up his hands. "Look what happened tonight. Someone tried to kill us because they think you're getting too close."

"We have to call the police," I say again.

"And tell them what? We have no proof that what happened tonight had anything to do with Shanahan."

"We can't just do nothing! This girl — AJ — she's been missing since June." I sit down at my desk chair and show him AJ's Facebook page. "One of the servers where she worked says they haven't seen her in almost four months."

"That doesn't make sense," Simon says. "If she ran because of something she saw that night at the Hi-Line why did she wait three years?"

I've been puzzling that out myself. "It must have been something in my story," I say. "It looks like she went AWOL right around the time the article came out. Maybe when she read my story she realized that the man who assaulted Amanda was Cass Osgood."

"But wouldn't that have made her *less* scared that he'd been exposed already? No

356

one would have had any reason to keep her quiet then. And then with him being dead, what would she be afraid of?"

"She might have been afraid of Shanahan. If you're right that Shanahan left the party to help Osgood —"

"I didn't say that —" Simon begins.

"But it's what you thought. That's the reason you didn't want me following the Hi-Line lead. Because you thought Shanahan was involved. What if Shanahan — or his people — threatened AJ?"

Simon shakes his head. "But why would he wait until the story came out?"

"I don't know," I admit. "Maybe something in the story worried them and they went looking for AJ and she got scared. We have to find her —"

"That's exactly what you can't do, Joan." He pulls my chair closer to him. His face is lit by the glow of my computer screen, his eyes are dark pits, the lines around his mouth deep grooves as if carved into stone. "You can't keep looking for her. It's too dangerous."

"I can't just ignore that she might be in danger," I say.

"She's gone to ground," he says. "And that's what you have to do. Just stay here and keep laying low. You'll be safe here. I'll find out if Shanahan is really involved in this. I-I'd never forgive myself if anything happened to you."

His voice hoarsens and trembles. I'm alarmed to see that he's on the verge of tears. I move closer to him — to comfort him — and his arms are suddenly wrapped around me. I freeze, paralyzed. I can feel his hot breath on my neck, the rough tweed of his jacket against my face, suffocating. I can't breathe. He must feel my muscles stiffen, because he pulls away.

"I'm sorry —" he begins. "I didn't mean —"

"It's okay," I say, getting up, not entirely sure what just happened. Was he making an advance? Had I given him a reason to think that's what I wanted? *Did* I want that? I've always wanted Simon's admiration, the validation of him thinking I was a good reporter. I knew that some people thought we were having an affair.

It's what people are saying about you and Simon Wallace, Roslyn had said.

Had I given Simon the wrong idea? Did he think I'd just been waiting for the story to be over?

Only, the story isn't over. The lamp light has fallen on the picture of the Black Rose pinned to my wall. Just as Lillian was still stuck in that moment at the Half Moon I am still reliving the attack in my East Village apartment. The story isn't over; it's still happening right now, right here.

Simon must see the fear in my face. "I don't want to leave you," he says. "Maybe I should sleep on the couch tonight."

I nod, too numb to even thank him, then I go down the hall to my room and lock the door behind me.

Early the next morning I hear Simon moving around the living room, but I pretend to be asleep, too embarrassed at last night's awkwardness to face him. All night I tossed and turned, reliving the attack in my apartment — only now it had merged with the memory of Simon knocking me to the ground even though Simon had only been trying to protect me from whoever the hell was shooting at me. Was I never going to be able to trust any man again?

I wait until I hear the front door close, then I hurry to get up and lock the door behind him. Then I go to my desk. My expensive view has been obliterated by fog and rain. I am cut off from the rest of the world, just as Lillian was. She went into hiding here right after she witnessed Abe Reles fall from the Half Moon Hotel — just as I have. *Gone to ground,* that's what Simon said. I see that he's left a note on a Post-it on my laptop. "Don't go out again until you hear from me. I've got a friend down in city hall I can talk to confidentially. I'll handle everything. You focus on taking care of yourself and staying safe. — S"

It almost makes me laugh. I don't need Simon's warning to keep me here; my own fear and trauma are prison guards enough.

I go to the kitchen to make coffee, moving as if through a fog trying to make out shapes in the mist. When I get back to my desk and check on my laptop I see that neither AJ nor Stacy has answered my messages. It's clear that they don't want to be found, so why should I risk my life looking for them? I can't think of anything else to do to find them. I look up at my wall and think about Lillian's story. Were she and Frank able to find Rose? Was the mystery of Abe Reles's death ever solved? I ask Bot to read me the contemporary coverage of Abe Reles's death.

While the official story was that Reles had fallen while trying to escape, there were suspicions that the police had been bribed to look the other way while Reles was thrown from the window, but no one was ever indicted. I ask Bot to find out what had become of Frank Maloney, the assistant DA whom Lillian was so fond of, but she's unable to find any reference to his future career. Maybe he decided he'd had enough of crime and politics after he lost his star witness for his big case.

I ask Bot to tell me about the DA in charge of the investigation, William O'Dwyer. He apparently had gone on to become mayor of New York City, but things didn't end up so well in the long run for him. In 1949 Mayor O'Dwyer was accused of associating with organized crime figures and was forced to resign from office. Was it such a stretch, then, to assume he'd had contacts with organized crime figures in 1941? That he was the one who arranged to let Eddie Silver and his thugs into the Half Moon Hotel to kill off his star witness? Maybe he was the man that Rose saw in the stairwell that scared her so much. I'm just about to ask Bot if there are any theories about O'Dwyer's role in Abe Reles's death when I hear a tapping at the door. I'm wondering who could be visiting so early, but then I look at the time and see that it's past noon. I've somehow spent the whole morning listening to articles about Abe Reles and Murder Inc. and Mayor O'Dwyer. I go to the door, embarrassed to still be in my bathrobe, and find Lillian.

"Oh, did I wake you?" she asks.

"Not at all," I say. "I just lost track of time. I was down a rabbit hole of research." I gesture at my desk, realizing Lillian probably isn't familiar with losing time on the Internet. She takes my gesture as an invitation to walk toward my desk.

"Your story got me interested in Murder Inc. —" I begin to explain, embarrassed for her to see all those references to her own past tacked to my wall like specimens, but she interrupts me by tapping her finger on a picture of AJ.

"Who's this?" she asks.

"A girl who's gone missing," I say.

"Like Rose," she says with a sigh, sitting down in the wingback chair. "She vanished after we split up beneath the boardwalk. Frank looked for her for weeks."

"You must have been worried about her," I say. Lillian points her toes to touch the floor.

"I was," she says. "Every time Frank visited I was afraid he was there to tell me they'd found her body in the river."

"Frank visited?" I ask, noting the wistfulness in her eyes when she says his name. What had become of him, I wonder. Maybe he died in the war. Maybe his picture is in the locket she gave me, which I haven't opened because it would feel like prying.

"Oh yes. Of course, it was part of his job. I was one of his star witnesses, after all. I could place Eddie Silver at the Half Moon on the night Abe Reles died. Frank said they were building a case against him, but his boss wanted to know who Rose saw coming up the stairs with Eddie that night before they could proceed. He kept asking me about that: What had I seen? Had Rose told me anything about what she had seen? Had she mentioned any names? I felt like I was disappointing him every time he came . . ." She pauses at the sound of a train whistle and looks out the window, as if hoping that Frank is on that train coming back to her.

"You couldn't help what you *hadn't* seen." I think about the man who attacked me whose face I never saw but who seems to be always with me. And I consider the invisible figure in the fog last night who shot at me and Simon. It all feels like a dream — or a nightmare. "But it must have been frustrating . . . a blank spot you could never fill in."

Lillian turns from the window to look at me, her eyes brimming, as if the river fog has filled them with watery light. "Yes, that's it exactly. There's always been this" — she splays her age-marked hand over her heart

363

— "this *hole.* I tried as hard as I could to remember everything about that night but all I could remember was that man lunging for me, the weight of his body on mine, the smell of the couch cushions, not being able to breathe . . ."

I put my hand on Lillian's arm; she's trembling. "You were sexually assaulted," I say. "That's a traumatic event. When I was researching the story on Cass Osgood I read about the science of what happens in the brain during a traumatic event. The chemicals released during trauma increase the storage of central details and make peripheral details fade. So the details of that policeman's face — the smell of the couch cushions, the song playing on the radio, the view out the window —"

I see myself on the landing of my old apartment looking for my keys. I hear a step behind me . . . A hand covers my mouth . . . A sickly sweet smell fills my head . . . My heart is pounding . . . I can't see anything . . . he's put something over my head . . . he knocks me to the floor and I struggle wildly . . . then my head hits the floor . . . *he drives my head into the floor . . .* and everything goes black. I have less to remember in my attack than Lillian but that moment is as indelibly burned into my memory as hers is.

"Those details are seared into your brain forever while the flight from the hotel, what Rose said about some guy on the stairs —"

Fragments from the night of the publication party swirl in my head — Sylvia and Simon arguing on the patio, Andrea Robbins telling me I was part of a new vanguard, a server handing me another glass of Champagne, Simon and Sylvia on the terrace . . . those memories feel faded.

"It's natural that you don't remember them as well."

Lillian nods. "Yes, that's it exactly. I remember that stupid freckled cop but not what Rose said to me under the boardwalk. She might have been telling me where she was going to hide, but I couldn't remember. I told Frank, though, that Rose had an aunt upstate in a town on the river — Barrytown it was called. Frank wanted to go up there but he was afraid she'd run if she heard a cop was looking for her. He thought that if we went together on the train maybe I'd be able to find her. To tell you the truth, I didn't think so. I thought that if Rose had gone to ground she'd not come out even for me, and especially not if she saw me with Frank. But I liked the idea of an excursion up the river with Frank . . ." She blushes. "I suppose you'll think it was vain of me. Here my friend was running for her life and I was dreaming of picnics in the country."

"I think you were very young to be locked up here with a bunch of dour nuns and it would be sensible to want to get out."

She gives me a grateful smile and then tilts her head. "Spoken like a girl who has an eye on a fellow of her own."

Now it's my turn to blush. Lillian's keen eyes have taken in my late-morning deshabille and made the obvious connection. "Well," I admit, "my editor did come by last night . . . but I don't . . . it's not like that . . . not that anything happened . . ." I debate telling her about what happened in the park, but that would only scare her. She misinterprets my hesitation.

"I'm sorry," Lillian says. "I didn't mean to upset you. Perhaps you'd better not rush into anything."

"Oh . . . I won't . . ." I blush again. "But what about your Frank? Did you go upstate together?"

Before Lillian can answer, a bell chimes on the computer, startling her. "What on Earth?"

"It's a message notification alert." I move my chair closer and see that Stacy has returned my Facebook message. "Oh, do you mind?" I ask. "It's from the friend of the girl I'm looking for."

"Let's see!" Lillian says, excited. "How do you get her message?"

The page is open to the picture of AJ and Stacy standing in a gazebo with a stretch of water behind them. Like all the pictures it doesn't show AJ's face clearly, but looking at her silhouette I feel like she reminds me of someone . . . but the image goes out of focus in my head before I can think who. When I open the message box I see with dismay that the print is too small for me to read. I'm thinking of asking Bot to read it but then Lillian volunteers. "May I?" she asks.

"Please," I say.

Lillian reads in a crisp, businesslike voice that she might have used to read back a transcription when she worked as a stenographer. "AJ would be happy that you're interested in her cartoons but she's not available right now. She's gone out of town to take care of a sick relative. I'll pass along your information to her, though, if you will give me your name and address and reporter credentials. Thanxxx!" Lillian drops the business voice. "She's misspelled 'thanks' and added some yellow dots with faces on them."

"Emojis," I explain to Lillian. "What do you think of Stacy's message?"

"That she's lying," Lillian says without hesitation. "There's no sick relative. This AJ is hiding because she's scared and her friend wants to know more about you before giving you any information. You can tell what good friends they are from this picture."

Lillian peers closer at the screen and reads the caption. "It says Camp Bernadette Forever."

"Hm," I say, peering at the picture. "A camp might be a good place to hide." I inch closer to the computer and type in "Camp Bernadette," but even before it comes up Lillian says, "I know where it is — that tall mountain behind them is Storm King. Frank and I passed it on our way up to Barrytown. Across the river is —"

"Stratford," I finish, recalling the town from my own train trips home.

"So," she says, her eyes flashing. "When are you going to go find her?"

Chapter Twenty

MELISSA

It's raining when I get up, and the morning news is ranting about a hurricane that's coming up the East Coast and is going to cause flooding and power outages and sea surges. They're going on like it's the storm of the century. It's the usual hysterical hype that Cass attributed to the television news outlets' hunger for ratings. Even Sandy, which was the worst storm New York ever had, wasn't really as bad as everyone made it out to be. Sure, we were without power and Internet for a couple of days, but it was kind of fun camping out with the kids, toasting marshmallows over the fireplace and eating by candlelight. Of course, if you were on the Jersey Shore or Staten Island it was worse, but those people should have thought twice before building in a flood zone.

Thanks to the rain, it'll take forever to go downtown in an Uber, so I'll have to take the subway. When I type the address into Waze my phone tells me that I can get the A train just a few blocks from my apartment and take it practically to the restaurant's front door. Easy-peasy. I'll take a selfie on the subway and send it to Whit and Emily. Won't they be surprised! Maybe I'll send one to Wally too. She'll die of shock.

I dress down so I won't intimidate Barbara but nice enough to show respect for her situation: black ponte skinny pants tucked into tall Hunter rain boots, cashmere sweater, and the classic Burberry Cass bought me in England ten years ago. I tie an Hermès scarf over my hair, put on the matching wide-brimmed rain hat, and grab an umbrella.

Enda offers to get me a taxi but I tell him I'm just walking to the subway. His eyes widen like I've told him I'm going out to rob a bank. Really, people stereotype the rich. (Not that I'm rich anymore; at least, not now, but once I sell *my* book I will be again.) Why doesn't anyone write about that? Maybe I'll do an opinion piece for the *Times*.

It's barely raining as I walk through the park. The cool, misty air feels good on my face and I imagine it's making my complexion all dewy even though it's probably not particularly clean rain here in the city. I make a mental note to do a charcoal face mask tonight since I can't afford to see my usual aesthetician.

The subway station is easy to find on the corner of Broadway and Isham. I'm a little startled by how tawdry the neighborhood looks over here, and when I go down into the station I can't help but notice what a mixed crowd it is. There *are* a few young professionals though, including a sweet redheaded girl who I decide is a safe option to stand next to.

When the train comes, I board with her, but after five minutes, we haven't budged. I turn to her and ask, "Why are we still sitting here? Are we waiting for someone?"

The girl laughs. "There's always a delay because there's only one track out, so they have to wait for it to be clear. The good thing is you always get a seat at 207th . . . oh look, the doors are closing."

The doors close but we sit for another five minutes. The redhead, who tells me her name is Chloe, asks polite questions about where I'm going and how many children I have and obligingly takes a selfie of both of us that I post on Facebook. Chloe seems like a well-bred girl, so I'm surprised to learn that she's working as a bartender/

371

dogwalker/babysitter.

"I interned at corporate offices but I hated it," she tells me. "I'm writing a graphic novel."

She shows me her sketchpad, which is full of drawings. I tell her they're very good but express concern that it must be hard to make a living that way.

"Almost impossible!" she says cheerfully. "But you gotta try, right?"

"Maybe you could go back to school," I suggest tactfully. "You could be an art teacher."

Chloe smiles. "Yeah . . . well, maybe. Only, I'm working three jobs to pay off my student loans from college so I'm not sure how I'd manage that."

The train finally moves. At each stop more people get on. By 168th Street there are no seats left. By 145th there's a solid wall of people in front of us. Chloe gets up for an elderly woman and stands in front of me. When the elderly woman gets off at 125th a large man takes her place and spreads his legs so wide I have to squeeze up against the guard rail. Chloe rolls her eyes and mouths *manspreader* to me.

"The train runs express from here to Fifty-Ninth," Chloe tells me. "I'm getting out at Fourteenth, and you're the stop right after. Take the stairs to your right and you'll be only a few feet from your restaurant. I think it's probably raining pretty hard by now."

"When do you take the train back up-town?" I ask, hating to see Chloe go.

"Around one," she tells me.

"In the morning? Doesn't your mother worry?"

She laughs. "Yeah, she's admitted she's tracked me on FindMyiPhone. . . . Maybe I'll see you around the neighborhood. My roommate and I go to trivia night at the Black Rose sometimes."

We exchange phone numbers and I tell her to text me if she ever needs anything. Chloe's made me miss Whit and Emily. I text them both but the texts aren't delivered because there's no service.

I ride the next couple stops alone and when the train halts at West Fourth Street, I exit to find water cascading down the station stairs and wind driving sheets of rain sideways. Thanks to Chloe's helpful directions, I make my way seamlessly to the correct sidewalk, but my umbrella turns inside out instantly and is torn from my hands to join the rest of the broken umbrellas littering the streets. I am soaked by the time I enter Buvette. I go straight to the ladies' to blot off my damp face and scrub my hands clean of subway grime. I'm seated at a table under a cooling vent and complain to the hostess to turn down the air conditioning. I order hot tea to make my point and prepare to wait.

Which I do for the next forty-five minutes.

I check my phone for messages. I'd given Barbara my cell phone number — de rigueur for meeting in real life, I'd thought — but I notice now that she had not reciprocated. Still, she could have Facebook messaged me or called the restaurant. But I suppose if she'd chickened out she wouldn't do either.

The waiter refills my sparkling water for the third time and asks if I'd like to order something while waiting for my guest to arrive. There's that hint of condescension in his voice that waiters reserve for the stood-up, but I somehow doubt it's employed for pretty young girls or powerful older men. The fact that I'm waiting for someone I was trying to help means nothing. I am still a middle-aged woman sitting alone in a restaurant in the middle of the day in the middle of a worsening storm. The idea of eating here alone seems embarrassing.

"I suppose my friend's been hindered by the weather," I say, rising to my feet and looking at my watch. "I should be getting home."

I step outside into the shelter of the awning and stare at the rain-swept street. Two taxis go by but they're off duty. I try my Uber app, but there's a fifteen-minute wait for the next car and it says my trip back home will take over an hour. The subway station yawns across the street, but the thought of going back underground into that fetid tunnel seems unbearable. Besides, I'm hungry — and angry at being stood up.

I check Waze and see that the Bosie tearoom is only a ten-minute walk south. Why not put some of Joan's research to work? Plus, their scones looked delicious in the pictures on Google. I put up my collar, fasten my rain hat, and step out into the deluge.

Unable to check my phone in the pouring rain and blinkered by my wide-brimmed hat I get turned around in the maze of West Village streets. It takes me more like twenty minutes to find the diminutive tearoom on a side street. I stumble in, drenched, shedding sheets of water like a large Labrador. A young woman behind the bar greets me by shouting, "Ahoy! Come aboard!"

I open my mouth to laugh, but a sob

comes out instead. I feel like I've been dragged out of the sea — a shipwrecked survivor. The tearoom even looks like a ship, paneled in deep honey-colored wood, the walls lined with round brass urns, the air steamy with exotic spices. The young woman behind the counter doesn't look at all fazed by a crying customer.

She offers me a table or a seat at the bar. I take the bar, huddling up close to this friendly girl as if she were a banked fire. She is wearing a black T-shirt that says Tea-Witch, a ruby glints from her left nostril, and half her head is shaved. She might be a pirate.

"Can I get you some hot tea to start? You look chilled."

I stare up at the wall of brass urns. There must be over a hundred varieties of tea in this little shop.

"We just got in a very rare milk oolong from Taiwan. It's very hard to get and flies off the shelves. That's what I'm drinking." She waves her hand over the teacup in front of her as if performing a spell and I catch a whiff of caramel and butterscotch.

"Yes, thank you," I say.

She measures tea from a canister and pours hot water into a china teapot while I strip off my sodden coat and hat and hang them on a wrought-iron coat rack. There are a handful of other customers — an elderly man reading a foreign newspaper, two Asian women talking low, their heads bent close together, a middle-aged woman tapping away at a laptop. The glass plate windows are steamed over, giving the tearoom an air of an underwater waiting room — but to what I'm not sure.

When I sit back down there's a delicate china teacup, a teapot, and an egg timer, white sand slipping steadily through its pinched glass throat. There's also a china plate with a scone and tiny glass jars filled with clotted cream and raspberry jam.

"These just came out of the oven," the waitress says. "I thought you looked like you could use a little sustenance."

Grateful and touched by the gesture, I take a bite of the scone, which is so good I nearly swoon.

"Good, right?" she says, pouring the tea.

I take a sip of the tea and it warms me down to the bones. "This is delicious," I say. "I heard about this place from one of my daughter's friends who used to work here. A girl named AJ? Did you know her?"

The girl is looking down at the tea she is pouring. When she looks up the warmth is gone from her eyes. "A lot of people have been looking for AJ," she says.

"Oh?" I try to look surprised. "Is she missing?"

"People are looking for her," she repeats, "that she doesn't want to find her. So, as you can imagine, I can't give any information about AJ to someone I don't know." Gone is the warm, tea-wielding waitress, replaced by a steely examiner.

"Of course," I say warmly. "You're protecting your friend. You must be so worried about her and you can't tell whom to trust. What kind of people have been asking for her? Reporters? They can be ruthless."

The girl makes a face. "You have no idea. There was one pretending to be her mother."

"Her mother? I ask, remembering what Barbara had said about the staff at Bosie being unhelpful.

"Yeah. This woman calling herself Barbara sent me a Facebook message saying she was AJ's mother."

"And that's not her mother's name?" I ask.

"Well, here's the thing." The young woman leans across the bar and lowers her voice. "AJ's mother died six months ago."

"Oh!" I say, feeling suddenly cold despite the warm tea.

"Is something wrong?"

"I just remembered something . . . at home . . ." I get up, knocking over the stool. Barbara — *my* Barbara — isn't AJ's mother. But why would she agree to meet me . . . Unless she wanted me out of my apartment just like I wanted Joan out of hers. Which means —

"I have to go," I say to the waitress. "How much do I owe you."

She shakes her head. "It's on the house, and here . . ." She hands me a card. It has the name Katy Morrison on it and under it the phrase "Tea Witch" with a drawing of a gloved hand pouring a cup of tea. "Let me know what you find out and I'll see if AJ would be willing to talk to you."

The streets are flooded and empty of taxis. There's no choice but to take the subway. I descend into the wet, slippery station and wait fifteen minutes on a sweltering platform before I'm rewarded with a humid, crowded car. I manage to grab the last seat between two enormous manspreaders, and then sit thinking about how I've been duped. I find the last message from "Barbara" and reply back, Who are you really?

Then I check the MataHari app to see if "Barbara" has been in touch with Joan. Two can play at this game. MataHari reports activity on Joan's Facebook with AJ's account, but it's not with Barbara; it's with someone named Stacy. Joan has sent her a message claiming she wants to do a story on AJ's cartoons — an obvious ruse that Stacy replied to with an evasive answer. Then Joan did a Google search for something called Camp Bernadette. I click on the link to the camp but the site won't load. We must have lost service.

The train stops and I look up to see what station we're at but there's nothing outside the windows but sooty cement. We're between stations, so why are we stopping? I look around but no one in the car looks alarmed. Everyone is either looking down at their phones or asleep. I remember what Chloe said about the train stopping between stations. Usually it's nothing —

Usually.

The man sitting to my right shifts, pressing his damp, beefy leg against mine. I try to inch over, but the man to my left is large and unbudging. I try to make myself smaller. I look across the aisle, hoping to make eye contact with someone sympathetic — a nice girl like Chloe — but the middle-aged woman in nurse scrubs across from me returns my gaze blankly. As if I'm invisible.

Then the lights go out.

A few people groan, but as if this is a common inconvenience, not a disaster. The conductor comes on and mutters something completely unintelligible. It's not just the lights that are out; it's the ventilation as well. As the car warms it fills with an odiferous *fug* that smells like wet dog and decomposing bodies —

It smells like Cass's open grave. It's as if I have been buried with him and these last few months have been a dream — or a nightmare. Which is what it's felt like. This isn't my life — living in a rundown building in a grungy neighborhood practically in the Bronx, breaking the law to snoop on my neighbor, riding the subway for an hour to be stood up. I've been sent to purgatory to atone for my sins.

But what have I done? Even if Cass did those terrible things — and how terrible must it have been if he'd paid out a million dollars to Pat Shanahan to make it go away? — *I* didn't know about them.

Girls all compliant like Melissa Osgood, Joan had written. Had I been compliant? Had I been willfully blind? The thought creeps down my spine and spreads into a warm, damp sensation through my legs —

No, that warm, damp feeling on my leg

isn't guilt; it's a hand. The man to my right has his hand, which is heavy and hot as a piece of cooked meat, on my leg. How long has it been there? Why am I still sitting here, anaesthetized, on the slick, clammy seat? That it's been there all this time without me realizing makes it feel as if I'm somehow complicit in its presence.

The lights go back on and the hand is gone. The train judders to life. I look around at the blank faces for someone I could tell, but why would they believe me? Would they care? I stand up and hang on to the pole, trying not to think about all the germs on it and trying to pretend I am somewhere else and that I am *someone* else — the person I was four months ago to whom this would never, ever happen.

As we pull into the next station, my phone chimes to life and I look down hoping that it's a text from Emily or Whit. Instead it's a landscape that might have been painted by a Hudson River School artist.

Camp Bernadette, where dreams come true and lifetime memories are made.

It looks like a good place to run to.

It looks like a good place to hide.

It looks like the place AJ might be.

Joan must think so too. She's looked up the Metro-North train schedule. But it appears she's looked up the timetable for tomorrow. She probably doesn't want to go in the storm. If I go now, I have a chance of getting to AJ first.

CHAPTER TWENTY-ONE

JOAN

I can see that Lillian expects me to go to the camp right away, but I told Simon I wouldn't go searching for AJ myself.

"I think I'd better wait until the storm is over," I say. It's a lame excuse — even I know that the real reason I'm not going is that I'm scared to leave the safety of the Refuge — and Lillian looks justifiably disappointed.

"She must be so frightened," she says, looking at the picture of AJ and Stacy. "Rose was . . . when I found her."

"So you did find her?"

"Yes . . ." Lillian is trembling.

I imagine she needs time to herself to regain her composure. She's reliving the trauma of an attack that took place seventy-seven years ago. "Come away from the window," I say, "and I'll make us some more hot tea."

"I like looking out the window," Lillian replies. "It makes me feel less shut-in. But I will take another cup of tea if you don't mind my company for a little longer. This storm has . . . *unsettled* me."

I tell her of course I don't mind, and go to make the tea. While I'm in the kitchen I email Simon from my phone to tell him what we found out. He replies right away, telling me to stay put and that he'll check out the camp. As I stand waiting for the water to boil I wonder if I will be reliving that moment on the threshold of my apartment seventy-plus years from now. It doesn't seem fair that we're marked by our worst moments. Shouldn't we get to choose what defines us?

Lillian must be thinking the same thing. "My life feels like this river," she says, not looking away from the window as I put her teacup on the desk. "I know it's out there rolling to the sea, but I can only make out bits through the fog and sometimes, when the tide comes in and the river flows backward, the only parts I can see clearly are the ones that are farthest away: my mother falling that day in the kitchen, Tommy's face when the police came for him, that cop's hand over my face . . . the rest of it feels like a dream."

"But you found Rose," I say, hoping to divert her from these painful moments with a positive accomplishment, "and had a picnic with Frank on the way?"

She smiles, her eyes still on the window. "It was raining so we ate sandwiches on the train. That's what I think about when I hear the train whistle — wax paper and pastrami and rye from Katz's Deli on the Lower East Side. Frank bought them downtown on his way up from the courthouse before coming to get me. I remember he laughed when I told him I'd never had a pastrami sandwich and he called me his *shayna maidelah*. That means —"

"Pretty girl," I say. "My grandmother grew up in Brooklyn and she said the boys in the deli called her that."

Lillian smiles. "I bet your grandmother was a pretty girl if you take after her."

"She always said I looked like my grandfather, but he died in the war so my mother never saw him and all the family pictures were lost in a fire so . . . anyway, you ate sandwiches on the train . . . ?"

"Yes, and cream sodas, which I'd never had either. It was all so delicious after the gruel and thin soup the nuns gave us here. Frank told me stories about the places we passed — Spuyten Duyvil Creek, which he said was named because of a Dutchman who swam across it to spite the devil. Henry Hudson anchored his ship, the *Half Moon,* there and people said you could sometimes see the ghost ship in the fog. When we passed Storm King Mountain he said that was where the ghosts of Henry Hudson's crew played nine-pins, which made the thunder that rolled down from the mountain. He said he had a cousin who had a farm on the other side and that someday he'd like to have a place in the country. He even . . ." She falters, her eyes welling with tears. "He even joked about how people would think we were headed for Niagara Falls and I thought . . . well, never mind what I thought." She wipes away a tear. "Frank got off in Poughkeepsie. The plan was for me to go on to Barrytown alone because we thought that Rose might be scared off if she saw me with a strange man. We agreed I'd come back on the first train after six P.M., whether Rose came with me or not. Frank would watch for us in Poughkeepsie, but he wouldn't join us until we were closer to the city. He didn't want her getting spooked and hopping off at an earlier stop. He told me he had undercover cops on the train to make sure I was safe."

"Frank was very protective of you," I say.

She nods but continues to look out the window as if she is trying to make out her past in the fog-and-rain-cloaked view. "I teased him about it. 'You won't be able to keep me locked up with the nuns forever,' I told him. 'I suppose not,' he replied with a serious look on his face. 'As soon as Rose tells us who was there with Eddie that night we'll be able to arrest him and you'll be safe and I can take you away from that place.' " Lillian smiles. "So you see, I had my own selfish reasons for wanting Rose to come back and give evidence."

"You didn't want to spend the rest of your life in hiding," I say, thinking that Lillian was far braver than me; she wouldn't have hidden here while Simon went to look for AJ. "That's only human."

"Yes, I suppose so . . . When Frank got off the train he kissed me. I watched him walk off onto the platform and vanish in a gust of steam from the engine. He looked like Humphrey Bogart in *Casablanca*. I sat gripping my handbag, perched on the edge of my seat until the next stop, afraid I'd miss it somehow. When I got off I thought there must be some mistake. There was nothing but the river on one side of the track and fields on the other. I heard a rooster crow! I'd never been in the country, and I didn't much like the looks of it. I asked the station-master where the village of Barrytown was, and he said I was standing in it. Wasn't there a post office where I could ask for my cousin's address (I'd decided I'd call Rose my cousin). He pointed up a steep road and said the post office was up there *aways.* The road was unpaved and muddy. On either side was more mud and cows. I was sure I'd come for nothing. Rose wouldn't last five minutes in a place like this.

"At the top of the hill was a tiny clapboard building with a row of columns on the porch that looked funny in all that mud. It was no temple inside though, just a single room with a potbellied stove and a couple of men in overalls sitting around drinking coffee. They looked at me like I'd landed from the moon! I'd worn my best dress and coat and my last pair of silk stockings, which were so mud-speckled they might have been polka-dotted.

" 'I'm looking for my cousin,' I said. I didn't say her name because I figured Rose might be going by a different one. One of the men said, 'Pretty city girl like you?' To which I replied, 'Prettier,' which made them all laugh. 'That'll be that gal staying out on Marge Mueller's farm,' one of the younger men said. 'I'm going out that way if you want a lift.'

"There was nothing to do but say yes, but when I got into the truck with him I was scared. He looked harmless enough, but so had Ernest. Ever since that night at the Half Moon I knew there was no judging which man might be harmless or not."

She turns from the window and gives me an appraising look. Her gray-green eyes are shockingly vivid in the muted light. "I expect you've found that same problem with the work you do. You can begin to suspect every man of intending you harm."

I nod, thinking of how I'd stiffened when Simon touched me last night. "Yes, I suppose so . . . but you trusted Frank."

"Yes," she says, looking back out the window. "And I got into that truck with that fellow and he drove me out to Marge Mueller's farm without laying a hand on me. He even offered to come by later to give me a ride back to the train station after my visit with Mary, which is what he called the 'city girl' staying on the farm.

"When I got down from the truck I hoped he'd leave before the girl came out, just in case it *wasn't* Rose, but the door flew open and I was nearly knocked off my feet by a whirlwind in gingham. Despite the affectionate greeting I didn't think this could be Rose. It had only been three weeks since I'd seen her last, but this girl had plain brown hair, was five pounds heavier than my Rose, and was wearing a dress Rose wouldn't be caught dead in. But when she held me at arm's length to look at me I saw it *was* her — a plumper, healthier, happier version of herself. It felt like it had been three years instead of three weeks we'd been apart.

" 'Well, *Mary,*' I said, 'the country certainly has agreed with you. Next you'll be telling me you've married a farmer.'

"She turned bright pink and cut her eyes over to the fellow who had driven me there and I saw in an instant that they were sweet on each other. Rose a farmer's wife! Or almost. There was no ring on her finger and she told the fellow — Joe, she called him — that she'd have those pies for him if he came back at four.

" 'Pies?' I asked when he had gone. 'When did you learn how to make pies?'

"She rolled her eyes and cocked her head toward the house. 'Aunt Marge put me right to work. Come on, I've got to get them in the oven or she'll have my head.'

"She took me into a tidy, well-scrubbed kitchen, where a dozen pie tins lay on a floured butcher-block table waiting to be filled. It looked like a cover of the *Saturday Evening Post*.

" 'I'm glad to see you, Lil,' she said as she rolled dough out on the butcher block. 'I was worried sick after we split up under the boardwalk, afraid Eddie Silver's boys had found you.'

" 'The cops found me first. They've been keeping me safe.'

"She looked up from her work. 'Oh, Lil, but it was the cops who looked the other way when Eddie's boys pushed Abe Reles out the window. You can't trust them.'

"Frank had told me that this was why Rose would be wary of the police. 'That was just a few bad cops,' I said. 'The DA's Office has taken care of them. The assistant DA himself has guaranteed my safety. Remember I told you about him — Frank Maloney? — he's the one who helped Tommy. We can trust him, Rose.'

" 'I go by Mary, now,' she said, laying the dough into the pie tins. 'It was my grandmother's name. Aunt Marge says I look just like her. She says she'll give me a piece of land for my dowry and Joe is saving up to buy the neighbor's orchard. I think he's going to ask me to marry him.'

" 'That's wonderful, Ro— Mary. I'd never thought you'd want that kind of life, but if you do, I'm happy for you. Only . . .' I paused, thinking of how to say what I had to say without scaring her, but then, I thought, maybe she should be afraid. 'If you don't identify the fellow who was with Eddie, then we'll both always be in danger. If you could just look through some pictures and pick out the guy —'

" 'Did you bring them with you?' she asked, crossing the kitchen to pick up a bushel of apples.

" 'No,' I said, wondering why Frank hadn't thought of that. 'You'd have to come back to the city and look through all their books of suspects. But it would be safe. Frank's got a dozen undercover cops on the train —'

" 'He's here now?' Rose looked up from the bushel of apples she'd brought back to the table.

" 'No,' I said, taking a knife and picking up an apple. 'He got off the train in Poughkeepsie and let me come on ahead alone.'

" 'And what if one of Eddie's men followed you off the train?'

" 'I got on the train at Marble Hill. No one could have followed me. I'm staying at the Refuge.'

" 'You mean the Magdalen laundry?' she asked. 'Oh, Lily! That's a terrible place!

How'd you end up there? You never . . . you're not . . .'

" 'I'm just hiding there. Frank said no one would ever think to look for me there. But you're right — it's not a very nice place but it's the only place I'm safe until Eddie — and that other man you saw on the stairs — are behind bars.'

"Rose picked up an apple and speared it on a contraption that cored and peeled it in one-quarter of the time it had taken me to peel one. She peeled and cored three more before answering. 'You could leave the city,' she said. 'You could come up here.'

" 'Do you really think this is far enough, Rose? Do you want to spend your whole life peeping out from behind the kitchen curtain? And do you really want to be peeling apples and making pies for the rest of your life?'

" 'I don't mind the apples,' she told me, attaching another one to the corer. 'But you're right about this not being far enough. Do you trust this Frank?' She speared me with a look as sharp as the knife I'd used to pare the apples. I told her I did. She nodded once and then cranked the handle. 'You always did have a good sense for people,' she said, then she smiled. 'After all, you picked me to be your best friend. I don't suppose it would be fair to leave you in the lurch, always having to hide. I'll come with you. . . . but you'd better help me get these pies done if I'm going with you tonight.'

"I got up and threw my arms around her. She wiped her face with her apron when I let her go. 'We'll tell Joe I'm going down to the city for a few days to help you pick out a wedding dress. Maybe it'll give him the idea to ask me.'

"We spent the rest of the afternoon peeling, coring, slicing, and arranging apples inside the pie tins, then rolling out more dough and crimping the top crusts. While the pies baked we took a walk through a pretty orchard.

"Have you been in an apple orchard?" Lillian asked suddenly.

"I grew up *in* one," I told her. "Not far from Barrytown, in fact."

"Did you now?" she asked, her eyes brightening. "So you know how pretty they are. Rose showed me all the different types of apples — winesap, Macoun, and one with the fancy name Belle de Boskoop. I teased her about turning out a farmer's wife and she teased me about being sweet on a copper."

I make a mental note to get some apples for Lillian when I go next to visit my mother upstate. She's given up asking me to come. Maybe I'll surprise her. I'd forgotten that you could get Metro-North at Marble Hill. I wouldn't even have to go down to Grand Central.

"Anyhow, when Joe came for us Rose was all ready. The pies were packed in cardboard boxes and she had a carpetbag. When Joe saw the bag his face fell. 'I'm only going for a few days to help Lillian pick out her trousseau.' She was so convincing I almost believed it myself. She jollied Joe along all the way to the station, teasing him not to eat all those pies himself and not to sign up for the army while she was gone. He went along with it all but when he handed me up to the train he looked me in the eye and said, 'You watch after Mary. She's too trusting.' Which made me wonder how well he really knew Rose.

"We sat on the right side of the train so we could see the river and I gave Rose the window seat since I had had the river view coming up. Also I wanted to keep an eye on the aisle for Frank. In Poughkeepsie the train doors opened on the left so I had the better view of the platform. I saw Frank get on one car back and I remembered what he'd said about not approaching us until we were closer to the city. I wanted to tell him it was all right; Rose was ready to talk to him. I told Rose I was going to walk back to find the ladies' room. When I came through the doors of the next car I saw Frank right away but he gave his head a tight, small shake and looked away. I saw that he didn't want me to approach him so I walked through the car, used the restroom at the end, and then walked back without looking at him. But I looked at everyone else on that car. If Frank didn't want me to talk to him he must be afraid one of Eddie's men was on the train. Was it the bald man reading the racing forms? Or the mustachioed gentleman in the tweed overcoat carrying a Gladstone case? There were half a dozen men it could have been. By the time I got back to Rose my heart was pounding.

" 'Everything okay?' she asked.

" 'Sure,' I lied, "I think I just ate too many of your apples.'

" 'Maybe they've got some bromide in the café car.' She started to get up, but I pulled her down.'

" 'Don't bother," I said, but now she was looking at me funny.

" 'You never were a good liar,' she said. 'Tell me what's wrong.'

"So I told her about Frank warning me

off. 'Maybe he's just being extra careful,' I said.

" 'Or maybe Eddie's got an eye on this train. I'm getting off at the next stop.'

"I told her I thought that could be more dangerous if one of Eddie's guys followed her off. 'We just have to sit tight. Frank will figure it out.'

"Rose nodded but I could tell she was scared. I was too. But I trusted Frank to figure something out — and he did. When the conductor took our tickets he handed me a note.

" 'Get off at Marble Hill,' it said. 'An officer will meet you and take you to the nearest police station. I'll meet you there.'

"I showed it to Rose, but she didn't like it. She wanted to get off at an earlier station — Ossining or Tarrytown — but I said no, we should do it the way Frank wanted us to and eventually she gave in even though I could tell she was upset about it. We didn't talk the rest of the way. Every time someone passed in the aisle I felt Rose tense up next to me, even if it was just an old lady or a nun. 'Do you think Murder Inc. is hiring nun assassins now?' I asked her. Which made Rose laugh. 'Sister Dolores would be up for it,' she said. 'She was one tough cookie.'

"When the conductor called Spuyten Duyvil I told Rose to get ready because Marble Hill was next. I could see the platform coming up and the oily black water of the Spuyten Duyvil Creek. We waited until the last minute to get up and then hurried to the doors when they opened at Marble Hill. No one followed us out and the platform appeared to be empty. I thought about the story Frank had told about the Dutchman swimming across the creek and Henry Hudson anchoring his ship there. . . . Have you been there?"

The sudden break in the narrative startles me. "Once, years ago," I tell her. "When I came down to visit the Cloisters with my mother. I remember she held my hand tightly because the platform is so narrow." The memory surprises me with its vividness. I remember realizing how wary of the world my mother was — an inheritance from her own anxious, overprotective mother.

"Yes," Lillian says. "A long narrow platform wedged between the rock face on one side and the Spuyten Duyvil Creek on the other, where Henry Hudson's ship the *Half Moon* had anchored. Somehow it was as if that tied the place to the Half Moon Hotel in Coney Island and that made me nervous.

As if I would never escape that moment in the hotel. The way the light fell on the platform through the slats of the stairs made it look like we were back under the boardwalk. There was even that same shadow of a man in a trench coat and fedora —"

"You mean it looked like the same shadow?"

"No," Lillian says, turning to me from the window. All the blood seems to have drained from her face. Her skin is the same watered gray as the fog pressing up against the window, as if coming for her, as if the waters of the Spuyten Duyvil have risen up bearing the ghost ship *Half Moon* to take her away.

"No," she repeats, "the shadow was real. I thought it must be the police officer Frank had sent to meet us, but then I saw the gun in his hand. It was pointed at me. I felt Rose pulling me backward, but to where? I wondered. We were already on the edge. And then I heard the gun go off and I was falling backward. Into the Spuyten Duyvil."

Chapter Twenty-Two

Melissa

I see that Joan had looked up the trains leaving from a station called Marble Hill. According to Waze, the station is only a ten-minute drive from the 207th Street subway station. There's a train leaving in thirty minutes that will take me to Stratford in forty-five minutes. I can talk to AJ today and hear her version of what happened at the Hi-Line before Joan gets to her. I know journalists; they like to think they're objective, but they can shape the facts to tell the story *they* want to tell. Joan has a vested interest in representing Cass in the worst light. Whatever AJ tells her she'll twist to fit her own version of the story and the truth will be lost.

I'm ordering an Uber on my way up from the platform but I spy a Green Cab on Broadway and commandeer it instead. It creeps slowly through the rain on Broadway for several blocks and then comes to a complete halt. "Why are we stopping?" I demand. "My train leaves in fifteen minutes."

"The bridge is up," the driver, an elderly Black man, says, pointing through the rain-spattered window. I lean in to look through the front windshield and see a looming iron structure at the end of Broadway. It looks like a prehistoric sea monster rising up out of the water.

"Why?" I ask the driver. "Why is the bridge up?"

"Ship in the canal," he replies laconically, as if we were in the Outer Hebrides instead of New York City. When we used to go up to Maine to visit Cass's cousins, the kids would find it exciting if we had to stop for the drawbridge. Cass would sigh and bitch but it was a quaint inconvenience, part of old-money island life. But who knew such a thing existed on the northern tip of Manhattan.

"Isn't there another way to get there?" I demand.

"Not unless you want to swim," he scoffs. "And I wouldn't recommend it. You know what that creek is called? Spuyten Duyvil. The Devil's Whirlpool 'cause of the riptides. Takes ships down to the bottom, especially in a storm like this."

"Oh, for heaven's sake," I say, "the storm is not so bad. The news just likes to make a big fuss to raise their ratings."

He cranes his neck to look back at me; his eyes are deeply lined and sorrowful. "I agree that the news media is not as dependable as it once was, but even a broken clock is right twice a day."

I hoot at the old-fashioned saying. "My grandmother used to say that."

"Your grandmother was a wise lady. Looks like the bridge is back down. Hold on."

He deftly swerves through traffic across the bridge and turns left just after it, climbing a steep hill. He makes a U-turn to put me right in front of the Metro-North station entrance. "You get on home before this storm gets any worse," he tells me after I've paid and tipped him. Of course. He thinks I'm heading home to my Westchester house. If only I were. I picture the white colonial in Ardsley, a fire in the fireplace, the deep ruby and gold Persian rugs, the gleaming hardwood floors, and polished oak bookcases — a snug sanctuary in which to ride out a storm.

Instead I'm heading down a wet and muddy metal staircase onto a cold, rain-swept platform wedged between cold black stone and even colder water. *Devil's Whirl-pool, indeed,* I think, looking over the edge of the narrow platform into the roiling water. It makes me shiver just to look at it. Gazing across the inlet I see the edge of Inwood Park and on the ridge above, partly shrouded in mist, the Refuge. It looks sinister from here, like something on one of those old Gothic Romance covers. All it needs is a fleeing girl in a white nightgown.

It's not entirely deserted here on the train platform. A woman with a rolling suitcase is sheltering on a bench under a plastic rain hat. Two teenagers huddle together behind the plexiglass map board, and a tall hulking figure at the end of the platform hunches into his hooded sweatshirt. Everyone is withdrawn into themselves against the rain that sweeps sideways onto the platform. I hadn't realized how isolated the station was — or thought about having to come back this way. Hopefully I'll have the girl with me — and if I don't I'll take an Uber back.

When the train finally comes it's an older model, the vinyl seats torn and patched with duct tape, smelling like stale chips and urine. While it creeps along the river, stopping at every obscure whistle stop — Ludlow, Glenwood, Greystone — I think about the best way to approach this girl AJ. She must be scared if she's been hiding, but of what?

I am the only one getting out in Stratford. There's no station waiting room, no taxi stand, no town that I can see. There is, though, an old weathered sign on the other side of the tracks that reads CAMP ST. BERNADETTE-ON-THE HUDSON. I cross a rickety trestle bridge, the planks and iron frame groaning under my weight and swaying in the wind. Hanging on to the iron railing as I descend the slippery steps I can feel the structure shaking and it occurs to me that the whole thing could rip free of its moorings and fly into the sky like Dorothy's house in *The Wizard of Oz.* What's the use of hanging on to something that's rotten at its core?

I walk up the hill and through an old wrought-iron gate that has the name of the camp spelled out in rusted letters. I pass a gatehouse and a stone chapel, the doors and windows of which are boarded up. Clearly Camp-St. Bernadette-on-the-Hudson has been closed for a long time; it's as empty as a ghost town. Had Joan bothered to check that?

Or — the thought intrudes as stealthily as the icy water creeping under my collar and down my back — what if Joan knew I was spying on her computer and she planted the suggestion that AJ was here? What if she's lured me to this isolated spot in the middle of a hurricane? How easy it would be to kill me and dump me in the river. When I washed up in some New Jersey swamp, people would think I'd followed Cass into a watery grave because I couldn't bear the shame of the scandal and my newly reduced circumstances. As if I were one of those rich, entitled women who couldn't survive outside of a pampered lifestyle. I'd show them.

My anger at my putative critics propels me up the hill toward a weathered clapboard house — the only building that has a light in the window. It looks like it had been an old farmhouse once, then converted into a dorm, and then abandoned. A chipped and worn rowing oar hangs over the door with the faint crudely painted letters: *St. Bernie's Forever! '78.* The building doesn't look like it's been occupied since then. Clearly I've come here on a fool's errand —

Only a curtain twitches at the window to the side of the door, blown by a stray breeze perhaps, or —

"AJ?" I call, knocking on the door. "Are you in there? I want to help you. I think you might be in danger."

The door remains solidly closed, barred to me as well as to the storm. And why not? Why should she trust me? I'm not really here to help her; I'm here to prove my dead husband's innocence.

"AJ, I'm Melissa Osgood. Caspar Osgood's widow. I know I'm the last person you want to talk to, but think about it. If you're scared because you saw something my husband did why should you still be scared? My husband is dead."

My words are greeted with nothing but the low moan of the wind and the lash of the rain. Perhaps the logic of my plea was too complicated for the girl. Even I can see its flaws —

The door opens.

A slim, dark-haired girl in jeans and a sweatshirt levels her large brown eyes at me. She looks frightened, but also defiant. I notice she's holding something in her hand — an aerosol can, which I think might be pepper spray but then realize it's just hair spray — the only weapon she has. The thought that she sees me as a threat makes me feel suddenly ill. What have I become that a girl like this — a girl who could be Emily — would be afraid of me? My heart breaks.

"I'm not here to hurt you, honey. I-I want

to help."

"And what if you don't like what I have to tell you?" she demands. "What if I did see your husband do something bad?"

It's what I was afraid of. Part of me wants to turn away. I don't want to hear what she has to say. But those eyes already have me pinned.

"Then you'd better tell me about it." It's what I'd say to Whit or Emily when they woke up with a nightmare or came home from school with red eyes. I can't tell this girl that everything will be all right. All I can tell her is the truth: "I'm here to listen."

The building is bitterly cold and damp, heated only by an electric heater that looks like a fire hazard. She has an electric kettle that she uses to make tea while I inspect her meager accommodations. A cot with a bare, stained mattress, a faded Dora the Explorer sleeping bag, a stack of paperback books — mostly those dystopian fantasies Emily read for a while — a bulging back-pack, and a flip phone plugged into a power strip. No wonder she's not posting on social media; she might as well be in a third world country. Watching her I notice what I hadn't in her Facebook pictures; she's Latina. Maybe I'll trot out my Spanish later.

She brings the tea to a rickety card table. "I don't have milk or sugar," she says, sitting down and blowing on her own tea. I notice a rose tattoo on her wrist when she raises the mug to her mouth.

"It's fine," I say. And then, pointing to the tattoo, "That's pretty."

"I got it when my mother died. Her name was Rosalita."

"I'm sorry about your mother. How . . . ?"

"Ovarian cancer, which they caught too late because she was afraid if she went to the clinic she'd get deported."

"I'm sorry," I say again. "My mother died of breast cancer when I was around your age. It's hard losing your mother when you're young. It makes you do . . . foolish things."

"Is that why you married Caspar Osgood?" she asks.

Well, that didn't take long. I take a sip of tea to give myself time. My best chance of gaining her trust might be if she thinks I've turned on Cass. "I never thought about it like that, but maybe that had something to do with it. I moved in with Cass after my mother died. I wanted to start my own family and Cass . . . well, he was very . . . *determined.* He knew what he wanted and that felt safe to me then."

"I can see that," she surprises me by saying. "He was very persuasive."

I try not to wince at the innuendo in her voice. "Why don't you tell me what happened? It was the night of that fundraiser at the Hi-Line, wasn't it?"

She hesitates, which I can understand; after all, she has no reason to trust me. But I see something else on her face, the look Emily would get when something bad had happened and she was afraid to tell me but she also wanted to get it out. I remember that the best thing to do at those times was just to be very quiet and still, like waiting for a shy woodland animal to eat out of your hand.

"Yeah," AJ says after a few moments. "This girl I knew from one of the bars I worked at asked if I'd fill in for her. It sounded like good money, so I said yes. I was helping out with the bills because my mother wasn't able to work."

"What a good daughter," I say. "Your mother must have been very proud of you."

"My mother would have told me to get out of there. It was, like, seventy percent men getting drunk on expensive scotch and smoking stinking cigars. My ass was black and blue from getting pinched after the first hour."

"The pigs," I say, meaning it. "Was my husband . . . did Cass . . . ?"

I'm almost hoping she says yes, that that's all this is, a little harmless ass pinching, as gross as that is.

"No," she says, "at least, not to me. I noticed him because he seemed upset . . . and . . . well . . ." She smiles ruefully. "He gave me a hundred-dollar bill at the start of the evening and told me to make sure his glass was always full."

"Oh," I say, "he didn't usually drink like that. But I suppose . . . well, I'd kicked him out a few weeks before."

"I know," she says. "I was taking a smoke break out on the terrace and he came outside with a girl. I hid behind a planter because you're not allowed to smoke on the job. They didn't see me, but I overheard what they were saying. He accused the girl of telling you about their affair, that she did it to force him to leave you."

"Did he?" I ask, surprised. "She didn't. Maddy Wensley, one of the other mothers at Emily's high school, saw Cass having an intimate lunch with Amanda downtown and took a picture of it. Here, I still have it on my phone." I scroll through my photos and find the photograph that had changed my life. It shows Amanda leaning across a table, showing a lot of cleavage and laughing too hard at one of Cass's jokes. Cass has his hand on her thigh. "Does that look like a woman who's been taken advantage of?" I ask.

AJ picks up her own phone and taps some keys. "Does this?"

The picture is so small — I'd forgotten those old flip phones could even take pictures — that at first I'm not sure what I'm looking at, but then I make out Amanda's blurry features. I look closer and see that she has a swollen cheek and a split lip. "You're telling me that Cass did this?"

"Yes. When he left I went to her to see if she was all right. I wanted to bring her down to the kitchen to get ice, but she said no, let it swell so everyone will see what a monster he is. She asked me to take a picture of her with my phone because her battery was dead and then she even asked me to make an audio recording of her saying what happened. She was so upset that I did it. I thought she was going to ask me next to go the police station and I was afraid if I did, it would be like a police record and I'd be deported."

"Oh!" I say. "Are you il— undocumented?"

"Yeah," she admits. "My mother brought

me here from Mexico when I was three. I'm in the Deferred Action Program."

"You're a Dreamer!" I say, excited to meet one.

She makes a face. "Yeah, those dreams aren't looking so bright lately. But three years ago I thought all I had to do was continue to stay out of trouble with the police. Anyway, it turned out Amanda didn't want to go to the police. 'I have other plans for this,' she said when I sent her the picture and voice memo.'"

I think of our vanishing bank account. "She was planning on blackmailing him."

"Maybe," AJ says. "I'm ashamed to say I was relieved she didn't want to go to the police. I left the terrace right after she left, thinking I would just grab my stuff and go. I was heading into the service stairs when someone came up from behind and put his hand over my mouth to keep me from screaming. I was terrified and dropped my phone. The man was talking and I couldn't even understand what he was saying I was so scared. Then I realized it was the man who had hit the girl — Caspar Osgood — your husband." She looks at me defiantly as if I'm going to contradict her.

"And then what?" I ask, trying hard not to look away. "Did he —"

413

"He didn't rape me," she said, "he just . . . talked. He told me that if I went to the police with Amanda he'd make sure I was sorry. That's what he kept saying over and over again. *You'll be sorry. I'll make sure you're sorry.* All the time he had his hands around my throat like he was going to strangle me . . ."

AJ's breath catches and I move closer to her. "I'm so sorry," I say. "I can't even imagine. How awful. Cass . . . well, he was under a lot of stress, not that that's any excuse, but as you say, he was drunk . . ."

"You don't believe me," AJ says, her voice flat, not even angry, just resigned.

"No — I mean, yes, I do, I believe he scared you, that he — my husband — behaved badly —"

"You don't believe he was threatening my life."

"Well," I say, "you didn't exactly say he was, just . . . I mean *you'll be sorry* could mean a lot of things."

"Here." AJ picks up her phone and presses some buttons until sounds come out of it. I can't make out what they are: a cry, then some whooshing that sounds like it's coming from the bottom of the ocean, and then out of that subaqueous roar comes a voice from the dead. The voice of my husband.

"This is what's going to happen," he says. "You're going to leave here and forget you were ever here tonight. If you don't you'll be sorry. I promise you that you . . . will . . . be . . . very . . . *very* . . . sorry."

Each pause between words is punctuated by a rasp that sounds like sandpaper dragged over barbed wire. It makes my throat ache just hearing it. It's the sound of someone choking. I look up at AJ and see that her hand is on her throat. I open my mouth to say something but nothing comes out, as if it's my throat that Cass's hands are around. A sharp crack, like a gunshot, ends the recording.

"He stepped on the phone and then left me there. It was only when I checked to see if it still worked that I saw it had been recording, and that was only because when he grabbed me, the recorder was still on from earlier when I'd recorded what Amanda had said."

"You had proof," I croak, my throat still tight. "No one could listen to that and not realize . . ." That Cass thought nothing of forcing himself on young women — *on a young girl no older than his teenage daughter!* And it wasn't just about sex. I'd told myself for years that Cass was just oversexed, a man of appetites, *virile,* but the man I heard on that recording was a man drunk on his own power. A bully. How had I lived with him and not seen it?

Because I had closed my eyes. I had gone through my life — my beautiful life with two perfect children and my handsome, successful husband and immaculate center-hall Colonial in Ardsley — willfully not seeing what Cass had become and what it had done to all of us — because I wanted to keep that life.

"I'm so sorry," I finally say to AJ. "He was a monster."

"That's what I thought," she says quietly. "I was still afraid of going to the police, but then one of the other guests saw me crying and took me aside and said he had seen what happened and that I should call the police, that he'd back up my story."

"Oh," I say, "that was . . . nice."

"Yeah, I thought so too. But after I called the police I saw him talking to one of Mr. Shanahan's interns. The intern — he was around my age — seemed worried and it looked like he was texting someone on his phone. That made me uneasy and I felt like I just wanted to leave, but then the police arrived and asked for me. Then Mr. Osgood came downstairs with Mr. Shanahan and the man who told me to call the police.

416

They wanted me to go to the station to make a statement. So I did, but the whole time I was talking I felt like the cop wasn't really listening. It didn't seem like any of the men had any intentions of believing me or taking me seriously. When I finished he left me alone in this creepy room without windows for a long time. I thought I was going to go out of my mind. I thought they had called ICE and I was going to get deported. Finally, the door opens and it's not the policeman, it's Mr. Shanahan and the guy from the club who said he would back me up. Mr. Shanahan introduced himself as the district attorney and he said he took the kind of charges I'd made very seriously. *Very, very seriously,* he kept repeating, did I understand the *gravity* of the situation? I just kept nodding and saying *yes, sir* and *of course, sir* like an idiot, until I was shaking all over. Then he said that Mr. Osgood had denied he had any interaction with me or the other young lady that night. So I turned to the other guy and said, 'But you said you saw what happened,' but he just shook his head and said, 'You must be mistaken, miss, I was with Mr. Osgood all night and I never witnessed anything like what you described.' "

"The bastard!" I exclaim. "Why did he

tell you he would back you up and then back out?"

She shook her head. "I don't know. I only know that it made me look like an idiot."

"What about the recording?' I asked. "And your neck . . . you must have had marks on your neck."

She passed me her phone again and pulled up a picture, a close-up of her neck with a ring of black-and-blue marks. "Yeah, I showed them. Mr. Shanahan said, 'We don't know who did that to you, and we have no way of ascertaining that that is Mr. Osgood on the tape, Miss Herrera.' Then he added, 'Another problem is that you don't appear to be on the list of employees contracted to work at this event. I'd hate to think you were impersonating another employee, as that would constitute a serious misdemeanor that would violate the terms of your work permit.' "

"He was threatening you." I'm appalled at the thuggish behavior of the man whom Cass had supported —

Had given a million dollars to since that night.

"Yeah," AJ says. "How could I have known that covering for someone could be called impersonating? It seemed pretty crazy, but here was this big man — the DA — saying it, so what was I supposed to do about it? I got out of there as soon as I could. When I left I ran into the intern I'd seen texting earlier. I asked him if he'd been texting his boss to tell him what was happening and he admitted he had, but only because he thought Mr. Shanahan could help. So I said, 'Look, man, I don't know who you think you're working for, but all these guys are assholes.' That seemed to really upset him. He tried to ask me more questions but by then I just wanted to get out of there, so I left."

"I don't blame you," I say. "I'm sorry you were treated that way by my husband and Pat Shanahan."

The man Cass had supported and given over a million dollars to. The man whose wife had been watching our every move. I see it now, so clearly. Wally had been keeping an eye on me *because* her husband had done this big favor for Cass and Cass was in his debt. When the *Manahatta* story was published they must have worried that it would come out that Pat had gotten those charges dropped against Cass. And then she recommended Greg Firestein so he could watch Cass to make sure he didn't tell anyone about the role Pat had played in getting him off the hook —

I recalled Cass yelling into the phone: *You'd better goddamn help unless you want me to go public with your part in this!*

He had threatened Pat Shanahan and then Greg and Wally came over and got me drunk on Veuve Clicquot (*The Widow's Wine*), and the next morning Cass was dead.

"Hey, are you okay? You're shaking."

I look at this slight, big-eyed girl. How easy would it be to get rid of her? If Shanahan hadn't balked at getting rid of Cass —

"The intern who was with Shanahan," I ask, "did you get his name?"

"No," she says, "but I saw him again at another party I worked. I'd recognize him anywhere."

"I think it must be Greg Firestein, a PR flak of Shanahan's." I open my phone. "I think I have a picture of him." AJ leans over to look as I scroll through my photos. She stops me at one from the gala and expands it.

"Him," she says. "He was the intern who was at the station."

I look down and see Whit, handsome in his tux and orange bow tie. "That's my son," I say.

"Oh," AJ says, looking embarrassed. "No wonder he looked so miserable. It couldn't have been easy finding out your father was

420

an asshole. He looked . . ." AJ screws up her face, thinking. "He looked like he'd just lost something precious."

He'd lost his father, his idol. A few days later he tried to kill himself. I remembered his face in the hospital bed looking up at his father as if he were drowning. I'd thought Cass had rushed to his bed out of love — but I bet what he'd really wanted to do was make sure that Whit didn't tell me anything about what happened at the Hi-Line. How much did Whit know? Was losing his belief in his father what drove him to try to kill himself? My God. I had to talk to him.

I shiver. "We need to get out of here," I tell her. "It's not safe."

"No one knows I'm here. Unless . . ." She glares at me. "Unless you told them."

"I didn't mean to," I say, looking away from those accusing eyes. I'm thinking of my laptop with its clever MataHari app on it. All someone would have to do is break into my apartment and look to see what I saw: the location of Camp Bernadette. They could be on their way here now.

I force myself to look back at AJ, but she's no longer looking at me. She's crawled over to the window to look out. "It's too late," she says. "Someone's coming."

Chapter Twenty-Three

Joan

"You fell in the Spuyten Duyvil?"

"Not fell," Lillian said. "Rose pulled me in to save me from being shot. The water was freezing and the current was so fierce, it might have killed us anyway. I remembered what Frank had said about the ghost ship *Half Moon* and I thought we were being pulled under the water by the arms of drowned sailors. The current was taking us out to the Hudson and I knew that if we got swept out to the river before reaching the shore we'd be lost. But then I remembered that Dutchman who had swum across the creek "to spite the devil" and I thought if he could do it, so could we — to spite Eddie Silver and all the men like him. I grabbed Rose, who was flailing beside me, and started pulling her toward the opposite shore."

She looks out the window, speaking as if

to herself. "Sometimes I feel as if I never did get out. That Rose and I are still drifting along the river — two girls who didn't matter, swept away with the trash out to sea."

She shivers and I reach over to pull the afghan around her shoulders. Her skin is so cold she might be a drowning woman I need to pull out from the river. "But you didn't drown that night. You fought the current. You wouldn't let yourself be a victim to those men."

She grabs my hand and squeezes with a surprisingly strong grip. "Yes, that's exactly what I felt. I think I got across that creek on sheer spite. Sometimes anger is the only thing keeping us going. I hooked my arm around Rose's neck like I'd seen the lifeguards do at Coney Island and I swam us to the other shore. We were nearly at the mouth of the river by the time we dragged ourselves out of the creek, on the spit of land just below the Refuge. When I caught my breath I turned to Rose. I couldn't see her in the dark, but I could hear her ragged breath. She was sobbing.

"It's okay," I told her. "We're alive. We just have to walk up this hill and we'll be at the Refuge. The nuns will help us."

She made a choking sound that turned

into a wheezing laugh. She seemed much worse from the swim than I was. I called her name but she only moaned. So I shook her — and felt warm, sticky blood on her. In trying to get me out of the way she had been shot. I couldn't tell where she'd been hit, just that there was blood on her arm and chest and that she was very weak. I had to get her help — and the closest place — the only place — was the Refuge. Some of the nuns had trained as nurses in the war and there was a full infirmary on the top floor . . . right here."

I remember Lillian saying that the infirmary was here, but it's still startling to have the story brought around to the present and to think of Rose and Lillian struggling up the hill, trying to get to this very room.

"You must have been scared," I say, "all alone in the park with your wounded friend."

"Yes," she says, her eyes brightening at the acknowledgment. "I got Rose to her feet but she could barely walk. It was a steep climb uphill through the dark and over uneven rocky ground. We were both shaking from the cold. I lost track of how many times we fell, each time Rose moaning more pitifully. I never thought we'd make it, but when we came up on the ridge I spotted the lights from the windows shining through the dark. I've never been happier to see anything. For the first time this place felt like a real refuge: a port in a storm. I was mostly carrying Rose by then and I felt as if I were a shipwrecked sailor carrying her dead crewmate to a lighthouse on a rocky shoal."

Her lip quirks and I see the spark of humor in her eyes, still there despite all she's been through. "Perhaps I was a bit delirious by then. I banged on the door, shouting for us to be let in. One of the younger nuns opened the door. When she saw me holding Rose up she sniffed and said, 'We don't take drunks here.' I explained that we weren't drunk, that Rose had been shot.

"She still looked disapproving, as if being shot was the inevitable consequence of living the kind of life Rose and I presumably had led, but she called for help and we carried Rose up here to the infirmary. Sister Agnes had served in the Great War and tended to gunshot wounds before. She told me straight off that the bullet had passed through Rose's shoulder and that it wasn't a serious wound in itself, but that she'd lost a lot of blood and might not survive if we couldn't get her to a hospital for more blood.

" 'I'll have to call the police,' she told me, 'if I take you to the hospital. So you'd better think what you'll say about how this happened.'

"I saw she thought we'd gotten ourselves into some kind of trouble that we didn't want the police to know about and I began to tell her it was all right, that we were *helping* the police, but then I recalled what Rose had said about Eddie having his own men in the police. I told her to please not call the police right away, but to wait. The assistant DA had been with us on the train. He must be chasing the man who shot us, but then he'd come here. She agreed and said she would give Rose what blood they had in the dispensary (they kept some on hand for miscarriages and hemorrhages after childbirth) to stabilize her for a few hours, but then we'd need to get her to the hospital.

"She left me with Rose and told me I should wash and get into clean, dry clothes. 'You'll want to look your best when you tell your story.' I did look a wreck and smelled like the river. I washed in a basin as best I could and put on the plain muslin dress that was the uniform of the Magdalens. It made me feel like a 'soiled dove,' as they called the girls here, but I knew it would only be for a short time. Frank would come after they caught the gunman. He would take Rose's statement and she would identify the man who had been on the stairs and they would arrest him and Eddie Silver and Rose would go back upstate to marry her fellow and I . . ." Lillian turned from the window and smiled at me. "Well, I had my own dream. I did hope Frank and I would marry someday, but I didn't mind if it took a while. I wanted never to feel as helpless as I'd felt in the water that night — or when my mother fell in the kitchen or when that cop pinned me to the couch at the Half Moon. I wanted to make my own way, to work and tell stories of girls like me who no one listened to . . . Oh, I don't know how I meant to do it. One moment I pictured myself a newspaper reporter like Rosalind Russell in *His Girl Friday* and the next I was over in Europe writing about the war or sitting in a room like this" — she sweeps her arm around my living room — "writing stories to sell to magazines. I suppose it sounds silly to a young woman like yourself who's done those things, but I had never really thought about myself as someone who could make a difference. But swimming

427

across the Spuyten Duyvil that night and carrying Rose up that hill had given me the feeling that I could do whatever I wanted to do."

"I don't think it sounds silly at all," I tell her. "I'm sure you did make a difference."

She shakes her head. "Sometimes, sitting here, looking out at the fog, the rest of my life seems like a dream. Everything that came after that night is less real than the life I dreamed for myself as I sat by Rose's bedside. I was right here, looking out this very same window. I drifted off to sleep at some point and dreamed I was back on that train platform facing that man with the gun. He was stepping out of the shadows into the light and I was just about to see his face when the gun went off and I woke up. I awoke with a jerk, my heart pounding, but I told myself that the gunshot was in my dream. Then I heard another one. It had come from below and it was followed by a scream and more shots and men shouting and women screaming. At first I couldn't move. I still thought I must be dreaming. How could danger find me here? This was the one place that was supposed to be safe, but then I realized that no place was ever really safe and I knew that Eddie's men must have come for us."

"You must have been terrified. What did you do?"

"I listened." She puts a finger to her mouth and whispers. "Listen now. What do you hear?"

I've fallen so far under the spell of her story that I do what she says. We both listen. At first all I hear is the rain beating a staccato rhythm against the glass and the high keen of the wind . . . but then, far below us, I *do* hear something — a murmur of voices and then the hydraulic churn of the elevator.

Just someone coming home.

"There were stairs where the elevator is now," Lillian says. "The gunshots and voices were coming from the stairs so I roused Rose and told her she had to get up, we had to go." Lillian gets up as if to show me what she had done. She's so shaky on her feet that I get up, too, and put my arm out to steady her. She grabs hold of me as if I were the shaky one and begins shuffling us toward the hallway.

"We had to take the back stairs," she says, guiding me down the hallway. "But first I had to find the key. Rose told me where the nuns kept a spare. Do you have the key?"

I'm confused for a moment but then I realize she's asking if I have the key for the locks now. How far, I wonder, will she want to take this reenactment? But if this is what she needs to do, who am I to deny an old woman some closure? I've left the back-door key on my night table, so I steer Lillian into my bedroom to get it. Then we continue on our way down the hall to the back door.

"I listened here," she says with her hand on the door, "to make sure there wasn't anyone coming up the back stairs . . . then I opened the door . . ." She gestures for me to open the door and I do. Cold, dank air hits my face as the door opens. The stairwell is dark. The bulb on this landing appears to be out. Watery, rain-shadowed light filters down from above. There's some kind of skylight up there. Lillian is looking down into the stairwell. "When we got here I heard footsteps coming up the back stairs and I knew Eddie's men were covering both ways out. There was only one other way." She points toward the roof. The dappled light falls on her face like a veil and for a moment I see a much younger, and very frightened, woman.

"You went up to the roof?" I ask.

"There was no other way," she says. "We heard them break through the front door . . ." As she points back toward my apartment I hear someone pounding on my front door. I jump at the sound.

"It's just someone at my door," I say. "It's probably Enda or Hector . . ." *Or Simon,* I'm thinking.

Lillian doesn't seem willing to move, though. She's frozen in time, reliving that horrible night. I can't leave her out here, though.

"Come inside, Lillian. I think I understand what happened. You can continue your story inside —"

"You have to remember," she says, fixing me with a keen stare and pointing up. "*That's* the only way out."

"I get it. That's good to know. Now, come back inside. It's freezing and damp in this stairwell."

"It's the laundry," she tells me. "The vats are in the basement. The steam rises through the house. Can't you smell it?"

I do smell something — a whiff of mildew and bleach — as I guide her back inside. I steer her down the hallway and into the living room. "Coming!" I call to the pounding at the door.

Lillian starts to shake as we pass the door. She must picture mobsters wielding shotguns right outside. I try to sit her down on the couch, but she wants to go back to the chair by my desk. I settle her in the high wingback chair, facing the river, and tuck my grandmother's old afghan over her chest. She closes her eyes and falls asleep almost instantly. Then I go to the door and look at the security camera.

It's not Enda or Hector or Simon; it's two wet and bedraggled women, a middle-aged one in a sodden and muddy trench coat and wide-brimmed hat, and a younger one in a soaked sweatshirt. A mother and daughter, perhaps, seeking refuge from the storm. Or some kind of ruse to get me to open the door and then invade my home.

"Hi," I say over the intercom, "do you have the right apartment?"

The woman looks up, her face furious — and somehow familiar. "This poor girl is in danger and it's all your fault, Joan, so let us in."

It's the imperious tone of voice that does it. Melissa Osgood. She's the last person I should be letting in, but then the girl with her looks up and there's something about her . . . I recall feeling dizzy, someone putting a note in my pocket . . . I unbolt the locks and open the door.

"You," I say to the big-eyed, dark-haired girl. "You're the server from the party who told me you had a story."

Chapter Twenty-Four

MELISSA

"I also gave you my phone number," AJ tells Joan. "But you never called."

The look on Joan's face — shamed and embarrassed — would be gratifying if we weren't soaking wet and still standing in the drafty hallway.

"Can we discuss this inside and out of view of the cameras?" I point up at the camera in the hallway and Joan's expression changes from shame to suspicion. I don't blame her. If the situation were reversed I wouldn't let her in. But then AJ says through chattering teeth, "Please. We had to run through the rain and we're cold and wet."

Joan relents and lets us in. "I'll get some towels," she says, disappearing down the hallway. AJ sits on a couch shivering. I go right into Joan's kitchen — I know where it is and I don't care if it looks bossy — and put on water for tea. I feel like I'll never be warm again.

When AJ saw the car coming up the drive, she grabbed her backpack and we ran out the back door of the house. She knew a footpath that took us down to the station without crossing the road. When we got there, though, AJ was afraid to wait on the platform in case someone was watching for us. We crouched behind the tall grass and cattails on the river's edge in the rain with God-knows-what crawling in the mud for half an hour waiting for the next south-bound train. Then when we finally got on the train the heat wasn't working. I thought we'd both end up with pneumonia. And it would be all my fault. I must have led Shanahan's men to this poor girl. I didn't even know where to take her. To a friend? But who? Who could I trust? I couldn't imagine showing up at any of the Brearley moms' doorsteps looking like a drowned rat with an undocumented alien. When I suggested we go to the police, AJ refused.

"They'll call ICE before I get two words out. That's how it is these days."

The only place I could think of was taking her home with me to the Refuge — but not to my apartment, where there could be someone waiting for us, but to Joan's so we'd have a witness.

When I come into the living room I see that AJ has changed into dry sweatpants and a sweatshirt. Joan is sitting next to her on the couch, her face arranged in an expression of concern. When she looks up, though, her expression changes to one of mistrust.

"I still don't understand how you knew where I live."

"Listen," I say, sitting on the opposite couch. "We don't have time for all that. The important thing is that I found AJ —"

"You're AJ?" Joan exclaims. "I've been looking for you!"

AJ rolls her eyes, just like Emily does when I've missed something obvious. I have to admit it gives me a little satisfaction to see Joan be the recipient of her disdain. "Like I said, I gave you my phone number."

"Which you apparently ignored," I add. "I found AJ, but someone followed me to her. Someone's trying to keep her from telling her story, which if you listened to in the first place —" I stop, hearing myself. "I suppose I can't really judge, seeing as I didn't listen to your story about Cass. Let's both of us be better listeners and let AJ tell her story."

Joan looks from me to AJ and then, for some reason, toward the window. Then she nods. "Okay," she says. "I'm listening."

AJ tells Joan what happened at the Hi-Line. It's hard to hear again, but not as hard as it was hearing it the first time. Maybe when I've heard it a hundred times it will cease breaking my heart, but then I think of Whit and my heart breaks all over again. When she gets to the part where the man at the club offers to back her up, she asks if she got his name.

"No," AJ says, "but I saw him again —"

"It must have been Greg Firestein," I say, taking out my phone to look again for a picture of him, but I get distracted — and defensive — as Joan asks me a few questions.

"Did you know about this at the time?"

"No," I say. "Cass was staying in the city because I'd kicked him out, and obviously he didn't say anything to me about it."

"Did you notice any unusual expenditures at the time?" Joan has the steno pad on her knee and pen poised to write.

"Not at the time," I say defensively. "Cass handled the finances . . . which I know sounds old-fashioned . . ." What it sounds like now is *stupid.* "But I discovered yesterday that he started giving large sums to Pat Shanahan's campaign after that night and supporting him at the *Globe.*"

"The *Globe* was the first paper to support

Shanahan's run for governor," Joan says.

"And most of the New York papers followed — even little *Manahatta* ran a positive feature on Shanahan last year," I say.

"I thought that was odd at the time," Joan says, "but then I heard that Sylvia was good friends with Pat Shanahan's wife."

"Sylvia's friends with everybody," I say. And then, recalling Sylvia's text to me the night of the gala and then Wally looking down at her phone, "I bet she tipped off Wally the night of my gala that the story was coming out."

Joan nods, "I remember she was on the phone a lot that night."

"Wally was glued to my side from that moment on. I thought she was being a friend —"

"But maybe she was keeping an eye on you?"

I nod, feeling the sting of it. "I think so. I imagine Pat Shanahan wanted to make sure that Cass wouldn't try to bring him down with him by talking about what happened at the Hi-Line. It would destroy Pat if it came out that he had taken campaign contributions to suppress a criminal investigation and threatened to deport a DACA immigrant while he was at it. Wally recommended a PR guy named Firestein, whom

Cass hired to help with the optics of the accusations. He and Wally came to our house the night Cass died —" I falter, recalling Wally plying me with Champagne and Greg groping me in the bedroom.

Joan leans forward, concern on her face. "What happened?"

I hesitate. Joan's a reporter — a *good* reporter, I'm beginning to see — and she's using just the tactic Cass would use to urge on a source. But then I meet her eyes and see the genuine concern there. Besides, what do I have to lose?

"I think Firestein slipped something in my drink to knock me out," I tell her, "and then he *groped* me while taking me upstairs. I'm guessing Cass must have said he was going to come clean about that night and Firestein killed him. All he'd have to do is slip something into Cass's scotch — he was guzzling it at that point — and carry him out to the pool."

"And the suicide note?" Joan asks.

"They had access to Cass's computer and his Twitter account. They'd have been able to go through his laptop, too, checking to make sure there wasn't anything incriminating Shanahan on it."

"That's what they were looking for in my files," Joan says.

"What?" I ask, trying not to look guilty. Does Joan know that someone has been hacking her computer?

She looks from me to AJ and then toward her desk as if she can't meet our eyes. "I was attacked," she says. "The night of the publication party someone followed me home and into my apartment. They — he — grabbed me from behind and forced me into my apartment. He had his hand over my mouth . . ." She makes a sound like she's choking and puts a hand on her throat. "I thought he was going to kill me. He pushed me down on the floor and covered my mouth with a cloth soaked in chloroform, but I struggled and . . . then he slammed my head into the floor. That's all I remember. I must have blacked out. When I came to it was morning; I could tell my stuff had been gone through, but everything seemed to be there. Only later I noticed one of my computer files was missing."

"Were you . . ." AJ begins, looking embarrassed. I must, too, because I know what happened to that file, but AJ's embarrassment is for a different reason. "Could you tell if . . ."

"I'd been raped?" Joan finishes for her. "I don't think so. But the truth is I don't know what he did . . ." Her voice breaks. "I'm not . . . the same. My vision is blurry and there are holes in my memory. It feels like there are pieces of me missing."

I'm about to ask if she's been to a doctor, but AJ speaks first.

"It's my fault," she says, her chin crumpling. "I followed you home after the party. I wanted to talk to you, tell you what happened, but when I got out of the taxi I saw someone go into your building after you. It was that man — the same one who was at the police station with the DA. He'd been at the *Manahatta* party, too, which is why I was afraid to talk to you there. When I saw him going into your apartment I thought you must know him and that meant you were all in this together. And then when I turned around to go, there was this woman standing in the middle of the sidewalk right behind me. She said, 'You're a long way from home, Alejandra, maybe you should go back there.' "

"She knew your name?" Joan asks.

"Yeah, that was the scary part, that and how polite and formal the words were, but the way she said them was like she was telling me that I'd better go away and keep my mouth shut *forever* if I didn't want to wind up dead or something. So I just left. I took the train back to my apartment, packed a bag, and went up to the camp. I knew some migrant workers who camped out there during the growing seasons. If I'd thought that man was going to hurt you I'd have gone to the police even if it meant getting deported."

"It's okay," Joan says, squeezing AJ's arm. "You didn't know. But that woman . . . can you tell me what she looked like?"

Before AJ can answer, the intercom buzzer rings. We all jump at the sound.

Joan looks uncertain but goes to the door. I follow her. When she pushes the button I see Hector standing in the lobby with a man whose back is to the camera. "There's a Mr. Simon Wallace for you, Ms. Lurie. Shall I send him up?"

I see Joan's shoulders relax. "Yes," she tells Hector, then turning to me: "Simon will know what to do."

"Who's Simon?" AJ asks, getting off the loveseat and coming over to the door. "Are you sure we can trust him?"

"Of course," both Joan and I say at the same time.

This *would* be the one thing Joan and I can agree on. Despite his harshness to me the last time I saw him I know that he is a crusader for the truth. He will love publishing AJ's story and exposing one last shameful episode of Cass's life. Since AJ told me

441

her story and I listened to the recording, I haven't questioned for a moment that she is telling the truth. And if Cass was the kind of man who would threaten a helpless girl to suppress her and tell his own son on his hospital bed to stay quiet, then he is the man who would bully and harass all those women. He is the man that Joan wrote about. I don't know when he became that man. Perhaps he always was and I just didn't want to see it. Perhaps he was never the man I imagined him to be. And as painful as it is to realize that I was married to a mirage, at least I can stop mourning for that man and begin reckoning with who I am for having believed his lies. Maybe I can help Whit and Emily face that truth, too, without it ruining them. The first step is being here with Joan and AJ.

We're all still standing at the door like a bunch of eager college students waiting for their dates. The door buzzer rings, automatically switching the camera to the hall view. I sense AJ tense next to me.

"That's him," she whispers. A statement, not a question.

"Him?" I ask as Joan unbolts the first lock.

"The man who was at the police station with Mr. Shanahan," she says. "The one who followed Joan into her apartment that night. That's the man who attacked her."

Chapter Twenty-Five

JOAN

"Simon?" I ask incredulously, turning to AJ, sure I must have misunderstood. "Simon's the man who followed me to my apartment? Are you sure?"

"Yes. I recognized him because he was the man who was with Mr. Shanahan that night at the police station and then I saw him at the *Manahatta* party."

"But that doesn't make sense," I tell her. "Why would Simon be with Shanahan? And why would *he* have offered to be a witness against Cass and then backed out?"

"Because he wanted to come to Cass's rescue," Melissa interjects, her face caught in the throes of a dawning realization, "to gain Cass's undying gratitude and approval. As far back as college, that's all he ever wanted. If he saw an opportunity to get Cass in trouble and then step in to help him, he'd do it to gain his approval."

"But then why run the story about him?"
I ask.

"Maybe Cass wasn't grateful enough . . ."
Another flash of realization crosses Melissa's
face. "The club membership . . ." she
begins, but the doorbell cuts her off.

I turn back to the screen. Simon is looking at the camera. "Joan?" he says, his voice
muted by the steel door. I had uncon-
sciously turned off the intercom when AJ
identified him. "Are you all right?" His voice
is all warm concern, a worry furrow creas-
ing his brow, the way he'd look when I
brought him updates on the Osgood story.
I'm not sure we have enough yet, he'd say,
keep digging.

He'd also said that a grudge was the best
motivator. And then what had Sylvia
said . . . something about not getting into
the Hi-Line . . .

"What about the club membership —" I
begin, but AJ interrupts me.

"I don't care about any club or why he
did what he did. That's the same man who
lied to me and then followed you into your
apartment. If you're going to let him in I
want to get out of here. Is there a back
door?"

"Yes," Melissa says. "We can go down the
back stairs." She grabs her coat and hat

445

from the hook by the door and puts it on while I wonder how she knows about the back stairs. "I think we should tell Hector that there's an intruder in the building, though." She reaches past me and pushes the doorman buzzer, which automatically switches the camera view to the lobby. There's Hector opening the door for a woman with a long black coat and a black rain hat tilted low over her face. Melissa gasps.

"That's my coat!"

AJ and I turn to look at her. She is, indeed, wearing a coat and hat identical to the woman in the lobby.

"That's weird —" I begin.

"It's Wally," Melissa says. "She took my extra Burberry to sell but she must have kept it for herself. But why —" Melissa's voice stops abruptly as the woman on the camera takes out a gun and aims it at Hector. And shoots. The sound is a muted pop from five stories below us, but it reverberates in my chest. Melissa shrieks and grabs my arm.

"Joan!" Simon calls from the other side of the door. "Are you okay? I think I heard a gunshot! I'm calling the police." He takes out his phone and begins tapping at the screen.

"Go! Take the back stairs," I whisper to AJ and Melissa. But as I speak I see the woman in the lobby walk toward the stairwell. "Damn, she's coming up the stairs."

"There's a skylight that goes up to the roof," Melissa says. "We can get out there and block her way and call the police —"

"You go," I say. "I'll keep Simon here. Maybe . . ." I want to say that maybe it's all a mistake, that Simon *can't* be here to kill me. But I realize how pathetic that sounds. I turn to Melissa and see understanding in her face. She knows what it's like to lose faith in a man you trusted. "Just go," I say, "keep her safe." I cut my eyes to AJ.

She nods and leads AJ down the hall to the back stairs as if she knows the place. I switch the camera back to the hall view. Simon is talking to someone on the phone. I turn on the intercom to hear.

". . . won't open the door. I think the others are there. Do you want me to meet you on the back stairs?"

He's probably talking to Shanahan's wife, planning their strategy. I can't let them reach Melissa and AJ.

"Simon?" I say through the intercom. "Who's that you're talking to?"

"Joan!" he cries, boyish worry on his face. "Thank God! Are you okay? I'm afraid you're in danger. I've found out something horrible about the way Cass died."

"Really?" I say, trying to keep my voice calm. "Tell me."

A flicker of annoyance passes over his face turning the boyish look into something else: pique at being questioned. "Why don't you let me in and I will."

"I think I feel better talking like this," I say. "Like you always said: a good reporter should always maintain a professional distance."

He purses his lips, the annoyance curdling into anger. I feel a stir of air beside me and nearly jump out of my skin thinking it's Shanahan's wife who's somehow gotten into my apartment. But it's only Lillian, come silently to stand beside me. She'd been so quiet sleeping in her chair that I'd forgotten she was here. She stands on tiptoes to look at the camera screen.

"He looks angry," she says.

"Joan," Simon says in his deepest I'm-your-boss voice, "I'm worried about you. All that junk on your wall, all that talk of conspiracies. I think you've lost the plot, as the Brits would say." He's trying for a more jocular tone, but I can see the tension in his shoulders, his right fist clenched as he reaches into his pocket.

"He has the keys," Lillian says. "We have to go." She's right. He's pulling a set of keys out of his coat pocket. He must have taken my extra set when he was here last night.

I turn away from the door and follow Lillian, who's moving surprisingly fast for someone her age. When she reaches the back staircase she holds a finger to her lips, listening. There are footsteps on the stairs coming up fast. Shanahan's wife.

"Mrs. Osgood? Melissa?" It's Enda shouting on the stairs from a lower flight. The steps coming up halt and wait for another set of footsteps. Enda thinks the woman on the stairs is Melissa — just as anyone who sees the camera footage will think it was Melissa who shot Hector and then shot me in revenge for exposing her husband and ruining her life. And now Shanahan's wife is waiting for Enda to reach her —

"Enda!" I shout down the stairwell. "That woman is not Melissa! She has a gun!"

Pounding footsteps follow, then a crash and a gunshot.

Lillian grabs my hands and pulls me toward the spiral stairs. "We have to go through the skylight," she tells me.

When I push on the skylight I remember that Melissa was going to block it to keep Sylvia out — but it opens. I shimmy through, scraping my hips on the splintery wooden frame, then turn to help Lillian through. She's so light I could practically carry her — and I might have to. How else is a ninetysomething old woman going to get off this roof?

She's thinking faster than me, though. As soon as she's through she looks around for something to block the skylight. "Here," she says, handing me a pole, the remains of some long-ago laundry rack. "Wedge it in the handle there. It won't hold long but at least it will slow him down.

It's as if she has done this before.

I thread the pole through the handles on the skylight, then stand and look around. The rain has stopped. Clouds are clearing in the west, letting through an orangey light, making the wet black tar paper glow like oil. Melissa and AJ are on the west side of the roof looking over the edge. I put my arm around Lillian and help her across the roof, worried that she'll slip on the slick tarpaper.

Melissa looks up as we approach. She looks puzzled, and I realize she must be surprised to see Lillian tucked under my arm, but all she says is: "We called the police. I told them an intruder had chased us onto the roof. I figured that was simpler than explaining the whole thing."

She's probably right, but it occurs to me that if the police think that it was Melissa who shot Hector they might also believe it was Melissa who chased me and AJ out onto the roof.

"What happened?" AJ asks. "We heard another shot."

"I'm not sure. Enda chased Wally Shanahan up the stairs. She may have shot him —" My throat tightens at the thought of another innocent victim.

A crash from behind makes us all turn toward the skylight. Someone is trying to push it open. Sirens sound in the distance. The police aren't here yet. By the time they arrive we could all be dead.

"There's a ladder," Melissa says, "but it's old and rusted."

"I used to go out on the fire escape in my old building," AJ says. "These things are stronger than they look, but you don't want more than one person on it at a time."

"You go," both Melissa and I say at the same time to AJ.

"Wait for us when you get down so we can go to the police together," Melissa says.

AJ looks at us and nods. "Okay, but you follow as soon as I'm down."

"Of course," we both say in unison again, in the same false tone.

"I mean it," AJ says. "No heroics. I don't want to face the cops alone."

"We won't let you," Melissa says firmly. "Here, take my gloves." She hands her a pair of leather gloves. "Hold on tight." She watches anxiously as AJ climbs down. I turn to Lillian, who's become a heavier weight on my arm. I lead her to a dry spot by a chimney and help her sit down.

"Rest here for a moment," I tell her.

Until what? I think. Lillian can't climb down the ladder. Would Simon and Wally hurt her if we leave her behind? My mind balks at the idea of Simon hurting a frail old lady, but then my mind is still struggling with the notion that he followed me into my apartment . . .

That he was my attacker. That he has been the dark, invisible presence I've been wrestling with all these months — the suffocating cloth over my face, filling my head with chloroform —

Which Simon had in his office from the story Ariel had done on the chloroform rapist. She had ordered it from a medical-supply company using a phony ID to demonstrate how easy it was to get and then Simon had locked it up in his office "for safekeeping."

So you reporters don't get any ideas about

knocking me out and taking over the magazine, he had joked.

Lillian is looking up at me, her face wet with tears. "I didn't want to think it was Frank either."

"Frank?" I ask, horrified that the terror of this flight has brought back her own trauma.

"When Rose and I got back up here, it was Frank who came through the skylight. I was relieved at first. I thought he'd come to save us . . . but then I saw the gun . . ."

A sharp crack of wood splintering cuts her off. I look toward the skylight. Glass shards fly up. Simon is breaking through the glass to get through. I pull over one of the splintery crates and drag it in front of Lillian. "You stay here," I tell her. "He won't know you're here. Wait until the police arrive."

She nods solemnly. "Don't worry about me. Save yourself and your friends."

My friends, I think as I turn away from Lillian. I hurry across the roof toward Melissa, who was so recently my enemy. She turns when she hears me behind her, face drawn and haggard in fitful light breaking through the clouds. "She made it," she says. "AJ's down."

"You go," I say. "I'll try to keep Simon talking until you're safe."

She looks toward the skylight as it crashes open and then down the long drop to the rocks below as if measuring her chances. But then she looks at me. "I think you'll be better at that than me. Just . . ." She grasps the handles of the ladder and turns to step on the highest rung. The metal groans. "Remember that Simon loved Cass once and there's nothing worse than realizing the person you loved was an illusion."

"Okay," I say, "I'll keep that in mind. Now, go!"

She starts the climb down and I turn to find Simon standing just a few feet behind me. There are glass shards on his shoulders and a streak of blood on his cheek, which gives him a manic, rakish air like it's a new fashion statement.

"For God's sake, Joan, what's going on?" he demands. "Have you gone insane?"

He says it so reasonably that I find myself considering the possibility. Isn't it more likely that I've gone insane than that Simon is here to kill me? I haven't really been the same since I got hit on the head. But then —

"I just saw Pat Shanahan's wife shoot the doorman in the lobby," I say. "So did Melissa Osgood." I don't mention AJ.

"I don't know what happened in the lobby. As for Melissa, I wouldn't trust her motives. Have you asked yourself what she's doing here? Did you know that she bought the apartment below you?"

"No . . ."

"Has it occurred to you that Melissa is the one with the motive to discredit you? Even to kill you? She blames you for ruining her life. Now she's gotten you up on this roof, scared to death of me." He takes a step toward me. "If you fell, what would people think?"

"I-I don't know."

"No? Use your brains, Joan." It's what he'd say when I brought him some piece of information he found questionable or if I failed to see the logic of some argument he was making. "Remember what's down in your apartment — a wall covered with Post-its and Internet clippings, half of which is about some murder case from the 1940s. People will say you went crazy. Melissa will say that your mania and obsession discredit our story about her husband. *She's* the one who benefits from your death. What benefit do I gain?"

He smiles and takes another step forward. I shuffle backward and feel the iron of the ladder against my calves. I want to turn and see if Melissa is down on the ground yet — *no,* I want to call her back up here to answer

Simon's accusations. I want a better explanation for Simon's guilt than that vague pablum about nothing being worse than realizing the person you loved was an illusion.

Simon standing right in front of me is not an illusion. The western light makes the blood on his face ruby red and the glass on his shoulders sparkle. "Joan," he says softly, taking another step toward me, "why would I encourage you to write the story and then try to stop you?"

It's a good question. Simon always told me to look at both sides of a question — to anticipate the counterargument. "You didn't encourage me at first," I say, remembering now that first meeting. "You told me I didn't have enough."

"That was being a good editor. I wanted you to make sure you had enough evidence."

"You delayed the publication for three years."

"To make sure the story was ready."

"You told me not to explore the incident at the Hi-Line —"

"Because it was unsubstantiated. There was no police record —"

"Because Shanahan had it erased."

A muscle twitches at his temple. "Who told you that?"

"Someone who was there. Someone who

said you were there too."

"So what? I told you I was at the party. I'm a journalist. It's my job to observe what the rich and famous get up to when they think no one's watching."

"Is that what happened?" I ask. "You saw your old idol getting hauled down to the police station and you saw an opportunity?"

"To do what?" he asks. His face, caught in the light, looks stony. "If I saw Cass taken into custody, why wouldn't I report that? Why would I keep it secret?"

"Because you wanted control, maybe? Or you never gave up wanting to impress the rich boy from college?"

Simon laughs. "Well, that would have been a fool's errand. Men like Caspar Osgood think it's their due for men like me to come to their aid."

"Is that what happened?" I ask, hearing the anger in Simon's voice. "You helped him out and then he wasn't grateful. I bet he ignored you even more, ashamed that you'd seen him at his worst. That must have made you angry. No wonder you agreed *eventually* to let me do the story. But you kept the Hi-Line incident back. You counted on using it as leverage if Cass threatened to sue you." I recall how blithely he'd burned those cease-and-desist letters we both received the day before the story came out. How confident he'd been, standing outside the restaurant. "That's why you didn't tell Sylvia about the story. You knew she was friends with the Shanahans and that she would warn them."

He looks at me skeptically. "And why would Sylvia think the story about Cass would affect Pat Shanahan —"

"Because she was there that night. You told me you were her plus one. She would have seen you go to the station with Cass and Shanahan and suspected you helped Cass. And it was Sylvia who called Wally Shanahan the night of my pub party." I picture myself preening in front of Andrea Robbins, bragging that there were other lines of investigation I could pursue, even one about an incident at a private club. "Sylvia overheard me talking about the Hi-Line incident and called Wally to warn her. Did Wally call you?"

"Why would Wally Shanahan call me?" he asks.

It's a good question. The truth is I don't know but then I have a hunch, and Simon always says that a good reporter follows their hunches. "She knew you were at the station and that you helped Cass get out of that charge. She knew that you had your own reasons for not wanting that information to be made public. You were the perfect person to make sure no one found out that her husband cleared Cass of those charges."

"Enough!" he barks. "You don't have an ounce of evidence."

"There's the witness who saw you with Shanahan at the police station and who saw you following me home the night the article came out."

He smiles. "Have you considered maybe that I followed you home for other reasons? That maybe" — he lifts his hand to my face and caresses my cheek — "I thought we could spend a pleasant night together."

At the touch of his hand I flinch, and with that flinch Simon's mask falls away. He slides his hand behind my neck and erases the space between us. The backs of my knees press against the metal frame of the ladder, the top part of my body tilting over into empty space. As soon as he has control over my body he no longer has to lie.

"I only meant to put you out long enough to retrieve the girl's phone number. Believe me, Wally suggested I do much worse, but I told her I could keep you under control. I didn't think it would be hard; you were always so hungry for validation. I was only going to tie you up and blindfold you to make it look like a burglary, but then you had to struggle and hit your own head on the floor."

He runs his fingers up my scalp. "Honestly, it was such a blow I thought you were dead. Oh, I was horrified at first! I even considered calling 911. But I had to search through your files first to make sure you didn't have anything about the Hi-Line incident in your notes and I realized that I might have left it too long, that I wouldn't be able to explain how much you had bled, and then I thought, *Would it be so bad if she died?* And I felt something turn inside of me. *Why should I be the slave to circumstances?* I'd wondered that since college when I met people like Cass and Melissa who had so much when I had so little and I thought that all I had to do was be their friend and then I could have what they had. I thought if I wrote his papers for him in college and his stories for the *Times* he would be grateful. I should have learned when he claimed I had stolen my stories from him that there was nothing he wouldn't stoop to. When I saw what he did to that server, I thought it was an opportunity to watch him fall, but then I saw that Pat Shanahan would come to his rescue and I knew he was going to get out of that too. Nothing would ever touch him. I thought why shouldn't I benefit from some of Cass's luck? I'd have something I could always hold over him."

"Was that the only reason?" I rasp. "Or did you think he'd be your friend again?"

He tightens his grip on my scalp. "That would have been stupid," he says. "No one likes the man who sees you when you're down. He avoided me like the plague after that. . . . He even —" He breaks off, his face contorting. I sense the moment of weakness, what Simon taught me to look for when interviewing a source.

"What did he do?" I ask. "You helped him out of a jam and then . . . he did something worse than just avoid you."

"The bastard had me blackballed!" he spits.

"Blackballed?" I repeat.

"From the Hi-Line. Sylvia nominated me and asked Cass for a letter supporting me and he wrote instead that I wasn't the *right sort* for the club. Of course, the letter was supposed to be confidential but Sylvia found out."

"That's . . .". I want to say *ridiculous*. Could Simon really have been motivated by something so petty? I say instead, "So you decided to get back at him. How fortunate that I showed up with my story."

He laughs. "You were the third ex-*Globe* intern whose résumé I forwarded to Sylvia. I figured eventually I'd get one with a complaint. The fortunate part for me was that you were so easy to control. Such a *good* girl, eager to please and follow the rules. As long as I kept you away from the Hi-Line incident I'd have something to leverage Cass with." He laughs, his mouth so close to mine I can smell his coppery breath. "Cass himself taught me that trick. When he accused me of plagiarism at the *Times* and I told him I was going to go to the editor in chief to defend myself he threatened to reveal that I'd lied on my college application to Brown — a tiny doctored recommendation letter, but enough to ruin *a man like me.* You know what Cass said to me the night I went to his house?"

He seems to expect an answer even though I can't speak or shake my head or, for that matter, do I know what he's talking about. When did Simon go to Cass's house? Then I realize with horror that he must mean the night Cass killed himself. His grip on my scalp is so tight it feels like a vise, cutting off the flow of blood. I make a grunt that doesn't sound like me at all, but he takes it as an expression of curiosity, a signal to go on with his story.

"He said that if I revealed that I was there at the police station and covered up for him it would go worse for me than it would for him. 'Men like me always land on their feet,' he said, 'while men like you end up on the garbage heap.' That's when I slipped the sedative in his drink and waited until he passed out. Suffice it to say he didn't 'land on his feet' when I dumped him in the pool, nor, I imagine will you . . ."

He bends me over the rim of the ladder and tightens his grip on my head. My vision blurs and stars, sunbursts raying off the glass shards on his shoulder . . . and landing on the woman standing behind him. Lillian, tiny and determined, holding up a splintery piece of wood as if she were Joan of Arc — her favorite saint — wielding a sword. She's not tall enough to reach Simon's shoulders, but Simon will kill her after me if he sees her.

"No!" I try to cry, although it comes out like a grunt. "Run!"

Simon whirls around, giving me enough space to step out of his grip and try to help Lillian, but then he stumbles back against the ladder, his face a mask of fear and confusion as Lillian rushes him. His arms windmill in the empty air for a moment, his

463

eyes searching —

For me, I wonder, or for something else? He looks like a man who's suddenly remembered a forgotten appointment.

— and then he falls backward.

I crouch at the edge to look down. Simon's body is splayed on the rocks below, red seeping over them in the orange-gold glow of the setting sun. That glow is spreading over everything. I look up and see Lillian through the red-gold mist, which matches her red sneakers. She is looking east, back toward the skylight as if she is watching someone coming through it. I look but there's no one there. Is she reliving that moment when she saw her Frank come up through the skylight and she realized he had betrayed her? She flinches, as if at a loud sound, and her face is stricken, but then the pain dissolves into something else, a radiance. She turns, her eyes briefly grazing me.

"It wasn't him," she says, a light dawning on her face. Then she tilts her face up to the setting sun and sighs as if she hasn't felt the sun on her face for decades. Her face is suffused with love, like something — or *someone* — has been restored for her. She looks . . . *free.*

As I reach for her the red glow expands, filling my brain, wiping everything else out.

I feel, for an instant, Lillian's fingertips brushing mine, and then I feel nothing but the empty space left behind after a sun explodes. And then I don't even feel that.

CHAPTER TWENTY-SIX

MELISSA

It was clear right away that he must have died instantly, spine broken on the rocks, limbs splayed, their looseness an uncanny reminder of the pose he'd struck in the library that day to imitate Cass. Now Simon had followed Cass into death. On his face was the same surprised expression he often wore in college when someone was unexpectedly cruel — or unexpectedly kind. It made me wish I'd been kinder to him more often.

I climbed back up the rocks to check —

On what? I knew he must be dead. But I had to make sure he wasn't suffering.

As I turned to go something bright caught my eye, a glitter of gold in a crack between two rocks. I knelt and reached down, thinking it might be something that had fallen from Simon's pockets. As my fingers touched cold metal I saw something else, hidden deeper in a crevasse, that made me freeze. I quickly withdrew my hand, pocketed the piece of gold, and clambered back down toward AJ.

"We have to find out if Joan's all right . . . if Wally got to her . . ." I stammered, still unnerved by what I'd seen in the rocks but determined to put it aside for now. I expected AJ to argue about going back but she didn't. She led the way, helping me over the rocks and climbing up the steep hill. By the time we got to the front of the Refuge there were police cars and ambulances outside. I saw a stretcher being carried out of the lobby. It was Hector, an oxygen mask over his face, which was drained of color. At least he was still alive. I'd find out what hospital he was going to, but first I turned to AJ.

"If you want to go now I understand."

She shook her head. "You need me to say what happened, and I'm tired of running. If they deport me . . ."

I squeezed her shoulder and promised I would do all I could to help prevent that from happening. I started walking toward the plainclothes detective who looked like she was in charge (partly because she looked just like Mariska Hargitay on *Law & Order*), but I stopped when I saw a second gurney coming out of the lobby. Joan was on it, unconscious, her face dead white beneath a plastic oxygen mask. She looked worse than Hector had. Enda was walking beside the gurney, his face grim.

"What happened?" I asked Enda. "Was she shot?"

Enda shook his head and pointed to a woman being led out of the lobby by a police officer. It took me a second to recognize Wally. Her carefully highlighted hair stood up in spikes, her face streaked with grime. Here was my "friend" who had plied me with Veuve Clicquot and told me to stand by my man. I wanted to ask her why she had been willing to risk so much to save *her* man. Was it love — or was it because her own sense of self was so wrapped up in his that she no longer knew who she was without him? But then I realized that I couldn't ask her those questions until I answered them for myself. Instead I turned to the officer. "I saw that woman shoot Hector Ramirez," I say, pointing at Wally.

"I heard the shot," Enda said, "and chased the woman up the stairs, disarmed her, and secured her to the banister while I ran up to the roof. I got there just as the man fell off . . ." He looked over to the detective. "He was trying to push Joan off and lost his balance." Enda paused, looking puzzled, then shook his head as if clearing his ears of water, and looked down at Joan. The EMTs were barking numbers at each other: blood pressure, heart rate . . . something about internal bleeding. "She just collapsed."

"She was hit on the head four months ago," I yelled at the EMTs. "She didn't go to the hospital. It could be an aneurysm." The EMTs looked at each other grimly. I was guessing that wasn't a good sign. "What about Hector?"

The detective shook her head. "Too soon to tell. They've taken him to Columbia Presbyterian — that's where they'll take Ms. Lurie too. I need you to come to the station to give a statement."

"I'm going to the hospital," I told her. "And so is she." I grabbed AJ by the arm and pulled her close.

A policeman drove AJ and me to the hospital, less out of politeness, I guessed, than to keep an eye on us. When we got to the ER I took one look at AJ and grabbed a nurse. "This poor girl's been out in the cold and rain for hours. I think she has hypothermia and shock."

I made enough of a fuss to get her into a bed, hooked up to an IV for fluids, and covered with heating blankets. I asked the nurse to keep us informed on Joan Lurie's and Hector Ramirez's conditions. When she asked if I was family I told her Joan was my sister and Hector was my domestic partner.

"And this one?" she asked skeptically, pointing at AJ.

"Mi sobrina," I told her.

"Aunt Melissa," AJ called me when the nurse left to get more blankets. "Who's my uncle?"

"Hector," I told her, adjusting the pillows. Now get some rest while Tia Melissa makes a few calls."

I went out to a waiting room and called the immigration lawyer Cass had hired to help Marta get her green card and asked him to come help AJ. Then I went to find out how *my sister* Joan was doing. The nurse told me that she had, indeed, suffered an aneurysm and was in surgery.

"Why didn't you make your sister go to the hospital after she was attacked?" she asked me.

"Because I'm a bad sister," I told her. "But I'm going to try to be a better one."

"You'd better," she snapped. "In the meantime, your boyfriend's daughters are over there."

She pointed to three women holding

hands in the waiting room. I introduced myself as a friend of their father's and apologized for telling the hospital he was my boyfriend.

"You're not?" the youngest of the sisters asked. "We were hoping Papa finally found a lady friend." The oldest of the sisters added something in Spanish that was too fast for me to follow.

"How's he doing?" I asked.

They told me that the bullet had missed his heart but that he'd lost a lot of blood. "He's a strong man," the eldest — Thea — told me. "He came here on a boat from Cuba when he was only thirteen and raised his two baby sisters and sent them both to college — us too. Family makes us strong, he always tells us."

As he had said to me while I used him to spy on my neighbor, I think with a heavy sigh. I left them praying for their father and went to sit outside for a moment. I needed air. I needed a moment —

I needed to find a way not to hate myself. I could blame Cass. He had set this all in motion with his lies, his cheating, and his entitlement. But I was the one who had turned a blind eye and enabled him. It had been so important for me to hold on to the idea of who we were — college sweethearts, golden couple — that I'd refused to see what was in front of my face. If I had seen, maybe I could have done something to stop all of it.

I take out my phone and open the MataHari app. Joan has a list of contacts on her computer. I call the one under "Mom." A woman answers on the third ring, her voice a tangle of hope and dread.

"Joannie?"

Joan's mother, Anne, arrives after midnight. She's a faded blonde with a few extra pounds on her and a beautiful peaches-and-cream complexion. I tell her that Joan is out of surgery and in stable condition. I help her find the on-call doctor and leave her to go see Joan alone. She comes out tearful. "They say they stopped the bleeding in her brain but that they won't know how bad the damage is until she wakes up."

I commandeer a sleeping chair, which I know about from when Whit was in the hospital and I wanted to sleep in his room, and bring Anne water, coffee, blankets — anything I can think of to make the waiting more bearable. I shuttle between her and Hector's daughters until I'm sure both Joan and Hector are stable.

At the end of the next day I suggest to

Anne that she come back to the Refuge and use her daughter's apartment to get some rest. I arrange things with Enda, and when he opens Joan's apartment for Anne I'm there with a bag of "essentials" I picked up. She walks straight over to the desk and stares at the wall of Post-its. I could kick myself for not coming in earlier to get rid of them. I know how it must look to Anne, like the work of a madwoman.

"Is this what Joannie was working on?" she asks.

"She did a good job," I say, pointing to the card with AJ's name on it. "She found the witness before anyone could hurt her, and she'll tell her story just as she told these women's stories." I point to the six women who were Cass's accusers, forcing myself not to look away.

Anne nods and then points to one of the articles about Murder Inc. "What's all this stuff from the '40s?"

"That I don't know," I say. "Maybe she was inspired by the history of this building? The story about Rose O'Grady is kind of a local legend. Maybe Joan saw in it a parallel to the story she was telling about young women who are victims of sexual assault today."

It's a lame explanation but Anne seems to

accept it. "She'd have gotten some of it from her grandmother," she says. "My mother was always telling these kinds of stories from her youth. 'Eat your vegetables; we didn't get any in the Depression.' Or 'If you go with the wrong boys you'll end up like the Kiss of Death girl.' I grew up hearing so many of them that I was scared silly of doing anything, but Joan's reaction was to ignore them and get out." She turns to me, tears brimming in her eyes. "Maybe she would have been more careful if she wasn't so busy rebelling against all those scary stories."

I shake my head. "You raised a brave girl who risked her own safety to help other women. You should be proud of her."

"Oh, I am," she tells me, the tears spilling down her face. "I just hope I get to tell her so."

After making sure Anne has everything she needs, I go down to my apartment. I sit at my desk and think about Joan sitting at hers, one floor above, trying to find a way to tell the stories of the women Cass hurt while struggling with her own damage and pain. Was it really all that strange that she had to find a side door in through another story?

I open my laptop. I'd meant to delete the MataHari app after using it to get Anne's phone number, but I haven't.

I open it up and, in spite of my resolution not to, look through Joan's files one last time. According to the timestamps, the last folder she'd opened is called "Lillian." I open it up and see that it's the story of a woman who grew up in the '30s in Brooklyn and came to the Refuge in the '40s. It's what Joan was researching, and it's written as if the woman herself was telling it, from her Depression-era childhood of bread lines and Catholic school, through the tragic loss of her mother and subsequent disintegration of her family, to her brothers ending up in orphanages and falling into lives of crime. It's like a '40s movie: young Irish girl struggling to keep brother out of jail joins forces with a handsome young assistant DA to put the bad guys away, but is ensnared in the crime world herself. When I get to the part about how Lillian was assaulted by a policeman at the Half Moon Hotel I see why Joan saw this story as a companion to the stories of her informants. I can hear all the women who were assaulted by powerful men and then silenced. Most of all, I see AJ, bullied and threatened by Cass and Simon and Wally and Pat

Shanahan, driven into hiding just as Lillian was —

By another DA.

I read the last bit about Lillian and Rose running from the train, jumping into the Spuyten Duyvil to evade the gunman, fleeing to the Refuge, hearing the gunshots and then escaping to the roof —

Just as we did.

The story breaks off with Lillian on the roof, turning to see her unknown assailant. Was it Frank, the handsome assistant DA? Had he been the one working with Eddie Silver? Did he send the killers to Abe Reles's room? Was he the man on the stairs at the Half Moon Hotel who Rose saw?

Poor Lillian! What a horror to find out the man you trusted, the man you thought was going to save you, was your destruction. Hopefully that's not actually what happened. But if not, then what did happen? Did Rose and Lillian escape? Did they ever get off that roof?

I search through the files for anything that gives away the ending, tears trickling down my face, as if the ending to some '40s pulp heroine's story could tell me the ending to mine. But there's nothing there. Lillian's story is unfinished. For all I know, Joan made her up and her resolution is trapped inside Joan's potentially damaged brain.

The last thing I do before I fall asleep is to call Whit. It takes three calls and several text messages to him and Drew to get him to pick up. When I ask him about what happened at the Hi-Line three years ago he breaks down in tears.

"Dad told me that he was trying to *help* that girl, but when I talked to her afterward she was so angry — and *scared*," he tells me. "I knew something was wrong. Then when Dad came to the hospital he told me it was all a big misunderstanding and if I told anyone it would hurt you, Mom, and that I'd already disappointed you enough by what I'd done."

I'm so floored by this tactic of Cass's — that he would use his own son's love and shame to hide his secrets — that I can't speak at first, but I swallow hard and make myself.

"You could never, ever, disappoint me, Whit. Never be afraid to tell me the truth — and I promise I'll always do the same for you."

We talk for another half hour and I make him promise to come down next weekend. It's too late to call Emily, but I text her with plans for a family weekend.

As soon as it's light I walk to the hospital,

taking the path through the park. I stop at the rocks where I'd found Simon's body. I had told the police what I saw in the rocks below where Simon's body lay, but I didn't give them the bit of gold I'd found first. I look at it now — and then put it away. As I turn toward the river I can almost see Lillian and Rose climbing the hill from the banks of the Spuyten Duyvil on their way to the Refuge.

When I get to Joan's room I see that she's awake, sitting up in her bed, looking out the window to the same view of the Spuyten Duyvil as if she, too, is watching the progress of the two fleeing girls.

What happened to them? I want to demand. Instead I clear my throat.

"Melissa!" she calls. "Just the person I wanted to see. I have so many questions."

"Me too," I say, relieved at the sharpness of her gaze. Whatever damage was caused by the aneurysm it hasn't quenched her sharp, inquisitive nature. As I sit down, though, I feel a tremor of dread at the thought of that sharp intelligence aimed at me. What if she asks how I found AJ or why I moved to the Refuge? But that's not what she says.

"No one will tell me what happened to Lillian."

"Lillian?" I repeat with a sickening drop in my stomach. "You mean the woman whose story you were writing?"

"Well . . ." She looks confused. "She was telling me her story. She was in my apartment when you and AJ arrived and then she came up to the roof with me. Don't you remember?" She lowers her voice. "*She* was the one who pushed Simon off. But then I blacked out and I didn't see what happened to her."

I swallow hard and take her hand. "Joan, there was no one else in your apartment when we arrived and no one else with you when you came up onto the roof and no one else who fell to the rocks." I squeeze her hand. "I'm afraid you must have imagined Lillian."

CHAPTER TWENTY-SEVEN

JOAN

The neurosurgeon, a pompous but frighteningly competent superstar from Columbia–Presbyterian, has an explanation for "Lillian." "The bleed in your brain produced hallucinations. Not uncommon. You're lucky you didn't die. You *would* have if your friend hadn't called me. You're welcome."

My new *friend,* Melissa, has another explanation. "Repressed trauma. You subconsciously knew that Simon was the one who had attacked you but you couldn't face that so you made up a sweet, dotty old lady whose story mirrored yours: innocent young girl in the city betrayed by charming older man."

"But I didn't make up all that stuff about Murder Inc. and Abe Reles and the Half Moon Hotel and William O'Dwyer," I object. "A lot of that really happened."

"You did research," Melissa tells me,

producing for me a file of articles she'd copied from the Internet on Murder Inc. "And then incorporated it into the story 'Lillian' " — she puts up her fingers in air quotes, which unnervingly makes me feel as if Lillian herself might appear in the air between her hands — "told you. It's a great story — I'm doing a little research myself right now to see if she was a real person. When you finish the book on Cass you should write one on Lillian."

One of the odder *sequelae* — a word I've learned from my occupational therapist — of my trauma has been acquiring Melissa Osgood as the most vocal champion of my book exposing her husband's misconduct. She's agreed to be interviewed for it, a coup that made my publisher more than happy to grant me a three-month extension. In addition, Melissa has made it her mission to oversee my recovery and get me in shape to write it by personally managing my "rehab team" of therapists. She also makes me get out every afternoon for a brisk walk together through Inwood Park, during which I am to report on my writing progress for the day.

Nor are there any interruptions from the little old lady next door. My *real* elderly neighbor is a retired accountant named Phyllis Breen (née Schwartzman), whom

Enda took me to visit when I got home to prove to me that no one was hiding Lillian Day in a closet. Phyllis is a congenial, sharp-tongued plump woman in a housedress who hasn't left her apartment since "the second Bush administration" and spends her days watching CNN and doing crossword puzzles. She thanked me for the Milanos, told me she preferred Entenmann's, and invited me to stop by for coffee anytime (*Tea? Blech! Might as well drink dishwater!*).

"I thought it was a little odd when you said your elderly neighbor was visiting you," Enda said after the visit to Phyllis, "but I didn't want to suggest . . ."

"That I was delusional?" I finished for him. Enda's become a friend as well. If tackling Wally Shanahan to keep her from shooting me hadn't been enough to endear him to me, the fact that he visited me every other day in the hospital, bearing grapes and gossip magazines, would have. He's still a little careful around me, though, as if I'm a cracked teacup that might come apart in his hands.

"Actually," he said, "I wondered if you might not be entertaining a ghost."

That was Enda's explanation for Lillian. "It wouldn't be the first reported ghost at the Refuge," Enda told me when I scoffed.

He produced for me a dozen "sightings" on a website called "Haunted Inwood" and a drove of data he'd unearthed from files left behind by the Sisters of the Good Shepherd in the basement when the Refuge was closed, including a file for one Lily Anne O'Day.

Lillian was real.

Or at least, she had been. She was born in 1923 in Brooklyn, New York, and was remanded, at age eighteen, on the charge of prostitution, to the Refuge. A note from the admitting nun read:

Lily is an intelligent and pretty young girl who had no trouble with the law until her mother died of rheumatic heart disease. Since her mother's death, though, the family has descended into crime and loose morals. Two of the boys, who were remanded to St. John's House, have been arrested for petty thievery and vagrancy. The younger brother, Tommy, was involved in a shooting in August and is serving a three-year sentence in Sing Sing prison on the charge of manslaughter. Lily herself spoke in her brother's defense at the trial and made frequent entreaties of the police to treat her brother with leniency in consideration of the hardship of losing their

mother. "He would never be in this dif-
ficulty had our poor mother been alive
today," Lily told me.

All of which was exactly what Lillian —
my Lillian, be she ghost or hallucination —
had told me.

But how had I known about Lillian's life?
She didn't appear in any of the coverage of
the Murder Inc. trials. The only woman
referred to was someone named Rose
O'Grady, a mobster's girlfriend whom the
press dubbed "The Black Rose." There were
stories about her: that she wound up at the
Magdalen Refuge in Inwood but then vanished mysteriously, never to be heard from
again. She was one of the legendary ghosts
of the neighborhood, celebrated at our local
pub, and clearly I could have read about
her and conjured her in my disordered
brain.

Only I hadn't been visited by a ghost
named Rose; I'd entertained her best friend,
Lillian.

Thinking about it made my poor recovering brain ache and so I put away the files
and took down the Post-its and articles
about the Half Moon Hotel and Murder
Inc. and concentrated on writing my book
and doing my physical therapy and getting

out regularly. By Christmas I surprise myself by finishing a (very) rough draft. I'll still need that three-month extension to get it in good enough shape to turn in to my editor, but at least I've got the bones of the story down. It's not quite the story I'd set out to write, but then I'm not quite the same person I was when I began it.

When I report my progress to Melissa she says, "Congratulations! Let me know when it's coming out so I can go out of town for a few weeks."

I know she's only half joking. Although she's been completely cooperative in our interviews, I know how painful it has been to face how deluded she'd been by her husband.

"You're not alone," I tell her. "Look at how I was fooled by Simon. I still have trouble understanding how he could have encouraged me to write the story when he knew that he'd helped Cass evade the law. And all because of some stupid club membership!"

"It wasn't just the club," Melissa says, "although I can see how galling that must have been to Simon. He wanted more than anything to belong to Cass's world. In college he thought he could get that by imitating Cass and writing his papers to buy his

485

friendship, and later, his news stories. That night at the Hi-Line he must have thought he could buy entry into that world by hiding Cass's secrets. When he found out that Cass had blackballed him he must have realized that he'd always be on the outside and the only hold he'd have over Cass was to hurt him."

"It seems so childish," I say.

She nods. "Yes, but who of us doesn't act like a child sometimes? Speaking of which, are you going to your mother's for Christmas?"

Since Melissa's been spending more time with her kids — who often slept over, brought friends, played their music too loud, got into shouting matches over dinner, came home late from trivia night at the Black Rose, and generally made their mother happy — she's become an advocate for me spending more time with my mother.

"Yes," I tell her, "so you can cross me off your to-do list." I'm immediately sorry for that last bit. Melissa's ferocious efficiency saved my life, got me off my ass, and kept AJ from being deported.

"Good," she says, "because I'm starting a new job next week as assistant editor at a new digital media company and I'll expect you to pitch me a story after the holidays.

Stop by before you go — I have presents for you and your mom."

There's a holiday air to the Metro-North Marble Hill station, passengers carrying festive packages, the sun turning the ice on the Spuyten Duyvil silver, the steam from the approaching train white and puffy as snowbanks, the brisk air shimmering with a crystal-line clarity that makes everything stand out like an etching. Or maybe it just feels good to be out in the fresh air, clear-eyed, taking a train home for the holidays. I sit on the left side of the train and watch the river glittering in the bright sunlight, thinking about Lillian riding on the train picnicking on pastrami sandwiches and cream sodas . . . But of course, I made all that up.

I root in Melissa's gift bag to find what she had given me. There were two packages for me: a thin, eight-by-eleven-sized package labeled "Open First" and a small jewelry box labeled "Open Second."

Leave it to Melissa to be bossy, even with gift opening.

Neither said "Don't Open Until Christmas," though, so I open the large package first. Inside is a handsome paper portfolio in a beautiful shade of duck's-egg blue embossed in gold with my monogram. It's the kind of thing people Melissa's age used to hold their résumés or copies of their newest reviews. Kind of retro, but classy. I open it up — and find three pages of typescript. A letter, I think, taking the sheets out.

It is a letter, but not to me. It's to Melissa from the New York City medical examiner. The subject line reads: *Remains found near recovered body of Simon Wallace.*

Not exactly cheery holiday reading. I put it away as we come into Croton-Harmon, where I have to transfer to the Amtrak train to Albany. Why would Melissa give me a letter about *remains*? I have tried not to think about Simon's broken body on the rocks below the Refuge. I have told myself that he must have lost his balance and slipped. There was no "Lillian" there to push him, and surely I had not been in any shape to do it.

Unless I've conveniently forgotten doing it before I blacked out.

When I get on the next train I open the portfolio, take out the letter from the ME, and read.

Dear Ms. Osgood,
I've been told that the information you requested has been made available since

488

the inquiry into Mr. Wallace's death has been closed. And since you were instrumental in directing the forensic team to the additional remains I am happy to supply you with what we have learned from them.

The bone fragments wedged in between the rocks below where Mr. Wallace's body was found (see figure 1) were, indeed, human remains. They belonged to a female, probably in her late teens to early twenties, who died from blunt-force trauma to the skull, likely caused by the fall from the roof of the building adjacent to the site. In addition, below these bones, the forensic team found remains of a male, age unknown. He, too, had signs of trauma to the skull and spine, but in addition there is splintering of the sternum and rib cage consistent with a bullet wound. It's impossible to tell if he died from the fall or the bullet wound, but it is clear that he was shot. The proximity of the bones and similar stages of decomposition suggest that they died at the same time. It cannot be determined with any certainty what that time was, but deterioration of the bones suggest sometime in the middle of the last century.

Any clothing the two subjects wore has long since deteriorated. There were a few metal buttons recovered with the remains and a discharged bullet, but it's impossible to tell if they were associated with the subjects. The only other evidence clearly connected to the remains is a thin gold chain around the female's neck. Any ornament that may have been on that chain broke off in the fall and was not recovered with the remains.

The medical examiner's office will hold on to the remains for sixty days, when they will be interred in Potter's Field unless a relative claims them, which seems unlikely. Do let me know, though, if you discover any pertinent information.

At some point in reading my hand has drifted to my throat, where it stays, fingers touching my breastbone in the spot where Lillian's locket had rested. I'd asked about the locket in the hospital but they said I hadn't been wearing one when I came in.

Of course I hadn't. There'd been no locket because there'd been no Lillian to give it to me.

And even if there had been a locket, it could have been an old piece of jewelry I'd found somewhere. Nothing to do with anonymous bones lying for decades amid the rocks below the Refuge. A woman and a man who fell together after the man was shot —

I remembered Lillian's face as she stood on the rooftop looking toward the skylight — a look of anguish, followed by a flinch as if at a loud noise, and then her face lighting up as if she had realized something. What was it she had said?

It wasn't him.

At the last moment she had realized that Frank was not there to kill her. He was trying to save her, only he was shot and they fell together to the rocks.

Except I had imagined all that.

I shake my head and open the smaller package with trembling hands. It's a blue Tiffany box. Melissa has probably bought me some overpriced bauble —

But the thing inside is clearly not from Tiffany's — at least, not recently. It's a gold oval locket, dented and corroded at the hinges, the design on its face nearly rubbed smooth. When I hold it up to the window I can make out, in the sharp light off the river, that it's two intertwined flowers — a lily and a rose.

■ ■ ■ ■

My mother picks me up at the station and drives us back to the house — up the steep hill, past the one-room post office with its classical columns, down a winding road lined with old dry-laid stone walls and apple orchards, to the old white farmhouse where I grew up.

Just as Lillian described in her visit to Rose. More proof, if I needed any, that I'd made up Lillian out of bits of my past (locket in my pocket notwithstanding). How far gone must I have been not to recognize the details of my own childhood home.

Who could forget the particular quiet and peace of the farmhouse surrounded by apple trees on a ridge overlooking the Hudson? The old house looks newly white-washed by snow and blue sky, framed against deep-green pines and the blue ridges of the Catskill Mountains on the other side of the river. Closer up, though, I notice the paint is chipped and the porch stairs slope to one side.

If the book does well it wouldn't kill you to put some money into its upkeep, I surprise myself by thinking. The house has always seemed more like a trap than a haven, but maybe all havens are a little of both. Inside it smells, as it always has, of woodsmoke and apples.

"Put your stuff down and come say hello to Grandma in the kitchen. She's been waiting all morning to see you."

I find that unlikely, but I drop my bags and obediently enter the old kitchen with its wide plank floors, tin sink, chipped enamel stove.

"Hi, Grandma," I say, approaching her favorite chair by the woodstove. She has a photo album splayed open on her lap and she's looking out the window at a view of apple trees and mountains. When she turns to look at me, her blue eyes are as vivid as the sky outside. She smiles politely. As you would for a stranger.

"It's Joan," I say, pulling over a kitchen chair and sitting down close enough that she'll be able to see and hear me. "Your granddaughter. Anne's daughter."

"Joan," she dutifully repeats. "Like Joan of Arc."

Yet another detail I cribbed for "Lillian."

"Yes, like Joan of Arc. I bet she was your favorite of the saints."

She looks confused and I immediately feel guilty. Then she looks down at the album in her lap and says, "No, but she was Lily's favorite."

"Lily?" I say, feeling suddenly chilled, as if I'd brought the contagion of my brain damage into this snug, safe kitchen.

She nods and opens the album. It is not, as I expected, a family photo album. It contains Xeroxed copies of articles and pictures. My grandmother turns the pages slowly until she finds one of an imposing stone building. "Poor Lily. I lost her here."

I look closer at the picture and see that it's of the Refuge. On the facing page is an article about two girls who went missing there. "Mom," I say, turning to my mother, who's studiously checking on something in the oven. "Where did you get these?"

"From your wall," she says, coming over and laying down a dish towel on the butcher block. "When I saw them I realized they seemed familiar. Some from your grandmother's stories . . ." She reaches over to turn the pages. "The Kiss of Death Girl, Eddie Silver, the Half Moon Hotel . . . I figured you must have woven those details into your . . . *projections.*"

"You mean my hallucinations."

"I thought it might help you understand them if you could connect the details to Grandma's stories. So I showed these to her and . . . well, at first they upset her . . ."

My grandmother turns a page and taps a blunt fingernail on a picture of Eddie Silver. "It was *my* fault Lily went with him . . ." Her voice warbles and then breaks off.

"Did you tell her about Lillian?" I ask as she blots a tear from my grandmother's cheek.

My mother bites her lip as she would when I went off on one of my teenage rants. "No," she says finally, pulling up a chair beside me. "I never mentioned any Lillian or Lily. But when I showed her this . . ." She flips to the drawing of the girl known as the Black Rose and my grandmother laughs.

"That's me," she says, tapping the picture. "When I was young and pretty."

"But your name is May, Grandma," I say, hating the prim tone of my voice — but hating more that my grandmother has somehow fallen prey to my delusions.

"Changed it," she says, leaning close and lowering her voice. "So Eddie's men wouldn't find me. Joe always called me Mary, but I liked May and when he didn't come back from the war . . ." Her voice warbles again and I reach out and squeeze her hand.

"You don't have to do this, Grandma, if it upsets you."

She squeezes back. "I wondered then if what Sister Dolores had said was true, that I was being punished for living a sinful life. First poor Lily —" She raises her hands to her eyes where they flutter like moths beating up against a lit windowpane. "She was trying to give me time to get down the ladder. *Go, Rose!* she told me. *I'll keep him back.* When I was halfway down the ladder I heard a gunshot and then I saw them both fall. Him first, but holding on to the chain at her neck, the locket I'd given back to her to keep her safe, with both our flowers, the lily and the rose. Only it didn't keep her safe at all." Her frail voice is rising into the panic so familiar from my childhood. "We're none of us safe. Not ever!"

"Lily is," I say, pulling out the locket and pressing it into her hand. "Lily's safe at last. She wanted me to give you this and tell you not to be afraid anymore. The bad men are all gone. They can't hurt you — or her — anymore."

My grandmother looks down into her hand and gasps. She cradles the drop of gold as if it were a fledgling bird and touches two fingers to its worn surface. She looks up at me, her eyes bright and shining. "My locket — it kept Lily safe?"

"Yes," I tell her, "it did."

EPILOGUE

My grandmother died two days later in her sleep, holding the locket her best friend had given her and she'd given back over seven decades ago. When we found her in the morning she looked more peaceful than she ever had in life. My mother burst into tears.

"I thought I was ready!" she wailed.

I knew exactly what she meant.

I stayed for three weeks, helping with the funeral arrangements. My grandfather Joseph was buried in the old family cemetery beside the apple orchard, but the ground was frozen, so we couldn't bury her yet, and my mother didn't like the idea of her body lying in cold storage until spring, so we had her cremated.

When my publisher paid me for the delivery and acceptance of my book I gave my mother half the money to fix up the old farmhouse. "Unless you want to sell it and take a trip," I suggested.

"Not yet," she told me, "but why don't we use some of it to take a trip together this summer. I've been thinking I'd like to go to Ireland to look up our ancestors."

I said I'd love to go. I could do some research for the book on Magdalen laundries I was planning to write next. I spent the rest of the winter "researching" with Enda over pints at the Black Rose, listening to him singing Irish songs (he played with a band called the Fighting McGlynns) and songs he had written based on his aunt's letters about the laundries.

In the spring we held a memorial service for my grandmother. I rode up on the train with Enda, AJ, Hector, and Melissa. Melissa carried a heavy package on her lap that she refused help with.

"You have no idea the bureaucratic nightmare I had getting hold of this," she told us all. "I'm not letting go."

It contained the cremated remains of the two bodies found below the Refuge.

"How did you do it?" I asked. "Did you steal them the way you stole my locket?" I touched the locket at my throat. My mother had given it to me after my grandmother died. I was debating whether to bury it with her in the apple orchard.

"You're lucky I grabbed that when I did!

If I'd let the forensics team have it, you'd never have gotten it in time to show your grandmother. But for this" — she looks down at the box — "I had to do some digging. No pun intended."

Melissa had arranged for a car to pick us up at the station to spare my mother the trouble. When we arrived at the house I was surprised to see the driveway and roadsides full of cars. I hadn't thought of my grandmother as having many friends, but it was a tight-knit community and my mother had taught at the local high school for thirty years. There were teacher friends and former students and neighbors filling the house and the porch and spilling out into the apple orchard. We'd gotten lucky with the weather. It was a mild day and the apple trees had just begun to bloom. I thought about what Lillian — *my Lillian* — had said about the apple orchard being the peaceful place she liked to imagine herself in. I was glad that her ashes would lie here, beside her friend.

As soon as we arrived my mother announced it was time to walk to the cemetery. She waved me over and deputized me to escort an elderly man with a cane. A younger man — his grandson I guessed from their similar builds — said if I walked on his granddad's right side he'd take his left.

"And I'll be in Scotland before ye," the old man joked in an amiable voice that had a trace of a Brooklyn accent.

"It's not so far as that," I reassured him. "Just to the cemetery on the ridge."

The old man grunted and I saw that he needed to save his breath for the walk, so I chatted with the grandson, whose name was Will, asking how far had they come (from Gilbertsville, Pennsylvania, where the grandfather lived), where he lived (Philadelphia), and what he did for a living (history professor at Drexel). He told me he'd read my recent article in *The New Yorker* about the traumatic impact on survivors of sexual assault. It was a congenial conversation but I was a little sorry not to have the quiet to think about my grandmother on this, her farewell procession. Maybe I'd never have enough time for that. Finding out about my grandmother's turbulent youth had made me understand her better. She had all the symptoms of PTSD — anxiety, claustrophobia, and panic attacks. I could understand how she struggled for the rest of her life to find some elusive sense of safety and why she worked so hard to keep my mother — and then me — safe. I could even understand how in rebelling against her chronic anxiety and the way it had narrowed my mother's life, I had become reckless in my own life and made some bad choices. I could *understand,* but I still felt torn in two when I thought about my grandmother, unable to find any resting place in my own heart for her.

When we get to the little cemetery on the edge of the apple orchard, just below the ridge, I suggest to Will that we sit his grandfather down on the stone wall, but the old man says he'll stand "to show my respect."

So we stand, the old man leaning heavily on my arm, as the Unitarian minister says a few words and my grandmother's and Lillian's and Frank's ashes are poured into a trench dug in between the roots of an old apple tree. I can feel the old man trembling and I realize he's weeping.

"How did you know her?" I ask as I help him to the overlook for the last part of the ceremony.

"She was my sister," he says in a choked voice.

"Your sister?" I repeat, thinking he must be confused. "My grandmother May didn't have a brother."

"Not May," Will corrects. "My grandfather is Lily Anne O'Day's brother. Your

501

friend Melissa tracked us down on Ancestry.com by posting DNA from my great-aunt's remains."

"She was my sister," the old man repeats as we walk to the edge of the ridge. My mother has a bag that she offers to the old man. He takes it, and when my mother pours out the remaining ashes of my grandmother he gives his bag a surprisingly vigorous shake and releases a cloud of gray dust. It's caught by the wind and eddies up, merging with the ashes of my grandmother and then floating down to the river below.

Some of her will stay in the orchard, where she felt safe, my mother told me a few days ago to explain the proceedings, *and some will go to the river, to be free.*

My mother turns to the old man. "Thank you, Tom. Lillian and Rose would both be glad you were here."

"Tom?" I repeat. "You're . . ." I undo the locket from my neck and hold it out to the old man. My hands are shaking too much to open it, but his grandson is able to. Inside is a picture of a pretty smiling girl, hair braided on the crown of her head, her arms around a young boy.

"That's me!" Tom says, pointing at the boy. "And that's my sister Lily . . ."

His voice cracks. He looks up at me with

sharp gray-green eyes that nail my heart to my spine. "She saved me," he says.

I see Lillian standing on the roof, red sneakers perched on the edge, her face tilted up to catch the light, breathing the open air at last. Free.

"Yes," I tell Tom. "She saved me too."

ACKNOWLEDGMENTS

I'd like to thank Kate Nintzel, Liz Stein, Vedika Khanna, Camille Collins, Andie Schoenfeld, and everybody at William Morrow for their work on this book through difficult times. Thank you, too, to my wonderful agent, Robin Rue, and to Beth Miller of Writers House for holding things together during these fraught days.

I'm indebted to all my early readers: Nathaniel Bellows, Connie Crawford, Gary Feinberg, Lauren Lipton, Wendy Gold Rossi, Scott Silverman, Lee Slonimsky, Nora Slonimsky, and most especially to my trio of Golden Girls, Ethel Wesdorp, Nancy Johnson, and Jan Zlotnick Schmidt for their encouragement and warm support.

I'd also like to thank my cousins Benjamin McGuckin and Lisa Tumbleson McGuckin for their gathering of the McGuckin-McGlynn clan and their research into family history, which filled in the gaps in my mother's — and Lillian's — history.

Finally, I owe a great debt of gratitude to Steve Dunn for welcoming me to the Norton Island Residency in the summer of 2019, where the final edits of this book were completed. I wrote this book about seeking refuge in a time before I knew what a rare commodity that truly is. Thank you, Steve, for so selflessly providing a refuge to all the writers and artists of Norton Island.

P.S.
INSIGHTS, INTERVIEWS
& MORE . . .

■ ■ ■ ■

ABOUT THE BOOK

■ ■ ■ ■

BEHIND THE BOOK ESSAY

Courtesy of the Author

THE SEQUELAE

Like many people watching Dr. Christine Blasey Ford's testimony on September 27, 2018, I found myself crying at her description of the assault she had experienced and the psychological aftermath — what she called the *sequelae* — of that attack. Many women reported reliving their own traumatic experiences as they listened to Dr. Ford. I am fortunate enough not to have experienced sexual assault or rape; the person I cried for as I heard Dr. Ford describe the claustrophobia, panic attacks, and anxiety that she experienced for years was my mother.

My mother slept with the light on her entire life. She shook when I took her to the doctor and had such bad claustrophobia that she needed to have the door to the examining room left open while we waited. I'd lived with my mother's anxiety all my life but, only in her later years, when the anxiety worsened and she had trouble sleeping, did I realize she had an anxiety disorder. Even then I didn't identify it as PTSD from a sexual assault.

My mother, after all, had survived many traumas, as I learned listening to her stories of her Depression-era childhood. The eldest of six siblings, and the only girl, she grew up in cold-water tenement flats in Bay Ridge, Brooklyn. Her family was so poor they often had nothing to eat but bread and milk, but her father would cut up the crusts, soak them in milk and sugar, and call it a "treat." Her father dug ditches for the WPA and she was grateful he had work and didn't come home drunk like some of the other fathers on their street. There were tragedies — two baby brothers who died in infancy — but she felt loved and cared for. She didn't think of herself as poor because "everybody was in the same boat." Everyone wore the same uniform at her Catholic school and her mother starched and bleached her shirt so it was stiff and white. There were no books in her home, but she went to the library and read every book on the reading lists the nuns gave her. She was a good student. Her eighth-grade English teacher, Sister Agatha Dorothy (called Sister Aggie Dot by the children secretly) said she had a flair for writing.

The relative comfort and safety of my mother's childhood ended abruptly in April 1941 when she was seventeen. Her mother, who had had rheumatic fever as a child, collapsed on the kitchen floor and died in front of my mother. "I felt so helpless," my mother would always say when she told this story. "I've always wanted to know what to do in an emergency since then." After the funeral, her father sat in her mother's rocking chair and it collapsed beneath him, providing an apt metaphor for what happened to the family. Her father, who had been sober through her childhood, began drinking and was unable to care for his children. Her brothers were placed in St. Vincent's Home for Boys. She was sent to her aunts in Coney Island, who, she told me, were not kind to her. She thought it might have been because they were jealous of how pretty she was. By the time she was eighteen she was living in a boardinghouse by herself, making her living as a stenographer. She didn't earn a high school degree until she got her GED in 1969 at the age of forty-five.

Coney Island, only a few miles from Bay Ridge, was another world. She'd never met Jewish people before and laughed when she overheard someone ask in a deli for "sour cream." The shopkeepers called her *shayna maidelah* — pretty girl. There were mobsters, too, organized crime syndicates like Murder Inc., with its notorious hit man Abe Reles, known as Kid Twist for his preferred method of execution by strangling. And my mother knew Evelyn Mittelman, the notorious Kiss-of-Death Girl. "She wasn't much to look at by then," she told me. "None of those girls were after they went with the wrong sort."

The fate of pretty girls who *went with the wrong sort* became a persistent theme as I entered my teens and started dating. "You had to stay on the right side of the tracks," my mother warned me, "or men would take advantage of you." One of the mobsters would walk her home from the subway station, but he never tried anything because he knew she wasn't *that kind of girl.* She wouldn't try drugs, either, although heroin was rampant in Coney Island (a cousin of my father's later died of an overdose), and she was careful never to leave a drink unattended lest someone *slipped a mickey in it.* Meanwhile, her brothers were being recruited by local mobsters from the St. Vincent's playground to do their errands. My mother often found herself going down to the police station or courthouse to speak on their behalf.

"Why did you turn out all right?" a police sergeant once asked her.

"I had a strong survival instinct," she told me years later.

It wasn't until I was much older that she told me she was sexually assaulted when she was eighteen. The incident occurred when she'd gone into the hospital to have her tonsils removed. During the night a nurse came onto the ward and took her to a darkened examining room. The doctor told her to take off all her clothes. Then, she told me, she started shaking all over. "He must have gotten frightened by how much I shook," she told me, "because he let me go."

I asked her if she reported him; she told me no. Who would believe her? He was a *doctor.* Afterward, she said, she couldn't walk on a street with a hospital on it without shaking. For over sixty years she kept this secret. Until she told me.

My mother's life by the time I came along in 1959 was pretty nice. She met my father on the subway a few months before Pearl Harbor. She liked how clean and neat he looked and that he didn't drink. He introduced her to his sister Leah before he shipped out to the South Pacific, "so we'd stay in touch while he was away." They married when he returned and he went to City College while selling TV antennas at night to support her and my newborn brother, Larry. They lived in Sea Gate, a pretty gated community at the end of Coney Island, had my brother Bob, and then my father took a job at an electronics company in Philadelphia, where I was born. My mother, as she often told me, loved being a housewife and a mother. She resented the 1960s for crashing into that safe world, but she was progressive enough to take us to peace demonstrations and buy the first *Ms.* magazine in 1971. She still slept with the light on and "worried a lot." She seemed to be always planning for a disaster — buying extra food, hoarding pennies in salt boxes, keeping candles in case of blackouts. She was the worrier, the pessimist; my father was the calm one, the optimist. They balanced each other.

When my father died in 1999 my mother grieved but seemed to manage all right. Because my father had traveled a lot she'd always been fairly self-sufficient and she had three grown children who lived nearby to help her. But during the next decade it became clear that her anxiety was growing worse. She became fearful that she was suffering some undiagnosed condition. I took her to a slew of specialists and noticed she would tremble in their offices. When they couldn't find anything I took her to a psychiatrist, who prescribed anti-depressants. She lost weight. She didn't sleep more than a few hours a night.

"Mom," I said, "maybe you should try turning out the light."

"No," she told me, "I can't do that."

In 2016, just a month shy of her ninety-third birthday, my mother died in her sleep with the light on. When I saw her the next morning she was curled on her side, one hand tucked beneath her cheek. She looked peaceful. I had thought I was ready to say goodbye. We'd been close. We knew we loved each other. She'd told me all her stories and I'd become the writer that Sister Aggie Dot had thought she could have become. I didn't think she had anything more to tell me.

Then two years later I listened to Christine Blasey Ford recount the story of her sexual assault and wept. My mother's anxiety, claustrophobia, and fear of the dark suddenly appeared clearly as the sequelae of that moment in the hospital, standing naked in a dark room at the order of someone she trusted. Why had I never realized that? Dr. Ford's eloquent and brave testimony enabled many women around the world to tell their stories and reckon with the long-term trauma of their experiences. For me, it opened a window into my mother's past. I learned from her brother, whom she hadn't spoken to for many years, that he and his brothers hadn't been sent right away to St. Vincent's. "Margie quit school to take care of us," he told me. He also told me that their father hadn't been so sober during their childhood. In fact, he used to go drinking with Bill O'Dwyer, the future mayor of New York City, when he was just a beat cop in Brooklyn. My cousin sent me the intake form for one of our uncles who was imprisoned at Sing Sing, in which his childhood home was described as "one of abject poverty," which sounded a lot different from the stories of bread and milk my mother had told. How much else, I wondered, had my mother left out?

Around that time, I also read an article about Michelle Thomas's research on the history of women's prisons in the United States (available at https://digitalcommons .butler.edu/jiass/vol17/iss1/12). I was surprised to learn that there were Magdalen Refuges in this country, and even more surprised to learn that there had been one in Inwood, a neighborhood at the northern tip of Manhattan near where my husband grew up and where both my daughters now live. When I told my husband, he was surprised too. Although his mother had grown up in the neighborhood and he'd played in Inwood Park, exploring the caves and the foundations of the old Guggenheim estate, he'd never heard of there being a Magdalen Refuge where the park is now. Nor does it appear in Reverend William Tieck's 1968 history of northern Manhattan. The existence of the Refuge seemed to have vanished from living memory for many years, as if it were an embarrassment. The few references I found were in a community website that led me to contemporary newspaper articles describing the Refuge's architecture, riots, and ill-fated escape attempts. I found myself thinking that this was the kind of place my mother could have been sent to, as her brothers ended up in Catholic orphanages, if she hadn't stayed *on the right side of the tracks.*

For the fictional world of *The Stranger Behind You* I resurrected the Refuge, kept it open until the early 1940s (the real building was demolished in the '30s), and had the building restored into a fancy apartment house with a sweeping view of the Hudson River and a reputation for security — a place that offers safety but is haunted by the ghosts who found no refuge there. I sent my two female protagonists, Joan and Melissa, there to reckon with the trauma of assault and the fallout surrounding the exposure of a sexual predator. I wanted them to find the safety and peace that so eluded my mother, but only after they had reckoned with the truth. I wanted to tell this story because we can't build a safe — or just or free — world by burying the secrets of the past or hiding injustices, or by telling only part of the story. We can only find true refuge by knowing the truth.

READING GROUP GUIDE

1. Joan doesn't report the attack. Why not? What do you think of this choice? Why is it that women don't always report sexual misconduct or abuse?

2. How culpable do you think Melissa is for living with a sexual predator? Should she have been able to tell what her husband was really like? Could she have done something about his behavior?

3. In her study on Magdalen laundries in the United States, the scholar Michelle Jones states that "we seem to have lost all memory of them" and that "this historical amnesia hinders our understanding of prisons and marginalized women." Were you surprised to learn that there really was a Magdalen asylum in New York City in the early years of the twentieth century? Do our history books focus enough on the

history of how women were treated in the past? Why is it important to uncover this history?

4. Both Lillian and Joan have suffered a traumatic event. What are the long-term effects — the "sequelae" — of trauma? Is there any way to heal from this kind of trauma?

5. What do you think the #MeToo movement has accomplished? Why did it take so long for women to speak up against their abusers? Do you think there are any negative aspects to the movement?

6. Joan feels that her mother gave up on her dreams of becoming an artist and gave into her own mother's fears when she moved out of the city and went back upstate. Do you think Joan's assessment is correct? Are there times when it's better to give up on a dream and choose safety?

7. Joan becomes increasingly agoraphobic after she moves to the Refuge and begins to feel as trapped there as the inmates of the Magdalen Refuge had. Why does she feel that way? How do our choices some-

times cause us to feel trapped — and how can we escape?

8. Melissa is determined to uncover the truth about her husband, and she goes to extreme lengths to find out what Joan knows. Do you think she is justified in her actions? How ethical is her behavior? How do our priorities sometimes get in the way of doing the "right" thing?

9. Do you think that Lillian was a hallucination caused by Joan's concussion or do you think she was a ghost?

10. In the final scene the ashes of Lillian and Rose are disbursed between the orchard, where they felt safe, and the river, where they felt free. Are these two qualities — freedom and safety — always in conflict? Can we ever have both?

ABOUT THE AUTHOR

Carol Goodman is the critically acclaimed author of twenty-two novels, including *The Widow's House,* winner of the 2018 Mary Higgins Clark Award, *The Night Visitors,* winner of the 2020 Mary Higgins Clark Award, and *The Seduction of Water,* which won the 2003 Hammett Prize. Her books have been translated into sixteen languages. She lives in the Hudson Valley with her family and teaches writing and literature at SUNY New Paltz and the New School.